AN
HEIR
COMES TO
RISE

SHE WILL RISE

AN HEIR COMES TO RISE

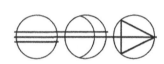

CHLOE C. PEÑARANDA

LUMARIAS PRESS

Published by Lumarias Press
www.lumariaspress.com

First Edition published February 2021

Map Design © 2020 by Chloe C. Peñaranda
Cover illustration © 2020 by Alice Maria Power
www.alicemariapower.com
Cover Design © 2020 by Lumarias Press
Edited by Bryony Leah
www.bryonyleah.com

Identifiers
ISBN: 978-1-8382480-2-4 (eBook)
ISBN: 978-1-8382480-1-7 (paperback)
ISBN: 978-1-8382480-0-0 (hardback)

www.ccpenaranda.com

DEDICATION

To you, the reader.

You can do anything.

CHAPTER 1

I N UNGARDIA, NOT even dreams were safe.

In fact, it was the one place humans and fae found themselves equal in their vulnerability. To fall asleep was to risk their minds falling to the mercy of the invading Nightwalkers; to be unaware of their chilling presence.

Such creatures, or anyone blessed with magick abilities, were born of the immortally supreme fae. A dark, invisible force among their ranks, the Nightwalkers possessed the telepathic ability to enter a person's unconscious mind and access their thoughts and memories, allowing them the deadly capacity to kill from within. To Nightwalkers, the mind was a playground of secrets and lies, and it was their eternal delight to release such thoughts from harmless containment and condemn their unwitting host.

Everyone has skeletons in the closet, and those who claimed otherwise were usually the ones with the most to hide.

Though rare, there were enough uniquely gifted fae in Faythe's home kingdom of High Farrow that the humans in the impoverished outer town did not revolt against the king or those living a life of luxury within the high inner-city walls. The imperious fae cast the humans out as though they were no more than dogs with the dreary town dwellings as their kennels, where they lived in fear of their immortal superiors. Uprising for equality would be futile. And fatal.

It was unusual to see the fae outside the wall for any reason other than work. There were no sights to behold in the old chipped brown buildings and uneven paths of the outer town, and nothing of interest in the very few amenities. The only regular sightings Faythe was used to were the fae guard patrols, though she could never be sure if they stalked the streets to protect the humans or as a further measure to control them.

The fae saw Faythe's kind as only useful for work; to be exerted until they died undertaking the tasks that kept the city and towns running, cycling on through generations. To an immortal, human lifespans were no more than a slight shift in time.

The inner city wasn't completely cut off to Faythe's kind, however. Some of them sought out work behind the fortification for better pay than anything they could get in the outer town, but humans needed unique or sought-after skills to be employed by the fae.

Faythe had no such skills. Her role was simply that of an assistant to a bustling bakery stall in the main town of Farrowhold's market square. She spent her days making runs from the home where Marie's daughters baked delicious goods to the prime spot on the square, occasionally making personal deliveries too. The pay was miserable, but it was made up for by a couple of breads and pastries she would get to take home each evening.

· She had never desired to work within the inner city, nor did she envy those who were deemed *worthy* enough to. She would rather suffer her long, grueling days and petty coin than be constantly looked down upon and forced to work for a pompous, arrogant immortal.

Faythe shuddered at the thought of immortality. Why anyone would want to live more than one lifetime in this sad, war-stricken world was beyond her comprehension. She supposed their opulent lifestyle offered more to be desired. Yet the fae were an unforgiving, power-hungry people, and despite her fair share of sleeping rough on an empty belly, Faythe was glad she wasn't one of them.

This workday was particularly busy. The merciless summer sun beat down, testing Faythe's strength by mid-afternoon. She was slick with sweat and panting, returning with her fourth run of pastries already.

"Grace says she's out of apples to make any more tarts today." Faythe set down the tray assortment, wiping her brow with the back of her sleeve.

Marie huffed her disappointment. Apple tarts were her best seller and Faythe's favorite.

"Well, we'll have to make do, I suppose."

Marie was a natural with the customers, always cheerful and smiling, which was probably why Faythe was hardly ever asked to work the front. It wasn't that she was unapproachable or hopeless, but Faythe was an open book with her emotions, and that never fared well with clients who were less deserving of Marie's warmth. Marie was also a generous woman and often felt guilty about the small sum she could afford to pay, but Faythe understood. Money was tight for most people in the outer town.

A lot of the small trades were stuck in a circular chain reaction. Workers were not able to be paid enough, and as a result, goods had to be sold at a far lower price than they deserved since no one had much left to spend by the end of each week.

"I have a couple of boxes ready for delivery!" Marie shouted to the back over the clamor of the midday crowd.

Pushing herself up off the crate she'd sat on for a few seconds, Faythe forced down a groan to collect them, her legs and feet starting to ache. Despite being in Marie's employment for two years, she never thought it got physically easier.

"And be quick! Mrs. Green likes her pies still warm," Marie grumbled, trying to balance multiple tasks of packing and serving at once.

With arms full, four deliveries to make, Faythe set off down the bustling streets. She knew the winding stone paths of Farrowhold better than anyone. To prove her point, one evening, her closest friend Jakon had even challenged her to a game of hide-and-seek, blindfolded. Faythe had maneuvered every corner, turn, and discarded crate like a graceful alley cat, and with her other senses forced to be on high alert, it didn't take long to track him down.

She considered herself too old for such games now, instead spending her free evenings sparring with Jakon in the square when trading ceased for the day, leaving it a quiet, ambient space to let loose from their stresses. They could never afford real swords. Jakon worked on the town farm and would steal broom handles to split in two every time they whittled the ones they had into twigs. Faythe had been trying to put aside what she could to buy a real blade one day, tired of hearing the thump of wood in place of the singing steel she longed for, but by her calculations, it would take most of a year to save for even a basic model.

After weaving her way through crowded streets and making her pleasant but swift stops, she still had one delivery left: the Greens' mill. Faythe added a slight skip to her step as she made her way there. It was always a comforting place for her as her mother had labored for Mrs. Green many years ago. After her death, Faythe would always find solace within the old decrepit building she was dragged along to as a child. Her mother had to fight against Faythe's protests every morning to get her to come along, but it was there she met Reuben, the mill owner's son. The once shy and timid boy with curly blond hair and dimples became a lively, playful spirit with Faythe's pestering for someone to play with. It wasn't long before she was more reluctant to leave than to go.

Once a week, Faythe would look forward to this delivery. Mrs. Green had remained a regular customer of the market stall bakery for years, though Faythe knew it wasn't only the delicious pies that kept her ordering; it was a way for both of them to keep her mother's memory alive. She purposely made her previous stops a little

4

quicker than usual to have a few minutes spare to spend with Reuben and Mrs. Green.

Rounding the corner to the mill, Faythe slowed her brisk pace when the large off-white structure came into view. She almost halted at the sight of a dark, looming figure emerging from the dainty front door.

He was cloaked and hooded—an oddity considering the suffocating summer heat—but that wasn't what made Faythe stumble in her tracks. The figure was tall and broad, way too much so to be like any of the men in town. Any *human* men at least. Faythe couldn't see this man's ears—to glance their delicate points that would confirm him as fae—but his stature alone made her think he was of immortal nature.

Faythe fought the urge to retreat as he glided toward her. She wanted to avert her eyes; to look at the ground and not pay any attention as he stormed forward. There was no other route to or from the mill without them crossing paths. Yet her eyes were fixed, compelled to track him. Her heart became the only sound, pounding loud in her ears in anticipation of the foreboding danger. She'd grown up with an instilled fear of the fae. Everyone had.

He advanced closer, and Faythe tried to catch a glimpse of his face in her curiosity to learn more about the strange male who held a poise different to any of the patrol she'd seen. He didn't march and stand intimidating like the others; he was elegant in his movement and inconspicuous in his demeanor. It was clear he didn't want to be noticed.

Faythe rarely looked twice at any of the fae guards who were a regular sight on the streets of Farrowhold. She found most of them to be carbon copies of the same brute force. But her intrigue was sparked by the mysterious fae stranger in front of her.

She expected him to float past without any acknowledgment of her, as they all did in their ignorance. Then, as he came a foot away, his head tilted upward, eyes locking directly on her. Their emerald color was striking, revealing deeper vibrant hues as he angled his head to the side and they caught the rays of the sun.

Time slowed in that second, or perhaps it was her heart as the loud thud faded to a distant hum. She thought she saw the same look of inquisition in his own eyes when they narrowed a fraction. Then he passed her completely in one long stride, and Faythe was broken from her trance.

She didn't realize she'd stopped walking until she took a long, conscious breath and her surroundings came into clarity once more. She dared a look back, but the streets behind were empty, and he'd disappeared like a ghost in the wind.

When she faced her destination again, realization struck Faythe. What reason would a fae have for being at the Greens' mill? Panic set in, and she pressed forward once again with a hurried pace.

Faythe didn't bother knocking as she rushed through the mill door. The aged floorboards cried loudly with every desperate step to locate Reuben and his mother. She couldn't call out for her worry.

In the large kitchen, she halted. Her relief at finding them was short-lived when she beheld the desolate look on Mrs. Green's face and noticed her eyes glittering with tears. Reuben had his back to her, but when he turned, his face was ghostly pale.

Her heart dropped at his solemn expression in place of his usual quirky smile.

None of them spoke for a painfully long moment. When she couldn't stand the suspense any longer, she choked out, "What's wrong?" The pie box in her hands became a heavy weight, and she set it down on the nearby table before taking a step closer to her friend.

Reuben opened his mouth to speak, but it moved without any sound as if he was struggling to comprehend the news.

"I—I have to leave," he finally got out in barely more than a whisper.

Faythe's frown deepened. "What do you mean? Reuben, what do they want with you?" she asked in urgency.

He shook his head. "I'm so sorry, Faythe. I did what I thought I had to. I… They threatened me in the woods, said they would kill you all if I didn't." He stumbled with ghostly terror.

Faythe clenched her trembling fists to hide the betrayal of her fear. She had yet to hear the rest of what had him so horrified.

"What did the fae want?" she pressed again through a shaky breath.

His look turned grave. "He was a Nightwalker," he said. Faythe's eyes widened, but she allowed him to go on without interrupting. "He…he came by to warn me, tell me to leave, before the king has one who isn't so forgiving bring me in. I've been spying information for Valgard—they cornered me in the Dark Woods some weeks ago. They asked me to find something, a stone of some kind, apparently hidden within High Farrow. I…I didn't find it. I… didn't…" Reuben trailed off, acknowledging the foolish and life-threatening act he'd committed.

His confession suffocated the air in Faythe's throat and struck her heart into an uneven rhythm. Of all the things she imagined his woes to be, this never even made the list.

Faythe had never left her home kingdom of High Farrow, but the histories were common knowledge. All children were raised with the lore through stories and song. She and Reuben even had lessons together as children in this very mill about the dangers and threats of the centuries-old war in Ungardia that still remained unresolved.

The nefarious kingdom of Valgard, east off the coast of the mainland, had waged conflict on the rest of Ungardia over five hundred years ago. The mainland divided its territory between five kingdoms: High Farrow, Rhyenelle, Olmstone, Dalrune, and Fenstead—the latter two having been finally conquered by Valgard over a century ago during the great battles. They had tried and failed to take the former three, who now held a close alliance. But the overhanging possibility of another great battle made everyone afraid.

Faythe's confusion and suspicion piqued, and the emerald eyes of the male outside flashed to mind. It was not often the fae offered mercy to her kind, and what Reuben spoke of was treason. King Orlon Silvergriff of High Farrow had his Nightwalkers rooting out those accused of such crimes to be sentenced to death immediately.

"What are you going to do?" Faythe had no answers, and she didn't expect to receive a useful solution.

Though he was a man now, Reuben still held onto his innocence. He was easily led, and his response to fear and pressure had always been to submit rather than fight. As much as Faythe had tried to whack the opposite into him through her brutal pestering to play with weapons and spar as children, it had always been Faythe's idea of fun, and Reuben's idea of torture.

"I—I don't know, Faythe. I'm scared."

At his tone of defeat, something in Faythe awoke: a need to help him in any way she could. She rattled through her mind trying to think of any possible resolve to save her friend's life. Fleeing would be no easy task—High Farrow wasn't the only kingdom with Nightwalkers in their royal service. He could be rooted out in any of the mainland kingdoms for treason.

Then one name sang above the rest in dawning: Lakelaria.

It was the one mighty kingdom that had remained clear of battles through the centuries. Lakelaria stood as its own great island to the west and was guarded by the wicked Black Sea, commanded by the queen herself, who was rumored to be the oldest ruler in the seven kingdoms of Ungardia—and the most powerful. Not much was known about the people or lands of Lakelaria. They had closed off their borders long before the conflicts started five hundred years ago and only allowed trade routes to remain open.

It would be a long shot to get Reuben across the seas and beg for safe entry. It was also perhaps his only hope. They had nothing to fear from Valgard and no reason to search for traitors. As far as anyone knew, no one left that island.

Mrs. Green's sob broke through her thoughts. Faythe had almost forgotten the mill owner's presence in her focused concern. Her expression softened at the hopeless look on her usually cheerful, bright face.

Faythe said, "I might have an idea." Then she turned her attention to Reuben once more. "Pack what you can carry. Every time you fall asleep, you're at risk. You have to leave tonight. Mrs. Green, you should be safe if you don't know anything."

She sobbed hard, and Faythe struggled to hold back her own sadness at the thought of her friend leaving, on the run with his life.

Mrs. Green approached her, and she accepted her embrace in solace. Her short, round form fit under Faythe's chin, and she closed her eyes for a moment as if she could feel herself absorbing the mill owner's pain and grief.

When they broke apart, Faythe offered a sad smile. Then she glanced at the clock perched on the wonky mantel behind and swore inwardly.

"I have to go," she said, then she looked once more at Reuben. "I'll meet you by Westland Forest, nine o'clock."

Reuben nodded. "Thank you, Faythe."

She gave a short nod of her own, then she twisted on her heel and bustled out of the mill before she could crumble under the intense sorrow in the room. Once outdoors, Faythe breathed in deep to calm her storm of emotion—then she broke into a run back to the square.

The day passed by quickly after her rocky encounter at the Greens' mill. Faythe's head rattled with ideas of how she could get Reuben across the sea to his only possible salvation.

As anticipated, Marie gave her an earful on how time was

money and didn't let her have a moment's rest upon returning. Faythe welcomed the distraction anyway, but all too soon, the sun was beginning its descent past the rooftops, and Faythe was heading home for the evening. Well—heading back to what she had come to call home, which was the very small one-bedroom hut she shared with Jakon. Its structure was poor, allowing harsh nights to whistle bitter wind through the cracks of its crooked wooden walls. Despite this, the humble setting brought the odd feeling of warmth and safety.

She burst through the threshold and spotted her friend lounging at the bench they used as a dining table in the open kitchen and living area. The place was shoddy and lacking in any color besides hues of brown. Neither of them was particularly bothered about interior design as they preferred to spend as little time indoors as possible.

"Whoa! Marie got you doing marathons again?" Jakon quipped, peering up from the piece of paper he was studying.

Faythe gave him a flat look, and he dropped the smirk.

"What's wrong?" He set down the parchment and stood immediately. She had to give him credit: he was always quick to detect her mood shifts.

Jakon was her closest friend. Older than her by three years, he'd saved her from the streets when her mother had died ten years prior. Faythe had no knowledge of who her father was, leaving her an orphan aged nine. Jakon had already lost his parents to sickness at the same age, so Faythe often thought they were like two sides of the same sad coin.

"Nothing. I'm handling it." She already knew her friend wouldn't let it go that easily, but she tried anyway to save putting another neck on the line.

"Do I have to force it from you?" His mouth set in a thin line, and she knew that cool, calculating look—had butted heads with it many times over the years from his unnecessary overprotectiveness.

"You have to trust me on this one. The less minds that know, the better."

He frowned deeply, catching on to exactly what she meant. "If you're at risk because of one of those bastards, you'd better tell me now," he growled.

There was no arguing with Jakon; they were both as stubborn as each other. Together, they were a force to be reckoned with, but against one another, it could be cataclysmic.

"Can't you put your male ego aside and trust I can take care of this?" Faythe snapped. Pushing past him, she grabbed her deep green cloak. The summer nights still held a chill to the air, but she slung the cloak on more for concealment than warmth.

Earlier that day, she had snatched some extra bread and pastries without Marie noticing. Finding an old bag, she piled them in to give to Reuben for his journey.

Jakon ignored her remark. "Fine. I'll just follow you until I figure it out for myself," he said, reaching for his own worn black cloak.

She glared at him. "You're insufferable." When he showed no sign of backing off, Faythe huffed, throwing her arms out. "Knowing only puts two of us at risk instead of one!" But she knew that if anything were to happen to her, Jakon would be right behind her to accept that fate too. "It's not even me who's in deep shit. It's Reuben."

His expression switched from relief to shock to fear in the five minutes it took her to ramble through her short encounter at the mill that morning. "And what exactly is *your* plan to help him? Gods, Faythe, why are you getting involved!" Jakon was pacing, which always set her on edge.

"He's our friend! What was I supposed to do—let him get caught?" she cried.

"Damn that boy when I see him for even telling you. He's practically tied his anchor to you as well," he seethed.

"He hardly had a choice," Faythe shot back. "You or I would have done the same if the other were threatened the same way."

His features softened a little, and he released a long sigh, fastening his cloak. "I would have gotten us the heck out of here before I risked both our necks. He's not safe in any kingdom now."

"I have a plan."

Jakon curved an eyebrow, waiting for her to continue. Faythe shifted on her feet.

"Lakelaria."

He huffed a humorless laugh. "Right, and your real plan?"

"That *is* my real plan, you asshole. Like you said, no other kingdom is safe. They're neutral territory."

"If they let him in!"

"I didn't say it was an entirely foolproof plan."

Jakon rubbed his hands over his face. "There's a ship docked at the harbor for trade tonight," he said reluctantly, offering a solution to the glaring hole in her idea: how to get Reuben across the sea.

She perked. "You know this for sure?"

He nodded. "I saw it this morning on my way to work."

She beamed at the knowledge. "Then let's go."

"You don't need to come, Faythe. I'll get Reuben out safely. I know more of the patrol timings than you do."

With a dead look, Faythe whirled for the door in response. She slid her hand into her pocket to retrieve the aged brass watch—one of the last items she owned of her mother's. It was nearly half past eight, and dark night had begun to blanket the town.

Jakon sighed. "I didn't think so."

CHAPTER 2

FAYTHE AND JAKON crouched low in the dark behind a stack of old discarded wooden pallets, their hoods pulled down to mask their faces. Neither said a word as they waited for the night fae patrol to pass.

Though they were allowed to be out, they didn't want to risk being stopped for questioning or possibly followed.

Any minute now, they would stroll down to the bottom of the intersection by the inn—if Faythe's pocket watch still kept the correct minute. Over the years, she'd had to adjust the handles when the minute hand occasionally stilled.

Right on time, they heard the sound of boots scuffling against gravel and faint voices, followed by the appearance of four tall, dark figures. Torches lined the sides of the buildings, casting intimidating shadows of their large forms.

The fae soldiers wore uniform colors of deep blue and black, and the sigil of High Farrow, a winged griffin, adorned their cloaks, clasped ornately at one shoulder.

Royal guards.

Even from her position down the street, their size and poise were something Faythe couldn't help but marvel at. She mentally chastised herself every time, but especially now, as she caught Jakon stealing a sideways glance at her obvious interest.

For a human, Jakon was handsome. Tall and well-built, his dark brown eyes and permanently disheveled brown hair made him easy on the eyes. The women in town were never subtle in their flirtation, but despite all this, he was still painfully human in comparison. They both were. Faythe's only standout feature was her eyes— her mother's eyes of bright gold. The rest of her was perfectly ordinary. She had chestnut brown hair and was a little too lean thanks to the days she didn't properly feed herself. There was only so much bland broth and stale bread she could stomach.

The patrol stopped outside the inn. They made quiet talk among themselves before a wicked-looking fae with a scar marring the left side of his face gave a nod and barged through the door with undue force. Faythe flinched at the sound of splintering wood, surprised the door still held on its hinges. They didn't appear to be heading in for an ale and a drunken chat with friends. No—they had business to do with someone inside, likely on the orders of the king.

"We have to move now," Jakon whispered beside her.

Faythe was rooted, her curiosity getting the better of her. It wasn't often she saw the king's guard taking action in the outer town. It was usually peaceful and boring.

Jakon hooked an arm around her elbow. "*Now*, Faythe," he hissed sternly.

She launched into a tiptoed jog behind him, quick but quiet, keeping to the walls for shadow cover. Once around the corner of a street further up, she heard a loud commotion exiting the inn behind her and dared a look back.

Faythe held in a small gasp at the sight of a young man being dragged out of the establishment with unnatural ease. His fight would be futile against one of them, let alone the four surrounding him. She knew him as Samuel, the innkeeper's son. They weren't friends. He was arrogant and a bully. Regardless of her feelings, she wouldn't wish anyone's fate to be in the hands of the fae.

He thrashed and cried out, but she couldn't make out any words from this distance. The fae with the scarred face kicked him behind his knees, and Samuel fell with palms splayed to the ground.

"We have to go," Jakon insisted, going to grab her elbow again.

She pulled her arm out of his reach. "We should help him." The idea sounded just as crazy as when she thought it. Even so, she couldn't stand to leave someone helpless—even someone like Samuel.

"Have you lost your mind? There's nothing we can do except earn ourselves a trip to the gallows with him," he hissed.

It took all her strength to close her eyes and block out the cries of desperation. Jakon was right: interfering would only instantly condemn them too.

As she turned her head to walk away, she almost collapsed with the weight of the fear that drowned her. It shocked her as much as it crippled her because she knew the fear wasn't for herself. She always did have a horrible sense of other people's emotions, and it was a curse she'd learned to live with.

As quickly as she felt it, the fear was gone. A sharp chill shot through her body, and she turned on her heel, once again snaking through the shadows like a nighttime bandit.

She was still trembling with the ghost of that terror when they reached the edge of the Westland Forest. Jakon led them into the dark woodland, where branches on trees swayed like wraiths. Straight ahead was cloaked in a veil of impenetrable black.

Faythe had never liked the forest. She didn't *trust* it. The wide-open space was an illusion of safety and freedom staggered with too many hiding places for an assailant to lie in wait. They only ever ventured here when she and Jakon tried their hand at hunting, more to cure their boredom than with any hope of catching wildlife. It wasn't just that they lacked the skills and experience; game was starting to become scarce in these forests.

There was no sign of Reuben. A feeling of dread grew in Faythe as the minutes ticked by, while Jakon paced the same few steps, his patience wearing thin. Then a rustling came from behind, and her friend drew his small dagger, taking a protective stance in front of her in a heartbeat.

Seconds later, the curly blond hair she'd come to love and hate bounced into view. Jakon released a sigh of relief and lowered the blade.

"You're late," was all he said to Reuben as he came to a stop in front of them.

Reuben was panting, adjusting the small backpack he carried. "I'm sorry. My mother wouldn't let me leave without triple-checking my supplies and saying many, many goodbyes."

Faythe's heart broke at the sight of her friend, his face grave as if he had already given up hope of escape.

"What are you doing here anyway?" Reuben asked him.

Jakon snarled. "You brought Faythe into your mess. I wasn't going to let her risk her neck alone."

Faythe knew that if he'd had the choice, Jakon would have left Reuben in his hopeless state rather than potentially risk her life by getting involved.

"We don't have time to waste on petty bickering. The night patrol will be changing shifts at the docks soon," she said to cut the tension.

They still had enough time, but she couldn't stand to look Reuben in the eye for long—not if it meant she had to feel the waves of fear and despair emanating from them. She fiddled with her watch in her pocket and brushed her fingers along the simple engraved symbol on the brass back, suddenly finding it very interesting.

"What's the plan then?" Reuben's voice brought her back to the gloomy forest.

Her eyes met his. "Lakelaria," she said, ignoring his wide-eyed look at its mention. "There's a supply ship leaving tonight."

Reuben blanched. "That's not a plan. That's suicide!" He turned to Jakon. "Please tell me you have something else?"

Jakon gave a silent shake of his head, and Reuben looked as if he might pass out where he stood. "It's the best chance you've got," Jakon said. Even Faythe was surprised at the gentleness in his tone.

"I can't... I—I won't..."

Realizing no number of soft words was going to get him to see sense, Faythe turned stern. "It's either stay here and be caught, or risk using that big mouth of yours to get safe entry into Lakelaria." When he still looked reluctant to agree, Faythe rolled her eyes, and with a shake of her head, she brushed past him and made to abandon him to his own fate.

She got all of a few steps before she heard, "Wait." His tone was weak. "Okay. I'll go if you think it's the best plan," he said in defeat.

She straightened, suddenly anxious he would entrust his life with her impulsive idea. She didn't let it show.

"Then we had better get moving."

They used the cover of trees along the forest edge to get to the adjoining coastline. Once on the rocky shores of Farrow Harbor, Faythe spotted the large cargo ship on the docks. Men were hauling crates on and off with haste.

They didn't have much time.

"What now?" she whispered to Jakon.

He gave a sly smile as he spotted what he was looking for. "Follow me," was all he said, darting out of cover.

Faythe and Reuben followed suit, keeping low and ducking behind whatever bushes or pallets they could find along the way. Two fae males stood guard at the docks while the human men carried out the work. Even though the fae were stronger and faster.

Typical, Faythe thought.

Ducking behind a pile of crates and barrels, Jakon let out a whistle-cry. Faythe shot him an incredulous look until she recognized the sound: a very convincing birdcall they often used to meet others in secret.

She looked over the large barrel she was crouched behind—which was among various other containers yet to be loaded on board—and noticed a familiar slender man with shoulder-length, rugged red hair glance toward them at the sound. Ferris Archer. What he lacked in muscle and height, he'd gained in wits and cunning. He had been a close friend of theirs for many years, though he had a reckless and impulsive disposition, and they usually got up to no good under his influence.

After making a dramatic show of looking as if he might suddenly pass out to one of the fae patrol, they jerked their heads toward the cargo, and Ferris made his way over. He thumped down on top of the barrel Faythe hid behind with an overexaggerated sigh before twisting his head and peering down to give her a quick wink.

"This better be good, Kilnight," Ferris said under his breath, using Jakon's surname. He took a long swig from a waterskin he'd picked up.

Jakon wasted no time explaining. "We need your help to get Reuben on that ship to Lakelaria," he said plainly.

Ferris choked on his water a little before regaining composure. "I don't think I heard you right—"

"It's his life if we don't," Faythe injected. Time was not their luxury tonight.

Ferris sat for a moment before taking a quick glance down at Reuben and squeezing his eyes shut with a groan. "I don't want to know what you did, but I can take a good guess, you foolish prick."

Reuben shrank back at the comment.

"Please, Ferris," Faythe pleaded.

He was quiet, and she prepared for his outright refusal. Then he stood, making a display of closing his waterskin, and stretched his arms.

"All these are to be boarded." He subtly gestured to the stacks around them. "The second to last on the left is only half-full of grain. You should fit, and I'll make sure I'm not one of the guys hauling your heavy ass on there."

One of the patrol shouted to Ferris to get back to work.

"How you get in there isn't my problem. We'll be hauling barrels for the next fifteen minutes. Don't let any of the others see you if you value your head—they're all whistleblowers." With that, Ferris turned to face them for a final stretch, flashing Faythe another wink. He was a shameful flirt. Occasionally, she would play along in amusement, but she'd never once desired any romantic or lustful relations with the red-haired deviant.

She smiled her thanks for his help, and Ferris picked up a smaller crate beside them before making his way back to the docks.

Faythe poked her head back over her hiding spot to scout. There were two fae patrol and six men loading cargo. The fae were lounging on the docks playing cards, not paying much attention at all. She supposed they didn't need to. Any foul play, and they'd be alert with swords drawn before any of the mortals could blink. Two of the men were on the ship securing the consignments while the other four journeyed back and forth with containers. She looked to her left. The remaining six large barrels would take at least two or three of them to lift each one.

Jakon seemed to arrive at the same idea as Faythe. They gave each other a slight nod, and it amazed Faythe how in tune with each other they were sometimes.

"It'll be a very small window. We have to be quick and quiet," Jakon spoke coolly. "Take this." He pushed his dagger into her hand. "We can't risk the fae hearing. We're too close for their ears."

Faythe didn't like where his addition to the plan was going.

He gave an arrogant smirk at her look of protest and said, "Don't worry, Faythe." He ruffled her hair, and she resisted the urge to bat his hand away and tackle him. "They're about to turn back to come for these. Be ready."

Faythe didn't have time to object to his completely stupid and reckless idea before he ducked out from behind his barrel and rushed for the docks. She fought in irritation not to launch the blade at him, but then the quickly alerted fae had her shrinking back.

She couldn't hear, but she watched in silence as Jakon stopped in front of them and made some desperate gestures toward the path leading back into town. One of the fae shouted over to the cargo loaders while the other roughly grabbed Jakon by the arm.

Faythe jolted, ready to jump out of position to intervene if his plan went badly. Reuben put a hand on her shoulder as if anticipating it, and she almost bit his fingers off—until she watched the patrol begin to walk in their direction, Jakon in tow. As they passed, he looked to her, a slight smile on the corner of his lips assuring her this was part of his impromptu idea.

Faythe's tense shoulders loosened just as the four men, Ferris included, returned from the ship to collect more supplies.

"This is it," Faythe whispered as they approached. She glanced at Reuben, and her heart cracked for him at the fear on his face. "Listen to me, Reuben. You made a mistake, and that can't be undone, but now, you need to focus. You *have* to live." She pulled him into an embrace, and he let out a breathless sound.

"I'm sorry, Faythe, and thank you for all you've risked for me— all of you. I'd be dead otherwise. Look after my mother, will you?" he said hurriedly, aware the crew were almost within earshot.

"I will," she whispered. "I really hope you make it, Reuben. I'll miss you."

They released each other, and she brushed away a tear from his face before crouching low, staying still as a statue. All four of the men returned, shifting the end barrel before lifting it two to a side and shuffling off again.

Without wasting a second, Faythe was on her feet, angling the dagger to pry open the lid of the container Ferris had indicated.

He spoke the truth. When it came loose with a faint *pop*, it was barely half-full.

Reuben hauled himself up onto the barrel beside it, hesitating for a second before lowering himself into the opening. He shuffled around until he was half-buried in sacks of grain and the lid could be sealed.

"It's not going to be a comfortable journey, but they say it only takes a couple of days to get there." Faythe passed him his back-pack along with the food she'd gathered earlier. When she was satisfied he was as comfortable as he could get and there were enough gaps in the wood for air, she grabbed the lid but paused.

He gave a weak smile. "I'll be okay," he said. But Faythe could hear the doubt in his voice and *feel* his overwhelming dread and panic.

There was no time for her to get emotional. "Goodbye, Reuben."

He gave her a thankful nod, and she threw the lid over him before he saw the tears forming in her eyes.

When she was confident it was sealed, she spared just a second to rest her hand on the wood before she pushed off it. Checking the men were still occupied on the ship and the coast was clear, she left.

Back at the edge of the forest, she couldn't help but pause to look back and watch them carry the last of the barrels onto the ship. When they finally got to Reuben, her face wrinkled in sadness at the thought of him in there, scared and alone.

Ferris stayed true to his word and did not partake in carrying that particular load. Instead, he went for the final barrel she assumed was also half-full since he lifted it alone with ease.

The fae patrol returned looking particularly pissed off, and with Jakon nowhere in sight, Faythe's stomach dropped. She had to go find him now. With everything loaded, the fae gave the men a nod to leave for the night before one of them went to haul up the ship's anchor.

Stealing a last look, Faythe mumbled a quiet prayer to the Spirits for Reuben's safe journey, not caring that her words would carry into chilled wisps of wind and offer no consolation in return.

She turned and disappeared through the dark curtain of the forest.

CHAPTER 3

F AYTHE WAS SILENT as she pressed her back to a cold stone wall in one of the alleyways in town. Cautiously, she dipped her head around a corner to check for the fae patrol. She had no idea where Jakon was, and she prayed the fae hadn't taken him to a cell for whatever he'd attempted to distract them with.

She was about to step out and dart across the intersection while the street was soundless and clear when she heard a familiar bird-call carry through the air above.

Whipping her head up, she squinted through the dark across the distorted line of rooftops until her eyes landed on an inconspicuous shape bulging next to the chimney of an adjacent building. Faythe didn't realize how tense she was until her whole body loosened at the sight. With feline stealth, she dashed in and out of the shadows before reaching the drainpipe they used to climb onto the roof, which had become a favorite hideout to evade the patrols and escape the hustle of daytime. It offered a bird's-eye view over the town, where the obscure array of dwellings and establishments were laid out like a dreary stone maze. The vantage point presented one sight that was always impeccable to behold: a distant view of the eternally glowing inner city. The battered brown building stood just tall enough for them to catch a glimpse of it over the rampart.

Faythe scaled the side of the wall, hauling herself up using the holes and sticking-out bricks in the worn structure. Jakon was sitting lazily against the chimney shaft, and even in the shadows, she could make out his playful smile. She crouched low and shot across the narrow flat of the rooftop. When she reached him, she gave him a whack across the arm.

"Ow! What's that for?" he complained, though he kept his grin.

"Don't be so reckless next time! They could have locked you up just because they felt like it." When he gave her a breathy laugh in response, she couldn't fight her own amusement and smiled. "Where did you lead them to anyway?"

He let out a huff. "I told them a fight had broken out at the inn. The place looked a little battered from those other fae bastards earlier, so it was plausible," he grumbled. "But when they showed up and saw there was nothing left to be done, they gave me two months' cargo load duty at the docks for wasting their time."

Faythe couldn't help her chuckle at his dismay and lightly punched his arm again. "Serves you right."

He pushed her back, then he brought her close to him in an embrace. She sat beside him, resting her head on his shoulder, as he draped his arm around her. She was so tired from all the emotions of the night, she wanted to fall asleep right there under the stars.

Sometimes, she wished it could be more with Jakon. Faythe loved him more than anything, more than *anyone*, and it always pained her when she occasionally caught the longing in his eye—as if even after all this time, he still held hope she might one day feel that love intimately too. He'd kissed her once, years past, and she'd returned it, if only to be sure it wouldn't spark their friendship into something deeper. It simply confirmed her platonic feelings toward him and made her feel horribly guilty for trying. Her life by his side would be mundane and conventional, safe, and no doubt happy for the most part. Perhaps that was what scared her the most.

After a moment of peaceful silence, Faythe heard the familiar whistle for the third time that night. The pair frowned at each other before Jakon returned the birdcall. There were only a handful she considered friends who knew about it.

She warily peered over the side and spotted Ferris by his swagger. He was carefully making his way over when he spotted them above. It didn't take him long to scale the building and join them.

He let out an exhausted sigh before lying flat on his back in front of them, tucking his hands behind his head. "You two have been busy tonight," he said in greeting. Neither of them replied. He continued, "Always knew it would be that kid who would end up in deep shit one day. I mean, you're all pretty stupid, but he the most."

Faythe rolled her eyes. Ferris was the oldest at twenty-five, which apparently made it acceptable for him to act like an arrogant asshole most of the time.

"What do you want, Ferris?" Jakon asked, bored.

Ferris rolled to the side, propping himself up on an elbow. "They came to me with the same offer, you know?"

Faythe frowned, ready to throw him off the roof, but he went on.

"I told them to go burn in the Netherworld."

She didn't believe Ferris would have used such tame words to tell someone where to go if they displeased him. His wicked smirk confirmed as much. They didn't have to voice they were talking about the same thing: the exact reason their mutual friend was currently a cargo load.

"Valgard must be planning something big if they're openly terrorizing people for information like this," Jakon mused.

"Indeed. They didn't like my rejection, and in response, they said they would hunt my entire family." Ferris laughed. "I told them to go ahead because I haven't seen any of them in years."

Faythe was trembling when Jakon put his hand on hers—either from the cold or fear, she couldn't be sure. They exchanged a look, and she could almost hear the words, *"I won't let anyone hurt you."* She smiled weakly, but then it faltered as she recalled the earlier events of that night.

"The innkeeper's son—do you think...?" She couldn't bring herself to finish the sentence.

Jakon gave her a grim look. "It's possible," was all he said.

She didn't want to think of the kind of torture and punishment he would endure at the castle prison to share what he knew about Valgard, and then he would be killed for treason.

Faythe looked to the stars, beyond them, and thanked the mythical Spirits' she had been able to help Reuben get away. She was hopeful that whatever met him on the journey or after would be a mercy in comparison.

Ferris's voice brought her eyes back down. "Just thought I should warn you, they have soldiers testing the borders, and some are managing to slip past. Stay out of the woodlands if you can, and don't go out of Farrowhold if you don't have to."

For all his cockiness, Faythe knew Ferris cared for them like family. They were all cut from the same cloth and had been dealt similar versions of the same misfortune.

"There's been talk of unrest in Galmire," he added sternly.

Faythe shuddered at the mention of Galmire, the town on the edge of High Farrow. It was home to the Dark Woods that made up part of the border separating them from the conquered kingdom of Dalrune. Valgard soldiers must be grabbing those who were foolish or desperate enough to wander through, and with the lack of game to hunt in Farrowhold, she couldn't blame the ones who did.

"Thank you," Faythe said fiercely. The two exchanged a warm smile—a rare occurrence since they were usually testing each other's patience—then she looked to Jakon. "Let's go home."

He nodded with a knowing smile.

The three of them scurried across the roof one by one and climbed back down to the street before parting ways.

Back at the hut, Faythe and Jakon didn't stay up much longer since they were both exhausted from the night's unexpected affairs. They changed and tucked themselves in, and Faythe was grateful they never talked about any of it. She thought her mind might burst from the exertion of emotion.

In less than ten minutes, Jakon was already lightly snoring in his cot beside her, but Faythe couldn't get her mind to settle. When she closed her eyes, a pair of bright green irises flashed, and she wondered why she couldn't get them out of her head.

She scrunched her eyes shut, willing herself to think of some-thing—*anything*—else to help her drift off. But if it wasn't the strange sighting of the fae male earlier that day rattling her thoughts, painful images of Reuben—cramped in a dingy wooden cell in the middle of the ocean, losing his wits in fear—crowded her head. The thought made her sick.

Faythe always had vivid dreams and usually awoke feeling more exhausted than when she went to bed. Tonight would be no different with the lattice of thoughts and emotions that wouldn't settle, not even when she felt the slow waves of sleep lap over her and pull her under all at once.

It was dark. Whorls of black and gray smoke engulfed her, and she watched tendrils of it entwine around her fingers as she lifted a hand to touch it. It had no scent and did not choke her when she inhaled cautiously. Above her head, she could make out an endless black void through the gaps in the smoke. Below her feet, her own obscure reflection was cast back to her by a pane of cracked black glass.

Faythe took a few wary steps into the abyss, and the clouds moved with her. She scanned and squinted through the infinite space to try to find something or someone, but she didn't trust her voice to call out. She was too afraid of what might call back...

Feelings of dread and panic started to rise within her, and she clamped her fists tight to stop them from trembling. She began to feel cold. So cold. She'd had her fair share of nightmares, but this —it felt...*different.* Every instinct told her to wake up.

The smoke shifted, and she gasped in horror as thick ringlets snaked up her arms before the translucent vines tightened like rope. When she tried to pull free, it was futile. The same phantom touch crawled up her calves, and she was fully ensnared in her sleep predator's trap.

Her panic spiked, and she squeezed her eyes shut. She had been able to wake herself from nightmares before, so she calmed herself and focused. Yet no matter how hard she strained her mind, it was as if something anchored her here.

"How brave you are to find yourself inside *my* mind." The threatening snarl came from behind.

She whirled her head only to find blackness chasing ghosts as the silhouettes shifted to trick her. A light caress went down her face, and she whipped her head around again—but still, she found no solid form.

The faceless monster was taunting her.

"I...I don't—" She tried to speak but was cut off as she felt another shadow-arm snake around her throat and apply light pressure. Terror doused her. *It's only a dream,* she told herself. *One breath, two...*

Slowly, her heart calmed a little. She would wake up soon; could *force* herself to wake up if she focused right. She clamped her eyes shut and willed herself back to consciousness once more, imagining her bed and Jakon, who would be sound asleep beside her.

After a moment, she felt no change and dared to open her eyes. Faythe found herself still trapped in the bottomless pit of her ghoulish nightmare. She let out a small whimper of defeat.

A rumble of laughter echoed around her, bouncing off phantom walls that made it impossible to pinpoint its origin. "Don't you know not to go wandering through people's minds when you don't know the way out?" the voice said.

Faythe went cold as ice. The ghost of an arm tightened around her neck, and she let out a strangled sound.

"No words?"

She detected a hint of amusement in the tone and knew it was enjoying its taunts and relishing in her fear.

Finally, a real, solid figure started to emerge across the dark space, and the mist cleared to reveal a striking fae male. Not exactly the terror-inducing, foul-looking creature she was expecting.

Her panic dissolved into pure shock as she matched the voice to the familiar face she had encountered earlier that day: the fae she crossed paths with on her way to the mill. Without his hood, he was even more beautiful than she imagined from her quick observation in town. His short, jet-black hair glistened in the light that had begun to chase away the shadows.

The black and gray mist now only swirled in a lazy circle around them, the vines that had stretched out to hold her firm loosening slightly.

The bright green of his eyes pierced right through her from the distance he still kept between them. They narrowed, and his strong, angled jaw tilted as he observed her. Faythe took the opportunity to gauge the threat.

His poise was elegant yet commanding. A warrior, perhaps. Though she noted his black leather pants and knee-high boots to be of exceptionally fine craftsmanship. If the fae had access to money and finer wares, he must be of high rank. His toned upper body was obvious from his loose-fitting white shirt, which only added to her assumptions the fae had likely seen the lines of battle; was honed for it.

He stalked toward her slowly, deliberately, looking over every inch of her. Faythe had never felt more exposed even though she was fully dressed in her usual sleep clothes. Her feet were bare, however, making her feel strangely inappropriate.

He stopped close enough beside her that she felt his warm breath across her neck as he angled his head down, still inspecting. Her heart raced at the proximity. He lifted a finger and traced it delicately over the curve of her ear, sending a jolt through her that made her whole body tremble at the contact.

It felt so *real*.

Faythe remained rooted to the spot. She knew she would be too frozen in fear to make any movement even without the arms of smoke still holding her.

"Human," he mused.

Her heart was a wild, erratic pounding in her chest, and she was sure he could hear it. She found her palms slick with sweat and her mouth so hideously dry she wasn't sure she would get any words out.

Finishing a full lap around her, eyes still fixed, his frown deepened when he came to a stop at arm's reach in front of her. "Do you know where you are?" he asked.

Faythe's lips parted slowly. "I'm dreaming," she whispered, more as a reassurance to herself than in answer to her sleep demon's question.

His eyes narrowed, and a sly smile twitched at the corners of his mouth. He huffed a laugh. "I remember you," he said, his voice smooth and eloquent. "From the town today. Or yesterday, so to speak." He folded his arms, resting his chin on one hand as he pondered. "What is your name?"

She debated keeping her mouth shut. She had to wake up at some point. This was only a dream; he couldn't really hurt her if she resisted. But that also meant anything she told him couldn't hurt her if he was just a figment of her imagination. She had nothing to lose if she played along in this cruel nightmare.

"Faythe," she answered.

"Fai-th." He drawled the single syllable of her name as if it

might offer some clue to his puzzle. He studied her for another painfully long moment. "Fascinating," he concluded.

She wasn't sure what intrigued him exactly. She stood in silence, waiting for him to turn into some beast and devour her or for something worse to come crawling out of the shadows and do the job.

"You should be careful whose mind you go walking into at night. You might not make it out so easily next time," he said in warning.

Her brow furrowed in confusion. She was about to retort that *he* was the one invading *her* dreams but quickly realized she'd be arguing with herself.

He breathed a long sigh. "Well, I should like to get *some* sleep tonight, Faythe," he said. "I will be seeing you again, however. Just not here, if you know what's good for you." His smile made her skin crawl.

She wanted to counter that she would never be seeing him again if she could help it; that she would banish all thoughts of him or never sleep again if this was what awaited her.

He spoke again before she could form a reply. "You can wake yourself up now. I won't stop you." He kept his grin as he motioned for her to leave through a door that didn't exist.

Faythe shot him a glare and was about to argue again that it wasn't for him to decide. But she was eager to get out of this conjured Netherworld, so, instead, she closed her eyes and imagined the warmth of her bed, the old wood smell of hut, and Jakon's soft-sounding snores…

Faythe jolted violently awake. She was panting, and her shirt clung to her with sweat. Sitting up in bed, she rubbed her eyes and scanned the hut, swallowing down the nausea from her nightmare.

Real. This is real, she told herself.

Jakon's breathing was a sure, comforting sound. She swung her legs over the side of her cot, taking deep, concise breaths to slow her galloping heart. Some nights, her dreams and nightmares were so vivid it took her a while to distinguish whether she was truly awake and hadn't jumped into another twisted scene in her unconsciousness. She could go through several a night sometimes and always remembered each one.

Jakon grumbled from his stomach-down sleeping position, one arm and one leg hanging off the cot he barely fit in. He peeled a lazy eye open. Faythe must have looked as awful as she felt because he instantly pushed himself up into a sitting position. After he scanned her over and determined there was no physical harm, he gave her a knowing look.

"Bad dream?" he sighed, rubbing his eyes sleepily.

She gave him a weak smile. "Yeah," she breathed. "Just a stupid dream. I'm fine."

Glancing out the small square window behind him, Faythe spied the first rays of sunshine piercing through the lapis-colored sky, signaling a new break of dawn. She hoisted herself up and went into the closed-off section of the hut they'd made into a semi-functional washroom. She cupped her hands in a bucket of icy water and splashed her face, the coolness nipping her skin. She welcomed the feeling that jerked her awake. *Real*, she told herself again, and she proceeded to strip down and wash her whole body under the bitter ice water.

When she stepped out of the washroom, clean and refreshed from her night terror, Jakon was already dressed for his shift on the farm. He wore his usual brown pants and over-the-knee umber boots with a faded white shirt rolled up to the elbows and braces strapped over his shoulders. In the midsummer season, there was no need for extra layers and cloaks during the day, especially with his type of labor.

Faythe dressed in her own plain clothes: a simple short-sleeved purple tunic with a pair of black pants and worn black boots. They were both in need of some new clothes. She slung a simple belt over her waist to give herself *some* shape.

"Are we still going to the solstice bonfires tonight?" she asked casually.

Jakon grinned. "Of course. It's your favorite holiday."

Summer was the season of nurture and growth before the fore-shadowing autumn withered its efforts to brighten the dull land with colorful blooms. The days were long, which left the cool nights to be appreciated and welcomed.

The solstice took place after dark on the hills at the edge of Farrowhold, decorated by tall, blazing stakes built by the fae. It was one of their king's very few acts of kindness. The celebration put everyone in the usually gloomy town in high spirits. The streets came to life with vendors and entertainers, people played music and danced upon the hills, children laughed and ran free, and for one whole night, it seemed everyone could forget the threat of war and their impoverished lives and just enjoy the moment.

Of course, the fae had their own celebrations inside the wall, and Faythe could only imagine the grandeur.

She beamed enthusiastically.

"I'll meet you back here at eight, and then we'll go," Jakon said, matching her joy before leaving for his day of work.

Faythe took a long breath, still smiling. Today, she would allow herself to forget her nightmares, the threat of Valgard, and her friend who would be well on his way to Lakelaria by now. Tonight, she would have fun.

CHAPTER 4

F AYTHE TOOK HER time lazily strolling back to the market. She'd made her deliveries as quickly as possible just so she could have these few minutes alone to enjoy the heat on her face and watch as people adorned the walls with banners and decorations for the solstice celebrations. It was uplifting to see vibrant bursts against the otherwise unsaturated colors of town. She could already feel the positivity and excitement in the atmosphere, and Faythe herself was in high spirits. But her break was over all too soon as she rounded the last corner onto the market square and headed straight for the bakery stall.

Marie was talking to customers and selling her goods as usual. Faythe glanced at the selection of pastries, and her stomach growled. When Marie caught her longing gaze, she wordlessly nudged her head with a knowing look, inviting her to take one. Faythe smiled sheepishly, leaning in to snatch a chocolate tart before perching on a discarded crate to eat.

She was halfway through the decadent dessert when she stopped mid-bite, nearly choking as her eyes caught glimpse of an out-of-place hooded figure leaning casually against a wall under the shadow of a veranda. To anyone else, he looked like a simple foreign merchant—one who would likely deal in unsavory goods from the way he casually picked at his nails with his dagger, holding a demeanor that dared someone to approach.

But he was staring right at her out of the corner of his eye, that damned emerald color piercing right through the blanket of darkness beneath his hood even from across the square. Faythe looked around, praying there was someone or something else catching his attention, but no one even slightly acknowledged him.

Bile rose in her throat at the quick passing thought that maybe she was still in another version of the same nightmare. But her instincts told her this was no dream.

He could just be here on more business like yesterday. She calmed herself. Of course, it was laughable to think she was memorable enough for him to recognize her from the quick glance he'd spared in her direction.

She suddenly lost her appetite despite not having eaten anything all day and set the tart down. Her throat was dry as bone from the quick surge of fear and chocolate consumption. She turned to ask Marie, "Would you mind if I hop out for some water?"

"Of course, dear, but be quick. We're running low on a few items—be sure to stop by the house on your way back."

When Faythe got up, she dared a glance back around, but he was gone, and she couldn't help but doubt if he'd ever been there at all. She released a long breath of relief and laughed quietly to herself. Perhaps her sleep-deprived mind was playing cruel tricks on her. She set off down the street, heading for the nearest water pump.

When she got there, she gulped the water greedily before splashing her face to jolt herself awake. The cold licks of wind against her wet face were refreshing and necessary in the heat. A slight breathless sound escaped her lips.

"Are you avoiding me, Faythe?"

She spun around so fast and, out of instinct, threw her fist out in attack, but her assailant stepped gracefully out of reach, and she connected with only air. Faythe backed up a good distance as she looked over at the fae male looming too close for comfort. He had his hood down this time, his face an eerie, picture-perfect vision of what she'd conjured last night.

His words finally registered in her, and she went cold despite the blaring sun. "How do you know my name?" she asked, sounding braver than she felt.

His head tilted. "You told me, remember?" She wanted to wipe the amused smile off his face. "You really have no idea what you are, do you?"

Cheerful voices sounded down the street behind her. Faythe turned to look, but he grabbed her by the elbow and swiftly pulled her around the corner and into a shadowed alley before she could bark a protest. He casually pulled his hood back up but kept his face in full view.

"I've done nothing wrong! What do you want from me?" she hissed.

He chuckled, and she fought the urge to swing at him again. "I don't *want* anything from you, Faythe. I'm merely curious." He was enjoying this, like a lion playing with his dinner. "You can't lie to me. You made the mistake of coming into *my* head last night, so tell me, how does a human come to be a Nightwalker?"

It took a moment for her to hear him right. Faythe, a Nightwalker. She laughed out loud, and his eyes narrowed at the outburst.

The only way her mind could process the encounter with the fae male was to think they had perhaps already caught on to her involvement in Reuben's escape, and he had been sent to bring her in. But until he made a formal accusation, she would maintain her innocence.

She calmed her face. "Look, I don't know what orders you're on, but that's a ridiculous charge to try to get me arrested." She tucked her long brown hair behind her ear and pointed to herself. "Human, remember?" she stated the obvious.

He laughed back at her—a sound that was quickly becoming a trigger for her violent thoughts. He crossed his arms and leaned against the wall.

"No one's trying to arrest you." He paused before adding, "Yet."

She stilled, and he took in her look of panic, flashing an amused, wicked grin.

Regaining her composure, Faythe straightened. "Well, if it isn't happening today, I have to get back to work." Not a lie, but a perfect excuse to get away and buy herself some time to plan her next move.

She felt sick to her stomach. Would she end up in a barrel sailing off into the unknown too? Jakon would be heartbroken; would likely go with her. She decided she couldn't tell him. She'd have to leave in the middle of the night, and...

Her racing thoughts were cut off by his smooth voice. "If you're not playing me for a fool, you're in even more danger than I thought." He frowned, his face turning serious. Peeling himself from the wall, he took a step closer. "Listen to me very carefully," he said, and she resisted the urge to flinch back at his sudden stern tone. "If you don't know how to control it, there are far worse minds than mine you can end up in when you sleep. If you wander into the mind of another Nightwalker, they'll know about you. They can trap you in their heads and kill you from there." He paused for a moment, assessing her with a look that made every nerve cell tremble.

A cold chill rattled down her spine. Her thoughts were a whirl-wind as she tried to make sense of what he was saying. She wanted to laugh again; to believe it was all some twisted joke. But the urge to ridicule the idea died when she beheld the fierce look in his eyes. The fae had no reason to imply such an impossible ability lived within her. It would confirm his insanity more than her guilt.

He continued, "You're different, Faythe—something the king doesn't take too kindly to. So until I've figured out exactly how you came to exist, I suggest you keep your head down. Don't engage with any of the fae on patrol as it seems when you do, you can't get them out of your head." His straight face twitched into a teasing smirk.

Her cheeks flushed crimson. "Last night..." She trailed off in disbelief.

He nodded, and it was all the confirmation she needed to know he could recall every detail of her nightmare because he had been there. Or, at least, his mind had been there—if that was how it worked.

He said, "There aren't many of us Nightwalkers. We can't enter a mind we've never seen the face of before, so you'd be wise to keep a low profile. Should be easy by the looks of you."

Faythe didn't have it in her to react to the insult. She took a long breath to calm her racing heart. It wasn't possible, *shouldn't* be possible...and yet her mind was already filled with clarity on so many things. Her *dreams*—

Oh, Gods.

"It's not true," she whispered, though the words tasted like a lie.

The world tilted for a second, and she shook her head to clear the dizziness. Too many questions and no one to turn to for answers. How could she trust this fae to keep her deadly secret and not turn her in at the first opportunity to earn favor with the king? She would be killed simply for being an uncharted threat. She couldn't even tell Jakon—it would be too much of a risk.

Then a thought crossed her mind that made her heart drop. Did her mother know?

For the first time since her mother had died, she felt completely and utterly scared and *alone*. The excited clamor of the town around her faded, and the sun dimmed dramatically. She had to calm herself. This was not the right place or company to break down in panic.

A rough pair of hands gripped her shoulders tightly. They shook her once, then twice.

"Look at me."

She wasn't sure if the words were spoken out loud, but they made her snap her eyes up to his, and the world came back into focus.

"I'm going to help you. But you need to keep your wits about you," he said sharply.

She willed herself to keep looking at the green eyes that seemed to hypnotize her. She couldn't trust him—he was fae and would betray her eventually. She was nothing to him.

"Why?"

He shrugged. "Maybe I like the challenge."

So casual and *friendly*. It was not what she had come to expect of his kind, but when she took race out of the equation...he seemed perfectly *normal*.

He released her shoulders, and she backed up a step, suddenly aware she would be expected back at the stall by now and hadn't even been to the bakehouse as Marie had asked.

"I have to go," she said quickly.

He gave her a knowing nod. "Don't tell anyone about this, Faythe, not even your friend. I'll find you again soon."

She didn't have time to ask how he knew about Jakon as he pulled his hood further over his face and turned to leave down the dark alley. Instead, she called, "What's your name?"

He stopped, his body twisting back a fraction while he seemed to contemplate. "Nik," he answered at last before swiftly disappearing through the shadows.

Oddly, she didn't expect such a simple name.

Without another thought, she was sprinting to the bakehouse.

CHAPTER 5

F AYTHE BARELY HEARD Marie's daughters rant about how their baked goods had already started to spoil and go cold. She didn't hear much back at the stall, where Marie also scolded her for taking so long and being late two days in a row. She did wince when Marie threatened to find a replacement if she was tardy again.

Her mind reeled. She thanked the Spirits when the workday came to an end earlier than usual in preparation for the festivities. Marie had given her the day off tomorrow. Many of the stalls would stay closed as a rest day from the solstice celebrations and for people to attend mass at the temple early in the morning.

When Faythe arrived home to the hut, it was only half past six. She figured Jakon would be working usual hours as he'd suggested they meet at his return time of eight. She was determined to forget everything she'd learned today as well as her new unlikely fae ally in the quest to keep her secret hidden. It still made her sick to think about her new incomprehensible reality and how she would be able to live with herself for lying to her closest friend. Even more, it terrified her to fall asleep if she had no control over where she went in her dreams.

She pushed the panic-inducing thoughts aside, and with plenty of time to spare, she decided she would use it to put a little effort into her look for tonight, if only to keep herself busy. Not that she had many outfit choices, but she opted for the only gown she owned in place of her usual pants and tunic. It had been a gift from Jakon on her eighteenth birthday.

The gown was a deep crimson color with ornate gold embroidery over the square-cut neckline and long sleeves—to match her eyes, he'd said. She dressed quickly, discarding her other clothes on the bed and going to the small, clouded mirror in the washroom. She took sections of hair from the sides of her head and braided them back out of her face. A small difference to her everyday untamed waves.

Once satisfied she had achieved all she could with her look, she huffed at her plain face in the mirror. Her eyes were her mother's, but Faythe couldn't help but wonder if she looked at all like her father. Whenever she asked about him as a child, her mother had refused to talk, simply saying they were better off without him.

Faythe had a long face and high cheekbones made slightly more prominent by lack of proper nutrition. Her jaw, while still feminine, was angled with a small, rounded square chin. Her mother had a round and tapered face, making her look almost pixie-like. Faythe smiled at the memory. Even ten years after her death, she would never forget the image of her mother's delicate beauty.

With nothing else to occupy the painfully slow minutes, Faythe leaned casually on the old but hardly used wooden kitchen counter as she picked at an apple to keep her stomach at bay. She glanced at the watch in her dress pocket, tapping her foot impatiently for Jakon to get home. The spare time gave her mind free rein to run wild over the huge revelation that could change her life. Internally, she became numb to the overhanging notion she was capable of the notorious fae ability, refusing to accept the impossible as fact or truth. She attempted to push the thought to the back of her mind for fear of crippling herself with panic and dread. No matter how hard she tried, a constant unsettling feeling remained in her stomach.

Close to eight, the door swung open, and she thanked the Spirits for Jakon's arrival at last to save her from her quickly spiraling emotions.

He stopped just past the threshold and gawked at her for a moment, but then his lips curved up into a grin. "You look incredible," he said.

Her cheeks flushed, and she mumbled an awkward thanks, smoothing down the skirts of her gown. Jakon kept his hands clasped behind his back, hiding something, and her face fell into a frown. When he noticed her stare, his grin widened.

"I have a surprise for you," he said, bringing the object into view.

She gasped, hands going over her mouth, when she beheld what her friend carried in both outstretched palms.

A sword!

He nodded at her to take it, walking forward slowly. "Happy summer solstice, Faythe," he said quietly when he was close enough for her to accept the gift.

Faythe stood in the same frozen position, hardly able to form words. "Jak, we… I can't. It must have cost so much money," she got out, feeling guilty he would spend it on her.

"Don't worry about it. I saved what I could, and Dalton owed me a favor, so I got a good price," he said, mentioning Farrowhold's blacksmith on the other side of town.

Faythe raised a hand to graze her fingertips over the large crystal-clear stone on the pommel.

"The blacksmith kindly offered the stone with no charge. Called it The Looking Glass—some ancient rock that's supposed to bring good fortune and all that." He huffed a laugh.

Tears welled in her eyes as she continued to trace over the intricate woven pattern of the cross guard that expanded confidently like the wings of an eagle into downward-facing peaks. She had no thoughts on what the symbols meant along the rain guard, only that they were beautiful.

"They had a rather artistic side," Jakon commented, also admiring the craftsmanship. "Take it." He pushed it into her hands.

She held it between her own palms, and the light weight surprised her. Gripping the crisscrossed leather of the hilt, she pulled it free from its scabbard with a satisfying cry of sliced steel. She could only marvel wide-eyed as the full glory of the brightly polished blade glinted in the candlelight, revealing every impressive contour of the masterpiece as she raised it skyward, the metal a little darker in tone than she expected.

"It's Niltain steel," he said as if reading her thoughts.

She gawked at him at the mention of the precious metal. It was a rare material and the most robust, only found in the mountains of the Niltain Isles—a small island off the south coast of Ungardia. Not much was known of the people or creatures who dwelled there, but they fell under the jurisdiction of the kingdom of Rhyenelle.

"Where did you get this?"

"Does it matter?" He grinned deviously.

From his look, Faythe knew she didn't want to know the answer. "What about you?" she asked instead, still feeling guilty at such an outrageously generous gift when she had nothing to offer in return.

He shrugged, nonchalant. "Swordplay is your thing. I do well with only my fists anyway." He gave her a playful push. "You'll just have to be the one guarding our backs from now on."

Faythe gave an excited squeal in acceptance, balancing the blade in each hand to get a feel for it. Jakon stepped back to let her use the space to swing it gently a few times. She couldn't find the words to describe how it felt: as if it had been made for her alone and no one else could wield it. The weight was perfect, with the hilt seeming to have all the right grips for her hand that made the control as easy as if it were an extension of her own arm. She made a mental note to stop by the blacksmiths and commend him for his expert craftsmanship.

After finishing her admiration and disbelief, she sheathed the blade and unwrapped the belt from its scabbard to sling around her waist.

"You're going to wear it tonight?" Jakon asked, pleased but wary.

"Of course." She beamed.

He smiled, more to himself, at the absolute joy on her face.

"I'm just surprised you'd trust me with a real blade against you," she teased. "We'll see how long your fists hold up then."

He barked a laugh and brushed past her. "I'll freshen up quick, and we can go enjoy the celebrations."

Faythe grabbed his elbow. "Thank you, Jak, really. You have no idea how much I love it," she said with absolute sincerity.

He brushed away a stray bit of hair that never fit in her braid and gave her a knowing smile. "I do."

CHAPTER 6

DUSK HAD SETTLED over the skies, lit by a glorious full moon and a glittering cascade of stars. Faythe breathed in the scent of fire—entirely wholesome and welcoming as it coaxed her to find where dancing flames brought the aroma to life. She linked arms with Jakon, and together, they strolled lazily through the bustling street, past multiple vendors offering unique treats and long sticks that sparkled a rainbow of color when lit.

When they came across a certain food stall, Faythe stopped to purchase two skewered sausages that made her mouth water. They devoured them on their way out of the stone town and up to the grassy hills, where she could already spy waves of orange and yellow dancing the tango with human silhouettes. The music was wonderful, and she found herself swaying to the lute band's ensemble as they walked toward it.

They passed another vendor, and she stopped again, grinning to herself. "I'm getting a drink," she announced.

Jakon's eyes wandered to where she was headed, and he laughed. "The last time you were drunk, you got us banned from the inn for starting a brawl."

She feigned shock. "They were *cheating* me at cards!"

"Actually, you were cheating them. You're a sloppy cheat when you're drunk," he countered.

"I would never resort to such measures," she scoffed with a playful smirk, heading to the stall anyway. She bought one glass of wine, downed it in a few bitter gulps, and went straight for another while Jakon rolled his eyes, sipping on his drink. She stuck her tongue out at his judgmental look and refrained from giving the stallkeeper the same response when he looked inclined to say something to her.

"Some of us still have to work tomorrow," Jakon said.

"That's never stopped you before, if I remember correctly." She grinned at the memory of last Yulemas. They'd gotten so piss-poor drunk Jakon had woken up among the pigs at the farm. Miraculously, he'd convinced his superior he had arrived early to get a head start. Still drunk.

"Never again," he said, reminiscing with a smile.

The first wine had already taken the night chill away and loosened Faythe's tense muscles. She wished she'd left her cloak at home. They reached the peak of the hills, and Faythe took a moment to marvel at the sight: people dancing, laughing, and just being *together*. It was a change from the usual gloom that coated the town under the same bland routine.

She drank, and when she looked into the raging fires before her, they seemed to beckon with arms of black smoke. For a second, her mind flashed to her dream—her *nightmare*—the night before, which she had now come to discover had been inside Nik's head. She raised a hand to her throat, the ghost of that phantom touch lingering.

"You okay?" Jakon asked, sipping his wine.

She nodded and smiled before knocking back the rest of her second cup and discarding it in a nearby waste container. She took his hand, leading him further into the mass of people around the largest center bonfire. She stopped at the edge of the flames as the song changed and women took their place around the burning inferno for a dance. It was one her mother had taught her as a child. Jakon released her hand and stepped back to watch.

Faythe was going to protest she hadn't participated in such dances in a *very* long time and would most likely look foolish, but his nod of encouragement—or maybe it was the wine—dissolved all the words from her mouth when the tune picked up rhythm. She watched the women carelessly flow with the music and flames, and then she joined in, twirling and bowing and moving her feet as she gave herself over completely to the melody.

Faythe felt as if she were floating, her dress and cloak fanning around her as she made spin after spin. She wasn't certain she was even still grounded. A sharp crackle exploded into falling embers in front of her, and she became one with the fire that lured her into a dance of danger and passion with its whispers of seduction.

Minutes that could have been hours passed, and the tempo finally slowed, coming to its final chapter. When it stopped completely, people clapped, and the women made their final bow toward the flames. But Faythe did not, for through the rippling gaps in the fire, Nik's eyes bore into her. Dizzy from the dancing or alcohol or seeing him, perhaps all three, Faythe turned to Jakon pale-faced and swayed a little as she stepped over to him.

"I think we should get you some water," he said, hooking an arm around her waist to keep her straight. "Can you walk?" He sighed when she shook her head sloppily, looking around before leading her over to a makeshift bench. "Stay here. I won't be long," he muttered, giving her a look over and making sure she wasn't about to pass out before he made haste back down the hill.

She wanted to protest, but the words were lost, and he was too far down to hear her anyway. Faythe got to her feet. She could walk. She could follow him. She took all of a few steps before her vision doubled and she tumbled face-first into the grassy slopes.

A hand went around her waist, hauling her upright before she could taste the dirt.

The arm was gone as quickly as it came, however, and it took

Faythe a moment longer than it should have before she registered the encounter. She snapped her head around, but her alcohol-clouded mind delayed her focus.

As soon as Nik's face came into full view, she glared at him. "Twice in one day. To what do I owe the pleasure, *Nik?*" She drawled out his name, the wine giving her a clumsy sense of confidence.

"You know that's magick wine you're drinking? One cup is enough to put you on your ass, never mind two," Nik scolded.

Well, that explained a lot.

She kept her glare as she muttered, "Killjoy." Faythe looked him over. He wasn't in the same casual attire she'd seen him in twice before. Instead, he wore a familiar uniform. She noted the colors and sigil and backed up a step. "So you *are* part of the king's guard."

She had suspected it, but seeing him dressed and armed like a guard made her very uneasy. He knew what ability dwelled within her. She couldn't decide if his being close to the king kept her safer, since he might know if anyone was suspicious of her, or if it put her in more danger.

"Does that bother you?" he asked with a hint of amusement.

"How do I know you won't just go running to the king with my secret? I'm sure he'd reward you handsomely," she sniped.

"You'd have been locked in a cell long before now if that were my intention," he countered.

She dropped her eyes. He had point. Unless he was waiting to find out more about her.

"How do I know I can trust you?" she asked quietly.

"You can't," he replied, "but you don't really have a choice either."

Also a good point.

When she didn't respond, he reached into his pocket and pulled something out. "Here," he said, pushing the item toward her after a subtle look around to check if anyone was watching.

She examined the small vial of liquid in his cupped palm and didn't immediately take it. "It's not poison!" he said incredulously.

"That's not what I was thinking!" she quickly shot back.

He gave her a look that said he knew it was exactly what had crossed her mind. "It'll basically help you to sleep deeper and prevent a wandering subconscious mind. Use only two drops per night," he explained.

She kept her eyes narrowed, still skeptical, but with a grumble and a mutter of, "Thanks," she pocketed the bottle. His eyes traveled to her hip as she did.

"Nice sword," he observed. "Though one might think it a little out of your…standing."

She shot him a distasteful look. "It was a gift, and it's none of your damn business."

His lips pulled up into an amused grin, and she held back the urge to whack him. *Stupid fae and their pretentious, arrogant, selfish—*

"I only meant for you to be careful. It's not often you see a human, especially a *female*,"—he winced at her pointed glare—"with a sword of such caliber. You wouldn't want to draw too much attention to yourself."

Unspoken meaning lingered between them: *"Don't give them a reason to look into you."*

She nodded her understanding at the silent words.

"Enjoy the festivities, Faythe, and I hope you sleep well." With that, he turned and weaved through the crowd with swift grace until she lost him in a distant blur of revelers.

Jakon crept up to her seconds later, and she jerked in fright, wondering if Nik had somehow known he was near and disappeared on cue.

The world still spun, and when she looked into the fire, she saw animals of flame leaping and roaring, chanting for her to join them. A cold cup was pressed into her hands, and she drank greedily, desperate for her head to clear.

"Let's get you home," Jakon said, sliding his arm around her waist and hooking her own around his shoulder to carry her.

She didn't recall much of the journey back to the hut besides blurred bodies and a loud clamor as the solstice celebrations went on in full swing. In the hut, she threw herself onto her cot, her head somewhat cleared from the fresh air and constant top-ups of water Jakon kept supplying, but the walls still tilted slightly.

Jakon removed her cloak and boots before standing over her. "Unless you want me to fully undress you, you'd better get up," he said.

She giggled. "Yes, please."

He groaned in response. "You're always a pain in my ass when you're drunk." He helped her to sit up and unlaced the back of her dress. He'd seen almost every inch of her many times before simply because it came with sharing such a small space.

She turned to him once he'd finished. Her bold, tipsy state mixed with her internal frustration when she looked into the warm brown depths of Jakon's eyes. It should be easy for her to fall in love with him... Was there something wrong with *her?* She had lustful desires, of course, and would occasionally give in to flirtations with single suitors on a night out at the inn—when Jakon wasn't there to make her feel guilty about it. She refused to tangle their friendship with lust, knowing it would mean something entirely different to him. But tonight, she was irrationally angry at herself for not being able to return his want for something more.

Impulsively, she leaned forward to kiss him, desperate to prove herself wrong in her platonic feelings. Their lips met just briefly, but then he pulled away.

"Faythe." He said her name as a quiet plea.

At the pained look in his eye, she instantly regretted the reckless move. It was selfish of her to try, and hopeless. He seemed to know it too—at least in her pitiful tipsy state—but he wiped away his disappointment with a teasing smirk. It eased her guilt as he stood and lightly tousled her hair.

"Drunken fool," he muttered playfully.

She gave him a sheepish smile, and he turned to leave their bedroom and let her change.

Faythe mentally chastised herself, standing to slip out of her dress, which hit the floor with a *thump*. She swore as she bent down to rustle through the pockets. She retrieved her watch and set it on the side table before reaching in again and breathing a sigh of relief. The bottle Nik had given her was still intact.

She quickly slipped into nightclothes and then sat on the edge of her cot to inspect the small vial. She unscrewed the top, tentatively lifted it off, and found a dropper attached to the lid. She sniffed it once and immediately flinched back at the awful odor. If it were poison, she would be none the wiser, and that made her sick to her stomach. But as Nik had said, what choice did she have but to trust him? Surely there would be no reason to kill her this way when he could benefit greatly from handing his rare catch to the king.

Then she decided. If it could put her into a deep sleep and she wouldn't dream of anything, she would take a chance for that shot of bliss.

Before she changed her mind or lost her nerve, she squeezed the top to collect the liquid inside and then brought it up to her tongue to let two drops fall. She cringed at the foul taste, then she screwed it closed and quickly hid the bottle under her bed before Jakon could return and ask her about it.

He came in seconds later and smirked at the sorry state she must've looked.

As they lay in the peaceful darkness, Faythe watched the dust dance in the air where moonlight pooled into the room. She began to feel drowsy, but she wasn't sure if it was down to the alcohol or if Nik's miracle tonic was really working.

"Lumarias," she mumbled, her eyelids suddenly feeling as if they weighed a ton. She heard the shift of Jakon's pillow as he turned his head to her. "My sword—I'll call it Lumarias."

CHAPTER 7

THE MORNING AFTER the solstice celebrations, Faythe awoke to find Jakon's cot already empty and was shocked when she fumbled for her discarded pocket watch to find it was past midday. She naturally surfaced back to consciousness. She'd slept through her entire hangover and even felt *refreshed*.

Faythe had never felt so bright and alert from a full night of peaceful rest before. For the first time, she hadn't found herself in a single dream or nightmare and had instead fallen into a dark pit of blissful, deep sleep.

She slept the same for the next seven consecutive nights by routinely taking the drops her unlikely fae savior had given to her. A full week later, she was exuding energy. Even Jakon and Marie commented on her glowing change of attitude.

But her drops were running very low, with only a dose or two left. She'd been on the lookout for Nik since the contents drained to halfway. So far, there had been no sign of him in any of the day or night patrols, and she was starting to panic.

Faythe needed the drops. They provided her only hope of protection against herself. She would take them every night for the rest of her life if she had to. After all, she couldn't risk accidentally wandering into anyone's mind—if that was what her ability meant —and better, no one could walk into *hers*.

She had to ask Nik for more or find out where she could buy the drops herself.

When the workday finished, she headed back to the hut to find Jakon had already returned. He was hunched over the table in the kitchen, devouring a bowl of stew and a slice of bread. He nodded for her to sit, the same waiting for her.

"You cooked?" She raised an eyebrow, taking a seat opposite and tucking in.

He chuckled. "Not exactly. Mrs. Bunsen had leftovers she insisted I take back with me."

The farmer's wife was a kind woman and would offer them food whenever she had extra that was going to spoil, usually in the form of cold pies and meats. The warm meal was a welcome treat.

"I think I'll go to the square tonight, break in Lumarias a bit more," Faythe said after a few mouthfuls.

Jakon's shoulders slumped. "We've been every night since the solstice," he complained.

They had, and while she'd enjoyed every minute of practicing with her new blade, Faythe had never told him the real reason she insisted on going every night. She wanted to see if she could spot Nik in the night patrols. She'd made them stay until midnight most nights, but still no sightings of him, to her dismay.

"I'll go alone. I've chopped through all your sticks anyway." Faythe sniggered. When she'd whittled his sticks to mere twigs, he'd resorted to using a dagger in each hand, which he was surprisingly skilled at maneuvering.

He shook his head. "No, it's fine. I'll come."

She knew it was a begrudging agreement and could see his fatigue. She rolled her eyes. "It's a couple of streets away, Jak, and there's fae patrol all over. I'll be safe, you worrywart." She tossed a piece of bread at him.

Jakon paused his eating, contemplating before heaving an exaggerated sigh. "Fine," he drawled, "but back by ten?"

"Eleven," she countered.

He narrowed his eyes. "Deal."

She smiled in triumph, eager to finish her meal and change to leave.

Faythe dressed in black leather pants with a tucked-in loose white shirt and her same old black boots. After she braided her hair back, she looped her sword belt around her hips and swung her cloak on. Bidding Jakon goodbye where he lay collapsed on his cot, she had no doubt he would fall asleep as soon as she was gone.

Slipping into the night, Faythe embraced the calm of the quiet streets in contrast to the bustle of daytime. She passed two fae patrol who didn't bat an eye as she walked her usual route. Most of them knew her face and likely where she was headed.

Arriving at the square, she discarded her cloak on a side bench as she began to swing at and block her imaginary opponent, letting the world disappear around her to fall into her usual focused calm. Close to an hour later, she was slick with sweat, ducking and swirling and striking in a graceful dance of combat. She could almost hear the high clank of connecting steel where her blade met her phantom adversary.

She paused, her breath sharp, when she heard voices and peered down each street connected to the square to check if it was fae soldiers. When a small group of drunk humans walked into the space and passed by, she didn't hide her sigh of disappointment.

"Not hoping for anyone in particular, are you?"

At the sound of Nik's voice, her heart leapt in relief. *About time!* When she turned, scanning each direction again, she couldn't spot him anywhere.

He whistled, and it sounded from above her. Flicking her eyes up, she spied him perched on the rooftop behind, watching her with a sly smile.

"If that little show was for me, consider me impressed," he said. "For a mortal," he added with a grin. He stood and went to jump.

She was about to bark her protest that it was far too high, but he leaped and landed on the ground below in silent feline stealth before straightening and leaning back against the wall in the shadows. She stared at him wide-mouthed until she remembered he was fae and the human laws of nature didn't apply to him. She snapped her mouth shut with a scowl at his arrogant smirk and noted he was in his casual attire again, his cloak hood shadowing most of his face. Not on duty tonight then.

"How long have you been there?" she asked irritably.

He simply shrugged, adding to her quickly escalating ire.

She asked instead, "Where have you been?"

He laughed quietly. "I didn't realize I was needed." His eyes flashed in amusement.

Faythe bit back her retort.

"You know, I'd have thought you'd be a little more...pleased to see me," he said.

Oh, he was enjoying this. She was doing a good job of holding her tongue. She needed him, though it pained her to admit it.

The scraping of boots and faint voices down the street to her left stole their attention. Nik pressed a finger to his lips and motioned for her to follow as he dipped into an unlit alley. She sheathed her sword and flung her cloak over her shoulders. Once the three fae patrol had passed with a quick glance, she darted after Nik.

It was so dark she had to squint her eyes to make out the different shapes and not trip over anything, but she still couldn't see his figure down the length of the street. She was about to call his name when a hand clamped over her mouth. Her scream quickly died in her throat as she was whirled around. Faythe could just about make out Nik's emerald eyes piercing hers in the eerie darkness.

"Did you not get my gesture to be *quiet?*" he hissed through his teeth.

She winced, muttering a low apology when he released her.

He continued walking farther down the narrow passage. She followed close behind as if something else might make a move to grab her. They stopped at the end to check for bodies before scuttling over to the next dark street.

Nik led them in and out of main streets and alleyways and up over the hills that held the solstice bonfires. She came to a halt before they entered the small wooded area.

Noticing she wasn't so close behind anymore, he turned to her. "You coming?"

No one ever entered these woods, claiming it was home to a whole horde of unrested spirits and other wicked creatures. She knew a boy who'd accepted a dare to go in there when she was younger. It had taken him weeks to recover, and he looked as if he'd seen monsters from a personal Netherworld. He never told anyone what greeted him in there.

She hesitated. "Aren't these woods, like...haunted?" She cringed at the risk of sounding ridiculous.

He laughed a little. "Yes...and no," he said cryptically. Seeing she wasn't about to enter on that basis, he clarified, "The woods has a natural defense mechanism. You might see things you don't like at first, but if it deems you worthy, it'll let you pass."

She swallowed hard. "And how can you be sure it'll find me worthy?"

He shrugged, taking a step closer. "I'm not," was all she heard before he vanished through a veil of black.

Faythe cursed him colorfully and repeatedly as she paced in front of the tree line. When she looked to where Nik had disappeared, she could see nothing but pitch-black past the first two staggered rows of trees. It was like a doorless wall into another realm. The more she stared at the misted veil, the more she felt its pull: a silent, chanting dare to enter. The only slight comfort was that she could hear no screams or shouts from Nik—unless the smoke shielded that too.

Seeing no alternative, as the fae guard had not returned and she needed something from him, Faythe held her breath and took a wide step straight through the blanket of dark.

It was eerily black just past where she entered, darker than the night in the open fields as the canopy snuffed out all hues of blue. The woodland extended further, and she was completely surrounded by endless scattered lines of warped, wrinkled tree trunks. Thick heads of black leaves that looked more like flapping bats grew above, leaving not a single trace of the bright moon and stars. When she turned to look back, she could no longer see the grassy hills she'd come from. There was no way to go but forward, so she took a step, and then another, cautiously making her way deeper through the charcoal bodies of timber.

Nik was nowhere to be seen. Faythe realized what made her skin prickle and every hair stand on end was not the gloom and ghostly appearance of the woods; it was that there was absolutely no sound. Not a single woodland creature made themselves known through song or movement. She took another step, and the crack of a fallen branch beneath her foot echoed through the still silence. Then she cried out as something gripped her boot.

Panic rising, she tried to yank free of the branch that laced its crooked fingers around her ankle, trailing its spindly limbs higher up. When she tried to move her other foot, she found it too was gripped by black vines that oozed a dark liquid where they grew around her calf. She pulled Lumarias free, but another vine lashed out beside her and began to snake up her wrist and arm, leaving a cold, wet trail.

Faythe dropped her only weapon, and it landed on the moss

with a faint *thud*. Another vine captured her limp left arm, leaving her completely bound and vulnerable.

She was going to die. This was a trap, and she'd fallen right into it. She would have buckled with fear if she weren't being held up in a tangled web of obsidian roots. She snapped her eyes shut and focused on her erratic heartbeat.

Then the vines stopped growing.

"Faythe," the shadows whispered.

She trembled and let out a shaky breath, clamping her eyes closed so hard it hurt.

"Why won't you look at me, Faythe?"

She tried to block out the sound—a female voice—but the words rang between the trees, piercing right through her ears to rattle in her mind.

"Look at me," it cooed.

She refused, hoping that whatever it was would kill her quickly and painlessly.

Suddenly, a rumble shook through the woods, vibrating under her feet to tremble up and into her very bones.

"Look at me!"

She snapped her eyes open with the command and let out a strangled sound at the sight. Those eyes—*her* eyes—but slightly darker in tone, and the rest of her appearance exactly as she remembered. Her mother.

"My dearest Faythe." It was her voice, likely plucked straight from Faythe's head, but also not her voice, as it was distorted by whatever had conjured the vision. "Tell me what you're afraid of, Faythe."

Tears streamed down her face. She could only stare at her in pain. *She's not real,* Faythe told herself. *A trick of the mind. A cruel, wicked trick of the mind.*

"What do you want?" she whispered back, her lip quivering.

A new voice spoke, and her heart leapt. Jakon.

"I want to know your deepest fear."

Twisting her head to see her friend standing beside her, she let out another sharp sob. His face was beaten and bloodied, and the sight splintered her heart.

"Stop," she pleaded.

"Say it."

She hung her head and sobbed in defeat, trying to get his image out of her mind. A part of Faythe knew she deserved this, and she wanted to curl up and submit to the demon taunting her. Even if it meant her life, she deserved it.

"You can't protect anyone," the ghost of Jakon mocked her.

Then she realized the woods already knew exactly what her greatest fear was. The key was getting her to own it; to face it. From behind the wooden silhouettes, more figures emerged. They were cloaked, hooded, and...faceless. She caught a glint of steel as they approached her mother and Jakon, floating like harbingers of death to the people she loved.

Faythe strained against the bonds that held her. *"Please!"* she cried in frantic desperation.

Each step seemed faster than the last until they all stopped, close enough to strike them. Her whole body shook violently while she watched in cold-blooded terror. They raised their swords in unison, poised to bring them down on the two people dearest to her.

Faythe instantly snapped. Fear struck her mind like a bolt of lightning, awakening her. She twisted the oily black vines around her wrists and gripped them tight—then she poured every ounce of strength she had through her arms, which contracted painfully against the ropelike restraints, and cried out with the force it took to break them.

They tore from their roots, and she released a harsh breath when she felt her hands free. Faythe didn't waste a second, not a single breath, before swiping Lumarias from the ground and swiftly twisting to sever the bonds at her ankles. She lunged forward, feeling time slow as she watched the fall of the blade that would seal Jakon's fate. Gauging the distance, she thought she would be too late. But she stepped up and lifted her own blade above her friend's head. The cry of connecting steel resonated chillingly through the still forest, mere inches from his neck.

"I'm not afraid; I'm *terrified!*" she cried in anguish, pushing off the faceless monster's blade. It backed away from her, the copies of the ghost mirroring every flicker of its movement. It didn't position to attack her again, but Faythe advanced as it went on the defensive. "I'm terrified the people I love will die, and it'll be my fault!"

Their swords crossed over and over, and Faythe poured all her anger and grief into each swing to cut down the foe threatening those she loved. Overcome with a deep fear she could never protect them, she cried out loud while raising her sword for the killing blow. She could do it, whatever it took to keep them safe. Yet in her cowardice, she closed her eyes as she brought the blade down, knowing it would strike through the dark, faceless demon.

As her blade came to a stop between her hands at her side, she felt nothing. She was panting hard but dared open her eyes to face the creature she'd slain. To her shock, it was Jakon who now stood before her, his face once again perfect and unscathed.

"Why are you so afraid, Faythe?" it asked in his voice.

She trembled from her sobs, and her tone dropped low. "It's my fault she's dead," she confessed. The truth she'd buried so deep to forget tore open an old wound in her heart. "My mother... She was out looking for me that night. I didn't stay home like she begged me to. I left to go play in the forest even though she warned me to never go in there. It was dark, and I heard a scream, so I ran all the way home, and I waited all night...but she never returned." Her voice cracked as the words tumbled from her. "I tell everyone she left, but I know... I know it was her scream that night. Whatever she warned me about in the forest came for her, and I lured her right to it. She screamed...and I ran."

The tears stopped forming, and Faythe went completely numb at her self-conviction. She forced herself to turn around and face the ghost of her mother. "I'm so sorry." Her eyes fell to the woodland floor as the surrounding darkness eased into a soft gray.

A glowing figure approached and stopped in front of Faythe, gripping her chin with a ghostly lightness and guiding her face to look up. She stared directly at her own bright reflection, and her phantom-self smiled softly back.

"It is not your fault," it said. "There is so much you are yet to discover, Heir of Marvellas. So much you are destined for."

Her mother stood to its left, and Jakon to its right. Relief overcame Faythe at seeing her friend unharmed. She was too late to protect her mother, but she would protect him—with her life if needed.

"Stay true to yourself, Faythe. Aurialis will be your guide." They parted to reveal a bright veil of white instead of obsidian black.

Faythe felt too hollow to take in anything the voice said and too angry to try a response. With one last look at her mother's soft features, she lifted her chin and wiped her face, stalking for the blinding white exit.

She didn't look back.

CHAPTER 8

T HE WOODS OPENED up into a bright, ethereal glade—a stark
contrast to the nightmare from which she'd emerged. She
flinched at the sudden change in light as the night shifted into clear
daytime.

The sky was a cloudless crystal blue that sparkled as if it held
eternal stars. The trees around the open space glittered, and there
was a wide lake with a beautiful shimmering waterfall, the sound of
its soft cascading water soothing her pain and grief. Colorful
flowers decorated the perfect green grass, and Faythe breathed in
pure, cool, clarifying air. It was like no place she had ever seen
before, untarnished by man or fae.

She spotted Nik leaning casually against a giant rock near the
lake. "There you are!" he exclaimed cheerfully, pushing off it and
stalking toward her. His grin faltered as he got close enough to take
in the sight.

Faythe had examined herself already. There was no trace of
the black liquid from the vines or dirt from the ground, but she
imagined her face was pale and grim.

"You're an *asshole,*" she hissed, not having the energy to shout.

He folded his arms. "What did you see?"

She pushed past him, stalking to the water. "It doesn't matter," she said flatly.

He caught up to her in a few steps and was silent for a moment before he spoke. "If you ever want to talk about it, just say the word." There was no taunting or teasing in his tone.

Faythe gave an appreciative nod that he wasn't pressing the matter further. She wasn't sure she could revisit those events so soon, and it wasn't something she wanted to share with a fae male who was still little more than a stranger.

"Why did you bring me here?"

"I wanted to show you this," he said, gesturing around them. "Plus, it's away from prying eyes and ears." He smiled—a warm, genuine smile she thought really suited him in place of his usually cocky, sly looks.

Faythe stared into the lake that rippled with iridescent waves.

"Not many people make it into these woods. I thought it'd be the perfect spot for you to…train," he said, trying to pick the right word.

She knew then that he wasn't talking about swordplay. "I don't need to *train,*" she said quickly. "I just need more of those drops— they work." The words came out a little more desperate than she intended.

"Too well, it seems. Even I couldn't get into your head," he marveled.

She recoiled in horror. "You were trying to get into my *head?*"

"Only seems fair, don't you think?" He gave a knowing smile.

Faythe clicked her tongue and shot him a glare. Right. She'd unintentionally invaded his mind, unwittingly exposed herself, and led them into this whole mess. She silently cursed herself and him and the damned Spirits—or whoever else she could blame for giving her the ability in the first place. She didn't want it, not even in the slightest. It only meant danger and trouble for Faythe and anyone associated with her.

Nik continued, "I had to be sure they worked and the dosage

didn't harm you." She spluttered at the last part, but he ignored her. "A fae would typically need four drops to stifle the ability. Half of that seemed like a fair guess to prescribe to you." He grinned, amused at her look of utter disbelief.

"And if it was too much?" she dared to ask.

He gave her one of those insufferable casual shrugs. "It wasn't," was all he said.

She stared wide-eyed as he strolled over to the edge of the broad lake, hands stuffed into his pockets. She didn't need him to confirm what she suspected would be the outcome of taking too much tonic at once. She swallowed hard, caught between a mixture of anger he could have killed her and gratitude because she likely would have taken the risk regardless.

Of course, who would ever suspect a *human* might need a potion originally concocted for a fae body?

He didn't ask her to join him as he settled on the grass, stretching his legs out in front and using his arms to prop himself up from behind. Faythe lowered herself down beside him anyway, sitting cross-legged.

"I can't give you more of the tonic. It was only a temporary solution."

She whipped her head toward him. "I *need* it, Nik, please—"

He cut off her desperate begging. "It's not something you can buy at the market, Faythe. It's rare and only really used as a weapon against our kind. The king has it in his personal collection of serums to snuff out all kinds of abilities. It was a last resort to give you that—and a risk. If taken for too long or in too high a dosage, the mind shuts down, convincing the body you're dead. The heart stops."

She didn't speak. It wasn't from fear that one drop too much could have spelled the end for her. Instead, her heart sank at her broken hope of being rid of the curse.

"In a smaller dosage, it can also be used to stifle your ability but still allow another Nightwalker to enter your mind. You'd be helpless to throw them out," he added quietly.

She let out a long sigh of defeat.

At seeing her solemn expression, Nik sat upright and faced her. "You just need to learn how to control it," he said positively. "If you do, you hold the keys to your own mind. You can choose not to use your ability and be aware if you find unwelcome guests in *your* head. You can hide things from them without them knowing. If you master it, no one will find out what you are."

It was a small flicker of hope. Faythe turned her head to look at him and found his eyes already fixed on her. She tore her gaze away, cheeks heating.

"What are you?"

"I don't know what I am," she said quietly.

There was a long pause in which neither of them spoke. She looked deeper into the lake and gasped as she noticed the tiny orbs of light dancing below the surface. Getting to her knees, she reached a hand in to touch them, but they darted away from her fingers.

"Yucolites," Nik said in answer to her curiosity. "They're rumored to heal any wound or illness, though I've never been able to bottle them." He frowned into the lake.

Faythe looked at the fae warrior and found herself forgetting what he was: different, superior even, a member of the king's guard. And yet he was so...*ordinary*. It surprised her. In fact, she even felt *guilty* for believing they were all the same—imperious and uncaring of human lives. Yet here he was, helping her when he had no reason to, and they were barely more than strangers.

He met her gaze.

"Why do you bother?" she asked quietly.

He knew what she meant. "Despite what you may think of my kind, we're not all heartless."

"It was you who told Reuben to flee."

He curved an eyebrow in surprise. "I did, and he wasn't the

only one. Some I couldn't get to in time. The king has ordered all of his Nightwalkers to root out those in the towns who are associating with Valgard."

"Is he killing them—the humans?" She knew the answer already, but it was confirmed by the grim look on Nik's face. Her stomach fell as if she were finding out for the first time.

Her mind flashed to the innkeeper's son, dragged onto the streets the night she and Jakon got Reuben out on time. They'd left him to that fate, and even though she knew there was no helping him, it didn't ease her guilt.

"It's not their fault. They're being left defenseless," she said. "Life's not easy for a lot of us in the outer town."

He nodded his understanding. "We're at war, Faythe, and have been for centuries. One small piece of information could mean all the difference. We've stood for a long time, but we're not untouchable."

It made her think. "How old are you?" she asked.

He laughed through his nose. "Old. To your kind anyway, but still fairly young to mine."

She rolled her eyes. He was avoiding a direct answer. He looked to be no older than twenty-five in human years.

"You look at least seventeen," he observed.

Faythe scoffed. "I'm *nineteen*, I'll have you know." She glared, but a playful smile twitched at the corners of her mouth. She figured her lack of shape and womanly development from going many days without a proper meal made her look young for her age. She was actually coming up on twenty.

He barked a laugh. "I'm close to three centuries old," he finally admitted. "Not around when the war first started, but the great battles." He paused, and she noted the dark look flash across his face at the recollection. He inhaled deeply. "Let's just say, I really pray to the Spirits we don't see carnage like that again."

Faythe gaped at him. A cold chill settled over her bones at the thought of the horrors and bloodshed he must have seen during that dark time long before she was born. The age that saw two mighty kingdoms fall. But if he fought and had seen his companions slaughtered, watched the streets be painted crimson with innocent blood, it seemed his spirit never broke. She could admire him for that courage and bravery alone.

Nik's age shouldn't have surprised her—he was immortal after all—but it made her feel strangely *very* young and inferior. She was sitting next to a male who had already lived more than thrice a mortal lifespan.

Before she could ask any further questions, he bounded to his feet and walked a few paces back to the large clearing with the brightest green grass she'd ever seen. Faythe watched him but made no move to follow.

Nik withdrew his sword. "Up," he said, motioning her to stand with the point of his blade. "Sword out."

She hesitated for a second, continuing to watch him remove his cloak and discard it next to the trees. Feeling a little self-conscious, she rose, copying his movements until she stood facing him. She suddenly felt very vulnerable under the sly gaze of the lion stalking its prey.

"I don't know if swordplay is going to help with my... *problem,*" she said warily.

He chuckled. "No, but we could sit and talk all night, or we could have fun while we do it." He gave her a predator's smile.

She swallowed hard, knowing she was about to thoroughly get her ass handed to her. While she was confident in her combat abilities against her *human* friends, she wasn't foolish enough to think she was any sort of match against a fae.

"Got a name?" Nik nodded his head at the blade tightly gripped in her right hand.

"Lumarias," she said.

He made a sound of approval. "The key," he translated.

Jakon had never asked her if it meant anything. She didn't

suppose it mattered, but she had chosen the word of the old language from a book her mother often read to her as a child.

"Well," Nik said wickedly, "let's see how she sings." Then he swung rapidly and without warning.

He missed taking her arm off by a split second as she brought her sword up with both hands, the force vibrating through her bones and translating to the sharp cry of connecting steel that echoed through the clearing. She looked at him incredulously but didn't have time to shout her complaints as she was forced to go on the defensive when he moved again. They parried back and forth for a short while, and she panted, using every inch of focus to keep up, while he hardly looked winded at all. She could tell he was holding back for her sake, which only made her anger rise in determination. She pushed harder, faster, ducking and swinging, but she was severely outmatched. Nik disarmed her, sending Lumarias flying from her grip, and had his blade to her throat in two maneuvers.

"Good." He grinned, lowering his sword and motioning for her to retrieve hers. "But you leave your entire right side exposed when you deflect like that."

She snatched her blade up with a frustrated groan. "Tell me how to control the...*Nightwalking.*" She winced at the word.

Faythe struck first, and Nik blocked with immortal ease.

"When we sleep, we don't automatically walk into someone else's mind. It's a *choice.*" He counterattacked, and she ducked left.

"I don't *choose* to enter anyone's head," she breathed, again on the defensive from his flashes of steel.

"You do—you just don't know it." He spun around her so fast she barely registered when they switched sides, still tracking each other. "There's a moment when your subconscious first wakes that you are completely in your own head."

Left, right, left, she blocked his onslaught of attacks.

"You can either focus on a target and arrive at the doors to their unconscious mind, or—"

68

Again, she found her sword being knocked from her hand as Nik's hovered over her heart.

"—you can simply give in to your own unconsciousness. Sleep, in other words." He lowered his blade and used it to prop himself up while she gathered her breath.

She folded her arms across her chest. "I don't choose it though; it just happens."

He chuckled. "You must have a very active mind at night to not be aware of it." Nik's head tilted. "Do you find it's usually people and events that have happened that day?"

Faythe tried to think back. Her dreams were always of people she'd seen in town. Now she knew they weren't just dreams but she was in their *minds*, it made her feel strangely guilty for trespassing on private thoughts and memories.

"I suppose," she mumbled.

"My guess would be that you let your emotions run too high. Whatever or *whoever* has affected you, good or bad, is likely what influences where you go at night." After a short pause, he grinned wildly at her. "I must have made quite the impression."

Her cheeks flamed. She wanted to hiss a retort, but words failed her. Instead, she swiped Lumarias from the grass and twisted it in her wrist a couple of times as it was already starting to ache against the force of his blows.

"Arrogant prick," she muttered.

In a flash, steel met steel, so close to her face she felt the phantom kiss of the razor's edge across her cheek. He looked down at her through crossed blades, their breath mingling. It was a battle of wills as they stared each other down, until she pushed with everything she had, and he backed up a step with wicked delight.

They circled each other. "The key is in your own awareness," he said.

She laughed without humor. "You're not really helping."

Nik stopped pacing and sighed. "It'll take practice. Try tonight. We all work in different ways. I can only guide you with words—

69

the rest is up to you." He gave her a pitiful look and sheathed his sword. "I think that's enough for tonight."

Faythe huffed, doing the same, and stalked over to grab her cloak. After a silent moment, she asked quietly, "What if I can't control it?"

"You can, and you will. Your life depends on it, and if that's not enough motivation, your friend's life may very well depend on it too."

He knew exactly which heartstring to pull, and she recoiled. "If it ever comes to it, you save him, not me," she said fiercely. "You get him out whatever it takes."

He frowned at her, contemplating. "It won't come to that," he concluded.

The question she'd been terrified to ask came rushing to the surface. "Would he kill me...for what I am?" Her breath shook.

"I don't know," he said honestly. "The king doesn't like what he can't control. He doesn't like surprises. He has many gifted fae in his service, but a human? He might not like the idea of your kind having a force that could be used against him." He ran a hand through his inky black hair.

"I'm not a threat," she said in horror.

"We don't know what you are yet, Faythe."

CHAPTER 9

F AYTHE CREPT SLOWLY and quietly back into the hut, breathing a sigh of relief that Jakon was passed out in his cot. It was half past eleven when she parted from Nik at the edge of town, and she would never have heard the end of Jakon's scolding that she was late back.

She discarded her sword and cloak, changing as silently as a ghost before sliding into bed. Her mind was a whirlwind of thoughts and emotions.

My guess would be that you let your emotions run too high. Nik's words replayed in her thoughts, and she clamped her eyes shut, willing herself to calm her mind from spiraling right into whoever's it landed on when she finally found rest. Still, she was terrified to sleep.

She tossed and turned for hours. Every time she felt her eyelids droop, she shook herself awake, not confident Nik's advice would register when she slipped into that space of *subconscious,* as he'd called it.

Faythe turned on her side and looked at Jakon, asleep like the dead and snoring peacefully. She silently cursed him in her state of grumpy restlessness for being able to sleep without any worries.

Her eyelids fell shut. She could rest her eyes for a moment. That was all she needed.

Just for a few minutes…

Jakon strolled down the street greeting everyone as he passed. No one paid Faythe any attention as she trailed behind him.

She vaguely recognized the far east side of Farrowhold and wondered what they were doing here since there wasn't much of interest in this end of town. She heard the loud *clang* of metal before she spied the blacksmiths near the end of the street. Did her sword need adjusting? She wracked her brain while the sounds got closer but couldn't remember when they had discussed it or planned a trip here.

Spotting them outside the open compound, the person inside stopped their hammering and set their tools aside. They wore a long apron and a welding mask.

Jakon moved further into the large space, and the blacksmith wiped their hands on their apron before removing their face shield. It shocked Faythe as the man she expected to see turned out to be a young woman. She was pleasantly surprised at the beautiful blonde lady who greeted them, and she couldn't help but stare with raised brows. Her hair was in a messy braid, and there was soot smudged across her cheeks and forehead, but Faythe gawked in admiration at the woman's crystal-blue eyes and effortless soft, feminine face.

"She's my best work," the woman told Jakon with a wide grin.

A strange feeling went through Faythe, and she recoiled in bewilderment, her heart fluttering a little. She'd never had these kinds of feelings for a woman before. They were mixed with giddy excitement, and Faythe couldn't understand herself as her eyes remained fixed on the stranger. Jakon grinned at her, and she retreated further into the workshop, behind a curtain, coming back with something under a black sheet.

"The stone was a perfect shape—it fit well," she commented, pulling the sheet off to reveal the magnificent sword beneath. *Faythe's* sword, Lumarias.

Faythe's hand shot to her side, which was now bare. When her eyes followed, she beheld her clothing, and—

Horror, shock, and realization paralyzed her all at once. *"The key is in your own awareness."* She wasn't here with Jakon—not really. She was in his mind; his *memory.* Her breathing came out fast and hard. Did he know she was here? It didn't seem like it, but she blanched at the thought of him knowing when he woke up. She had no right to be here.

Jakon looked over the sword in awe. "It's perfect," he breathed. "More than perfect. You've really exceeded yourself, Marlowe."

Color warmed the blacksmith's cheeks as he took the blade from her, balancing it in his palms.

Nausea overcame Faythe. She wanted to apologize profusely and explain she didn't mean to be here, beg him to forgive her. It wasn't her feeling those emotions before; they were Jakon's. Her own feelings mixed with his in the memory, and she found it hard to separate them. Now aware she was Nightwalking, Faythe found she could listen to his thoughts. Every thought he was having.

Dizziness struck her as she considered everything she would be able to know about him by being in here. Every personal secret and feeling, everything that made him who he was, laid right out in front of her. He would never know.

"She's a lucky woman." Marlowe smiled.

At the look she gave him, Faythe wanted to insist things weren't like that between them. But she couldn't. She was never there and had never even been to the blacksmiths before.

Faythe squeezed her eyes shut and covered her ears, trying to block out the thoughts interweaving with hers, causing her head to pound. She focused on her bed, her room, just as she had done trying to exit Nik's mind before. Feeling a thread, she pulled at it with everything she had, back into herself...

Bolting upright, Faythe struggled for breath as she tried to get the world to come into focus. Hands appeared instantly around her shoulders, and she thought she could hear Jakon's voice but couldn't distinguish whether it was real. She trembled violently and snapped her eyes to look at him, lifting a shaky hand to touch his face.

Real.

"—just a dream," she heard, the words distorted as if her head were underwater. Jakon brought his own hand up to gently hold her chin. "It was just a dream, Faythe." His voice became clearer.

Oh, Gods, if he only knew.

Vomit rose in her throat, and she pushed him away to run to the bathroom basin, barely making it in time before heaving up her meal from the previous night.

Jakon rubbed a hand soothingly over her back and held her hair out of her face until she slumped, resting her back against the wall and tucking her knees up tight.

"Do you want to talk about it?" he asked quietly from beside her.

She breathed a sob as tears welled in her eyes. She couldn't tell him and wouldn't even know how to—or if he would ever forgive her nonconsensual invasion of his memory. Shaking her head, she buried her face in her hands. Jakon only pulled her into his side and held her as she cried out of guilt and shame. But mostly, she cried out of hopelessness and fear she might never be able to control herself.

When she'd finally calmed enough to stand, Faythe took her time to wash and dress before finding Jakon at the kitchen table. He'd made a bowl of porridge for them both and was halfway through his when he looked up.

"Feeling better?" he asked softly.

She gave him a weak smile and sat down. "Yeah, I'm fine," she said, her voice hoarse.

She had no appetite, but she forced herself to eat so she didn't risk fainting from having nothing left in her system.

"Maybe you should ask Marie for the day off. You look like a ghost."

She shook her head. "No. I'm fine, honestly. I'm on thin ice with her now anyway." When Jakon lifted an eyebrow in question, she clarified, "Too many leisurely strolls between deliveries." It wasn't a complete lie.

He rolled his eyes with a light chuckle. "If you're sure. Don't want you passing out in one of her pies. You'd certainly get the sack."

Faythe mustered a smile and pushed her breakfast around to distract herself from the drop in her stomach she felt every time she looked at him. He was completely oblivious to what she was and what she was capable of.

Jakon finished his porridge and bid her goodbye after checking several times that she wasn't about to combust. Faythe left the hut shortly after, needing the fresh air before the workday started. The morning was just warming up, and she welcomed the slight chill breeze as she strolled slowly over the dusty cobbled streets, deciding to take the long route to the square since she had time to spare.

After a minute, she had an impulsive thought and twisted on her heel before she could change her mind. As she weaved through the eastern part of town, she knew it was a bad idea but wanted to confirm what she had seen last night was definitely a memory of Jakon's and not just her own dream. A desperate part of her still held onto the foolish hope she didn't really possess the ability Nik thought she did. In any case, she wanted to thank the blacksmith for their work on her sword. Having not known it was a *woman*, Faythe greatly admired the young blacksmith for her talents.

Turning the last corner, she paused for a second when the compound came into view. It was *exactly* as she had seen it last night, and as she approached the blacksmiths, everything was unnervingly accurate. She had to lean over and touch something as her own mind flashed from viewing it through Jakon's memory. She had never been here before and seeing it in person now ruled out any possible doubt it wasn't a dream of her own.

"Can I help you?" a man grumbled.

Her eyes darted up and landed on a rugged, slightly rotund older man. Faythe quickly deduced this must be Dalton, the man she thought had crafted her sword.

"I... Yes, I'm looking for, um—" She stumbled like an idiot, still in her own mind about the realism versus Jakon's recollection of the place. "Marlowe," she finally choked out, recalling the name she'd heard from her friend.

He skimmed her from head to toe, determining she wasn't going to be a threat, before shouting to the back. After a moment, the curtain lifted, and a striking resemblance to what she remembered of the woman last night came into view. Faythe blinked at the sight. *Real. This is real,* she reminded herself. But she couldn't stop the trembling and clamped her fists shut. It confirmed what she already knew as the woman she'd only ever seen in her friend's dream—his *memory*—became flesh and bone before her.

"Hi!" she chirped. Even her voice was uncanny.

Faythe shuddered. "Hi," she responded in little more than a whisper.

Marlowe stared at her expectantly but kept a welcoming smile as she leaned sideward against a beam at the front of the structure. Dalton made himself scarce in the back.

Faythe shook her head clear as she realized Marlowe was waiting for her to speak. "I...I, uh, I came to say thanks," she got out. "For my sword, I mean. My friend Jakon came to you." She cursed herself for stuttering so badly in her nervousness.

The blacksmith beamed. "Yes! I remember. You're Faythe, right? How does she swing?"

Marlowe was a picture of natural beauty—even more so

standing in front of her in real time. Her hair was in the same type of braid, but her face was as fresh as day. Her expressions lit up her entire face and made all the difference from the projection in Jakon's memory. She could tell why he would be attracted to her, both in looks and spirit.

Faythe nodded and smiled. "Like a dream," she answered.

"He did a lousy job of trying to describe your height and weight. Guys never do have a clue, so I balanced a lot of it based on my own measurements plus what he gave me." She looked Faythe over. "Seems like an accurate guess."

Indeed, they were both of similar height and build, with Faythe having about an inch of height on Marlowe and her bones protruding a little more. Looking at the healthy weight of the stunning blonde, she really felt the need to fill herself out.

"I named it Lumarias."

Marlowe beamed again. "I love it!"

With nothing else to add, Faythe said lamely, "Well, I'd better go. Can't be late."

Marlowe straightened and gave a warm smile. "Don't be a stranger."

Faythe nodded in silent promise and turned, walking a few steps before she spun around again in a last-second thought. "Oh! Jakon and I… It's not like that."

The blacksmith's cheeks flushed, and her mouth popped open. Faythe grinned deviously before turning to stalk away with a quiet chuckle.

CHAPTER 10

T HE MARKET WAS fairly quiet for the rest of the day after she visited the blacksmiths, and Faythe thanked the Spirits for it. Her energy was at an all-time low, and she didn't think she would survive a day of running errands.

Marie left her in charge of the stall for a while after deeming the flow of customers small enough for her to handle—much to Faythe's insult. She sat idly picking at an apple on a makeshift stool behind the counter. As much as she enjoyed the peaceful day, it also made it a struggle to keep her mind off her increasingly heavy eyelids.

Faythe leaned her head back against the wooden beam of the stall, closing her eyes and chewing on a bite of the ripe fruit. A cough sounded in front of her, and she jumped, her apple jolting from her hand and landing on the ground with a *thud*.

Nik smirked as she straightened and scowled at his unexpected intrusion. He had his usual black cloak on with his hood up, making him look very out of place in the summer heat.

"Not quite the place to potentially fall asleep and wake up... *elsewhere,*" he commented.

She glowered at him. "I wasn't going to *sleep.*" Though she understood it was risky to even close her eyes with how tired she was.

"How'd it go last night?" he asked, but her pale face and flat look must have said it all because his grin faltered. "Bad?" He winced.

She gave a long, defeated sigh and slumped back against the wooden post. Nik came slightly around the counter so she could speak without any potential listening ears picking up on their conversation.

"I was in *Jakon's* head." She cringed. "I invaded his private thoughts, and I can't even tell him. I can't forgive myself."

He gave her a solemn look, and she hated it. She didn't want his pity or for him to see her as a lost cause.

"There was no *in-between,* no *subconscious space*. One minute I was awake, and the next I was walking alongside him in one of his *memories.*" She hissed the last word under her breath.

He hummed and was quiet for a moment as if deliberating. "I have an experiment I'd like to try," he said at last. At her skeptic look, he rolled his eyes. "Meet me in the woods tonight, alone," he emphasized.

Faythe wouldn't even think to bring Jakon into this anyway, but she knew it would be difficult to get him to stay at home *again.* "Fine," she said. She would think of something. She had no other choice but to trust Nik, and quite frankly, she was desperate enough to try anything he could throw at her.

He peered over his shoulder, checking the area, before stepping back. "See you tonight, at nine o'clock." With a last mischievous smile, he disappeared as stealthily as he had arrived.

The rest of the day passed by painfully slow, and Faythe was grateful for the setting sun as she started her short walk home. She got a few streets away before an idea came into her head. With a cunning grin, she spun on her heel and decided to take an exceptionally long detour to pass by one specific compound.

Her nerves rose when she stood outside the blacksmiths for the second time that day. This was the best idea she could think of to occupy Jakon for the night, and she commended herself for the stroke of genius.

Marlowe was nowhere to be seen, nor was Dalton, but she could faintly make out voices from behind the back curtain. Faythe wrung her hands together before stepping into the front of the workshop.

"Hello?" she called weakly.

After a second, the familiar blonde peered out from behind the sheet. Seeing Faythe, Marlowe beamed and stepped out fully, but then her face fell in concern.

"Is there something wrong with your sword?"

Faythe shook her head quickly. "No, I...I was actually hoping you could do me a favor." She winced.

The blacksmith frowned warily. "Sure. What's up?"

Faythe hesitated, and then she rushed out the words. "I need you to help distract Jakon for me."

Marlowe raised her eyebrows in surprise before shaking her head vigorously. "I can't. I... How exactly am I supposed to do that?" she stumbled, looking flustered at the suggestion.

Faythe felt guilty for asking, but without something to keep Jakon busy, he was usually latched to her side. She cursed him for being so annoyingly overprotective.

"Just for tonight. I need to be somewhere, and he's like a little puppy dog I can't shake," she pleaded in light humor, praying Marlowe wouldn't ask questions.

The blonde laughed nervously, and the red in her cheeks only flamed more. "I don't know, Faythe. Is there no one else you can ask? He barely knows me." She bit her lip.

Faythe shot her a knowing look. "I'm certain you're the best distraction I could find."

Marlowe gaped at her. "He doesn't like me like that!" she hissed in embarrassment.

Faythe chuckled. "Trust me, he does." She didn't need to know exactly *how* Faythe had come to the knowledge. When Marlowe didn't respond, her grin widened. "So is that a yes?"

She stood chewing her lip, contemplating. "Give me five minutes. I need to wash," she grumbled, gesturing to her soot-covered face and hands.

Faythe gave a squeal of excitement before ushering her to be quick. Jakon would be expecting her back home by now. She perched on a stool inside the workshop, fiddling with the various hammers and spanners and marveling at the intricate tools scattered about that she wouldn't have the first clue how to use.

Close to ten minutes passed before Marlowe emerged again, clean-faced, with her hair now unbound in lazy waves running past her breasts. Again, Faythe found herself struck with envy at her effortless beauty. She'd changed into a light blue cotton gown that matched her eyes and had her deep blue cloak folded over her arm when she shouted through the sheet a quick goodbye to Dalton—who Faythe discovered was her father even though they looked nothing alike.

Marlowe was a picture of nerves and uncertainty as Faythe stood beaming at her. She hooked her arm through hers in silent encouragement and to prevent her from voicing the protests on her face. Then, together, they took off down the street.

When they stood outside the hut a quick ten minutes later, Marlowe paused, fidgeting with her skirts.

"Come on—he doesn't bite," Faythe said with a hint of suggestion.

Crimson flooded Marlowe's cheeks as she glared at Faythe. "You owe me," she hissed under her breath.

Faythe swung the door open with a cunning smile and saun-tered in, immediately spotting Jakon in the open kitchen, seated at the table. At the sight of Faythe, he smiled—but then it dropped, and he fumbled to his feet when he spied Marlowe behind her.

"I hope you don't mind," Faythe said innocently. "I swung by the blacksmiths to pay my thanks, and we got to chatting." She gestured to Marlowe still standing shyly by the door. "You failed to tell me my sword was crafted by such a skilled and pretty *female.*" She was teasing, but a part of her felt guilty for using Jakon's attrac-tion to Marlowe, which she only knew about from feeling it in his memory. An even bigger part of her thought it was worth it for the floundering look on his face.

Neither of them spoke, so Faythe continued. "She didn't have any plans for tonight, so I asked her to join us for dinner. You don't mind, Jak, do you?" She was enjoying this.

"What do you think you're doing?"

She maintained her air of innocence at Jakon's pointed look and the silent words she heard.

He choked out, "Of course not! But, uh—we don't really have anything here, so—"

"We'll have to go out then!" Faythe interjected cheerfully. "I'll just quickly freshen up, and we can go to Harbor Hall. Keep our guest occupied, will you?" she said to Jakon before retreating to the back bedroom to change out of her workday clothes.

Faythe dressed in her usual training attire as she had the night before and secured Lumarias at her hip. Then she threw her cloak on so Jakon wouldn't ask why she was armed when they were only headed to the restaurant on the harbor for food. She wasn't sure if swordplay would be a part of Nik's *experiment* or if she could even muster the energy to lift her blade, but she thought it best to be prepared.

When she emerged again, she paused at the sight of Jakon and Marlowe chatting at the table. They appeared relaxed in each other's company, and he had a gleam in his eye she'd only seen a handful of times when he'd looked at *her* in that way. She had never been able to return it—not in the way he hoped. Yet Marlowe did. Faythe smiled at them as a warm feeling settled in her. Jakon deserved to be happy with someone.

"Ready to go?" she chirped, not wanting to break their conversation, but she had less than an hour before she was due to meet Nik.

They nodded simultaneously and stood, heading for the door. Faythe followed after them, and the trio took off down the pleasantly calm streets toward the harbor. It was a ten-minute walk, which they spent getting to know their new female friend a little more.

Faythe found Marlowe's energy wonderfully contagious as she chatted in depth about her creations and blacksmithing experiments among other things. She was two years older than Faythe and had found intrigue in her father's craft since she was a young girl. Her mother had passed from the same sickness that swept the town and took Jakon's parents thirteen years ago. It was one tragedy the duo had in common, and even though Faythe had lost her mother by different means, she still connected with them on their level of grief.

When the blacksmith wasn't working, the beauty seemed to never stop using her brain. She had a deep passion for reading and knowledge, and Faythe perked at the mention of her interest in swordplay too. She was excited to get into the sparring ring with her sometime.

They approached the beautifully lit Harbor Hall overlooking the sea—one of the prime spots in Farrowhold's outer town. Faythe and Jakon had only been a handful of times, usually on occasions such as birthdays when they'd saved a few extra coin, but they had been careful with their spending recently, and she knew they could afford to eat a nice meal tonight.

Pushing through the small white wooden doors, Faythe was immediately hit with the delicious scent of fresh seafood and breathed in deeply. It was moderately busy in the large, ambient space, mostly filled with couples seated in the intimate booths. The three of them were warmly greeted and guided to a small four-seater table in the corner. Faythe tried not to think of herself as a third wheel when she took a seat next to Marlowe and let Jakon sit opposite her. It was a subtle tactic on her part for them to engage eye contact and conversation.

Faythe tried her best to stay engrossed in idle chatter with her friends, but her head was elsewhere, and she bounced her knee in an anxious tic while checking her pocket watch every ten minutes. Marlowe seemed to notice and kept shooting her knowing looks.

The food came, and it took Faythe's mind off the time for a while as she savored the delights of hot and cold seafood fresh from that day. But when they'd finished and the clock closed in on nine, she cleared her throat and made a show of trying to cover her wide yawn.

"I think I'm going to head back. I'm *really* tired," she said. Not a full lie—she certainly was exhausted, and Jakon would realize exactly why thanks to her epic display that morning.

He gave her a nod of understanding and said, "Of course. I'll get the bill—"

"Don't let me ruin your night," she cut in a little too quickly, shooting Marlowe a glance for help. "I mean, it's still really early after all," she recovered.

Marlowe chimed in casually, "They have great desserts here." She smiled sweetly at Jakon. "If you'd like to stay."

Faythe had to give her credit: even she could be tempted to stay with the look the blacksmith gave him. "Natural flirt" could be added to her new friend's list of fine traits.

Jakon's cheeks flushed, and he smiled back nervously. It amused Faythe immensely to see her best friend so flustered. She had never witnessed this side to him in their decade of friendship. She'd never actually seen him take an interest in *anyone*. Like Faythe, Jakon had never committed to a serious relationship before.

"I...I would—but, uh, Faythe..." he stumbled.

Faythe waved a hand. "I'll be fine, you big worrywart. Stay out for as long as you'd like and don't do anything I wouldn't do." She fastened her cloak before she stood, reaching into her pocket and placing a few coins on the table despite both of their protests. Then she swiftly left the establishment with a final good night.

She'd already hashed out some details with Marlowe on their trip back from the blacksmiths, so Faythe knew she would try to occupy him until at least midnight. Still, she had no clue how long Nik's plan for the night would take and didn't want to risk Jakon returning to an empty hut and sending out a search party.

Mercifully, Marlowe hadn't asked what she planned to get up to, but at her few curious and concerned looks, Faythe had promised her it was nothing dangerous.

That was only a half-truth, however, as nothing with Nik seemed to be certain.

CHAPTER 11

F AYTHE PULLED HER hood up as she left Harbor Hall and made haste down the streets. She was already running late. In her hurry, she skidded to a halt around the next corner, nearly colliding with four fae patrol to her complete horror.

She stepped aside instantly and bowed her head low, not daring to make eye contact as she moved out of their path. She recognized the brute of a warrior leading the patrol from her quick glimpse. The unruly scar that marred the left of his face was a distinguishing feature, allowing her to single him out as one of the royal guards who had detained the innkeeper's son with undue force.

Her breathing stilled as they halted beside her instead of marching past like they usually did. She kept her eyes to the ground, playing the part of the scared human girl so they might continue on without questioning her.

But one spoke. "Where are you off to in such a hurry?" A deep, rough voice—one that sent a spear of ice through her.

"Home," she said quietly, still not raising her head.

She heard the scuff of gravel before large black boots came into view on the ground right in front of her. She swallowed hard, her heart skipping a beat.

"You will look at me when you talk, girl," he warned.

She didn't move.

In a second, Faythe barely had time to blink when large, calloused fingers gripped her jaw, yanking her head up so fast she couldn't hide her wince of pain. The guard gave her a vicious grin.

"Better," he said.

She supposed he was handsome, beautiful even, despite the disfigurement. He had sharp facial features, with eyes of stark black and wavy brown hair that fell above his shoulders, half-tied back in a small knot. Yet as she held his stare, his feral eyes only delivered a promise of violence and despair to anyone who crossed him. She couldn't mask her anger, forced to stare back in his viselike grip. Everything in Faythe screamed at her to *run*.

"What is your name?" he said in a playful calm.

She debated not answering, but at the guarantee of pain, she hissed, "Faythe," while hoping her tone wouldn't land her in the same trouble as her silence.

One of the others spoke quietly from behind. "She frequently trains in swordplay in the square, Captain. She's harmless."

The captain held her for a moment longer, contemplating, before releasing her with a grunt. She wanted to thank the young fae guard who spoke up for her.

Faythe winced, her jaw throbbing faintly from his unnaturally tight hold. She knew it would bruise.

His eyes flicked to the hilt of Lumarias before they pierced into her golden ones again. "A mighty blade for such a lowly *human girl.*" He chuckled mockingly, and her hands twitched at her sides in a flash of rage.

"It was a gift," she said through her teeth.

His eyes narrowed on hers for a moment, and she didn't balk. *Don't give them a reason to look into you...* She dropped her eyes to the ground again in a silent bow of submission as Nik's advice echoed through her.

With a disgruntled sound, the captain stepped away. "On your way then, girl," he said, bored.

Faythe didn't hesitate, twisting sharply and making off again in a brittle walk. She spied a dark alley, and once she turned the corner, she ran.

She sprinted the rest of the way, taking the darkest streets and running all the way up the hills until the woods came into view. She spotted Nik immediately. He leaned idly against one of the trees. Relief calmed her storm of nerves. She didn't even realize she was shaking until she slowed her pace upon approach.

"You're late," he said, and then he took in the sight. "What in the damned Spirits happened?" Nik stormed up to her, scanning her body for signs of physical injury. "Who hurt you?" he snarled, catching her jaw, which still ached.

"The patrol." She breathed hard, not knowing how to form the right sentence. "The captain," she added between pants, bracing her hands on her thighs as the exertion from the short journey caught up with her all at once.

Nik swore. "I thought I told you to keep a low profile."

Faythe stared at him, incredulous. "I was keeping a *low profile!*" she snapped. "It's not my fault your kind are just savage, ruthless beasts who will take any opportunity to show dominance and belittle us *humans!*" She shook out of anger more than fear now.

His lips thinned as his eyes softened. "That's just Captain Varis." He ran a hand through his jet-black hair. "He's a wicked bastard and a sadist, but he's one of the king's most talented Nightwalkers. Don't ever underestimate him." His tone wasn't scolding; it was laced with concern.

Her face blanched. It was just her luck a Nightwalker would find reason to stop her when she needed to be invisible now more than ever.

Reading her thoughts, Nik said, "You need to be able to understand your own abilities. Damn it, Faythe, it's a wonder no one's found out about you yet with your recklessness."

She cringed and wanted to argue, but he continued.

"If you learn to control your ability, you won't need to fear any of the others being in your head. You can block things you don't want them to see and only give access to your completely ordinary life to keep them satisfied."

Her head spun at the new information. Nik only motioned for her to follow as he stepped into the woods.

She hesitated. "Will I see...*things* again?" she asked quietly.

He shook his head and held out his hand. "No. You've already proven yourself."

She looked at the offer of comfort in his outstretched palm and then to his eyes as he smiled in encouragement. Maybe it made her foolish and naïve, but she couldn't help but *trust* him. The feeling unnerved her. He knew of the one thing that could condemn her and had so far chosen to help instead of turning her in. She wasn't sure if that made him an ally, a friend, or if he was simply fueling his eternal curiosity. Whatever it was, she was grateful for it.

Faythe slipped her hand into his, and he led the way through the dark, veiled entrance. Afraid he would vanish and she would once again be alone, suffocated by dark mist and black vine webs, she didn't realize the strength of her grip until he chuckled down at their joined hands. They'd made it through the perfectly ordinary woodland and into the waterfall clearing, and her knuckles had turned pale from her viselike grip.

She released him immediately, cheeks flaming.

Nik slung off his cloak and walked to the middle of the open space before laying it flat on the grass and sitting on it. Faythe watched with a frown and didn't immediately follow until he wordlessly gestured for her to do the same.

"I take it this is part of your *experiment?*" she said, matter-of-fact, copying his actions.

He grinned in response before reaching into his pocket and producing two vials of liquid. "It's just a simple sleeping tonic," he said at her hopeful look. "It will put you under as you would fall asleep naturally, but your ability will still awaken your subconscious," he explained.

"We're going for a nap?"

He flicked her nose. "Smartass," he muttered, handing one of the bottles to her. "I'm going to try to catch you in that space between before you launch yourself to Gods know where."

She looked at him wide-eyed. "You're going inside my head?"

He gave her a devious smile. "What dirty little secrets do you have to hide? You look so horrified, Faythe."

She whacked his arm with a glare, and he barked a laugh.

"I'll have to take mine first. It'll be at least five minutes before it works. Once I'm out, you'll take yours. I'll be able to feel when you slip under, and, well…" He paused. "I'm not really sure if it'll work, but it seems worth a try."

Worry creased her forehead. "And if it doesn't? What if I end up somewhere else?"

"I should still be able to enter your mind. You'll feel me there, and I can hopefully coax you back, but—" Another one of those pauses she'd come to dread. "Well, it's new territory. I don't know if your ability works the same as ours."

Faythe nodded. She knew he was referring to the fact she was a human.

Nik sighed. "We won't know unless we test the theory."

She supposed she had nothing to lose at this point. She had to get this under control, and if that meant letting Nik inside her head, she had to try.

"Just know," he said, "I'm putting *a lot* of trust in you not attempting to kill me after I take this." He popped the cork off the top of his vial, lifted it to hers in cheers, then took the whole dosage before discarding it beside him.

Faythe rolled her eyes and watched him lie back, his eyelids closing with a dramatic, relaxed sigh. She sat with her knees tucked up and studied the rise and fall of his chest for a couple of minutes.

For a moment, she was struck by his vulnerability. A full-grown warrior fae male lay perfectly at her mercy. Though he'd said it in humor, she felt a small burst of warmth that he really *did* trust her enough not to attempt anything. This would perhaps be her once-in-a-lifetime opportunity to do so; the only time she would come face-to-face with a fae who was incapacitated enough for her to strike. Yet even if it were the malicious Captain Varis lying there unconscious before her, she was confident she would never take such a cheap and dishonorable blow.

When his breathing slowed and became heavier, she looked at her vial. *Here goes nothing,* she thought, tipping the contents down her throat and lying flat beside Nik. She turned her head to look at him, so peaceful and innocent, not a wrinkle or frown disturbing his smooth, pale skin. Handsome. Nik truly was a picture of immortal grace.

Her eyelids fluttered a few times as she felt herself drift away, and with it, her rising panic faded…

"Faythe," a distant voice called.

She felt as if she was being projected one way but another force was tugging her in the opposite direction. She grabbed onto that phantom thread and pulled herself toward it, against the current that wanted to cast her into oblivion. It wasn't long before she saw light piercing through the pitch-black void she was in and followed it all the way until it blinded her and she had to squint her eyes, blinking rapidly to adjust.

Then she was standing in an endless room of swirling gold and white mist. She was awake inside her own head. She could feel it; *see* it. The mist cleared around her to show a reel of memories that flashed from one to another. She saw memories from when she could barely walk, right up until this very day—her whole life, in perfect clarity.

She thought of one person in particular, and it stopped, playing in real time the memory of her mother not long before she was taken. They lay in bed together, her nine-year-old self tucked warmly under her mother's arm as she read to her. Tears wet her face, and her lip quivered, but she made no sound as she walked closer to the moving picture. It stopped as she willed it on her mother's face. Faythe reached out a hand to touch her, but it passed right through, and she sobbed once.

Suddenly aware of another presence, all the images around her faded instantly, leaving only clouds of white and gold. She turned her head to look at Nik, who stood silently behind her with his hands in his pockets. She supposed he had been there the whole time. His theory had worked, and she didn't care what he saw before she blocked the memories out.

"My mother," she whispered.

He gave a small nod. "I know," he said. After a short, solemn silence, he continued, "I used to spend endless nights in my head when my mother passed. It's different, seeing it in front of you like that. Over time, memories can become faded, and we forget the details. But in here…we can keep them *alive.*"

She gave him a sad smile, grateful he would share such a personal piece of information with her. She didn't know he too had mourned a parent and suddenly felt guilty she knew very little about him at all while she was so selfishly wrapped up in her own problems. She wanted to ask when he'd lost her and what happened, but it didn't feel right in the moment.

"I guess it worked," she mused instead, trying to change the subject and lighten the somber mood.

He smiled, seeming glad for the switch. "I almost lost you for a second, but you had the good sense to follow my lead." He looked around and made a curious sound.

She too observed the colors of her mind. "It looks like yours," she said, "but less sulky and gloomy."

He laughed. "Think of it as your aura. The colors reflect a part of you."

She crossed her arms in amusement. "So what exactly does black say about your soul?"

He shrugged impassively. "Perhaps that I'm damned to the Netherworld," he answered with a smirk.

She stuck a hand out to weave it through the mist. It sparkled, and she thought it beautiful as it entwined through her fingers. Wherever she moved, it followed, and she found she could bend it to her will without any movement, creating a small golden butterfly in the palm of her hand.

"You've really not seen the inside of your own subconscious before?" he questioned as he studied her.

Faythe shook her head. "I either dream——" She winced. *"Night-walk,"* she corrected, "or I don't remember seeing anything when I wake. But that's rare, mostly. I guess all this time, I was exploring the townspeople when I slept." She laughed a little, trying to find the humor to keep herself sane.

The butterfly took flight before dissipating into the rest of the mist.

Nik released a long breath. "Do you find yourself exhausted the next day? When you've been Nightwalking, I mean."

She huffed. "I'd forgotten what a good night's rest was like until the week you gave me those drops."

He raised his eyebrows. "No wonder, Faythe. You've probably not had more than a couple hours' proper rest in *years.*" At her look of confusion, he clarified, "When we Nightwalk, our mind is still active. If you spend a night in someone's head, you've not really rested. It's why we can't do it every night—we'd wear ourselves out and become sloppy." He shook his head in disbelief. *"Gods,* it's a miracle you've kept it up for so long without going insane. But it also explains a lot about your lack of control."

She blinked in horror. "So how do I turn it off?"

"You have to figure that part out for yourself," he said. "For me, it's like there are two doors, metaphorically speaking. I can either focus on a target and walk through the door that will take me straight into their mind...or I can take the other door, and it all becomes black."

She pondered, "So we can never have dreams of our own?"

"We don't have random visions that make no sense, if that's what you mean. But your mind is limitless; you can stay in your subconscious and conjure up your wildest desires. It can be fun." He grinned at her suggestively, and she rolled her eyes. She didn't want to think of what his "wildest desires" might be. "But again, you're not getting proper rest if you stay here, so we can only do it sparingly. The darkness is the only way we get full, energy-reviving sleep," he concluded.

All this information was both daunting and exhilarating for her. After thinking the worst and hating her newfound ability, it was uplifting to discover there could be a positive side. She could vividly see her mother in her memories and apparently create fully unrestricted and immersive dreams for herself. But she really longed for nothing more than getting frequent blissful, undisturbed *rest.*

Doubling back to what Nik said, she swallowed nervously. "What do you mean by 'become sloppy'?"

He took a long inhale, and she could see he was deliberating whether to expand on it. "This is the part you won't like, Faythe," he said carefully. "You already know that our specific *talent* is often used as a weapon. We can find out everything about a person. We can *plant* feelings and ideas if we're strong enough. And we can also shatter their mind with a single thought." His look turned grave. "If we exhaust ourselves by trying to Nightwalk, our heightened negative emotions from the lack of rest can either lead to discovery or... accidentally kill the host."

Faythe went cold all over, feeling the world get pulled from under her. It took a few seconds to fully register, but then she almost collapsed where she stood as his words triggered a dark memory. She replayed it over and over in her head, putting the pieces together as its new reality dawned on her. That couldn't be true. She wasn't capable of that. Because if she was…

"Oh, Gods," she whispered to herself.

He took a step closer. "I know it's a scary thought, but you'll be able to learn control now. You'll never—" His words faltered when she brought her eyes up with a look of absolute terror. Nik froze at the sight, his frown deep with concern. "Faythe, what is it?"

She was too stuck in her own pit of guilt and disgust at the likelihood of what she'd done to respond. Faythe focused and started to push him out. She was close to screaming in anguish and wasn't sure what her emotions could do to him in here.

Very quietly, just before he disappeared altogether, she whispered, "I think I already have."

CHAPTER 12

Faythe felt something trying to pull her from her subconscious where she sat alone with her knees tucked tightly to her chest. She didn't sob; didn't do anything but give herself over to the hollowness she felt as she recalled the memory over and over again, hoping with everything she had that it didn't mean what she thought it did.

The mist swirled around her as if she were a planet and it was her stratosphere.

She wasn't sure how long she sat there after casting Nik out, but the force was becoming too strong for her to fight any longer. She found herself giving in to the tug that brought her back to full consciousness.

Faythe smelled the grass first, like fresh, crisp rainwater. Then she heard the gentle crash of the waterfall and lapping waves where it joined the lake below. She felt the fabrics of her cloak under her fingers as she moved them. Taking a deep breath through her nose, she forced her eyes open and stared into purest shade of sky blue she'd ever seen. Finally, she felt *him* as Nik's warm hands registered, encasing one of her own.

When she at last turned her head to look at him, he wore a

mask of concern, sitting on his knees looking down on her. He said nothing, waiting for her to speak first in fear of her falling apart with one wrong move. She pulled her hand out of his, sitting for a second before standing and striding aimlessly closer to the water.

It took a moment for her to gather herself. "How do you know...?" She flinched, not wanting to ask but needing the answer. "How do you know if you've done it? Shattered a person's mind, as you say?"

She heard him shift off the grass and stand, but she didn't turn to look at him, only watched the water ripple instead.

"It's like..." He paused, and she noted the slight pain in his voice. "A mind, to us, is like holding a hollow sphere of glass in one palm. All it would take is one slight squeeze to watch it splinter into a million pieces, and one more for it to explode and turn to dust."

Her stomach twisted at the thought. "You've done it before," she stated more than asked.

"It's not something I'm proud of. I remember *everyone* I've ever done it to—"

"Murdered," she cut in bluntly, finally turning to face him. "Everyone you've murdered. That's what we are really, aren't we? *Weapons.*"

"We don't have to be."

Faythe could *feel* the regret and remorse in his eyes, and for a slight moment...she pitied him. Until she remembered he'd always had a choice over what he did; control in the ways she didn't.

"Why do you do it? Why work for a tyrant king who would let humans suffer and kill without a second thought? He's a self-serving monster, and you are nothing but a spineless puppet to do his dirty work," she spat.

She couldn't stop herself. Perhaps he didn't deserve her anger, and a part of her knew she was only deflecting the feelings she felt toward her own self—what she was, and what she'd *done*. But she would never come face-to-face with the male she really wanted to scream at to relieve the pain and hatred that had built inside her for a long time. At least, she wouldn't face the King of High Farrow and live.

"Careful, Faythe," he warned.

"Why should I be? It's only a matter of time before I'm next."

His eyes flashed dark. "You won't *ever* be next. Not if I have something to say about it," he said with surprisingly fierce determination.

She reeled in her anger and let out a sigh of defeat, slumping down on the lake's edge. She swirled her hand in the water, aimlessly chasing the yucolites as they darted from her touch.

Closing her eyes, Faythe recalled the memory that haunted her. "There was a man in the town a few years ago." She didn't hear when he took a seat close to her, but she felt him nearby. When she glanced to her side, Nik was sitting with his knees tucked casually under his extended arms, his emerald gaze fixed intently on her. She looked away as she continued, perhaps out of cowardice for what she was about to confess. "I used to pass him every day on my way to the market. He owned Farrowhold's butchers and ran it with his wife on the main street to the castle. Everyone knew him." Her expression soured as she recalled his face. "He was a rotund, unkempt man who looked like he never knew the concept of a bath. But it wasn't his appearance that made me balk every time I saw him.

"He was cold-hearted, violent, and I knew he didn't treat his wife well. No one ever saw him strike her—he liked to keep that for private quarters." Her tone turned dark. "It was obvious though. She was marred by cuts and bruises, and everyone knew what was going on, yet no one stepped in to help her." She shook her head at the grim vision.

"One day, when I left early for work, the streets were empty. I heard the commotion before I saw it, and I cowered behind the corner leading to his butchers shop to watch from afar." Faythe took a pause, clenching her teeth. She felt the bite of her nails in the palm of her dry hand. With a shaky breath, she forced herself to continue. "He hit her so hard she fell face-first onto the stone and bled. I wanted to help her, but I was scared. I was only fifteen—what was I going to do against a man of his size?" She said it helplessly, though it didn't ease her guilt at her cowardice.

"Two fae patrol passed, and I felt relief that they would surely help her, punish him…but they didn't. They passed, and they did nothing, said nothing." She seethed through her teeth. "What's one lowly human life to them, huh?" She couldn't help the accusatory glance she made in his direction, but Nik kept silent. "That night, I couldn't get the scene out of my head. I couldn't stop hearing her cry and the sound of her face colliding with the ground. I wanted to *hurt* him, to make him feel the pain he liked to inflict on others. I'm not proud of thinking it, but that night, I…I dreamed of it, though now I suppose it's safe to say I was *Nightwalking*…in his head."

A humorless laugh came from her. "Even after all these years, I can still remember it—*feel* it—so clearly. He had so much hatred for everything, and violence was the only way he knew to find release from the demons that plagued his thoughts." She shook her head in disbelief she hadn't realized sooner. "The scene played out exactly as I saw it, except when he lifted his hand to strike her, I…I screamed as loud as I could. He looked me dead in the eye, and I *felt* his shock and horror for a split second before the scene obliterated and it was only darkness. I woke up straight away, paralyzed by a gods-awful feeling. It was so unlike any of my other dreams or nightmares."

She looked into the water and found some of the yucolites had latched themselves to her fingers as she continued her lazy swirls. "That morning, I went to work as normal, and the day passed by without any surprises. It wasn't until later on that the whispers began circulating around town… He was dead. The butcher on Main Street. His name was Tom Crestler, and he was found dead in his bed that morning. No trace of any physical wound—they said he must have died from some kind of heart failure. Some of the skeptics even accused Nightwalkers, but those who knew him insisted he had done no wrong to the king to warrant his execution." She knew she didn't have to conclude the obvious, but still, she whispered, "I think I killed him."

They were both silent for a long moment. Faythe couldn't bring herself to look at Nik to see his reaction. It made her no better than him in a sense—no better than any of the fae Nightwalkers who were used to ending lives.

A hollowness opened up inside her as she realized she didn't really know who she was anymore. She wanted desperately to go back to her life of ignorance; to just be a simple human girl who loved her friends, did the work she needed to stay fed, and enjoyed her spare time swinging a blade that would never see the lines of battle. All of that was gone now, and she tried to grasp her new reality. She was a weapon forged to be a masterful thief of thoughts and a silent assassin of minds.

Nik's voice snapped her from the dark pit she was slowly falling into. "You don't know that for sure," he said quietly.

She shook her head. "It would be easy to turn a blind eye in ignorance, wouldn't it? But when the pieces fit so perfectly together, it's impossible to ignore the truth."

Nik knitted his eyebrows. "Is his wife living a better life without him?"

Faythe nodded. His wife had taken over the butchers shop and made it flourish. Instead of it being a grim establishment she would dread passing by every day, she now cast a warm smile at Mrs. Crestler, who would often be out front smiling and laughing and enjoying the company of her customers instead of cowering away like before. She hated that some part of her—a *large* part of her— had been glad when she heard the news of Mr. Crestler's passing, only so she knew his wife would be free of him.

"Then wouldn't you agree," Nik said carefully, "he deserved the end he met no matter how it came about?"

She knew he was only trying to lighten the burden, but it didn't help to clear the oily coat of disgust she felt at the heavy knowledge she'd been the one to give it to him.

"He was still a man; still a life," she said. "What right did I have to take it?"

They looked at each other, and she could see it, the understanding: two soundless assassins of the same kind. Only, one was unwitting, and the other...

"How do you live with what you've done?" she asked, still staring into the depths of his emerald eyes as if she could see right through them and into the black-and-gray smoke of his soul.

Nik's frown deepened, and his mouth set in a thin line. "I live with it by never forgetting. Some people I've killed deserved it— murderers, traitors, rebels—while others were less deserving but still guilty of crimes against the crown. I have to follow orders I don't always agree with." His look left room for unspoken words; he was being careful with the information he disclosed. "I live with it by never forgetting any of them. By remembering who I am and what I've done, owning it, and never letting the dark part consume me."

Faythe nodded in appreciation of his honesty. She would find a way to live with what she was, what she had done, and what she was capable of. She had to, if only to be able to control herself and make sure she never used her ability again.

"Your face," he mumbled softly.

In a knee-jerk reaction, she reached a hand up to touch her jaw. The pain and tenderness had gone completely. Her eyes shot to the lake, where the yucolites had returned to dodging her touch. She withdrew her hand from the water, and as she stared at it, she was sure it was glowing. Yet one blink, and it was gone.

"I guess the legends are true. They must like you."

She imagined the purple and blue fingermarks that had started to pepper her lower face would be completely gone too, and she looked back into the water in silent awe and thanks. When she caught the fae guard's eye again, she couldn't stop her curiosity and figured it was a good opportunity to ask, while they were still deep in personal subjects, "What happened to your mother?"

She knew it was the wrong move when his eyes darkened and his jaw twitched. He said nothing for a moment as he held her stare, and then he pushed himself to his feet.

"I think there's been enough dark conversation for one night," he said emotionlessly.

Part of her was annoyed he would evade talking about himself when she'd all but laid herself bare to him in the short weeks they'd known each other. But she also understood what she wanted to know was sensitive and something she wouldn't push. He didn't owe her anything either. In fact, she owed *him* for everything he'd risked by helping her.

"Let's get you home," he said quietly.

She stood and pulled out her pocket watch. It was half past eleven. She prayed Marlowe had come up with enough reasons to keep busy and Jakon wasn't back at the hut already.

In a few minutes, they were cloaked and ready. Neither of them spoke another word as Nik led the way out of the woodland.

She would never get used to the magick that kept the woods in eternal daytime. As they emerged again onto the hills that held the starry night sky, she couldn't decide what she enjoyed more: the serenity of midnight lapis dazzled with bright constellations, or the exuberance of energy under a crystal-blue blanket teeming with peaceful life.

At the same spot they parted time last, Faythe muttered a weak goodbye, and Nik strained as if he wanted to say something else. Quickly, he dropped it and offered his own farewell before silently misting into the dark. Faythe also kept to the shadows, her hood pulled up, as she made her way into the town to avoid any more run-ins with the fae. Especially Captain Varis.

Her relief dropped like a weight at the sight of the empty hut. She discarded her cloak and sword clumsily and dressed quickly, slipping under the covers and pulling them up to her chin.

Faythe lay in silence for a while before she heard Jakon creep in and dip into his own cot. She thought she heard him ask if she was awake, but she kept her eyes closed and breathing steady, facing away from him. Soon after, she felt herself slipping into that familiar oblivion, confident she would be able find the space Nik had guided her to and sleep. *Really* sleep.

CHAPTER 13

FORCED TO TUNE in to the monotone voices of pompous fae nobles, Nik's eyes strained against the weight of boredom. Regardless of his disinterest in the petty politics they squabbled over, he sat poised and attentive, but his mind was elsewhere.

Nik had to keep his eyes off the Captain of the Guard stationed by the door across the hall. Every time he caught a glimpse of the wicked scar that had disfigured Varis during the great battles, it made his fists curl in anger at his brutal display of dominance over Faythe. It shouldn't bother him as much as it did, but imagining his cruel hand curled around her jaw made him want to tear the whole limb from the captain.

Instead, Nik diverted his focus to the bleak faces of those in attendance at the council meeting. Most were creased in anger and distaste as they took it in turns to parry their discontent across the table in the hope the king, sitting at the head, would take their woes into consideration. Nik knew it was all wasted breath. These meetings were a formality; a guise to keep the lords and other highly positioned fae dormant—for a while.

King Orlon of High Farrow rarely took on the advice and suggestion of his close councilmembers and had even less regard for the personal anguish of the high fae who offered him little in return. But the king was smart and knew just how to make them all feel as if they were included in the running of the kingdom. They had all been disillusioned to feel *important*. It kept them on his side so when it mattered the most, they were all more inclined to vote in favor of the king's propositions even when Nik hoped they wouldn't.

Orlon's voice boomed through the hall, silencing the nobles immediately, as he recited his conclusion for the grueling meeting. Finally, everyone stood, and idle chatter arose while the high fae started to file out of the grand council chamber. Nik remained seated, as he always did, to hear the afterword from the king; his *real* verdict on the adjourned congregation.

Nik couldn't stop his gaze from flashing to the captain one last time before he too filed out through the main doors. Varis turned to face them and bowed low, ever the submissive lapdog to the king. Except the captain liked to add his own flare of malevolence to the orders he was given. Nik blazed at the sight of him, relieved when Varis twisted sharply and marched from the hall. It curbed his impulse to challenge him.

A thick silence fell when everyone—even the rest of the guard —had left the room, leaving only Nik and the king still seated. Nik glanced at the great throne seating the King of High Farrow, but the ruler didn't meet his eye. Instead, crooked fingers propped up his powerful jaw in quiet contemplation. Nik took it upon himself to rise, standing straight but not making a move to exit unless dismissed.

When the king remained within his own head, Nik opened his mouth to request leave, but Orlon's commanding voice shook the silence. "I don't like to be made a fool of." The king echoed his thoughts. "And I feel Lord Hellias thinks I am just that."

Nik couldn't hide his hint of a frown. Nothing about the high fae in question had seemed suspicious to him, but he knew better than to debate the king's observations. He let Orlon continue.

"Some of the humans with warrants of arrest have been conveniently slipping out of High Farrow before they can be brought in for questioning."

Nik felt the air drop in temperature, but he focused his breathing to keep his heart steady. He knew the king's fae ears might be able to pick up on an increase in tempo and give away his nerves.

"As you know, Hellias has the Nightwalker ability, and my spies have tracked his movements into the outer town on several occasions. It almost fits too perfectly to be coincidence." The king's lips twitched up cunningly. He believed he had uncovered the truth of the human disappearances all on his own. It would have been Nik's head long ago if he really knew the truth—that *he* was the one warning the targeted humans to flee.

He kept his face placid, remaining stern and attentive as he had been trained to do. The king rose from his throne at last, and Nik tried not to let his size and poise intimidate him.

"You'll understand why I raise this matter to you specifically. I need his mind searched, and I gather it is no easy task to remain undetected in another Nightwalker's head. You are the most powerful in my service with the gift, and you have not disappointed me before." His black orbs bore into Nik's emerald eyes, and he raised his chin in confidence.

"It will take time, but I will find out what you seek." Nik spoke firmly, offering a small nod of obedience—though, internally, he was cursing the male for bestowing the task. He didn't doubt he could achieve what the king asked, but he always hated being used as a weapon for his dirty work.

"Good. Though I don't like to be kept waiting on results. If there are traitors in our midst, I want them exposed and dealt with swiftly. Any accomplices, I want them searched as well."

Nik flexed his fingers behind his back in irritation. "Of course, Your Majesty. Though it will require great strength and focus to enter another Nightwalker's subconscious without detection. I will have to be well rested between tries."

The king hummed his disappointment, which irked Nik further. "A pity the Nightwalking ability has such…restrictions."

It wasn't a direct insult as there was no one more qualified for the job than Nik and no ability that could get him the information he sought quicker. But Orlon's lack of patience and understanding of what it took, and what Nik was risking for it, riled him to no end.

Nik already knew Lord Hellias was innocent of what the king suspected, but he still planned to carry through with the task in the hope of uncovering *something* that would satisfy the king's quest to bring down the perpetrators. Selfishly, he needed to sway suspicion from himself too. He wasn't as foolishly naïve as the lord who clearly lacked the competency to cover his tracks. Nik knew of a labyrinth of tunnels that ran under the inner city and led out just beyond the wall. From there, he was aware and stealthy enough to remain perfectly incognito and evade the king's secret spy force in the outer town of Farrowhold. He almost felt as if Hellias deserved to be caught for his amateur attempt at discretion.

"If that was all, Your Majesty…" Nik said, desperate for release from the formal setting.

The king didn't bother to respond with words, simply raising a lazy hand in dismissal. Nik didn't take it personally; the High Farrow ruler was never one for pleasantries.

He stepped away from his chair and strolled for the exit. In the wide, bright hallways, he found himself immune to the pristine glamour and luxury of the castle. In fact, despite its grand size and maze of hallways and passages, Nik had started to feel suffocated within its confines. The inner city wasn't much different. It was why he had started to venture into the humble dwellings of the outer town some months ago. He found it somewhat comforting to walk inconspicuously among the humans and see how their lives in the unruly brown town fared in comparison to the fae inside the gleaming white city. The contrast was stark, and he couldn't shake the guilt of living in such prestige while the humans were cast out to live impoverished lives. So he'd taken to Nightwalking through them, to offer those he could get to on time a chance to flee rather than be executed for something that wasn't entirely their fault.

Though the king sent out fae patrols to the towns, they were sparse and had lax protection orders. Nik always believed he could do more to prevent Valgard from infiltrating the kingdom and preying upon the innocent human citizens, terrorizing them for information. The prospect of another dawn of carnage like the great battles shook him to his very core. Whenever he approached his concerns on the matter, Nik was immediately shut down by his superior, the ruler of High Farrow.

His mind was too preoccupied to dwell on the matter. Saving the convicted humans had come to a halt when he'd stumbled upon the impossible; discovered an anomaly that challenged the order and hierarchy of the species—or, rather, she found *him*.

"You're a hard male to get a moment with these days."

The eloquent voice of the king's ward didn't come as a surprise. He'd already slowed his brisk walk when he picked up on her quiet approach from behind. Nik cast her a sidelong smirk as she fell into step with him.

"Have you been missing me, Tauria?"

Her golden-tanned cheeks flushed a shade of rose at his teasing response. Rolling her eyes, she looked away. Nik took the moment to admire her beauty. The tone of her skin was radiant against the green of her gown, the rich emerald a proud reminder of who she was; where she came from.

Her standing as the king's ward was only a title to keep her safe, and High Farrow wasn't her native home. It was known to everyone on both sides of the wall that Tauria Stagknight was the sole heir to the Fenstead throne and had fled here over a century ago when her homeland was invaded and conquered by the merciless Valgard. A day he knew still haunted the female behind her mask of resilience.

The King of High Farrow wasn't the most loved ruler, not since those dark battles that had turned his heart. Since then, he'd ruled with little mercy and ruthless punishment to those who even slightly displeased him. One of the last acts of kindness Nik was grateful for among the king's wickedness was his taking in of the terrified Fenstead princess who'd fled to their doorstep as the only surviving royal from the Kingdom of the Stag.

"If I have to suffer the company of court ladies and imperious lords one day longer, I'm going to go insane," Tauria complained, her bottom lip almost falling into a pout.

Nik chuckled softly. "And I suppose you want me to help you get out of it?"

A sheepish smile tugged her lips in response.

Nik felt guilty then. That he'd been so absent these past few weeks and had failed to check in on his friend. Over the century of her living within the castle of High Farrow, they'd become very close companions and confided in each other about everything. Without her knowing of his antics in the town, it twisted his gut to think she might believe he didn't care. In truth, he couldn't tell her what he'd been up to with the humans *because* he cared. He cared immeasurably for her safety, so he wouldn't risk her having any knowledge of his treason and possibly be implicated if he were ever to be caught.

"I'm sorry I haven't been around," he said quietly, dropping the amusement. She gave him a look of understanding that pained him. He hated keeping things from her. "How about we take the horses out tomorrow?"

Tauria beamed wide, the smile creasing her hazel eyes. It instantly brightened up Nik's mood.

"You know I always beat you at horse racing," she gibed with a nudge of her elbow.

"In my defense, I never know we're in competition until you

announce you've won. With forewarning, I might get the chance to put in a little effort."

The princess barked a laugh. "As if! You just can't stand to be bested by a *female.*" She teased the word.

Nik offered a crooked smile but felt hideously guilty another female surfaced to mind in that moment—one he wished he could tell Tauria about.

Faythe. The name struck him with both thrill and fear. Not for what she was capable of, but for the dire fate that could befall her in the hands of the king. A human girl. A *Nightwalker!* The thought was inconceivable, yet Nik had a daunting feeling he was yet to scrape the surface of what truly lay dormant beneath her beauty and innocence.

CHAPTER 14

F AYTHE LAY SPRAWLED across the flat of a rooftop, basking
under the intense heat of the midday sun. She finished the
final bite of her apple and tossed the core, not bothering to check if
there was anyone passing below.

Two weeks had passed since her last night in the woods with
Nik. She'd only seen him when he invaded her subconscious on a
couple of nights to check she wasn't self-destructing or doing any
more unwitting Nightwalking. But they never spoke of anything
else, and his visits were quick before she pushed him out.

It wasn't that she was upset or angry with him, but since she'd
learned what she needed to do to prevent her mind from
wandering at night, she didn't see reason to delay the inevitable.
His status would never allow them to be *friends*, and she had no
desire to explore her ability any further since she had absolutely no
intention of using it—ever.

Mercifully, she had managed to keep herself in her own mind,
finding the darkness Nik had tried to explain that pulled her into
blissful, deep rest every night. She hadn't lingered in her subconscious either to explore what she could do with her *own* memories
and imagination.

Marlowe and Jakon had spent many evenings together since she'd played Cupid, and it brought her joy to watch their relationship slowly blossom. Faythe found release and comfort through the swinging of her sword most nights, but she wasn't always alone. Occasionally, Ferris would happen to be passing by and offer to be her sparring partner, which usually meant a colorful vocabulary of curses on his part when she bested him time and time again, much to Faythe's amusement.

She'd also spent a lot of time alone with Marlowe, finding immense joy in the company of a new female friend. It was a different kind of comfort she was missing with Jakon, being able to chat about topics he would have no interest in, such as clothes, the men Faythe found attractive in town, and other harmless gossip. It brightened up her days.

Everything seemed normal, as if she didn't harbor a deadly secret none of her companions knew about. She dared to hope that would be the end of it and she could continue to live her perfectly plain and ordinary life as she had been before she knew anything of her ability.

She had the day off today, but Jakon did not. She'd had a lie-in and taken extra time to laze around before deciding to get ready and make something of her day. She'd pottered about the streets, gushing over clothes and accessories she'd never be able to afford— at least not on her pitiful salary. The miserable feeling made her decide she would one day find a more rewarding job for herself, a purpose, and something to bring in more coin so they could live a little better. She didn't have many skills without a sword in her hand, but perhaps she could apprentice in some trade.

Faythe sat up groggily, the midday sun making her seriously drowsy despite her extra-long rest. Standing, she made her way over to the edge of the roof and shimmied herself down the drain-pipe, landing with a quiet thud in the empty alley. Deciding on a destination, she strolled lazily, in absolutely no hurry to do anything at all.

When she eventually approached the blacksmiths, she spotted Marlowe in the front of the workshop intently examining something through a magnifying eyepiece.

"Find anything cool?" Faythe asked in way of greeting.

Marlowe looked up and flashed her a grin. "Magestone," she said, holding up the iridescent black sliver of a rock. "They say it's the one material in the realm that can render a fae...well, mortal, I suppose. Diminish their strength, speed, abilities, and the like," she said casually.

Faythe's interest piqued, and she walked over to examine the rock closer. Marlowe held it out to her, and she took it in her palm. It was surprisingly ice-cold. Faythe held in the urge to flinch at the contact, in stark contrast to her clammy hand.

With a glance behind her, she said, "Should you really be flaunting this out in the open if it's possible that's all true?"

Marlowe waved a hand. "It's just legend now. No one's seen a significant quantity of magestone in very long time. Apparently, it used to be a component in the Farhin Mountains of Lakelaria, but it was mined and destroyed many centuries ago. All that remains is the occasional useless shard." Marlowe snickered. "What could be worse for a fae than being made to feel like a *human?*" She teased the last word.

Faythe examined the rock. Colors bounced off its flat surface at all angles.

"Keep it if it interests you so much. I found it in a pile of scrap metal I bought off a merchant from Olmstone last week." She leaned back in her seat. "It's pretty though. I could make it into a pendant for you if you'd like?"

At the offer, Faythe smiled. "Thanks, but it's yours. Make a pendant for yourself. Or sell it. Could be worth a small fortune if it's as rare as you say." She gave the stone back to her.

Marlowe shrugged. "Perhaps." She pocketed it in her apron. "What brings you my way today?"

Faythe perched on the table in front of her. "Can't I come see a friend without wanting anything?"

"Of course you can. But I don't finish for at least another couple of hours," Marlowe said, abruptly standing and retreating into the back. Something Faythe had quickly come to learn about the blacksmith was that she could hardly sit still for a minute and would always look for something to occupy her hands and mind.

Faythe followed her. Behind the curtain was where they kept the furnaces and heavy equipment for bigger projects. Marlowe picked up a blade and began to sharpen it. Faythe winced at the loud scraping of steel but watched her work in admiration.

After a moment, she asked over the noise, "How is it you know about the magestone?"

"They're called books, Faythe. You should try picking one up sometime."

Faythe rolled her eyes at the playful gibe, but knowing her friend probably knew a lot about ancient legends and beings, she asked, "What do you know about the...*Nightwalkers?*" As much as she tried to convince herself she was content with not knowing anything else other than what she needed to keep control and survive, Faythe couldn't help the burning curiosity that there may be things she was yet to discover about her ability.

Marlowe paused, the space going silent as she curved an eyebrow at her. "No more than what everyone else knows, I suppose," she answered. Faythe wasn't sure if it was disappointment or relief she felt. "Although," Marlowe continued as if she'd just remembered something relevant, "I did read something once about a higher *kind* of Nightwalker."

Faythe straightened, her attention piqued.

Marlowe set the blade down, turning to lean with crossed arms against the bench. Her face contorted with concentration as she tried to recall the details, and then she said, "I mean, none have been known to exist for centuries, if they ever did at all, but the book I read told a legend of those who could enter both an unconscious *and* conscious mind. Complete telepathic abilities and absolutely lethal." She shuddered. "The Nightwalkers are bad enough. Just be glad we don't have their superior mythical ancestors among us."

At Faythe's blanched look, Marlowe laughed. "Relax—it's just an old scary story," she teased, spinning around to resume her work.

"Indeed," Faythe said quietly.

Her thoughts whirled. Perhaps Nik would know more; would be able to confirm if such an ability did exist—in his three centuries of existence at least.

"Why do you ask?"

Faythe cleared her throat and found something to fidget with. "Just curious. I wonder what other fae abilities there are," she said, hopeful it came off as a bored question.

When Marlowe showed no sign of suspicion, Faythe internally sighed with relief. "There are quite a few: elemental, shades, shapeshifting…" She went on to list a few more before adding, "But gifted fae are fairly rare. Most of them are just as normal as you and me, save for the immortal strength, speed, and grace." She huffed.

Faythe forced a breathy laugh. She wasn't *normal*. Would her friend be disgusted if she found out what invasive ability she possessed? The thought of any of her friends looking at her with hatred or disappointment made her stomach sink.

"There's some books on them over there if you'd like to learn more." Marlowe jerked her head to the corner.

Spotting the lazily discarded pile, Faythe walked over to them, brushing off dust and soot to read the titles. One in particular caught her attention. Grabbing the old leather book, she held it up.

"Are Spirits a favorite topic of yours too?" she asked, flashing the title: *The Forgotten Goddess.*

People sometimes referred to the Spirits of the Realm as Goddesses. They were supposed to be the forces that kept the world in balance to stop the species from destroying each other. But with the war and destruction that had raged for centuries, it amazed Faythe how people could still believe in such nonsense.

Marlowe peered up from her blade. "Ah, that's a good one, actually. You can borrow it if you'd like. Did you know, some people believe there was a *third* Spirit? She was supposedly cast out of the realm over a thousand years ago. People speculate why, but no one really knows." There was genuine passion in her tone.

Faythe scoffed. "I don't believe in any of it. Spirits, Gods, and Goddesses—where are they now, when we actually need them?" she said, putting the book back down.

Marlowe huffed at her. "Believing or not is irrelevant. It's a good read. Or do you not know how to enjoy a story?"

Faythe scowled at her. "Fine. I'll read it, and I'll give you my *informed* reasons for why it's all absurd." She swiped the book, tucking it under her arm. "If you need me, I'll be out front, fully engrossed in the wonders of the *Spirits.*" She drawled the last word.

"Don't mock them, Faythe. You never know which ones are listening," Marlowe sang as she passed.

Faythe only rolled her eyes and pulled a seat out front to bask in the sun. At least she had something to pass the time while she waited for Marlowe to finish up for the day.

About halfway through the book, Faythe cursed Marlowe for being right. It was captivating, to say the least, and she found she couldn't turn the pages fast enough. The feel of the aged, worn leather binding in her palms and the sweet, musky scent of old paper rekindled a lost passion for her favorite pastime. It had been years since she'd picked up a book, as it was something she had enjoyed with her mother, but reading now brought her comfort instead of sadness. Her excitement for new stories sparked again.

She read various different tales on the mythical appearances of

Aurialis, the Spirit of Life and Goddess of the Sun, and her sister Dakodas, the Spirit of Death and Goddess of the Moon, over the past millennia. But it was the legends of the long-forgotten third Spirit Marvellas, the Spirit of *Souls* and Goddess of the *Stars*, that took precedence as the tales Faythe found the most interesting.

One of her favorite theories about the lost Spirit was a tale dating back nearly one thousand years ago when she had vanished. The legend depicted she had fallen in love with a fae warrior and, with her sisters' help, relinquished her powers and titles to be bound in the same form as her lover. She still didn't believe any of it to be truth or real history, but regardless, Faythe found herself moved by that particular story. Perhaps foolishly, she hoped such a love could exist in her world.

Alternatives to Marvellas' disappearance were not so poetic. Some theorized she was consumed by her sisters for her powers or she broke her sacred duty and was cast back to her own realm.

A familiar voice pulled Faythe from the fantasy. "How is it?"

She peeled her eyes from the captivating text and had to blink rapidly to refocus from reading for so long. She took in the sight of Marlowe: clean-faced, apron off, and leaning against the wall with crossed arms.

"Is it that time already?" Faythe asked, not realizing how fast time had gotten away from her.

Marlowe smirked. "I'll take that as a thumbs-up." She pushed off the wall, grabbing her cloak and folding it over her arm.

It had become a regular thing for Marlowe to join them most evenings. The three of them had pretty much become inseparable over the past couple weeks. It surprised Faythe how well they got along considering her lack of previous female friends, but everything was so *easy* with Marlowe. If Jakon was her partner in crime, Marlowe would be her confidante in conspiracy.

The blacksmith had also expressed her appreciation of their company, telling them of her isolated days spent in her father's workshop and how her evenings had been spent building on her already impressive knowledge through reading. It put Faythe to shame sometimes when she thought of how smart her friend was in comparison.

"Do you mind if I borrow it?" she asked as she stood, closing the book with a satisfying *thud*.

Marlowe's irises twinkled. "Of course! I knew you'd like it."

Faythe fought her sheepish smile as Marlowe looped her arm through hers and pulled her into a lazy stroll down the street.

CHAPTER 15

F AYTHE AND MARLOWE picked up some meat pies and bread on their way back to the hut after the blacksmith's shift and were sat at the kitchen table eating when Jakon sauntered through the door. He flashed them both a grin before excusing himself to freshen up after his day on the farm.

When they were all together again, he greedily tucked in. "I was thinking we could take a walk down to the harbor tonight," he suggested to no one in particular.

It sounded like more of a romantic thing to do, and Faythe was about to exclude herself from the invitation when Marlowe cut in.

"Actually, I thought maybe we could all go to the square tonight. I've yet to see Faythe in action."

Faythe perked up at the mention, and Jakon chuckled. "You two in a sparring session? That's something I'd pay good money to see."

Both women flashed him a devious smile.

"We'll need to stop back at the blacksmiths to get your sword," Faythe said.

Marlowe shook her head and jerked it to the side. Faythe's gaze followed, landing on the blade that lay over her cloak in the corner.

She had been too caught up in her storybook to even notice Marlowe was equipped with the sword when they left. As she looked the woman over now, she registered her casual attire of a fitted tunic and pants in place of her usual cotton gown.

Reading her exact thoughts, her friend smirked. "That book really took you away for a while."

"You can read?" Jakon teased.

She scowled at the remark and tossed a piece of bread at his mocking laughter. He caught it and leaned over to tousle her hair. Batting his arm away, Faythe rose and stuck her tongue out at him, then she eagerly skipped to retrieve Lumarias and ready herself for sparring.

No one stopped them on their journey to the square, and mercifully, she'd had no more run-ins with the fae captain since their first unpleasant meeting either.

The two women discarded their cloaks next to Jakon, who took a relaxed, laid-back position on one of the benches. His eyes gleamed with boyish amusement.

They were in the midst of stretching and warming up when they heard a low whistle. All of their attention snapped to where a head of rugged red hair emerged into the square with a feline grin.

"Where was my invite to this magnificent showdown?" Ferris quipped.

Faythe smirked, twisting her sword in her wrist. "I suppose you could do with a few lessons on what a *skilled* opponent looks like," she taunted playfully. "Take note."

"Now, Faythe, everyone knows I *let* you win, being the gentleman I am." He bowed slightly in arrogance before throwing himself down beside Jakon.

Faythe's eyes flashed in challenge. "Perhaps we should put all doubt to rest after this?"

He shifted, deciding whether he should back down or rise to it, and said, "No, thanks. I quite like my balls and don't feel like losing them tonight."

"Smart man," Jakon commented.

Faythe faced Marlowe again. She was flexing her sword between her hands, looking slightly nervous. "It's been a while," she admitted, taking up a defensive position.

Faythe took her counter stance. "If you want me to go easy on you, just say it."

Marlowe's eyes twinkled, and with a smug grin, she said, "Never."

Steel met steel in a ballad of action and combat, every note sending a pulse of energy through Faythe that compelled her to dance in time with each twist and swing of her sword. Nothing focused her more than feeling the clash of her blade against her target. She forgot her two friends who sat as onlookers, tuned out every other sound, and gave herself over to the guidance of her blade as it harmonized her movements. It didn't matter that it was a match of practice and fun—every time she felt the cold leather hilt of her sword in her palms, it awakened Faythe's desire to fight, her need to protect, and her want to win.

Marlowe was an excellent opponent and certainly challenged her as good as Jakon did. Faythe brought her sword up once again, halting in a killing strike that had her friend bested for the third time in the half hour they'd been sparring. They were both panting when they called it there and slumped to the ground.

Ferris clapped slow and loud. "What a show indeed, ladies. We could have charged good coin in an arena to have people watch." He smirked suggestively. "Even more so if you were naked."

Jakon punched his arm, and Ferris howled his laughter. "Don't pretend you didn't think it too," he said in deviant delight.

Faythe shook her head at their boyish bickering as Marlowe passed a waterskin. She took it, chugging the cool liquid down her burning throat greedily.

"You're quite the swordswoman," Marlowe said in admiration.

Faythe beamed at the compliment. "You're definitely worthy opposition."

She nodded her appreciation with a smile.

Ferris stood and loudly announced, "Well, if that's all the action I'm getting tonight, consider me satisfied." He gave a wolfish grin. "Seriously though, Faythe, you could turn a good profit in The Cave. I happen to work for a man who finds sport in it. I can get you in."

At the mention of the notorious cave, she stiffened. It was rumored to be below the inn and only accessible by those in the know. An underworld of gambling, violence, and illegal trading, The Cave was a domain of nighttime pleasures for the wealthier members of town and those who foolishly gambled their short earnings, or occasional fae guards who enjoyed betting on humans like dogs.

"Not a chance in rutting damn," Jakon growled.

Ferris cast him a bored look. "Are you her keeper?"

Jakon was on his feet facing off with him in an instant.

The two women also shot to their feet, Marlowe moving close to Jakon so he wouldn't swing. Ferris didn't balk in the slightest, instead choosing to smirk. This only riled Faythe's stupidly protective friend further.

While Jakon stood a foot taller and packed a bit more muscle, Ferris had a cunning wild side that would make any man think twice before crossing him. Faythe didn't want to see the outcome of that fight.

"Let's tone the male-ego dominance bullshit down a notch, shall we?" Faythe cut in. She couldn't deny Ferris's offer tempted her a little, if only so she could earn money—*decent* money—doing something she was actually good at. Even if it was considered unsavory practice. But at risk of having Jakon blow his top, she forced down the urge to inquire about it further. "I'm not exactly welcome at the inn anymore, and I doubt I'd be a match for anyone down there."

Ferris shrugged casually. "I've seen the pathetic talent they choose to show. They're sloppy brutes who have little actual weapon skill. Trust me, you'd stand a good chance of holding out well." His eyes flashed to Jakon, who blazed at the thought, then he looked back at Faythe. "And you wouldn't be going as yourself." He grinned mischievously. "Think on it. You know where to find me if you change your mind." Turning on his heel, he strolled away.

"Damned prick," Jakon muttered after him.

"Let's go," Marlowe said sweetly, linking her arm through his to simmer his anger.

It worked, and Faythe was surprised as Jakon looked to her and his face instantly softened. Even she couldn't calm him down so quickly. With a smile, he allowed Marlowe to lead him over to where she retrieved her cloak and sword, and together, they began the walk home.

Faythe felt a pang of something she wasn't used to, and the feeling saddened her a little. *Jealousy.* Of the special thing they had between them that she'd never had before. A closeness. A bond that couldn't be matched by anyone but a partner...a lover. What she had with Jakon over the ten years they'd known each other was special. She loved him, would give her life for him, but there was never that deeper connection clear between the two souls walking a few paces in front of her.

As if sensing her brooding, Marlowe turned and held her free arm out for Faythe to loop hers around. She gave a small, grateful smile and obliged.

The three of them walked linked together back to the hut, three friends who shared a different kind of life bond. Faythe dared the damned Spirits to try and break it.

When they arrived home, Faythe made her way inside and bid Marlowe good night when Jakon insisted he walk her home. Entering the bedroom, she halted at the item she spotted laying on her bed.

Warily taking it in her hands, Faythe held up the familiar-looking iridescent black stone that dangled from a black rope necklace. She didn't know when Marlowe had secretly left it for her to find or even when she'd found the time to craft it while Faythe was stuck between the pages of *The Forgotten Goddess*. Still, she smiled at the magestone pendant that had been delicately carved to form a teardrop shape. It glittered beautifully in the moonlight, and Faythe slipped it around her neck, feeling the coolness nip against her bare chest.

With a yawn, she dressed for bed, eager for sleep now her muscles had started to ache from the exertion of her workout with Marlowe. She tried and failed to wait for Jakon to arrive back, feeling her eyelids grow heavy and shut of their own accord. Then she drifted off into darkness.

CHAPTER 16

THAT NIGHT, FAYTHE awoke in the usual confines of her subconscious. The mists of white and gold always stunned her; *moved* without needing her command. She was about to let go and fall into a pit of dark, restful sleep—she never did stay there for long—but she paused as a thought crossed her mind. Maybe it was from reading the soppy love story of Marvellas, or perhaps it was seeing her own two friends engage amorously, but she couldn't shake a feeling of longing for someone to share such a deep connection with.

It was an embarrassingly foolish thought, and Faythe was about to abandon the idea—but this was her mind. No one was around to watch or judge, and she had yet to try anything with her imagination. She cringed a little at what she was about to do but sighed and closed her eyes anyway.

As she stood there in the dark, Faythe tried to conjure both the image and emotion of what it would be like to have someone touch her; make her pulse race. She wasn't a complete stranger to such feelings. There was no shortage of young, attractive men in town, and she'd occasionally give in to their innocent flirtations to satisfy her lust. But she wanted *more* than just sexual desire.

A part of her felt silly as she waited for something to happen. She was about to banish the thought and give up...when she felt it.

A warm breath caressed the length of her neck. She sucked in a sharp breath as the feeling sent a cascade of tingles down her spine, and she tilted her head in response. A strong, muscular force materialized behind her, and then there were hands...trailing down her bare forearms, sending shockwaves through her. It felt so *real* Faythe leaned into the force.

More... She wanted more.

She could have sworn she heard a soft chuckle right before phantom teeth scraped along her neck in a teasing response. Her heart beat a wild frenzy as desire pooled at her core. Eyes of the brightest sapphire blue pierced through her closed lids, and she snapped them quickly open.

The strong, powerful hands became real flesh as she watched them continue their tender strokes along her bare forearms. Blood throbbed in her veins, and Faythe wasn't sure she was even still breathing when she moved to twist out of his grip.

Just as she was about to face the man with the intense dark blue eyes, she recognized the invading force. When she fully turned, her imaginary seducer had vanished, leaving her staring into Nik's deep green eyes instead from a few meters away.

She couldn't hide her look of disappointment, especially when her emotions still ran wild from the heated encounter. She wanted desperately to put a face to those sapphire orbs that pulled at something deep within.

"What do you want?" she demanded.

Nik smirked. "I see you're discovering *exactly* the kind of things you're capable of experiencing in here."

Her cheeks caught fire. "Get out!" She pointed in no particular direction.

His grin only widened. "You don't have to be embarrassed, Faythe, but if you long for release, you need only ask." His eyes danced with amusement.

She gaped at him. "You're the last person I would go to for...*that.*" She cringed as she said it, her blood near boiling from the humiliation.

"Ouch. And here I thought we were starting to become friends." He held a mocking hand to his heart.

In a flare of anger, she began to push him out of her mind when he said, "Wait."

She paused, giving him one sentence to convince her not to kick his ass.

"I thought you could use some more lessons on how to use your ability," he said. "Meet me in the woods?"

She folded her arms. "Like you said, I'm discovering for myself just fine, thanks."

"That part, yes, but you haven't learned how to block others." He gestured to himself as an example. "Or how to control what they see so you don't get discovered. You also need to learn how to not get *yourself* discovered in someone else's head. Another Night-walker or not, it can be deadly for you if you don't."

"I don't plan to do any Nightwalking ever again."

He gave her a knowing look. "You should still know how. You never know when you might need to use your ability. We may be deadly weapons, but we can also be useful tools to help others." There was a hint of encouragement in his voice.

Faythe hadn't thought of her ability as anything but invasive, cruel, and deadly...but if there was a way it could be used for good, she supposed it couldn't hurt to learn.

"It's been weeks. Why are you only now claiming it's important I learn this?"

"I've been busy."

"Not too busy to invite yourself here whenever you feel like it."

"Someone has to check you're not wreaking havoc with your untrained mind. Perhaps you'd prefer I hand the job over to Captain Varis?"

With a glare, she muttered, "Stupid fae prick." He only

chuckled in response. "Tonight?" she asked, not even knowing what the time was or if Jakon was home yet.

Nik nodded. "Meet me there in twenty minutes." Then, with her reluctant agreement, he left, dissipating into swirls of gold mist and leaving a faint outline where he'd stood.

Faythe swore to herself for conceding to his plan and forced her mind into full consciousness.

Her eyes opened onto darkness. Moonlight poured in through the box window. Turning her head, she spotted Jakon sprawled out in his too-small cot, snoring softly. Faythe pulled herself into a sitting position, swung her legs over the edge of the bed, and silently reached for her pocket watch on the side table between them.

Half past midnight. She mentally cursed at the late hour. She knew she wouldn't be returning to her warm bed in time to get much proper rest tonight.

Barely daring to breathe, she maneuvered through the small space with feline stealth. Changing swiftly, she didn't bother to equip her sword as she swung on her cloak and left the hut. She muttered a silent prayer Jakon wouldn't wake to discover her absence.

With her hood up, Faythe made herself a living shadow as she floated through the dark streets, keeping her ears on high alert for fae patrol. She stopped at a corner leading onto Main Street, hearing a quiet clamor of voices and shuffling boots. When she peered around, her heart froze at the sight of the patrol—at the sight of Captain Varis in particular. They stopped outside the inn, and Faythe had a horrible sense of déjà vu. This was where she'd seen them dragging the innkeeper's son out onto the street weeks ago. But they didn't appear to be there on any urgent business tonight, and instead of making a brute show of forced entry, the four guards casually strolled inside as if it were a normal night to grab a drink.

Faythe tried not to think too much about it.

Once they were fully out of sight, she darted through the intersection into the next dark pocket and continued her inconspicuous trek to the hills. When she approached the woods and didn't spot Nik, she decided to go in alone rather than risk anyone else spying her waiting on the outskirts. Darkness opened up into light, and as always, she took a moment to breathe in the clarity of the air and appreciate the ethereal brightness of her surroundings.

At the waterfall, Faythe was imagining what it would be like to swim in the crystal-clear waters surrounded by the tiny dancing glow of the yucolites when her thoughts were disturbed by a rustling nearby. She opened her mouth to say something witty to Nik about being late, but the words died in her throat as she turned to find a magnificent giant stag. It was staring directly at her.

She immediately froze at the sight of the creature that could kill her with one jerk of its hoof. She didn't know if she should gawk or run from the huge white beast with antlers of shimmering silver. Faythe had seen stags in the forest before when she'd hunted with Jakon, but she'd never seen one of such grace and beauty. The animal in front of her was not of any mortal nature. No—it must exist by some form of magick, or at least be enhanced by it.

Faythe knew the smart choice would be to run and hope she could reach the edge of the woods quicker than it could catch her. A risk considering the length and might of its legs; she could easily be impaled on its antlers if it got close enough.

"Follow."

Faythe jerked at the sound but held the beast's stare. It was impossible, foolish even, to imagine she'd heard the animal talk to her. But it dragged its hoof on the ground with a huff, flaring its large nostrils, and flicked its head in time with the word.

Then she realized it was not spoken out loud.

Perhaps the woods took all logic and reason out of a person, or perhaps she was just more reckless than she realized, but she found herself walking toward the beast that could end her in a single blow. Stupidity or bravery, she wasn't sure. She stayed a cautious distance behind it as it turned, and then she followed it through the trees in a direction she hadn't ventured before. She had yet to explore any of the woods besides the waterfall clearing and could only imagine what else was lurking around, good or evil. It made her shudder. She wasn't in any hurry to go investigating on her own.

The yucolites weren't the only life form that glowed here. She looked up to notice the aerial equivalent weaving around the branches of the tree canopy, creating a peaceful hum. Fireflies, she deduced, though it was strange to see them in the daylight.

After a short walk, the trees opened up into another large clearing, this one brighter than the waterfall, which she didn't think was possible. It was as if the invisible sun that blanketed the woods in the daytime, through some ancient form of magick, was shooting a beam directly to this glade alone. A solitary feature stood in the middle: a grand stone temple that glittered a soft gray. Faythe followed the stag a little closer to the structure and then halted. It turned its massive head to look back at her once and, with another huff and a nod, gestured her over to the closed doors inside the portico. The beast stalked up the steps in a couple of powerful strides and disappeared right through the solid stone entrance in front of her eyes.

Faythe blinked once, twice, and stood gaping where the creature had vanished. She suddenly went cold. Maybe she was still in her mind, and her own thoughts were mocking her, or perhaps she was Nightwalking...

She quickly shook her head to dismiss that conclusion. While her subconscious was vivid and very convincing, she'd learned to distinguish the difference; *feel* what was truly real. Her instincts knew this was definitely no illusion of her own making.

She approached the temple slowly and with caution and then ascended the few steps past the colonnades to stand in front of the massive stone doors. Raising a wary hand, she reached out to touch the rock. Solid. She pressed her whole palm to the door, then her other one, and gave a push. Nothing moved. She pushed harder, using all her strength, before giving up and stepping back with a grunt.

Her eyes trailed the faded gold lines that made up a pattern across both doors. Faythe had to step back down the steps to get a view of the whole picture. She squinted and tilted her head a few times. It was a circle with three lines struck through it, overlapping its circumference. Simple and familiar, she wracked her brain for a few seconds, until...

She gasped, and her hand darted into her pocket. She'd seen that symbol—it was the same as the engraving on the back of her mother's watch. Pulling it out, she flipped it over in her hand and stood with her mouth gaping. Her eyes darted from the stone door to the brass watch, back and forth, until she was certain they were exactly the same, not a line different. But her discovery raised far more questions than it answered. She was sure her gentle, innocent mother wouldn't have been in these woods. She would have no reason to be...

So what did it mean?

Faythe stormed up to the doors again and held out the watch. She tried pressing the engraved side to the stone and waving it in any possible way she could think of, achieving nothing but looking like she'd lost her mind. She groaned in frustration. Why did the stag bother to guide her here if she couldn't get inside?

"There you are!" Nik's voice bellowed from across the glade.

Faythe jumped at the sudden noise and whirled to see him stalking over to her. He didn't look pleased.

"I had to follow your scent," he grumbled. Then he paused, taking in the structure around them from below the steps. "How did you find this place?"

"You've never been here before?"

He shook his head. "I've been to these woods many times over the centuries, but I've never seen this."

"I don't know how you could have missed it," she mumbled

sarcastically. When he didn't respond, she asked, "Do you know what this means?" She gestured to the large symbol adorning the entrance.

"You don't know the mark of Aurialis?" At her clueless look, he rolled his eyes. "Goddess of the Sun? The Spirit of Life, you might call her?"

A spark of remembrance came to mind. She'd read about the Spirit as well as her two sisters in *The Forgotten Goddess* earlier that day. The revelation only raised more questions.

Faythe thought for a moment. "Do you think it's just some old place of worship?"

His head angled back as he ascended the steps. "Maybe, but these woods don't open to everyone. Perhaps it was meant only for those chosen by Aurialis." He smirked.

She gave him a flat look.

Nik braced his palms against the door and strained as he tried and failed to push them open. If his fae strength couldn't open them, she felt foolish for even trying.

"Strange," he muttered.

She wasn't about to explain she had been led here by some giant, mythical stag at the risk of sounding completely insane. She was hardly confident she wasn't slowly losing her mind. Perhaps it was a side effect of having an ability that was never intended for a human body.

She supposed there was nothing more to do. "Let's just go," she huffed, stomping down the stairs and stalking away. If there was no way in, it was a waste of time following the stupid stag. She made a mental note to act on her first instinct and *run* next time. However, she seriously hoped there would be no repeat sightings of large, ethereal animals to worry about.

CHAPTER 17

Nik paced a few steps in front of Faythe, much to her irritation, as he went over various techniques of guarding the mind against unwelcome visitors.

"So when you feel that pressure on your mind, you have to be able to pull your walls up so they can't enter," he lectured.

Faythe poked aimlessly at the grass with a stick. She'd picked it up on the way back to the waterfall clearing, bored stiff from listening to him ramble on about control, focus, and everything else so painstakingly dull it made her eyelids grow heavy. He stomped over to her, moving to grab her shoulders and steal her attention, but as soon as he gripped her, his arms immediately dropped as if she were made of fire.

Nik's eyes flashed to her chest. "What is *that?*"

She looked down, innocent, and weighed the small teardrop pendant in her palm. "This? Marlowe made it for me. Pretty, isn't it?"

"I didn't know magestone still existed, especially not on this continent."

She arched an eyebrow in growing interest. "It's true then, what it can do to a fae?"

He assessed her, debating whether he should share the information he knew about a material that could be used as a weapon against his kind. At last, he said, "I wasn't sure. No one's seen it in a very long time. Most believe it's gone completely, but—" His lips thinned. "Touching you just now, it felt like a magnet sucking out a small piece of strength. Almost undetectable and not nearly enough to incapacitate me. At least, not in such a small quantity."

She dropped the stone to her chest with a curious hum. Faythe wanted to tell Marlowe the myths were facts, knowing the blacksmith would relish in the information, but she quickly realized that would mean giving away her meetings with Nik. Her face fell. She hated having to keep secrets from either of her friends, but she *couldn't* tell them about Nik—it would put her at risk of them finding out about her impossible ability.

"Be careful," Nik spoke, still frowning at the pendant. "It could lead to unwanted questions if anyone else happens to sense it." He meant the fae guards. The *king*.

She nodded in understanding, tucking it under her shirt. To test her theory, she had deliberately made sure to wear the necklace when he invited her here, and she was glad for the answers to her question. In a larger quantity, if magestone still existed, it could be a mighty weapon to nullify the fae's strength and abilities and even the playing field for humans in battle. It was no wonder they wanted it gone.

Thinking back to her conversation with Marlowe, Faythe recalled a burning question she wanted to ask Nik. She hesitated before blurting, "Has such an ability ever existed that was *more* than just Nightwalking…like in a conscious mind, for example?" Her stomach twisted as he looked at her curiously.

"There are legends, but I've never known anyone who's met someone with such a talent. Why?"

She wasn't sure if it was relief or disappointment she felt. In his three centuries of existence, Nik could neither prove nor disprove the fact. She knew it was outlandish, completely irrational, and he would laugh at the thought that had swirled in her head since the blacksmith unknowingly enlightened her to the possibility.

She was about to pass it off as mild curiosity, but instead, she said, "Sometimes…I think I *feel* things that are not my own…or *hear* things that were never spoken." She laughed as she heard her thoughts out loud. He'd think her insane and abandon all hope of training her. She should never have said anything about it. Yet when her friend had mentioned the uncharted ability, Faythe couldn't help but think of all the times she'd heard and felt things she had no explanation for. And since she'd already defied the impossible, she didn't see the harm in asking Nik about it. If there was even a slight chance, she wanted to rule it out completely for the sake of her own sanity.

She waited for the laughter, the mocking, the teasing, but none of it came.

"Like what?"

Surprised he hadn't immediately shut down the idea, she shifted, suddenly self-conscious. It was her turn to start pacing with her eyes on the ground, more out of nerves than anything.

"Mostly, it's just like a burst of emotion. Or I hear words, phrases, when they've never moved their lips… I've always assumed I'm good at reading people, but what if it's more than that?" She dared a look at him. "I know—it's impossible and probably just my own heightened emotions running away with my thoughts, but—"

"No—I believe you," he cut in, folding his arms and maintaining the intensity of his stare. At her raised brow, he continued, "I mean, I shouldn't… I should think you're absolutely losing it and convince you to take a vacation as soon as possible." He smirked. "But I think you did it to me one time—answered a question I never even asked. I thought nothing of it, of course, but if you're saying it's happened a lot before…by the Gods, Faythe, your existence becomes more inconceivable by the day." He shook his head in disbelief.

"It might not be what I think it is," she said quickly.

He ran a hand through his hair. "There's one way to find out." He grinned in mock challenge. "What am I thinking?"

She gave him a dead look. "It doesn't work like that. I only hear and feel projections."

"Yes, when you haven't been trying." He tilted his head. "Who knows what you could truly be capable of? A force like no one's known before."

"I don't want to be a *force* to be used against anyone."

His face turned serious. "You can't run from yourself. Stop being so afraid of your own abilities and *face* them, Faythe, or the things you're trying so hard to hide from may very well be your undoing."

"Why do you care, Nik?" she said nastily. "What are you even doing here?" She was deflecting her anger at herself again, and he knew it too.

His face softened. "Don't make your gifts a curse. They are what you make them, not the other way around. There's a reason you have them, so embrace it. Don't fight it."

She knew he was right. She'd spent so long trying to convince herself she was still that same ordinary human girl; that she could lock up all this and try to forget she even had an ability. But the more she discovered about herself, the more she realized she would never be that girl again. The idea scared her to no end, but she would learn to embrace herself—every part of herself—and know that despite it all and no matter what came of it, her heart would not be tarnished.

"It could just be very weak clairvoyance," she offered nervously.

"We can't be sure until you actually *try* to tap into it instead of waiting to hear things you never intended to."

"Another time," she said. "I think I might implode if I try anything tonight."

He kept his gaze fixed on her, a smile tugging at the corners of his lips.

"What?" she said, feeling her face flush.

Nik shook his head and huffed a laugh. "You're a gods-damned miracle, Faythe."

CHAPTER 18

A FTER THE ROCKY discovery of her possible extended ability, Faythe and Nik stayed a while longer in the woods. The fae guard spent most of his time trying to explain how mental barriers worked and how to Nightwalk without risk of discovery.

It unnerved Faythe to think others could be aware—that *Jakon* could have been aware she was in his mind if she'd made a wrong move. Luckily, it wasn't common for the unwitting host to detect Nightwalkers, and this only tended to happen with unrested or less experienced walkers. Again, Nik expressed great disbelief she hadn't been found out by accident. Faythe was relieved more than anything.

He had brought more sleep tonic, so they spent some time in her mind practicing the barriers. She learned how to show him edited versions of her memories without appearing too suspicious. Then, when Nik announced it would soon be daybreak, she raced home and thanked the Spirits not a soul was around to stop her as she darted through the streets. Mercifully, Jakon was still sleeping when she arrived, so she changed into her clothes for the day and pretended she'd woken up earlier than usual.

Almost a week passed, and Faythe was grateful when her day

off rolled around. She was desperate to visit Marlowe at the blacksmiths. She had new questions she didn't want to ask in front of Jakon. He had a tendency to pry, and it would only raise his suspicion. Marlowe, on the other hand, had a wonderful nature of answering questions without any cynicism. In fact, it was like she relished in the unusual topics Faythe brought to her. She was a pocket of knowledge and enthusiasm, which was what Faythe loved the most about her friend.

She stopped by the market just as they were opening and picked up a few pastries from Marie's stall while the mild morning sun streamed down. One of Marie's daughters, Grace, had filled in to do the deliveries at least one day a week to allow Faythe some time to herself.

She was practically skipping down the streets when she rounded the corner to the blacksmiths. She couldn't see Marlowe, but she could hear the hammering of metal in the back. Peering through the curtain, she spied the blonde bent over another masterpiece of hers.

"I come bearing food!" Faythe exclaimed over the loud clanks.

Marlowe startled before whipping around to spot Faythe. She relaxed, flashing her a grin, and replied in greeting, "Apple tarts, I hope?"

"Of course. I wouldn't get you anything else." Faythe set the paper bag on a nearby bench.

Marlowe held up her creation: a fine steel blade. Simple but elegant. "It's supposed to be a gift for Jakon since he doesn't have one. What do you think?" she asked, biting her lip.

Faythe raised her eyebrows in wonder. "It's truly perfect, Marlowe. He's going to love it!"

At her enthusiasm, Marlowe relaxed and grinned widely. "It's not finished, but you said his birthday was coming up in a couple of weeks. I thought it could be a gift from both of us." She shrugged.

Faythe's face fell. "I can't take any credit for that. You give it to him. I've got something in mind anyway." She smiled reassuringly.

It was a lie. She had no idea what to get him, and now, seeing Marlowe's gift, she felt even more lowly. She could never compete with a gift so thoughtful and handmade. Not that Faythe ever saw it as a competition to lavish her friend with grand gifts, but it still bothered her she could never afford anything close to her own sword or even the materials for the one Marlowe crafted for Jakon.

"Oh, okay. If you're sure," Marlowe said, setting the blade down. "So what brings you down here?" she asked, wiping her hands on her apron before going over to the bag of pastries.

Faythe watched her take a few bites, hesitating before saying, "I was actually hoping to pick your brain about something, but if you're busy, I can come back another day?"

Marlowe waved a hand. "I have time. I don't have any major work at the moment, so I've just been messing around."

Faythe let Marlowe finish her tart and chuckled as she reached in for a second. She dipped a hand into her pocket and retrieved the watch that was starting to burn a hole through it. Her thoughts had been churning to find out what the symbol on the back—the mark of Aurialis—meant in connection to the one at the temple. If there even was a connection. Perhaps she was reading too much into it, but she figured if anyone might know, it would be Marlowe.

"Does this mean anything to you?" she asked, walking over to where Marlowe perched.

She finished her second tart and dusted her hands off before reaching to take the watch from Faythe's outstretched hand. In typical Marlowe fashion, her brow creased as she flipped it over in her palm a couple times, held it up at various angles, and studied everything she could see with the naked eye.

Faythe chewed nervously at her fingernails as she watched the blacksmith ponder over her mother's old pocket watch. Marlowe hummed once and went to take a seat with it at a small bench, picking up a magnifying eyepiece and continuing to study the watch further. Faythe didn't disturb her but moved to lean idly against the table while her friend examined the brass gadget with an expert's attention.

Eventually, she spoke. "They haven't made them like this in a *very* long time," she drawled, not looking up from it. "I'm surprised it still ticks."

Faythe already knew that and was waiting for her to say something about the engravings on the back, but her focus remained on the front as she squinted through her eyepiece.

"I'd be fascinated to see its inner workings." She looked up at Faythe in silent question. Faythe was about to protest when Marlowe quickly added, "I'd be able to put it back together, of course." Though a little smug, there was a plea in her eyes.

Faythe was hesitant. She didn't doubt her friend's abilities, but it was one of the only things she had left of her mother's, and she was wary about it being tampered with.

"I don't know, Marlowe. I'd rather not risk it to see old cogs and screws," she admitted, anxiety getting the better of her.

Marlowe didn't give in. "Who knows what strange workings could be in such an ancient device! Wouldn't you like to find out?"

Faythe had no interest in watch mechanics and didn't match her friend's enthusiastic wonder. Though one word had her deliberating while Marlowe waited with an eager look: *ancient.* If the watch was as old as Marlowe suggested, perhaps there was a chance something about its interior could offer clues to explain the Spirit symbol engraved on the back and if the item had any connection to the temple.

Faythe sucked in a subtle breath. What if the answer or the *key* to open the spiritual dwelling was not on the watch's exterior, but within its inner workings?

Her giddy thrill overcame her wariness, and she gave Marlowe a small nod to go ahead. She didn't waste a breath reaching for a bunch of small tools in a nearby pouch.

Faythe watched in nervous anticipation as she took a miniature screwdriver to the back but still said nothing of the engraving. If Marlowe knew what it meant, her face gave nothing away.

Once the plate was loose enough to be removed, she peeled it back to reveal a bunch of cogs and screws that made absolutely no sense to Faythe. Marlowe, however, frowned deeper in concentration as she reached for her magnifying eyepiece once again and went in close to investigate. A few minutes passed before she hummed at her findings.

"No wonder the minute hand stutters. There's an extra piece that doesn't seem relevant to the main mechanics—it just gets in the way," she pondered out loud, picking up a small pair of tweezers.

Faythe stood upright. "Are you sure?" she asked skeptically, fearful of the watch breaking.

Marlowe shot her a dead look. As if she really had to ask. Faythe backed down and nodded for her to continue. She stayed close behind, peering over Marlowe's shoulder and holding her breath as she watched her go in with steady precision. Marlowe gripped the small misplaced pin and pulled. It came out with a *click*, followed by a *thud*.

Faythe could only gape in disbelief as she watched the front part of the watch come away from the back completely. Marlowe jolted her head back in shock, lifting her hands away.

"I don't understand. It was a dud piece of metal!" she cried out.

Faythe didn't want to shout at her friend for being wrong, so instead, she took a breath to hold in her dismay and paced to the back of the workshop in silence, hoping Marlowe would be able to mend it swiftly.

She was flicking through more discarded books when Marlowe said her name to quietly beckon her over. If she'd already fixed the watch, Faythe owed her friend some appreciation for her quick work. When she strolled back over to the bench, she held in her whimper at the sight of the thing still in two pieces.

However, her watch wasn't what Marlowe was focused on anymore. She held up a tightly folded piece of parchment between her tweezers and said, "Did you know this was in here?"

Faythe's eyebrows knitted together. "That was in my mother's watch?"

Marlowe gave a nod before extending it to her. "It seems you have a concealment watch. I've heard of them before. They were used a long time ago to smuggle information between allies," she said with no small amount of relief she hadn't broken it after all.

Faythe took the parchment carefully. It was worn and slightly yellowed with age. Did her mother know it was in there? She didn't immediately unravel the sheet. What if it was a message *from* her mother?

Handing the paper back to Marlowe, she said, "You read it," and damned her own cowardice at the thought.

Marlowe didn't say anything as she took the parchment from Faythe's outstretched palm and cautiously began to fold back the edges.

The suspense was killing Faythe. She held in her snap to hurry up, tapping her foot in a nervous tic while she watched Marlowe finally unfold it to its full size, which was no bigger than the palm of her hand. The blacksmith read over it a few times with a deep frown of concentration.

Faythe couldn't stand it anymore. "Well?" she said with a bit more bite than intended.

Marlowe shot her a glance and shrugged. "It's like a poem, but not in a language I can read."

Faythe's whole body fell with disappointment and a little sadness. It wasn't a note from her mother. The old inscriptions and clearly aged paper weren't connected to her at all. If Marlowe was right, the parchment was likely a scribe from a centuries-old battle and wouldn't provide the answers she needed to gain access to the temple.

"An old war message?" she asked in bored curiosity.

Marlowe tilted her head. "Perhaps. I might have a book that could translate. I recognize some of the symbols." She shot up from the bench and wandered over to the books in the corner.

Laying the parchment down beside them, she began to sift through the mix of black and brown leather covers. When she found what she was looking for, Marlowe beamed and flicked through the pages, scanning over inscriptions that were no more than pretty decorations to Faythe. A language of elegance and affluence, she gathered from the delicate swirls and coils of the ancient text.

"It might take a while, but I'll try to translate what I can."

Faythe peeled her eyes from the book, finding it of little interest, while Marlowe ran her finger across the lines. She was irrationally angry at the hidden message that had turned out to be nothing of use. The small, hopeful feeling she'd let herself have—that it might be something to bring her closer to her mother—left a hollow void.

She looked at her friend still deeply engrossed in the texts. "I think I'm going to wander the town for a bit. Meet you at the hut later?"

Marlowe glanced up for a quick second, her only reply a small nod and smile before she dipped her head low again.

Faythe left her to it.

CHAPTER 19

AYTHE STORMED THROUGH the streets after her disappointing trip to the blacksmiths. She wasn't sure if it was her exasperation or complete lack of sense and rationality that influenced her destination. Perhaps she had a death wish, she thought, as she found herself strolling up to the standalone white house in the wealthier part of town.

Without giving herself time to cower away, she rapped on the wood door twice and took a polite step back, hoping the person she wanted was working today. After a short wait, the door swung open, and a familiar mop of red hair and brown eyes stared at her in surprise.

Ferris worked as a personal servant for the occupants of the house, though Faythe had always thought it a generous job description since he was essentially employed to carry out their dirty work. Ferris suited the work—was actually good at it—with his deviance and ruthlessness when it came to doing what needed to be done. She had to admire him for that.

Realizing he was waiting for her to explain her unexpected appearance, she blurted, "I want to take you up on your offer."

For a quick moment, she wanted to steal the words back and scold herself for even thinking of fighting in The Cave. She wanted to believe she was above such a barbarous sport. Yet she couldn't deny the dark part of her that itched to feel what it would be like to swing her sword in real combat. She was fed up with feeling useless, tired of holding back the desire that truly lived under her skin, and sick of being so impoverished she couldn't even afford a decent birthday gift for her best friend.

Ferris arched an eyebrow at her before a wild grin spread to his eyes. He stepped out over the threshold, closing the door behind him, and leaned with arms crossed against the frame.

"Does your guard dog know you're here?" he quipped.

She rolled her eyes at the gibe—he meant Jakon—and quickly considered abandoning the idea. It was a mistake to come to him. Even so, she found herself saying, "No. And he can't find out about any of it."

Ferris chuckled. "Good to know you have a mind of your own, Faythe. I was beginning to doubt it."

She scowled. "Don't make me regret coming to you."

He laughed again in response, and she fought the urge to swing at him. "I believe I'm the one doing you a favor here," he said before raising his chin. "I want a cut of your profits as your sponsor." His eyes twinkled darkly.

"I might not win."

His smile only widened. "I'm going to be putting in good money for you, Faythe, and I expect a fantastic return." He straightened. "I have every confidence you won't disappoint." He turned, bracing a hand on the doorknob. "Next fight is in two days' time. I'll find you some suitable…attire." He gazed over her at the comment, and she shifted. His final wink made her blood go cold and pump faster at the same time.

Had she just made a deal with darkness?

Without another word, he was back inside the house, and she was left staring at the white chipped door.

She stood there for a second after he vanished, unsure if the darkness was in her or Ferris. Then, twisting on her heel, she retreated with haste back into the main part of town, giddy with nerves, excitement, and…fear. But the thrill drowned out the voices telling her this could be the most foolish thing she'd ever agreed to.

CHAPTER 20

Faythe's mind reeled on her return from signing Ferris's phantom contract. She would be entertaining with her sword at no small risk to her life. She composed her rattling nerves at the thought, surprised to find Jakon already home when she arrived back at the hut. He sat at the kitchen table with his head in a book she had never seen before, looking up to flash her a welcoming smile as she walked through the door.

"She's got you reading now too?"

"Apparently, it's a wonder I've lived here this long and not learned about the wonders and histories of Ungardia."

Faythe chuckled and walked over to catch a glimpse of the text he studied. Jakon shifted as if trying to conceal the pages. She frowned deeply, about to question it, until she glanced the bold heading: *Legends of Lakelaria*. Her stomach dropped, and she cast Jakon a sad, knowing look.

"I've been asking at the docks if there's been word of anything unusual over there, in case there was talk of a stowaway from High Farrow, you know?" Jakon admitted.

Faythe's heart cracked. She'd been riddled with the guilt of not knowing Reuben's fate, but she didn't know Jakon was also silently suffering. She put her arm over his shoulder in quiet comfort, and he embraced her around the waist in return as they both stared down at the pages in solemn silence.

Some of the illustrations were beautiful: glittering channels of water and wonderous mythical lake creatures. Faythe leaned forward to flick over a few pages, but she wished she hadn't. Other depictions of what possibly dwelled in the Kingdom of the Water Dragon were not so welcoming. Man-eating sea beasts, half-human sirens with wicked pointed teeth, fae with the lethal ability to command the flow of water...

Jakon must have noticed her rising panic because he leaned in to close the book before she could work herself into a frenzy. She looked to him wide-eyed while her mind reeled at the horrors she might have sent her friend straight into the arms of.

Jakon stood, hands going to her shoulders. "They're only myths, Faythe. Anyone I've asked, those who have *real* knowledge of Lakelaria, have assured me it's just as ordinary and boring as any kingdom." He tried to reassure her with a faint smile, but he was a horrible liar.

She didn't call him out on it. For both their sakes, they had to *try* to believe Reuben was safe and they hadn't blindly sent their friend to a terrible fate in the lands of the unknown.

Jakon pulled her into a tight embrace, and she allowed herself to breathe and regain a sense of calm in the comfort of his arms, composed by the time she stepped back. She gave him a weak smile, walking past him to the washroom.

His voice halted her.

"I've been meaning to talk to you, Faythe. Uh—"

She turned back and cocked her head. "What's up?"

Jakon scratched the back of his neck nervously. "About Marlowe and me. It's not... It doesn't bother you, right? That she and I—"

Faythe's lips curled up in amusement at his flustered look, and she cut in, "Not in the slightest, Jakon. I'm happy for you. For both of you!" she assured.

He smiled awkwardly back. "Good... That's good." He cleared his throat. "I just thought, you know, it might feel weird or something. Since it's always just been you and me, but you never, um..."

She knew what he wanted to say. Faythe had never returned his feelings of affection; never wanted to be more than friends.

"Look, Jakon, I love you. I always will, but not in the way I know Marlowe loves you and you love her back. You two are made for each other, and I'm happy for you both as a couple. I'm grateful Marlowe came into my life too."

Relief washed over his face. "I love you too, Faythe." He made the few strides over to tousle her hair. "You'll always be my number one, you know?"

She batted his hand away with playful ire. "There's room for two of us to share that top spot now."

He looked at her with love and gratitude, giving a nod of appreciation at the comment. Faythe replied with a warm smile before scooting off to change.

That evening, Faythe insisted Marlowe and Jakon go out without her, claiming she was too tired to accompany them. It wasn't entirely a lie—she *was* tired—but she really wanted to go alone to practice her sword skills in preparation for her first fight.

It hadn't fully settled that she was about to face off in a real challenge that could harm or kill her if things went horribly wrong. She could already hear Jakon's fury if he found out, and it made her nauseatingly guilty for keeping yet another deadly secret from him. But she knew what she was doing, and she didn't need his lectures on what was best for her.

Faythe decided to avoid the square, not wanting to risk running into her friends or any of the fae patrol. Instead, she found herself scaling the hills toward the woods, figuring a tree trunk might at least provide her with stationary target practice.

Her boots crunched over fallen branches on the woodland floor as she passed through the maze of staggered trees, making for the waterfall glade ahead. When she emerged, she got all of a few steps before stopping dead in her tracks at the cold pinch of pointed metal on her back. Not daring to move or breathe, she remained paralyzed to the spot until the assailant on the other end of the blade spoke.

"Please state your name and business."

At the sound of Nik's mocking voice, her shoulders fell in relief —which quickly turned to annoyance as she spun around to glare at him. "You're an ass," she muttered. "What are you doing here?"

He laughed and lowered his sword. "I believe you're in *my* secret hiding spot." He cocked his head in amusement. "What *are* you hiding from, Faythe?"

"Nothing," she mumbled. "I just came to practice in peace." She emphasized the last word.

Nik shrugged. "Don't let me get in your way." He sheathed his sword at his hip. "It's all yours." He walked past her and took a seat on a large rock near the lake, pulling out a dagger to fidget with and making a show of looking like he wasn't paying her any attention.

She grumbled, irked already that she didn't have the place to herself. She hadn't considered the possibility he might be here and realized she didn't know much about him at all, such as what he got up to when he wasn't being an annoying bastard in their lessons or when he wasn't on whatever guard duty the king assigned him. She never saw him around the outer town at least.

Not in the mood to converse, she swung off her cloak and drew Lumarias, trying to block out his presence. Taking up poise with her sword, she began to duck, swing, and dodge, releasing herself to that glorious calm until it was only her and the air she cleaved.

To her surprise, Nik went a good while without saying anything.

He didn't move from his lazy position on the rocks, but when she stopped to dare a glance at him, she found him studying her intently. It made her squirm inwardly, and she fidgeted, flexing her sword in her wrist. Then he was on his feet, cloak discarded and sword drawn, coming to a stance in front of her.

"Now, let me correct everything you're doing wrong." He smiled arrogantly. She was about to retort when he said, "You've got great skill, Faythe, but a load more potential if you have the right person show you." There was no mockery or insult in his tone.

"So you're going to be my teacher?"

He nodded. "In mind skills, sword skills, and…other skills, if you find yourself lacking," he added suggestively.

She gaped, lifting her sword to poke him with the pointed end. He batted it away with his own blade before she could, and the clang of steel echoed through the clearing along with his bark of laughter.

"You really can't help yourself, can you?" she grumbled.

He crossed his arms, still holding his sword. "I've never been with a human before. I'd be curious to see if your kind is as… fragile as you look." He grinned deviously.

She didn't hesitate and brought her sword up in a flash reaction, going for his neck.

Faster than she could blink, his blade was up and connecting with hers once again before it could land. His bellows of laughter resonated through the open space. She only glared at him, her temper flaring.

"Good. Now, when you left step, be sure to be in a position to cover your right flank from attack." He demonstrated her error by darting for her side and kicking her feet from under her.

Faythe landed on the grass with a thud, wide-eyed in disbelief. She wanted to shout that he had caught her unaware and hadn't given her time to even attempt a defense, but her anger blazed and fused any words, leaving only a burning need to respond with the steel in her palm.

She shot to her feet. In a burst of blind rage, she swiped for him over and over, in a quick round of lethal blurred steel, until she was panting. He deflected every strike and swing with immortal ease. Tears welled in her eyes out of frustration and fury—or the fact she was realizing she wasn't as good as she thought or Ferris believed. She was very likely to only embarrass herself in The Cave...or worse.

"Faythe, stop," Nik said calmly.

She didn't. She continued her onslaught of unfaltering attacks. Every time he effortlessly stepped out of the path of her blade, he only made her blood pump harder and fueled her determination.

He ducked the next blow and spun around her so quickly she didn't have time to register the move until she was again falling flat on her back against the cool green floor. She panted and clamped her eyes shut, cursing the tears that escaped.

"You need to learn to channel your rage, not let it consume you," he said quietly from above.

She didn't know why she was so angry. Or why when she held a blade in her hands, it seemed to open the floodgates of indignation and grief she spent so long holding back with weak fortification.

"Thanks for the advice," she said sarcastically, pushing herself to her feet. She walked a few steps away before twisting to him, her sword angled again. "Teach me something of use, will you?"

He didn't balk or position himself to fight at the challenge. "Where does the anger come from?"

She went on the offensive once more, but he still didn't raise his sword as he ducked from her blade. "I don't want to be weak," she spat, thrusting forward. He dodged her again. "I don't want to be defenseless." Another swipe of her sword. "I don't want to be afraid." He kept dancing around her blows, and she felt her temper rise again. "I don't want anyone else to ever get hurt because I was too cowardly and incapable of protecting them!" she screamed in frustration.

Her eyes locked on his as the last words left her. She brought her hands up, blade poised—and then she *saw* his next move before it happened. In a split-second reaction, she twisted her sword and felt it connect with the edge of his thigh, slicing right through where, just a second sooner, he would have stepped fully out of range.

Faythe stopped, breathless, and stared at the shallow gash in Nik's leg that had started to bleed through the fabric of his pants. Her eyes snapped to his, and he stared back at her in surprise.

"I'm sorry," she breathed.

She dropped her sword, only now returning to her full senses as she realized what she'd done; the feral *rage* she'd let consume her.

"How did you do that?" was all he said.

She shook her head in disbelief. "I don't know. It was like—*oh, Gods,* I'm sorry. I didn't mean to," she stuttered. All at once, her other emotions returned and threatened to drown her now the anger had subsided.

As if sensing it, he said, "It's nothing. I heal far faster than you. It'll be completely gone in less than an hour." His eyes bore into hers in bewilderment, awe, curiosity... Faythe wasn't quite sure what it was.

"I lost control. I don't know what happened," she muttered weakly.

His face softened. "You have a fire in you. That's a good thing —if you can learn to harness it." After another assessing look, he went on, "You're faster than any mortal I've ever seen, but *that*... It was impossibly quick, even for you."

She swallowed, her throat suddenly bone-dry. "I don't know how to explain it... It was like I could *see* your intentions before you physically moved."

He was quiet for a moment. "Your ability is more impressive

than I thought. It could be an invaluable skill in combat," he said at last.

She blinked. "Wouldn't that be…cheating?"

"If you have an advantage, why not use it?"

She pondered for a moment, deciding it couldn't hurt to see what she was capable of. "I don't know how to read a mind. It's always been *accidental.*" She cringed as she glanced at his leg, slightly relieved to see the wound had already started to knit together.

"Then we'll have to figure it out—together," he said with a small smile.

She was grateful to have him as her friend. That was what she considered him now, whether it was mutual or not, and she felt bad she had ever doubted his motives when he'd given her no reason to. Most of all, she was glad to not be alone.

At the thought, she perked up. "Where do we start?"

His wicked grin returned as he motioned for her to retrieve her sword with a flick of his own. "First, the basics. You're good—great even, by mortal standards." His green eyes flashed. "But you can be better."

CHAPTER 21

F OR AN HOUR, Faythe and Nik parried back and forth with deliberate slowness while he demonstrated a range of new maneuvers, as well as how to attack and deflect using more than just her blade. They even ditched the swords at one point and practiced dodges, kicks, and how to get out of compromised positions. Faythe felt wonderfully drunk on the combat knowledge and techniques he shared with her and was in utter awe at the way he moved, a centuries-old fae warrior honed for the battlefield.

She wanted to continue, thinking she could never get enough, but Nik insisted they take a break. They sat on the rocks by the lake, Faythe catching her breath, though Nik didn't look winded in the slightest, much to her irritation.

"What did you mean earlier?" Nik broke the silence. "When you said you don't want anyone *else* to get hurt?"

She didn't answer immediately as she decided whether to share the personal information with him. But she already considered him a friend, and at his look of genuine concern, it didn't scare her to reveal the most vulnerable part of herself: her fear.

She looked away. "My mother. She's dead…because of me. It's what I saw the first time we came here. I think it wanted me to admit it—face it. My fear of losing someone else to my own cowardice," she said into the lake as if whatever governed the woods was listening too. She told him the events leading up to and after what happened that night, and he listened in respectable silence. When she finished, they remained in quiet thought for a long moment.

"Valgard soldiers have been breaking through our borders for years—it was likely they who took your mother for information. You were just a child. It was not your fault," he said solemnly and with a hint of anger she knew was directed at the ruthless kingdom of Valgard.

She appreciated his attempt to console her, but she had already come to terms with that night and accepted her role in it. She gave him a weak smile regardless.

"What about your mother?" she asked carefully, noting the shift in his face. His jaw flexed, and he refused to meet her eye. She waited for his refusal to speak of it again, expecting his silence in answer.

"She was killed nearly one hundred years ago by an intruder. They were never caught," he said quietly.

Though a great measure of time separated their trauma, Faythe felt herself tragically bonded to him through their mutual grief in that moment. She knew verbal condolences would offer little comfort as they never had for her, so she didn't bother with them. Instead, she shuffled down the rocks until she was close enough to touch and didn't wait to see if he would retreat. She reached a hand over and placed it on top of his. To her surprise, Nik twisted his wrist and reached his other arm over to encase her small hand between his calloused palms. A burst of warmth shot through her chest at the acceptance, and they sat like that in comfortable silence. It was never awkward; they simply tuned in to the quiet murmur of the woods, content at having company nearby.

Then his voice broke her mindless thoughts. "Your conscious

abilities seem to surface when something's being projected at you or when your own emotions are running too high," he pondered and looked at her. "You need to find the focus to block yourself from hearing loud thoughts in passing and the discipline to reach into a person's mind and find information at your own will."

"You make it sound like choosing to sleep or stay awake."

He gave a soft laugh. "I would imagine it's similar, actually. At least to your Nightwalking."

She winced. "I haven't even tried to do that yet…knowingly."

"You have to try. Pick someone who won't make you feel as guilty as you feel doing it to your friend."

She was beginning to wonder if Nik was a conscious mind reader himself with how often he knew exactly what she was thinking. "I'll try," was all she said.

His eyes met hers, and she found herself being swallowed by the emerald pools.

"What do you want, Faythe?"

A provocative question. From his teasing grin, she knew he was projecting it to her on purpose. Hearing her name in his voice inside her head sent a ripple down her spine. She refused to let it show, but she also couldn't bring herself to look away.

"You need only ask," he whispered seductively in her mind.

Gods, she could even hear his change in volume. It sent a pulse through her as if she were feeling his breath on her ear even though he kept his distance.

"Stop that," she hissed, ripping her hand out of his as her cheeks flushed red.

He chuckled. "I'm just testing your abilities." From the way his pupils darkened, she had no doubt he could hear the increased tempo of her heart; could possibly even *smell* the effect it had on her with his fae senses. "Though that's with *me* trying. Now, you try. I'll let you past my barriers just enough to test the theory."

She stared at him in horror. Did he really trust her enough to let her go poking around in his head?

Reading her expression, he said, "Don't worry, I have every control over my mental walls. You'll only be able to see the things I let you."

Right. Of course he wouldn't offer himself as a test host if she could rifle through any of his thoughts and memories. She took a wary breath, straightening before focusing her eyes fully on his. She pictured what his walls would look like; imagined his black-and-gray smoke like that in his subconscious. Then, as she pierced past the deep green of his eyes, she found herself arriving at a thick black veil, which she somehow knew was the entrance to his mind. She gasped a little at the strange feeling.

"Good. I can feel you," she heard faintly, but his voice was a background blur like the rest of the woods as she honed in on the image of his mind. It felt like being in two places at once.

The wall was solid, but then she felt a small crack open up and slipped inside. It was pitch-black until color soon appeared in a blur of rainbow hues and a scene unfolded around her. She was looking at herself through waves of spitting amber fire, and she was dancing. His memory of the summer solstice, she realized. When she locked eyes with herself at the end of the song, her heart skipped. But was that Nik's heart she was feeling? He walked around the fire with eyes fixed on her as she walked—more like swayed—away from him to find Jakon. She felt something else. Curiosity? At the man who held Faythe from falling. When she was sitting by herself, Jakon having gone to get her water, Nik started his walk toward her. When he got closer, she stood up, yet to notice him as his eyes grazed over her, appreciating the effort she'd made for the event. She could hear his one thought in that moment: *Beautiful.*

Faythe pulled herself from the memory and focused once again on the green eyes and surrounding noise of the woods. She averted her gaze immediately, cheeks aflame.

"What?" he asked innocently.

She glared at him. "You know *what.* Why did you choose to show me that?"

"Just in case not enough people told you how wonderful you looked that night," he teased, and the heat on her face reached boiling point. His eyes twinkled in amusement before he asked, "What was it like?"

"It felt like I was *you,* obviously."

"It's not obvious though." He looked ahead, brow creased in thought. "When we Nightwalk, we don't see through the host's eyes; we shadow them through their memories. Most with the ability don't usually know emotion unless it's relevant information, and even then, memories don't always capture true feelings." Another contemplative pause. "Your reach far surpasses the typical Nightwalking ability to be able to shadow *and* embody the host. With training, you might be able to know what a person is thinking and feeling in real time, not only in memories. You could maybe even alter thoughts in real time too." Faythe paled, and he quickly added, "Only if you choose to, of course. You've gone this long without knowing what kind of power you have, so you only need to train your mind to enter another's at will."

"Is that all?" she said sarcastically at the wave of new information.

He gave her a look of understanding. "It may seem like a lot, but it will become as easy as breathing. Trust me."

She did trust him. She trusted him to help her, and she knew that with his guidance, she might one day be able to master both sides of her ability. Never in her lifetime did she imagine she would be putting her trust—and her life, in some ways—in a centuries-old fae warrior. But Nik was different. He was *good.*

"Thank you," she said sincerely.

Something changed in the atmosphere between them, but she didn't balk at the intimate look they shared. Slowly, he reached a hand up to graze his fingers under her chin. Her heart pounded when he seemed to shift slightly closer, their thighs now touching where they sat side by side on the rock, and she felt the soft caress of his breath over her mouth. Only a sliver of space remained between them, and it became a noticeable coolness. She wasn't sure if she was still breathing. She longed for him to close that distance.

"What is it that you want, Faythe?"

She caught the question at the edge of his mind. He wouldn't kiss her without her asking for it, and it was enough hesitation for her to snap into her own senses.

Nik was fae, an immortal, a royal guard. And she...

She was human, a nobody, and that was how it would always be. They couldn't be seen together. She could never tell her friends how she came to know him or anything about him. No one would understand, and no one would accept them.

She backed away and stood, letting his hand drop where it had held her face. She felt cold from the absence but shook her mind to clear the thoughts and calm her racing heart.

"I think that's enough of a lesson for today," she said a little breathlessly, not daring to look at him again as she stalked over to her discarded cloak and fastened it around herself.

Neither of them spoke as they left the woods and walked over the hills, barely muttering their goodbyes when they parted on the edge of town as usual. But Faythe couldn't stop her rattling thoughts and still felt the echo of his touch as she made her way back to the hut in the dark.

CHAPTER 22

F AYTHE SULKED THE whole way home after departing from
Nik. She knew it was for the best that they keep it strictly
friendly, or professional, or whatever it was they were doing, but it
didn't help her sting of disappointment. There was no changing
who they were or the differences that separated them, and she
couldn't give in to the feelings she had for him.

Perhaps a kiss would mean nothing to Nik. Maybe getting
everything from her wouldn't mean anything to him either. The
thought delivered a different kind of pain.

When she swung open the door to the hut, she was immediately
confronted by Marlowe sitting at the table while Jakon paced the
small space in front of the door. Upon seeing her, he let out a deep
sigh of relief, but his eyes blazed.

"Where have you been?"

She winced at his tone. "I was just out practicing as usual," she
said, flashing the pommel of her sword under her cloak.

"Practicing! It's one in the morning, Faythe! We went by the
square—you weren't there!"

Her eyes widened. She hadn't realized the time. Her hand dove
into her pocket only to find it empty.

"Shit. I'm sorry. My watch is still at the blacksmiths. I lost track of time."

He ran a hand through his hair. "We were worried sick. You can't do that."

Her eyes flashed in vexation. "Can't do what, Jak? Go out on my own? I'm not a *child!* I can look out for myself."

He didn't deserve her anger, and she knew deep down she was only riding on the back of her indignation over everything that kept her from pursuing her feelings for a certain fae guard. Not being able to talk about it only made her resentment grow more.

Jakon recoiled at her tone and then straightened. "You have friends who care about you. I don't know what's been up with you lately, but your secrets and selfishness affect us both," he shot back.

Faythe felt the words hard. He knew right where to strike. She couldn't help herself in her flash of rage, and she focused on his mind to see if he meant any truth in them. Jakon was an open book; no walls like she saw in Nik's head, and completely vulnerable to her.

"You don't think your actions affect me too. You only think about yourself. I wish you would just let me in."

The thoughts were loud, and Faythe could *feel* the anger in him. Tears pricked the backs of her eyes, and she glanced at Marlowe who had yet to say anything.

"Where were you? It's not your fault. He only wants to help. We both do."

Pity resonated in her words, and she hated it.

"You two have each other—you don't need me anymore. Consider yourselves relieved of the burden of *caring,*" she said sourly. Shutting them both out, she turned on her heel and stalked to the bedroom.

Jakon called her name but didn't follow.

The tears fell silently from her eyes as she stripped down and pulled herself into her nightclothes before curling up in her cot. They kept falling as she thought of everything she was and wasn't. Everything her friends thought about her; everything she couldn't have with Nik; everything that made her a screwed-up waste of existence. She didn't deserve her abilities. She didn't deserve her friends. She didn't deserve to be *loved*. She would only end up disappointing everyone in the end.

After a long moment, she heard shuffling, and then, from her position facing the wall, she felt the dip of her bed and a warm body curl around hers. The petite female form fit neatly behind her own.

She released a sob, and Marlowe stroked her hair without saying anything. She only held her tight and let Faythe cry it out. And she did. Sadness poured out of her like her anger in the woods. She wanted so badly to tell Marlowe everything in that moment—and Jakon too. It pained her more every day, the walking lie she was to them.

When her sobbing ceased, she felt hollow and tired. She was starting to fall asleep when she heard more shuffling and the creak of Jakon's bed as he sat in it.

Neither woman moved, but Jakon spoke. "I'm really sorry, Faythe. I didn't mean what I said."

She didn't respond. She knew he'd meant it from peering into his thoughts, and for once, she didn't feel guilty for it.

Jakon didn't press the issue further, and she heard him lie back in his cot.

As silence filled the room, she embraced the fall into darkness, still safe in the warmth of Marlowe's arms.

Faythe sat in her subconscious idly playing with the mist between her fingers. She intended to guide herself to full unconsciousness at first, but she had been toying with an idea for some time now.

She couldn't get Marlowe and Jakon's thoughts about her from her mind and was tempted to walk into Marlowe's head to see if they ever spoke about her when she wasn't with them. It seemed petty, but she was desperate to ease the pain and insecurity. She could deal with it from anyone else—herself, even Nik—but she wouldn't be able to live with herself if her friends truly thought of her as selfish and uncaring…or worse.

She could control it, only see what she needed to see to put her own mind at ease and not pry into anything she had no business seeing. At least, she hoped she could. Which was why she had sat on the idea for all this time, out of fear she might accidentally walk into Marlowe's private thoughts or memories and never forgive herself.

She stood abruptly. Nik had said she needed to try; to practice. If anyone would understand, it was Marlowe, she was sure of that. So, without giving herself time to back out again, she closed her eyes and thought of her friend until she felt a pull…and just like that, gold changed to hues of vibrant purple when she opened them.

Marlowe's mind.

It shocked her how easy it was, but Nik had warned her not to stay in this part of the mind for long and to find the memory she was looking to jump into. She began sifting through memories of Marlowe and Jakon, quickly flicking through them to rule out the ones in which she was physically present, until there was only one prominent memory left.

The scene unfolded around her as she willed it to, and she stood behind Marlowe as she and Jakon walked hand in hand down by the harbor. Faythe recognized the path just past Harbor Hall, beautifully lit with amber torches. The moon was bright, catching the ripples of lapping water and making the sea glitter like the stars in the night sky above. It was the perfect romantic setting, and Faythe couldn't help but feel like she was intruding.

Find the relevant information.

The memory skipped forward, and they were sitting on a bench, Marlowe resting her head on Jakon's shoulder while he wrapped his arm around her. Faythe's heart stung at the sight. It was jealously, she realized, at their completely effortless, carefree relationship.

Finally, Jakon spoke. "Do you think Faythe is okay with this?"

Marlowe lifted her head, knowing he meant the two of them. "Why wouldn't she be?"

He shrugged, looking out over the tranquil sea. "She seems distant lately."

Faythe's face fell at his pained look.

"It was never like this between us—you know, like what you and I have," he started. "But I feel like she's been pushing me out ever since. Or maybe I've been pushing her away by not including her as much as I should. It's always just been the two of us, and now…" He trailed off.

Marlowe put her hand on his thigh. "She's a grown woman, Jakon. She's headstrong and fierce, but her heart is always in the right place. She knows how to look out for herself."

He nodded. "Gods, I know she does." His frown deepened as he put his hand on hers. "I think…I think I'm scared to let her go. To accept that she no longer needs me."

"You've looked out for her since she was a child. She'll always need you. But she also has her own life to live."

He was silent for a moment before admitting, "I love her, Marlowe. I always will."

She gave him a warm smile. "And nothing will ever come between that." Squeezing his hand, she added, "I love her too."

Faythe felt the damp trails on her cheeks before she realized she was crying. She didn't stay to see if they said anything else, only projected herself back into her familiar gold-and-white mist.

She sobbed loudly in the comfort of her own head, feeling awful she'd ever had doubts about either of them. Jakon, who had been by her side since she was orphaned at nine years old and always put her first. Even now, when it came to Marlowe, he made sure to confess his love for her. Not as a lover, but no matter what, he would always choose Faythe. It made her feel hideous he ever thought he'd have to choose between the two. And then there was Marlowe, who showed absolutely no sign of jealousy or resentment for it.

Faythe felt crippled with guilt and undeserving of their love and loyalty. But she wouldn't let herself fall into despair; she would rise and prove herself worthy.

CHAPTER 23

W HEN FAYTHE AWOKE the next morning, both of her friends had already left. She pushed back the disappointment she felt at not getting to tell them she was sorry and that they didn't deserve her display of anger last night. Her words of apology would have to remain unspoken until she saw them later.

For now, she hopped out of her cot and washed, feeling fresher and lighter than she had in a long while. It was as if a weight she didn't realize was slowly crushing her had been lifted—that uncertainty of who she was and what she meant to the people who mattered.

She was dressed and heading out the door when she paused on the threshold, nearly tumbling over a package on the doorstep. She frowned and gave it a light kick, making sure nothing live or combustible was inside. When it remained stationary and silent, she warily picked it up and took it into the hut. She gave it another look over before gently pulling at the string that bound the box shut and peeling back the lid cautiously. Inside, a note on the top was the first thing to catch her attention. She picked it up and read:

Faythe,

This cost me a month's wage,
but I expect the debt to be paid
in full in good time. I'll meet you
on Crow's Lane at ten o'clock
tomorrow night.
Don't be late, and be sure to
leave your guard dog at home.

Yours always, darling Faythe.

Ferris didn't have to sign his name; there was only one person she expected this particular delivery from. Faythe discarded the note and looked into the box. As promised, the contents consisted of more "suitable attire" for her first fight. She pulled out the first item: a scarf, one that would cover her head and act like a mask over her nose and mouth to leave only her golden eyes on show. There was also a pair of plain black gloves.

The next item stunned her for a moment. She pulled it out fully and held it up for a quick inspection. It was a matte-black, textured leather suit. It looked to be a tight fit, but the material flexed and stretched, and she could imagine the freedom of movement it would allow. A real fighting suit.

The final matching items were revealed to be a pair of black boots and a long black cloak.

Faythe marveled at the ensemble laid out on the table. She'd only ever dreamed of owning such a set for use in professional combat. She didn't dwell on *where* Ferris got his hands on such items. The suit certainly wasn't from anywhere in this town—perhaps not even this *kingdom*.

Folding everything together, she stashed the clothes under her bed. It would all be over if Jakon found out about it. Then, giddy with new excitement and thrilling nerves, she skipped out of the hut.

After a deliriously dull workday, Faythe was left alone to close up the stall. She'd spent most of her shift trying to stay busy and offering to run extra errands to keep her mind off her friends—and Nik. She'd tried and failed to push the fae guard from her thoughts.

She had just boarded up when a voice appeared behind her. "I thought you might want this back."

Faythe whirled, and a small sound came out of her at the sight of Marlowe. She was holding out her mother's pocket watch as if it had never been tampered with at all. Faythe gave her a weak smile and took it in her own hands.

There was a small silence before she blurted, "I'm so sorry, Marlowe. You didn't deserve my anger last night, and neither did Jakon. I—"

She was cut off when Marlowe lunged at her, flinging her arms around her in a tight embrace. All of Faythe's sadness and worry dissipated instantly. She didn't know how much time passed as they held each other, nor did she realize just how much she needed it from her friend. It felt as if a small weight had been lifted from her shoulders.

Marlowe pulled back and didn't remove her hands from Faythe as she looked her in the eyes and said, "You know you can tell me anything, right?"

Faythe swallowed at the intensity in her ocean-blue irises and gave a small nod. Marlowe waited another second as if hoping she would say something to explain her moods and absences. *Gods*, she wanted to. But she couldn't. It was better for both their safety if Marlowe remained oblivious.

Finally taking a step back, Marlowe gave her a small smile, but she couldn't hide the slight disappointment on her face at Faythe's silence. Regardless, she linked her arm through hers to start their walk to the hut.

"Actually, there is a favor I need to ask of you."

Marlowe pulled them to a stop and unhooked their arms so they could face each other, giving Faythe her full attention while she waited for her to continue.

Faythe cleared her throat. "I—uh…I need you to keep Jakon busy again tomorrow night." She had no right to ask her again, especially not after her outburst yesterday.

Marlowe crossed her arms. "If I'm going to do that, you're going to tell me exactly what you plan on getting up to."

It was a fair bargain, and Faythe knew she could trust Marlowe with this secret. It was a perfectly normal *human* activity, albeit stupidly dangerous and reckless.

"I'm going to fight…in The Cave. I went to see Ferris, and he's arranged it." She waited for the outcry of horror; for Marlowe to shout at her for being completely out of her mind and run straight to Jakon to talk her out of it. None of that came. She couldn't read the expression on her friend's face as she stared back for a moment, contemplating.

"You're sure you can win?"

Faythe blinked in surprise. "Well, no, but Ferris seems pretty convinced I have a good shot." She winced. His judgement of her skills wasn't exactly solid ground to go on, and even she felt foolish for trusting it.

Marlowe huffed, but a small smile tugged at her lips. "I hope he knows if he's slightly wrong and you come out with even a scratch, it won't be Jakon's wrath he has to worry about."

Faythe sagged with relief and grinned widely. She didn't deserve such a loyal friend. Marlowe simply looped her arm back through Faythe's without saying anything more of it, and they continued their walk. Her heart swelled. Although it was yet another secret she was keeping from Jakon, it was a relief to have at least one of her friends to talk to about it.

Back at the hut, Jakon strolled in no more than ten minutes after them. His lips parted to speak, but Faythe hurled herself at him before he got any words out. Jakon's solid arms wrapped around her waist, lifting her slightly as she clamped hers around his neck. They stayed like that for a long moment. Faythe was overcome with emotion, but she had exhausted all her tears last night.

"I'm sorry," he mumbled into her hair.

She pulled back to look into his brown eyes and shook her head firmly. "It's me who should be sorry. I don't know what came over me. You had every right to be angry."

"I'll always need you, Faythe, and I'll *never* stop caring about you," he said quietly.

"I know," she barely whispered. "I'm sorry if I've been distant lately, but it has *nothing* to do with you or Marlowe. I'll always need both of you, and I'll never make you choose between either of us." She stepped out of his arms.

Marlowe smiled warmly at her while Jakon gave her an appreciative nod. The air between them finally returned to full, bright clarity, and Faythe filled her lungs with it in relief.

"I think we should all go to Harbor Hall tonight—my treat." Marlowe beamed.

Faythe grinned in answer, grateful for the change in topic to shift the mood. Her stomach grumbled loudly at the mention of food, and as soon as Jakon was freshened up from the farm, they swiftly left the hut.

They strolled lazily together down the quiet street toward the harbor. Torches lining the buildings aided the fading sunlight as it finished its descent over the horizon. At Harbor Hall, they were guided to a table by the window overlooking the sea. This time, Marlowe and Jakon scooted into the booth together, and Faythe sat opposite them. She had been worried about feeling out of place in the trio, but it surprised her just how comfortable she was. They dined and laughed and talked about everything and anything. She relished in the normalcy and joy at seeing her friends so carefree.

She hadn't realized just how much she missed and needed this. If she was going to learn how to control her anger and sadness to become more in tune with her abilities, the key was balance.

Their spirits were elated, and Faythe felt drunk on laughter as they paid their bill and left, making the short walk back home. But as they rounded the last corner before the hut, Faythe stiffened, all joyous feelings snuffed out in an instant. Marlowe noticed the change where their arms joined and followed her gaze.

The trio faced another force of three walking toward them from the bottom of the street. Two fae guards...led by Captain Varis. Marlowe said nothing but subtly pulled Faythe closer into her side as if sensing her fear. Faythe tried to keep her eyes fixed on the ground and not pay them any attention, hoping the captain wouldn't remember their last encounter. But his dark voice rumbled through her mind.

"Look at me, girl."

A show of dominance. He wanted her to look at him as they passed, to taste the fear in her eyes and prove to himself he had succeeded in evoking the terror he wished upon his inferiors. She knew that if she didn't oblige, he would stop them and physically try to satisfy his sadistic desire for violence.

When the guards were only a foot away, she forced her eyes up to meet his. She didn't balk at his black stare, though the waves of hatred and malice that radiated off him turned her stomach, nearly knocking her off-balance. At seeing her defiant stance, a flash of rage stabbed her chest. *His* rage.

Maybe she was foolish for not giving him the reaction he wanted, but in that moment, her own vexation took over from logic and rational thinking. She would not cower. Never again.

They held each other's stares as they passed, arms almost grazing, one second feeling like a lifetime. When Varis didn't stop to punish Faythe, she released a long breath and offered Marlowe a weak smile as her friend squeezed her arm. It seemed she'd managed to pass the encounter off as her general wariness of the fae. A wariness everyone had, and justifiably so.

"It's as if they have nothing better to do with their immortal existence than invoke fear and stand pretty," Marlowe quipped once the guards had passed.

Jakon laughed at her lighthearted comment, and just like that, Faythe banished all thoughts from the past few minutes, remembering the great night she'd had with the best company instead. Back at home, she hugged Marlowe good night before Jakon walked her to the other side of town as usual. Then, safe and tucked up in bed, for the first time in a long time, Faythe fell asleep with a smile on her face and glee in her heart.

CHAPTER 24

T HE FOLLOWING DAY was a series of pastry deliveries, pleasant chatter, and Marie complaining Faythe wasn't focused when she messed up a couple of orders. Her scolding was justified. Faythe's mind was elsewhere today—on the fight that loomed closer with every tick of her watch. She'd barely put the thing down, checking relentlessly as the hands drew closer and closer to the ten o'clock mark when she'd meet Ferris down Crow's Lane.

When she got home after the workday, she sat at the kitchen table and made herself look immersed in the book splayed out in front of her. Her foot tapped nervously against the wood, the only sound echoing through the painful silence as she waited for the door to swing open, announcing Jakon's arrival. But he was late.

Jakon was usually quite punctual with his return time of eight o'clock, but it was approaching half past nine, and Faythe was starting to grow worried. He'd been late home before, when work had needed him for an extra hour or so. It was just her luck this would be one of those days.

At the sudden creak of the door, Faythe jumped up—but it was only Marlowe who strolled across the threshold, and her disappointment was obvious.

"He's not home yet?" she asked, brow furrowed.

Faythe shook her head and huffed as she sat back down.

"What time do you have to be there?"

"Ten," Faythe muttered, checking her watch yet again.

"Go change—I'll distract him from coming through if he gets home." She ushered Faythe to her feet.

Faythe was wary but nodded and retreated into the bedroom to slip into her new attire. Discarding her tunic and pants, she stepped into the suit, pulling it up and sliding her arms into the long, tight sleeves. When she zipped it up, she took a moment to marvel at the feel and fit as it became like a thick second skin. Around her forearms, bodice, and knees, the material was reinforced but blended in with the gritty matte texture of the rest. A fixed belt went around the hips, and she noted the various slots for potential daggers and other weapons.

Although she owned no mirror big enough to see herself, Faythe knew the suit was stunning. She would have to thank Ferris. She was sure he expected her to pay him back through her earnings if she was successful, but she had to give him credit for his taste and for matching her fit perfectly.

She had just slid into the boots when she heard the front door swing open, followed by shuffling and the murmur of voices. Faythe swore, throwing the rest of the items back under her bed. She looked around wildly to find something to conceal herself from Jakon. With minimal options, she decided to quickly throw her bedsheets back and slide herself in, tucking them up under her chin.

She closed her eyes, feigning sleep as the voices grew closer.

"I think she wasn't feeling too well and headed to bed," she heard Marlowe say louder than necessary, and Faythe knew it was really intended for her ears. She thanked the Spirits her brilliant friend had come up with a similar excuse to her own in the heat of the moment.

The door to the bedroom creaked, and Faythe slowly peeled

her eyes open, trying to muster a drowsy, disoriented appearance. "Hey, Jak," she said hoarsely.

His face fell with concern as he took her in. "Sorry I was late home. They kept me back for extra work."

She gave him a weak smile. "It's okay. I'm only going to sleep anyway. I don't feel so good."

"We can stay in tonight, make sure you're—"

"I'm fine, Jak. Go have a nice night together," she insisted a little too quickly. She didn't know what time it was now, but she was sure she would be late if she didn't leave very soon.

He opened his mouth, about to protest further, but Marlowe chimed in, "I had something planned for us tonight. I made sure Faythe was seen to and tucked in before you got home."

She dared a look at her friend that would show her gratitude. It wouldn't be easy for Marlowe to keep this from Jakon either.

He gave her a grateful smile and then turned his attention back to Faythe. "Are you sure you're okay?"

"Absolutely stellar." She grinned, hoping that would be enough to convince him. With a final glance, he nodded and turned to leave.

Marlowe flashed her a wink and mouthed, "Good luck," before following him out of the bedroom.

Faythe stayed in bed for an anxious few minutes more until she heard their mumbled voices fade and, finally, the last click of the front door closing behind them. She didn't waste a second before whipping back the covers and launching herself up. Fitting Lumarias swiftly across her back, she pushed the gloves on and slipped the scarf around her neck, deciding she wouldn't cover herself fully just yet so she wouldn't look too inconspicuous on her short journey to Crow's Lane.

Swinging her new black cloak over her shoulders, she darted out of the hut and became a living shadow, blending in seamlessly with the dark night. She was a stroke of black smoke as she weaved through the streets with feline precision. The suit granted her a new freedom of movement she had been missing out on in combat. Not a single piece rubbed or itched, and despite its thick material, she felt utterly *weightless*.

She rounded the corner onto Crow's Lane, suitably named as one of the darkest alleys in town where crows feasted on discarded scraps from the inn and butchers. The sounds and smells were vile enough that no one ever took this route if they could help it.

She could only faintly make out a figure leaning sideways halfway down the alley. She prayed it was Ferris and not some unfriendly foe. After all, she would have little chance of defending herself in this darkness, and her cries wouldn't be heard from down here either.

The figure pushed off the wall as Faythe neared. "I was starting to worry you'd bailed," Ferris jested, though it was with no small amount of impatience.

She stopped in front of him and began to make out his features as her eyes adjusted. "I'm here, aren't I?" she retorted.

"Indeed." He looked her over in admiration. "How exquisite you look, Faythe. Like death incarnate."

She shifted. "Who would have thought you had taste?"

"The suit is straight from Rhyenelle. The female warrior fae wear such a garment. It was not an easy thing to get hold of."

She gaped at the mention of the legendary warriors of Rhyenelle. Their legions of mixed-gender fighters rivaled even those of High Farrow. Suddenly, Faythe felt very unworthy of the garment and considered removing it immediately to avoid insulting such skilled combatants.

"A simple black leather pants and tunic would have sufficed," she mumbled.

He shrugged. "If you plan to be the best, you should look it. And I expect you to pay it back and then some. Tonight even, perhaps." He gave her a cunning grin.

She swallowed hard. No pressure then.

He continued, "We go in, you don't speak to anyone. I'll do all the talking. You need only show up, put on a performance, and leave. I'll deal with the rest. Got it?" His voice was stern. This was business to him, and she was his wild card.

Her nod was her only answer, nerves swallowing her ability to speak.

"Don't act cocky. Don't show off. The less people bet on you, the more money in our pockets, understood?"

Hustling—that was his plan. Faythe didn't have the option to back out now, she realized, as this lethal game she was about to enter had just become all the more deadly.

CHAPTER 25

F AYTHE FIXED THE scarf around her face as a mask and pulled the hood of her suit up as they exited Crow's Lane and rounded onto Main Street. She clenched her gloved hands into tight fists to stop from trembling as nerves and adrenaline coursed through her veins.

A few wandering humans gawked and retreated as she swaggered past. She tried hard to muster every ounce of confidence to portray the character of a ruthless assailant like the kind they would expect to find in a place such as The Cave.

They approached the inn, and Faythe took a deep breath before she followed Ferris inside without allowing herself to falter a step. She hoped the owners wouldn't recognize her. They weren't on particularly good terms since she'd played a part in destroying furniture and glass bottles in her drunken brawls.

The establishment was peppered with small groups of men chatting and drinking. A couple glanced at her, their curiosity piquing, as the mysterious hooded figure glided past. She continued to follow Ferris's back while he didn't so much as peek in any direction, making a beeline straight through the tables, past the bar, and down a dimly lit hallway toward a descending staircase. No one seemed to stop him or ask his business, and she wondered just how often her friend visited the notorious cave below.

Her hands grew slick under the leather of her gloves. She flexed them as more of a distraction than anything else as the torches lining the walls became less frequent. At the bottom of the stairs was another short hallway, and two giant human men stood guard on either side of the large iron double doors at the end of it. She tried not to balk, hoping she wouldn't be fighting anyone of *that* size.

She had no idea who she would face in the fighting pit, actually, and if Ferris knew, he hadn't given anything away. Maybe it was out of fear she would change her mind, or perhaps his silence was a blessing so she wouldn't get herself worked up beforehand.

Ferris stopped walking and turned to her. "I've put a lot of money in for you tonight, Faythe, and I've persuaded my master to as well. Losing isn't an option. You're quick, you're smart… Don't disappoint us," he said quietly, so only she could hear. He wasn't scolding her or trying to spark fear and pressure so he wouldn't lose his coin. No—from the look in his eyes, Faythe knew this was her friend's way of building her confidence.

She took a deep breath and rolled her shoulders back with a new flare of determination. Losing would *not* be an option. Not tonight or any other night.

Ferris turned on his heel and stepped up to the guards. He spoke quietly, so she couldn't make out what they said, and then he flashed something to them from inside his fitted black-and-silver jacket. They looked him over before they did the same to her a foot behind him.

For the first time, she really took in the redhead's appearance. He was dressed in finer clothes than he usually wore, and it made Faythe wonder what kind of audience would be waiting inside to greet her. She could faintly hear the clamor of voices and cheering, but it was mostly drowned out by the thick wrought iron doors behind the guards.

It all came to life a moment later when the guards nodded and each pulled a handle that opened into the massive space: The Cave. It truly lived up to its name, and she followed closely behind Ferris as he stepped into the cavernous dwelling.

The smell hit her first. It wasn't the odor of bodies or the sting of alcohol that turned her stomach; it was the copper tang of *blood*. Her vision swayed a little. She hadn't expected it. She was a fool not to, but she had hoped she could get away with quick wit alone and not have to draw blood.

Ferris put a hand on her back, guiding her further in, when she slowed to take in her surroundings. He leaned in close to her ear.

"You only have to strike enough to put on a show. It is not a fight to the death, Faythe."

His reassurance eased her nerves a little. She would not be able to go through with it if she had to kill someone.

He led her over to a balcony—not too high—that overlooked a huge stone ground pit. A fight was well underway, and she caught sight of two bloodied men engaged in savage combat. There were ghastly stains on the pit floor and walls, and Faythe almost turned on her heel and stormed right back out at the gruesome display.

Revelers cheered and relished in the gore, some leaning casually over the rails and watching in silence with predatory grins. Others stood looking nonchalant as they observed the fight, casually drinking from finer-looking pitchers than could be found in the inn above. The crowd was mostly men, all finely dressed like Ferris. Faythe recognized no one and figured they were the minority humans who actually possessed some wealth and didn't venture into the same parts of town she did.

There were some women too, dressed in scandalous gowns that left little to the imagination. But they were beautiful. Some clung to the arms of their male companions like proud trophies, while others stood more independent but still clearly with company as they smoked from long ornate pipes. They seemed to enjoy the show as much as their male counterparts from their sly smiles and seductive eyes.

The contrast of finery and savagery made The Cave an interesting hot spot for the elite.

Faythe again fixed her eyes on the fight below. The sight did nothing to ease her nerves, but at least she could take in what she could of the arena and figure out what angles she could use to her advantage.

The men fighting held daggers in each hand. The smaller of the two looked close to conceding—or passing out—as he sluggishly stepped around the ring. Ferris had said nothing of rules or weapons, and so far, she assumed there were none; anything was fair game.

The beast of a man leading the fight showed no mercy to the other as he attacked again and again. Faythe could only watch the ruthless beating in horror, her heart increasing in tempo at the thought of facing off with such an unhinged opponent. *Gods*, if Jakon could see this place—see *her* in this place and what she was about to do...

She shook her head. She couldn't think about that just now. She had to stay focused.

"Come," Ferris said into her ear above the clamor. Keeping his hand firmly on her back, he led them around to the opposite side of the balcony just as she heard the crowd roar and assumed the weaker man had finally fallen.

There was a downward staircase through an open gap in the stone. Faythe knew it could only lead to one place.

Ferris stepped behind her, and she felt his arms over her shoulders before he reached to unclasp her cloak. It fell away, and he came to stand in front of her with it draped over his arm.

She suddenly felt very bare and very vulnerable. A wave of panic washed over her.

Oh Gods, *oh Gods*, what had she been thinking? This was no

place for a novice human woman to practice her swordplay tricks. This was a place of merciless brutality, and she was going to get herself hurt—or worse.

Strong hands gripped her shoulders hard enough that the pain broke her frenzied thoughts. The crowd had settled again as if waiting for the next dose of carnage. A sharp shake snapped Faythe's eyes up to meet hazel ones.

"Get yourself together, Faythe. You know you can do this. Your size is your biggest asset—they won't see it, but I do. You're fast, you're observant, you're smart. They won't expect it," Ferris spoke directly, a coach gearing up his prized fighter at the edge of the ring.

"Next fighters!" a voice bellowed.

It shook Faythe awake. She took a deep breath, and the pair exchanged a nod of understanding. It was a final good luck from him.

Faythe turned for the entrance down to the pit and began to calm her turbulent mind into a smooth river of focused calm. The loud pounding of her fear faded to a quiet hum, leaving only enough to awaken her senses, not shut them down. With every step, she counted her breaths, slowing them to steady the tempo of her heart. She dove deeper and deeper into the well of lethal tranquility that forced her to hone in on every teaching, every practice, every trick that made her a force to be reckoned with in the face of threat or challenge.

She would not be weak.

She would not cower.

She would not lose.

Her foot hit the stone floor of the fighting ring, and she emerged a different person than who she was on the balcony. The crowd had gone utterly silent. Faythe stood tall, unflinching, and cast her bright gold eyes up—the only part of her identity on display—to scan the onlookers. Everyone watched her, even those who had been chatting idly with mild interest before.

Death incarnate, Ferris had described her. And it was exactly what she would become in this arena; how she would win.

The pit master, a tall, skinny man, stood in the center of the ring. His eyes grazed over her, and at the promise of pain in her eyes, his throat bobbed.

"And the opponent!" he hollered.

She looked over at the other entrance to her left. After a short pause, a dark-skinned, dark-haired man stepped out. The crowd broke into murmurs and gasps as they took in the sight of the tall brute—pitted against *her*.

He stood over a foot taller than Faythe, and he was built like stone. He wore a beaten-up brown leather tunic, completely sleeveless to show off his incredibly muscular arms and draw attention to the fact he wouldn't need much protection against any challenger. He was a fool, and it was a weakness Faythe had already noted.

If they wanted blood, she knew exactly how to give it to them.

Another weakness was his sandal-clad feet. Faythe felt insulted by his obvious confidence he would to be able to wipe her out without much movement. A fool indeed. She had every intention of making him dance.

His eyes scanned her, and his look was nothing short of feral. "Is this all you can give me?" he called loudly, throwing his arm out as though she were a mere cockroach for him to crush. He wanted to rouse the crowd and assert his status as the victor before the match had even begun. Faythe knew the tactic and let him belittle her as she kept still and silent.

Ferris was right. No one would bet on her given these odds, and it would work right to their advantage.

Beneath her mask, she smiled deviously but didn't let it reach her eyes.

Her opponent got the response he wanted as the crowd roared their laughter. Some even booed at the weak competitor who wouldn't offer up much of a spectacle before she was wiped out.

"Last bets!" the pit master yelled before motioning for them to take stance.

Chatter rose on the balcony, and she looked up again to see people flashing their coin in a wild frenzy, likely not in her favor. She couldn't blame them. To anyone, this looked like a shoo-in for the wild beast against the tame doe.

Then she spotted Ferris leaning on his forearms over the rails as he stared at her. He was grinning, but she could also see his look of concern. She gave him a subtle nod to assure him she was not about to fall apart upon seeing her opponent. She even surprised herself as she felt the complete opposite.

"Weapons?" the pit master said.

The brute scoffed as if he didn't think he would need any but drew a simple steel sword from his side in one hand and took a dagger from his belt in the other.

Slowly, deliberately, Faythe drew Lumarias from its scabbard on her back, not taking her eyes off his for a second. They were wild as he stared at her, a hunter primed to strike his feeble pray.

"Good luck to both. You may begin." The pit master made himself scarce quickly at his final announcement.

They circled closely, and Faythe watched his every flicker of movement. Just as she predicted, he launched forward in a lazy attack meant for a quick knockout with brute force. She ducked and stepped right, missing the blow with ease.

He grunted and immediately swung with his blade this time. She stepped out of his path in a steady motion. His nostrils flared at her taunting maneuvers.

Faythe was yet to lift her sword, instead getting a feel for his steps and going on the defensive until she tired him out. Not out of breath, but patience.

It wouldn't take long. She could already see his temper rising.

He swung his sword again, faster, going in with his dagger straight after in an attempt to catch her unaware. But she knew that trick. Jakon had been the first to show her how to block and maneuver around the attack of two simultaneous blades, and Nik had built on that knowledge significantly.

She ducked and dodged around his onslaught of quick jabs and long swipes, enjoying the look of absolute rage and disbelief on his face that he had yet to strike her.

The crowd had long disappeared to Faythe as she honed in on her moving target with cool calm. Deciding she'd grown tired of the foreplay, with his next lunge forward, she twisted around him, concurrently bringing her sword up and slicing down toward his exposed left arm. She felt the slick tear of flesh under her blade and repositioned herself once behind him, noting the deep cut that began to bleed from his shoulder to his elbow.

Once, she would have balked at the sight; at the fact she'd caused the wound. But this was a fight, and it was either he or she who had to wear the scars when it was over.

She vaguely heard the gasps and murmurs above but didn't dare look up or lose focus as he whipped around with a loud, animalistic sound that would send any sane person running. She stood her ground as she faced off with the bull. He saw red as he dragged his feet across the stone, poised to charge.

And he did—fast. Faythe barely had time to register the movement as she instinctively ducked low, pivoting. He practically flew over her, and she swiped her sword to catch his upper thigh as they switched sides again.

He roared once more and didn't leave a second before he was upon her. Their steel connected over and over in a battle of feral rage against cunning defiance. Faythe had to recall all her teachings with Nik to deflect with her sword while being aware of his dagger and veering from that too. But with all her tricks and training, she would soon falter against his brute strength if she continued this way for much longer.

She feinted right, and where he went to strike, she raised her sword skyward, bringing the pommel down to connect with the wrist that held his dagger. It went flying from his hand, and in the same breath, she leaned back and put all her might into a kick that sent him stumbling back. In his shock, he didn't recover fast enough before she brought her sword up and sliced low across both of his thighs.

Crying out, the giant fell to his knees.

In a flash, Faythe was standing over him, the point of her sword resting over his heart. She panted heavily as she looked down at her opponent. His face contorted in rage, and she could *feel* it coming off him in waves mixed strongly with embarrassment and disbelief.

"You'll pay for this, bitch."

The thought was so loud she couldn't have blocked it if she tried.

Despite the heat and the sweat that had formed a layer under her suit, Faythe went utterly cold at the promise in those words. Her senses opened up as if she had just remembered they were in an arena and there was a crowd cheering and shouting.

"The victor!" she heard the pit master announce as he emerged into the fighting ring once again.

She backed up a step, lowering her sword. Her eyes flicked to the skinny man beside her who stared back with wide-eyed disbelief. Some people cheered for her, but many, she noticed, were livid at her victory; at their loss of coin for betting against her.

All of a sudden, Faythe realized the real danger was never in the fighting; it was in the repercussions of *winning*.

She looked to the fallen man still on his knees and the threat that lingered in those eyes. Had anyone lost enough coin tonight to also want a target placed on her back?

Twisting on her heel, she hastily retreated to the exit and hurled herself up the stairs where no one could see her. Once she emerged at the top, she didn't pause, marching for the exit. Onlookers parted, opening a clear path for her as she passed.

Lumarias was a dead weight in her hand, the edges of the

blade still slick with its first taste of blood in real combat. She hadn't drawn too much from her opponent and doubted it was enough to satisfy the more bloodthirsty members of the audience like the previous fight. But she had done what she needed to do.

And she had won.

CHAPTER 26

F AYTHE SAT ON a discarded wet crate in Crow's Lane under the
safe cover of darkness. She had removed the scarf, pulled
back her hood, and unzipped her suit from under her neck. She
almost moaned at the cold lick of air that swirled around her head
and over her chest, feeling her breath start to come easier. She
discarded Lumarias on the ground next to her, needing to find
something to clean off her opponent's blood before she returned it
to its scabbard.

She leaned over, putting her head in her hands while her mind
replayed the events of the night.

"You'll pay for this, bitch."

Such promise and malice in his thoughts—in his *feelings*—it
made her uneasy he might try to fulfil his wish one day. She might
not be so lucky next time.

Faythe had humiliated him. A giant brute taken down by a
woman. His mind had told her he was not going to let it pass
without punishment and retribution. This was a man of little
forgiveness and much vengeance.

Hearing a scuff of boots to her left, Faythe rose to her feet,
swiping up Lumarias and extending it toward her intruder in a

single breath. Still skittish and hostile in the aftermath of her first real combat, when her eyes adjusted, she beheld Ferris holding his hands up in surrender with a wide grin.

She lowered her sword with a disgruntled sigh of relief, and he came closer. Then she felt a surge of anger and pushed his chest with both hands. He stumbled back a step in surprise.

"You bastard!" she hissed, careful to keep her voice low. "You've put us all in danger! A man like that isn't going to bow down and accept a humble defeat, Ferris!"

"Whoa, relax! Faythe, you're forgetting no one knows what you look like. You're as good as a shadow to those people!" he defended.

She retreated in realization and relaxed slightly, but she maintained her edge as the echoes of her opponent's feelings haunted her. Her ability was a blessing and a curse—though she was finding it far less positive.

"You're safe. Don't worry too much about it, okay?" Ferris said calmly.

She nodded warily and took a seat again, still not trusting herself to stay upright.

"Here." He held a small package out to her: a coin pouch.

Faythe took it in her palm, and her eyes widened. It was heavy. Drawing the strings, she emptied some of the coins onto her hand, and her face blanched at the silver. These were no mere coppers. She could already tell this was more than what she'd make at Marie's stall in a whole month.

"That's for your participation and victory. And this..." He reached into his tunic and pulled out another brown leather pouch, which she took from his outstretched hand.

More silver coins—and a couple of gold, she realized in absolute shock.

"This is your share of the betting profits. After I took back what was owed for the outfit and claimed my cut from what was left, of course."

She gaped at the money. There was so much coin she didn't know what to say. They had already made enough for her debt to Ferris to be paid off in full. This was all completely hers.

"Are you sure this is right?"

He chuckled. "You did a lot better than I thought. People were betting like crazy for the other guy to make a sure handsome return on their coin."

Her face fell, and her stomach turned. "Won't a lot of them be pissed and want to get back at me?" She winced.

"Like I said, no one knows who you are. Besides, this business is a sport to them. Sometimes you win, sometimes you lose. They'll get over it, and it won't stop them from betting in future, trust me."

Ferris was not one to coddle or sugarcoat situations—another trait she admired when the circumstances called for it. Like now. She eased a little as he continued.

"Keep it up, and we'll be living the good life in no time." He stuffed his hands in his pockets.

Her face fell in dread. "You want me to fight again? I think we made more than enough tonight," she said quickly.

"And when it runs out? Do you want to go back to running pastries all day for a wage that can barely keep you fed?" He looked her over.

Faythe knew he was talking about her particularly lean stature. She didn't respond.

"One fight a week, and you can keep your day job to maintain appearances. Just tell that guard dog of yours you got a raise or a promotion."

It was tempting. Too tempting. She could do this once a week and make a better life for herself and Jakon. When she thought of what it could do for him, there was no question anymore. After all, it wasn't blood money. She hadn't killed anyone or done anything criminal to earn it. No—she'd put her own life at risk and won in complete fairness thanks to her skill with steel and her stealth.

With a deep breath, and without giving herself a chance to second-guess, she said, "All right. I'm in."

Ferris beamed darkly, and in his eyes, there it was: the understanding she had just signed away her soul. Whatever lay in the pits of the Netherworld would claim her soul instead of the blissful Afterlife.

CHAPTER 27

FAYTHE FIDDLED WITH a strange compass device she'd picked up from the workshop bench in the blacksmiths. Next to her, Marlowe was completely engrossed in the old book of words and phrases that was apparently older than the king. She was at least halfway through translating the strange note they'd found in her mother's watch.

It had been nearly three weeks since her first fight at The Cave, and she had fought and won two more fights since, with her fourth only a couple of days away. Faythe had never felt more alive and confident in herself. She finally had a way of putting her skills to use that would benefit her and her friends.

They had spent many evenings together in Harbor Hall, dining and drinking wine. Jakon had bought into her story that the bakery had picked up and Marie had entrusted her to run the stall alone on a higher wage. He was skeptical at first, so Faythe had to be careful with just how much she spent to avoid raising his suspicions about her unsavory weekly activities. She had also been shopping with Marlowe during the week and purchased a couple of new gowns, tunics, and pants. Again, not buying anything too expensive to keep her roommate from finding out about her new unorthodox source of income.

She had not heard from Nik since their last encounter in the woods, and while she didn't expect him to think of her enough to warrant even a short visit to her subconscious, she felt his absence more than she cared to admit. Had she messed up whatever friendship they'd formed because of her stupid overactive thoughts and emotions? Maybe he thought he had nothing more to teach her—and besides, she was not at risk anymore, so perhaps he no longer saw it appropriate.

Her mind had been too occupied by the fighting to think about him, but now the initial thrill and adrenaline of an approaching challenge was wearing off, she found herself *missing* the fae guard.

"Have you heard the rumors of the Gold-Eyed Shadow?" Marlowe's voice pulled her from her thoughts. "Apparently, she's like a deadly ghost and haunts the town."

Faythe scoffed. "Sounds like an arrogant fool who's in over her head." She flashed Marlowe a grin.

Her friend chuckled. "I thought so too." She was quiet for a moment before she added, "You need to be careful, Faythe. I've never seen a set of eyes quite like yours before. Unless you fight blind, it's the only thing you can't hide, and it's your most distinguishing feature. Luckily, Jakon doesn't tune in to petty gossip, or he would have put the pieces together by now. But I've heard mention of you here—clients inquiring about new weapons to challenge you with—so you should know."

Faythe cursed herself. She hadn't thought about her eyes possibly attracting attention and had tried not to stare at anyone for so long they would take notice. But with Marlowe's warning, it seemed she hadn't done a very good job of that.

"Don't worry about me. As Faythe, no one is exactly looking in my direction for anything anyway. No fool in this town would be able to make the connection." She gave her a reassuring smile—the best she could muster while also trying to convince herself she wasn't in danger of being discovered. Changing the subject, she asked, "Is everything in place for tonight?"

All concern wiped from Marlowe's face in an instant at the mention of Jakon's birthday. "Of course! He's going to be so surprised. I can't wait to see his face." She beamed.

They had planned a surprise party at Harbor Hall and invited everyone they were acquainted with in town, some friends closer than others. Faythe was to meet Jakon at home and take him down there for a meal, just the two of them. Little did he know, Marlowe would already be there with everyone ready to surprise him.

The profit from each fight was still substantial despite Faythe's reigning title of victor. With her winnings, she had been able to afford the whole space for the night as well as hire the hall to cater a spread of food, treats, and wine. Jakon would never suspect anything like it. They usually celebrated each other's birthdays by going out for a modestly priced meal and exchanging a small gift if they could afford one. She already planned to say Marlowe had helped with the costs when he undoubtedly asked.

He had left early this morning, and Faythe was yet to give him his gifts. She had splashed out on a selection of new jackets, shirts, and pants as well as a pair of new boots. He was in desperate need of it all. Marlowe had finished crafting the sword for him from scratch, and it was impeccable just like her own. She had an eye for detail that stood out as her maker's mark. Jakon was about to be spoiled like he'd never been spoiled before by both women, and they had been giddy with excitement all week.

"Good. Well, I should probably go. I want to be home before Jakon gets back." Faythe pushed herself up from the bench.

Marlowe gave an excited squeal in response, and Faythe left her to finish up for the day.

When she arrived back at the hut, she decided to get herself ready while she had some spare time. Earlier that week, she and Marlowe had gone shopping for new gowns just for tonight. Her dress—a white crystal-embossed corset that overlapped long, lilac chiffon skirts—made her feel beautiful and showed off the woman's body she was slowly filling into from eating well these past weeks. Faythe had never thought she'd be able to wear such a fine dress and still marveled at her new wardrobe, embracing the femininity.

She went to work on her hair, pinning half of it back in various places until she had some form of braided knot at the back, leaving the rest in its loose natural waves. She applied a thin, flicked line of kohl to accentuate the brightness of her eyes and powdered her cheeks to give herself a natural rosiness. As she was finishing off, she heard the door swing open and dropped what she held to skip out and greet her friend.

Jakon paused across the room at the sight of her, but she ran and threw herself at him anyway. He caught her around the waist as she flung her arms around him, squeezing tightly.

"Happy birthday, Jak!" she squealed.

When he put her down, she stepped away and found him still staring wordlessly at her. Her cheeks flushed as he looked her over from head to toe.

"I thought I would put in the effort for your birthday," she said, shifting nervously.

"You look…" He trailed off. She knew it wasn't lust in his eyes as he observed her, wide-eyed; it was friendly admiration. "Incredible." He settled on the word and then regained his usual composure. "You didn't need to go to so much trouble. I'm going to have to spend my birthday fending off lustful men all night now," he teased.

She huffed. "I hardly think so."

"Trust me, all eyes will be on you tonight," he said playfully. "Let me just go change. Except now, I think I'm going to be severely underdressed in comparison." He scratched the back of his neck with a hint of embarrassment.

"Actually," Faythe drawled, "that's where your gift comes in." She didn't wait for him to say anything before she scurried off into the bedroom and returned beaming, carrying three different paper shopping bags.

He gaped at her, not immediately going to them when she placed them on the kitchen table and gestured for him to take a look. "Faythe, I... Where did you get the money for all this?"

She knew the inquisition would be coming and rolled her eyes. "I was saving long before I got the raise. Now, stop worrying and open them!" she lied, pushing him over to the table so he wouldn't question her further.

Jakon pulled out each garment one by one, stopping to gawk at her after every piece. She watched like a kid on Yulemas morning, grinning at every new item as if it were the first time she was seeing them too. Marlowe had played a part in some of the choices, and she had to admit, together, they had impeccable taste in men's attire.

"I want you to wear the royal blue jacket tonight. The rest, you can pick," she said, specifically choosing that one because she knew it was the same color as Marlowe's dress for the party.

He looked at a loss for words as he finished fishing through all the articles, but he finally said, "This is too much... Far too much. We can return some of it if—"

"You're really killing my buzz, Jak, and I'm starting to get offended," she cut in with a look. He seemed like he wanted to protest more, but Faythe held her gaze firm, letting him know she would kick his ass if he did.

Instead, he smiled, and with a long sigh, he said, "Thank you, Faythe. It's way more than I could have ever asked for, so thank you."

She embraced him again with a squeal of delight. "Now, go change. I made a reservation for the best seats, and we'll be late!" She gathered up the clothing and pushed him into the room before moving to wait in the kitchen, reeling with excitement. She couldn't keep still and paced around humming a tune to herself to distract her from checking her pocket watch as she'd done twice already since he retreated to the bedroom.

When he finally emerged, she had to clasp her hands and bring them up to her face to hold in her cry of happiness. He could have been a painting; she almost didn't recognize him in his finery. He wore black leather pants that had silver studs down the sides to match with the studs on his deep blue jacket. His white shirt underneath was crisp and much better fitted than his old ones. Finished off with his new black leather knee-high boots, he looked the part.

"Now who's going to have to fend off lascivious females...*and* males, perhaps?" she gushed.

He nervously pulled at the jacket with an apprehensive smile. "It's not too much?"

Faythe shook her head quickly. "Not at all." She held an arm out to him and sang, "Shall we?"

Jakon gave a soft laugh and linked his arm through hers. His eyes trailed over her again, and he smirked. "Look at us—you'd have thought we just robbed the wealthy part of town."

She chuckled, her lips pulling up in a deviant grin. He wasn't too far from the truth.

Faythe practically skipped down the streets, unable to keep herself still from the thrill of nerves. If Jakon noticed, he didn't comment on it as they idly chatted about his day and what she had been up to earlier. She edited the details of her particular activities.

Harbor Hall came into view, and it took every ounce of Faythe's control not to jump from her burst of excitement. No one was sitting at any of the tables she could see through the windows, and she prayed Jakon wouldn't question the unusual quietness before they could get inside.

She let him go in first. He gripped the handle and pushed the door...

"SURPRISE!"

Jakon nearly knocked her over as he launched backward, going to grab her from any threat of danger. Faythe howled with laughter —so much so, her eyes started to well with tears, and she doubled over, clutching her stomach. He gaped between her and the crowd of their friends inside in utter shock and horror.

Marlowe came bounding to the door and grabbed his hand to drag him in as he stood there frozen. Faythe followed inside just as some lute players started their ensemble, and everyone flooded over to wish Jakon a happy birthday.

Every ounce of stress and lost nerve had been completely worth it for that moment alone. In fact, Faythe decided she could die right now and be happy that was the last thing she saw.

Inside, the party fell into full swing. They had moved the tables away from the center of the hall, allowing space for people to dance and chat together. Candles burned low, and Faythe admired her own handiwork as the glittering decorations made the room sparkle beautifully against the amber flames.

The food was delicious. Faythe was already on her second glass of wine—perfectly normal *human* wine, thankfully—while picking at some finger sandwiches and watching the revelers sway in time with the lute players.

"You look magnificent tonight, darling Faythe." Ferris's voice carried over the music as he came up beside her with a glass in one hand.

She mumbled her thanks, taking in his own fine attire as they both watched the party.

"I see you're not letting a single coin of your hard work go to waste." He gestured around and gave her another look over.

She smirked. "I'd barely call it hard work."

"How *do* you make it look so easy in there?" His eyes danced.

She shrugged. "Give me some real competition, will you? It's starting to get boring." Smug, she took a casual sip from her cup.

"Profits are starting to decline. People expect the Gold-Eyed

Shadow to win nowadays," he remarked, using her newfound nickname.

She hummed. "I'm not throwing a fight if that's what you're suggesting."

"Never, Faythe. I wouldn't diminish your talents like that." He paused and then said, "But we should find you someone more…challenging."

She lifted an eyebrow. "And you have someone in mind?"

He hesitated as if even *he* thought it was a dangerous idea. That spoke volumes, yet she still couldn't have braced herself for what came out of his mouth.

"How do you think you'd fare against a fae?"

She choked into her wineglass and met his insane proposition with wide eyes. "Do you want to get me killed?" she hissed, the music hiding her tone.

"All you'd have to do is outsmart him. Go on the defensive until you can get into a killing position," Ferris said nonchalantly.

She glared at him, trying to hold back her expression of outrage so people wouldn't question their encounter at the edge of the party. "If that's all, then you can bloody well try it yourself," she snapped.

He chuckled in amusement. "It was just a suggestion—and one that could rake in a much higher sum than even your first night."

She contemplated—actually gave the senseless, absolutely ridiculous idea some thought. There was no chance of her besting a fae. Their speed alone was simply not a match for any mortal—not even close. She had dabbled in swordplay with Nik, and he had never even been *trying.* It would be near impossible to dodge their attacks. Unless…

Faythe straightened, sucking in a subtle breath.

Unless someone possessed the ability to foresee their movements beforehand.

Her heart's tempo increased as she thought it over. She had done it once—had caught Nik's leg before he could fully move out of the way because she'd *seen* him plan his next move. It would be a risk. A *huge* risk. And it would be her life on the line if she took it. There was a high chance her death at the hands of a fae would go unpunished, accidental or otherwise. Especially as she'd be foolishly and *willingly* putting herself in the line of peril.

She shuddered. This was a very, very dangerous game she was playing.

"I'm in," she blurted.

His eyebrows raised at her agreement.

"But not yet. I'll need a couple of weeks…for experience and practice. I'll need to be fully prepared," she said with all the bravado she could muster.

She *would* need to practice—just not in the way Ferris assumed. She had only foreseen movement once, by accident, and since that time with Nik, she hadn't really tried to tap into her conscious abilities and see what else she was capable of.

He stared at her for a moment, an eyebrow still cocked in surprise, giving her one last chance to take it back. When she held firm, he gave her a single nod in answer; a phantom handshake for the deadly deal she'd signed.

The song slowed, and Faythe stood drinking while she watched couples join and sway to the romantic melody. Her eyes drifted to her friends, and her heart melted at the sight. Their outfits matched perfectly, and together, they brought the starry night sky to the dance floor, dark blues and silver accents creating beautiful floating constellations where they swayed. They were laughing, eyes bright, as Marlowe's hands draped behind Jakon's neck and he held her tightly by her waist.

She knew she should look away from their moment of intimacy, but she couldn't help the sting in her heart at the way they looked at each other. A set of emerald eyes flashed in her mind, and Faythe hated herself for exactly *who* she pined after in that moment.

"Dance with me?" Ferris's voice broke through her thoughts.

She turned to find his hand held out to her. Grateful for the distraction, she took it and let him lead her into a space where they could join and dance together.

After a quiet moment, he said, "You are some woman to behold, Faythe. Both on and off the fighting field." His eyes darkened.

A playful smile tugged at her lips. "It's a shame I don't mix business with pleasure."

He chuckled softly. "A shame indeed."

CHAPTER 28

T HE PARTY CAME to an end at one in the morning, and they all left together while the hall staff cleared up as part of Faythe's generous rental sum. Marlowe had booked a room for her and Jakon at the East Town Inn so they could have a night alone for once, not wanting to stay with her father in the cottage behind their compound. They dropped Faythe off at the hut and said goodbye with no small amount of teasing on Faythe's part about what they would get up to. Her friends flushed in embarrassment, to her great amusement.

She didn't change into her nightclothes, instead pulling on a pair of leather pants and a loose white shirt and sliding into her boots. Maybe she was being foolish, but she hadn't been able to get a certain arrogant, annoying, irritatingly handsome fae guard out of her head all night, and she was tired of waiting to see if he would seek her out—in her head or otherwise.

As she slipped into bed fully clothed, she closed her eyes and waited to fall into darkness. Then she awoke, standing in the gold-and-white mist of her mind.

Her hands became slick with sweat, and her heart raced with nerves. The last time she was in the black-and-gray clouds of Nik's subconscious, she'd had no clue about anything she was—or what *he* was. So much had changed since. That day seemed like another lifetime ago.

Nik could very well push her out with half a thought or not let her enter at all. He would be aware the moment she tried to project herself into his mind, just as she was whenever he visited hers. Without giving herself time to cower, she closed her eyes and thought of him. When she felt the pull and didn't immediately hit a mental wall, she knew she had made it through. It didn't stop her from slowly peeling one eye open first to check, though, a part of her hoping to still see gold. But it was the starkly contrasting whorls of black and gray she was met with when she opened her eyes fully, and she wasn't sure if she felt relief or fear at being back.

After a short moment, Nik came into view. She almost stumbled, gaping at the sight of him bare-chested, hands casually slid into his sleep pants. His usual loose-fitting white shirts had hinted at his toned upper body, but *this…*

Seeing him bare made Faythe's cheeks catch fire. She was at a loss for words and screamed internally to channel herself out of his mind. She'd clearly interrupted his deep rest.

"I…I can go if you, uh—sorry," she stumbled like an idiot.

"I was planning on a full night's rest, but I couldn't deny you, Faythe." A wicked smile twitched the corners of his lips at her obvious embarrassment. "Why are you here?"

At least he was back to his insufferable cocky ways. Their last awkward encounter hadn't tainted the air between them.

"You haven't been around in a while…" She trailed off, having no idea where her train of thought was going.

"I didn't realize I was needed."

"You're not," she snapped instinctively. Then she recovered. "I mean, it would have been nice for you to check in or something," she said lamely.

"Why?"

Faythe gawked a little. "Sorry. I guess I made the mistake of thinking we might be friends." She turned to leave as if there were an imaginary door when the mist shifted to wrap around her middle and hold her still. Even her mind felt a weight upon it as she was held from projecting anywhere.

Nik had once told her it was possible to become trapped in another Nightwalker's mind. It was why they didn't often risk it. Now, she was stuck here against her will.

"You could just as easily have visited me anytime as well, you know?" he said softly.

She turned to him. All the anger she was about to unleash faded at the remark. He was right. She had been just as absent as he, and she hadn't even realized, stupidly waiting on him to make the first contact, thinking he wouldn't want to see her again after their intimate moment in the woods. It had been nothing.

"You're right. I'm sorry. I've been…distracted," she said with a weak smile. She wouldn't tell him about The Cave, not wanting a lecture on the dangers and her recklessness like Jakon would give her. "Can you meet me in the woods?" she asked.

Nik curved an eyebrow. "Tonight? It's almost two in the morning."

"Please?"

He released a long, dramatic sigh. "Fine. Twenty minutes," he said begrudgingly. She felt the mist release her, and then the pressure lifted off her mind too. He gave a smug smile. "You're free to go."

She childishly stuck her tongue out at him and heard the echoes of his chuckle before she was back in her own mind. Rising to consciousness, she immediately shot out of her cot.

Faythe arrived first, emerging into the waterfall clearing and taking a big gulp of pure, fresh air. She sat near the water's edge, idly picking at the grass and letting the calming sound of running water hypnotize her.

After another few minutes, rustling came from the tree line, and a familiar head of polished black hair and piercing green eyes came into view. She beamed at the sight of Nik. It struck her just how much she had missed his company these past couple of weeks. It felt different, clearer, seeing him in person compared to in their minds.

"So what is it you have to tell me that couldn't wait?" he said by way of greeting. He dropped down next to her, casually leaning back on his hands as he observed her with his usual arrogant smile she'd come to love and hate.

"I was actually hoping you'd help me with…my conscious abilities," she said warily. He looked at her in curiosity, waiting for her to elaborate. "I want to learn how to control them better—in combat specifically."

The air was silent as she waited for him to quiz her further. She had no doubt he would force her to reveal her completely futile plan to challenge a fae in a fighting pit.

"I suppose I could volunteer to be your test subject," he said casually. She grinned in response. "But if I release my mental barriers to you, I trust you won't go poking around where you shouldn't," he added in playful warning.

Faythe frowned. "How does that work? Your barriers. I was able to slip right into Jakon's mind and Marlowe's. There were no walls." She cringed as she admitted to what she'd done.

"Did you now…? And how was it? Being in their minds, I mean."

"You didn't answer my question."

He chuckled. "I'm curious too, you know? You're something that's either never existed before or hasn't for a very, very long time." When she didn't respond, he rolled his eyes. "They have them—they just don't know how to use them. And not because they're mortal. I'm a Nightwalker and a powerful one," he said, not out of arrogance. "Mastering the mind is part of who I am, and I've centuries of practice. I don't think you'd get past my barriers even if you tried. Most of us are the same. With weaker immortals, you might stand a chance. But those without our gift, fae and human, don't naturally have the instinct to protect their minds and wouldn't know how to even if they did. Some have trained specifically against our ability and are able to form solid mental barriers, but it's not common."

She hummed her interest. "Have you ever come across someone with a barrier?"

Nik nodded. "Many times, but none I haven't been able to shatter through."

Faythe shuddered. Was he really that strong in his ability? At her unspoken question, he went on.

"I guess some may have held out against a lesser Nightwalker." Again, there was no haughtiness in his tone as he explained the facts. "It's risky though. If the host discovers you're in there, it's as good as killing them. Their fragile mind can't handle the confusion of having two essences consciously present at once; they don't tend to recover mentally. It's also dangerous for us. A lesser Nightwalker might never recover. It takes a lot of strength to keep the separation and get out before both minds mingle."

Faythe swallowed hard at the new information, knowing now why he was so worried about her being discovered. Not just for her physical well-being, but the mental danger it presented.

"When I was in your mind, you said you could feel me," she said, more as a question.

"The other side of your ability is different in that respect. When we Nightwalk, our whole mental being gets projected into another's. With your gift of consciousness, you're still completely awake and in your own head at the same time. It's fascinating," he said in awe.

Faythe felt more bewildered than fascinated by the concept.

"But I would be cautious," Nik continued. "While I believe you could dive as deep as you wanted into a person's mind without causing them harm, every ability has its limits. With you, I'd be wary of having your feelings and emotions become too entwined in another's that you lose yourself in there in the heat of the moment. You need to always be able to separate yourself from the host."

A silence settled while she pondered over the new information. Then she spoke.

"I only heard what I wanted to know…when I looked into their minds," she began quietly, finding the grass suddenly very interesting. "I haven't tried going any deeper—only what's been on the surface. Thoughts that were just…there. It was easy to hear them."

Nik made a curious sound.

Since she was getting all her truth out, Faythe added, "I Nightwalked through Marlowe too."

Sitting up straight, Nik's arm grazed hers as he scanned her face, possibly looking for any sign of guilt or anger. "On purpose?" he asked carefully.

She winced and nodded.

"Good," he said, leaning back again. When she whipped her head to him, he shrugged. "You needed to practice. I assume it went to plan, or you'd be taking out a tree by now."

She chuckled softly, grateful he didn't hold any judgment or disapproval in his response. It was a relief being with him, she realized. She didn't have to hide anything about herself, and he never looked at her with any kind of distaste or hatefulness. He didn't fear her for what she might be capable of.

"Now, are we going to get some progress made here so we can both get back to sleep tonight?" he asked, getting to his feet.

Neither of them had brought their swords, but Faythe didn't need a blade to practice reaching into his mind and predicting his movements. She stood too, going over to where he waited. Nik braced himself as if he were going to pounce. And he did. She couldn't stop her squeal of surprise as he lunged impossibly fast, ducking and lifting her over his shoulder.

Not even winded from the sudden movement, she was astonished by his delicate hold. "Put me down!" she shrieked.

He rumbled with laughter beneath her, but just as fast as he'd scooped her up, she was once again on her own two feet, dizzy from bewilderment.

"Sorry. I thought we were starting."

She gaped and then dropped her face into a scowl. Changing stance, Faythe braced herself this time. She took a breath and locked eyes with him.

"Are you ready?"

She heard the question at the edge of his mind. The corners of her mouth twitched up in response—and in taunting challenge.

"Don't hold back," she said.

He answered with a wicked grin.

She saw his first intention to go for her legs again a split second before he physically moved, and she jumped right to narrowly dart out of his path. Turning around, he straightened, giving her an approving side smile. Nik didn't waste a second, the thought of his next attack flashing from his mind to hers, and she twisted around him in the nick of time.

Her heart raced from the concentration she had to hold to keep track of him and his speed. She saw his following maneuver, but she was a second too late in avoiding it before he swiped her feet from under her with a side kick. He caught her with an arm around her waist before she could hit the ground, their faces coming intimately close as he straightened, and in a flash, the feelings from their last near-kiss pulsed through her.

They were gone the moment he released her and stepped away. Faythe noticed his taunting grin had also vanished.

Clearing her throat, she said, "I need to be faster." She was already panting—not from physical exertion, but the mental toll it took.

He gave a short nod. "Try again."

They practiced for another hour, and she gained speed on her reaction time—slightly, as the thoughts flowed into her more naturally. Still, she couldn't keep it up for long before he had her beat.

She sprawled out on the grass, feeling both mentally and physically drained. Nik sat beside her, looking completely unfazed.

"Do you ever get tired?" she remarked in irritation.

"Of course I do." He smirked down at her. "Just not nearly as easily."

They sat in a long minute of silence, and when her breathing was once again normal, she lifted herself upright next to him. "We could work out a schedule," she said, "to meet here for practice. If you can, that is."

He shot her a side glance, thinking it over. "I suppose I could dedicate some of my nights to helping. I'm nothing if not charitable."

She pushed his arm playfully, but he barely budged, her palm feeling like it connected with a slightly cushioned stone.

Breaking through their peace, a loud, animalistic scoff sounded behind her. Faythe whipped her head around, then she shot to her feet at the sight.

The mighty white stag!

It took her a moment in her shock to ask, "You see it too, right?"

"The giant beast? Yes, Faythe, I think it's pretty damn hard to miss," he retorted.

She didn't respond to his sarcasm, relieved she wasn't hallucinating. "Do you know what it is?" she asked instead. Before he could state the obvious in that irritatingly derisive way of his, she added, "I mean, what it wants?"

It was uncanny how similar this encounter looked to the last. The stag once again threw its head sideways as if beckoning her to follow.

"I would say that's pretty obvious too. Wouldn't you?"

She bit back her retort but managed a glare in his direction. "Have you seen it before?"

He shook his head. "Never."

Since he wasn't offering any help or encouragement, she went to follow it of her own accord and didn't glance back to see if he joined her. Just like the time before, it led her through the uneven rows of trees and right to the same temple in the clearing, motioning her toward it before disappearing through the stone doors. She knew Nik had followed and witnessed the whole encounter from his footsteps nearby, and she shook her head, trying to make sense of what she'd just seen for the second time. Not a movement was different on the stag's part.

"It was exactly like before," she mumbled, confusion creasing her forehead.

"You mean, you've seen it before?" he asked with piqued curiosity, coming to stand beside her.

A vacant nod was her only answer as she trailed up the stairs of the portico and pressed her palms to the doors. "What do you want?" she pondered out loud. Resting her ear against the solid, cold rock, she strained to hear if there was something—or *someone*—inside.

"You need the Riscillius, Faythe."

She pushed off the stone with a gasp. "Did you hear that?"

"Hear what?" Nik said from behind her.

Perhaps she was going crazy. That seemed like the only logical explanation. She dared to press her ear to the door again and waited.

Nothing.

Huffing her frustration, she marched back down the stairs and turned to look at the structure. It offered no clue or insight as to why she should be here, and she wanted to bellow her annoyance at the still stone building for wasting her time.

It must be mere chance. The stag could have appeared to anyone. Maybe it was on some centuries-old magickal loop no one had bothered to stop; a message for someone long since passed. These woods were bound to be full of ancient tricks and mysteries.

Faythe shuddered, not wanting to stay longer and discover them—or they her, since that was how it seemed to work around here. Yet as she held her eyes on the symbol of Aurialis that branded the door, she swore it started to glow slightly as if beckoning her to discover what lay beyond. She wanted to turn from the structure and vow never to follow the damned stag again, but the reckless, impulsive side of her dominated her sane, rational brain.

One word became a chant in her mind that she couldn't silence: the *Riscillius*. It had to be the key to get inside. Fortunately, there was one book-loving blacksmith in the kingdom who might hold the answer of where to find it.

CHAPTER 29

T HE EARLY-MORNING air held a chill to it as Faythe made her way to the market for work. Autumnal equinox was only a week away, and eager revelers had already started decorating the buildings with banners of vibrant fall colors in anticipation of the full bloom of the new season. She pulled her dark green cloak tighter around her and glared up at the sun that mocked her by not offering any warmth. Still, she was a little relieved the days were no longer so clammy and dry.

Over the past week, she had met with Nik every second night to practice her mind skills for combat—which was a fancy way of saying "to get put on her ass every five minutes." She was getting better though. Slowly. She was all too aware the fight with her fae competitor was looming closer. Two weeks' time, Ferris had told her a few days ago. She'd had to force back her panic that it might not be enough time for her to be competent in her ability to foresee their impossibly fast movements and stand a chance. But she couldn't tell that to Ferris.

Rounding the last corner, she strolled up to the bakery stall and offered a cheerful greeting. Her smile fell when Marie looked at her sadly without responding.

"We've been thinking, Faythe. I know you've helped us for a long time now, but we just can't afford the cost to keep you any longer. Grace has agreed to help with deliveries, but we don't expect it to be as busy here with the cooling weather." Marie spoke quickly and nervously.

She was being let go. A month ago, Faythe would have perhaps embarrassed herself by falling to her knees and begging Marie to reconsider. The small, insufficient wage was all she had to make ends meet. But now...

She smiled warmly. "I understand, Marie. You're doing what's best for your family, and I wish you and your daughters well."

It obviously wasn't the reaction Marie expected. Her mouth popped open in surprise. She came around the small counter and took Faythe's hands.

"You'll be all right, dear?"

Faythe answered with a squeeze and a nod.

The baker embraced her tightly. "Could you run one last errand for me though?" she asked, shuffling back around the stall and producing a small box. "Mrs. Green hasn't made an order for a while, but would you take this to her? I would hate to think she might have had a bad lot the last time."

Mrs. Green!

Faythe frowned, taking the box. How had she not noticed when Mrs. Green was one of her most frequent and joyous delivery stops? She had been so wrapped up in her own problems, she hadn't even realized how long it was since she last saw her, and Faythe felt riddled with guilt at her selfishness.

Then a dark feeling settled over her. The last time she'd seen Mrs. Green...

Faythe nodded with a weak smile and offered Marie one last farewell before setting off. She quickened her pace, the urge to get there as fast as she could drowning her with overwhelming dread.

Her nerves were irrational, she tried to reassure herself, and she would be breathing in her relief the moment she walked into the mill and saw Mrs. Green sitting in her usual spot at the kitchen table doing something to occupy her hands. Still, she was almost jogging by the time she rounded the next corner and the large off-white building came into view.

She hurled herself through the door, not bothering to knock or call out.

When the familiar chirp of Mrs. Green's voice didn't greet her straight away, her stomach dropped further. Faythe walked into the kitchen and found it empty. She called out in the hope someone would echo back. Leaving the box on the table, she continued her search as a daunting feeling set her on edge.

Everything was too still and untouched.

Too *quiet*.

Hearing movement from outside, she loosened off slightly. One of the workers! They would know where she was.

Out the back door, she spotted an older man by the shed grinding some contraption she assumed was full of grain. She practically ran to him, blurting out, "Have you seen Mrs. Green?"

He jumped in surprise at her sudden outburst, and Faythe mumbled a quick apology.

"You haven't heard?" he said.

She blanched immediately. "Heard what?"

His face fell grave. "She was taken near two months ago now, to the castle. She never came back," he said solemnly.

Taken… Just as they had gotten Reuben out. Faythe had told Mrs. Green she would be safe.

Her hand shot up to cover her wide mouth, and she backed up a few steps as if the news were a physical blow. The pain was similar. Her chest tightened painfully, and the air around her refused to fill her lungs properly.

The man muttered something else, condolences she could faintly hear. "Some fae guards came in the middle of the night. One had a particularly nasty-looking face with a long scar," he recalled.

The man tilted. No—it was her own vision that wavered and threatened to make her collapse at the malicious face that flashed to the forefront of her mind. Captain Varis. He had been here, and he had seized Mrs. Green. Had she been brutally handled like the innkeeper's son?

Oh Gods, oh Gods!

Faythe's stomach twisted as nausea washed through her. It was her fault—she had told Mrs. Green she would be safe if she didn't know anything and had sworn to Reuben she would look out for his mother. She had to blink fast to stay present through the waves of dizziness while her thoughts became a whirlwind. She didn't know what to do, think, or how to react.

Twisting on her heel, she took off.

Her feet slapped loudly against the cobblestone as she sprinted down the streets, barely dodging the pedestrian traffic. Her cloak bellowed behind her, and she didn't stop for a second even when her lungs and throat caught fire, begging her to rest. She kept running through the grass and all the way up hills, across long fields, until she saw him.

Jakon glanced up from his work, then he did a double take when he spotted her hurling herself over the plowed fields toward him. Dropping his shovel, he briskly walked to meet her.

Faythe came to an abrupt halt in front of him but couldn't get her words out as the exertion of her long sprint caught up with her all at once. She panted hard and nearly doubled over to throw up, but Jakon grabbed her by the shoulders, his face chalk-white as he frantically looked her over.

"Faythe, what's wrong?" he asked in panic. "What's happened?"

She gathered enough breath, and her eyes burned as she said, "Mrs. Green... They took her."

Jakon released a rush of breath at the information, disturbed but apparently relieved the grave news wasn't about her or Marlowe. He embraced her as if she might collapse, and she very well might have if he didn't hold her as she released her grief into his shoulder.

He let Faythe cry and compile herself before pulling back to look at her. "Tell me what happened."

They retreated into a barn and sat on stacks of hay as Faythe relayed the vague information she knew.

"Shit," Jakon swore, pouncing to his feet. "What reason would they have for taking her?" He began to pace the floor.

Faythe shrugged weakly. "Maybe she knew more than she was letting on, or maybe they're more ruthless than we thought and are eliminating whole households that displease them."

Jakon ranted a colorful array of curses and insults to portray exactly what he thought of the fae, their guards, and the royals. Faythe was too hollow in her own grief—her own *guilt*—to have room for anger.

"It's my fault. I should have got them both to leave, but I...I told her she'd be safe."

Jakon sat next to her and put his hand under her chin, tilting her head so she could look him in the eye. His remained fierce as he said, "This is *not* your fault. Her death is not on your conscience, not even for a second."

Neither of them considered the possibility she could still be alive. The fae didn't take human prisoners. But it still stung Faythe's heart to hear the word that was so final.

Death.

"She must have known they would come and didn't want to risk ruining Reuben's escape. We can only hope she sacrificed herself with the intention of saving her son—that it wasn't in vain," he said, and Faythe picked up on his slight tone of uncertainty.

If they had failed—if Reuben hadn't made it to safety—her death *and* his would be in vain.

Faythe couldn't dwell on it further for fear she would fall apart completely. She left Jakon to finish his workday and headed back to the hut. She didn't plan to tell him she no longer had a job at

Marie's stall. She would keep up the pretense to justify her income. It was yet another lie, and she hated herself more every day for the master deceiver she was becoming.

At home, she sat in utter silence and let her mind reel. She barely registered Jakon coming home or the small idle chatter he tried to engage in over supper. When he was asleep, snoring next to her, she shot out of her cot and dressed swiftly before quietly leaving and storming all the way to the woods. She spotted the fae guard with his back to her through the tree line, but he didn't turn when she emerged.

"Did you know?" she said with icy calm. Her rage boiled beneath the surface, but she wouldn't release it—not until she heard it from him.

Nik twisted slowly around, his face unreadable. "You're going to have to elaborate a little, Faythe."

Her anger spiked and then simmered. "Mrs. Green—Reuben's mother. Did you know she was taken the night after we got him out?"

He was silent, deliberating, and her patience began to run dangerously thin.

"I did."

She expected it, but it didn't make the blow any less. "You kept it from me all this time?"

"I didn't think it was something you needed to know."

She had to close her eyes and breathe for a moment or else she would erupt. "He was my friend, and I swore I'd look out for her!" she seethed, opening her eyes again to blaze at him.

His face fell a little, the only display of regret he would show, but then he wiped all expression away and started at her blankly.

"Did you have any part in it?" She braced herself, not sure how she would handle the knowledge if he had.

Nik shook his head. "No, but Varis found out about Reuben the night before I did and had plans to bring him in. When they found he was missing, they took his mother instead. He doesn't like to be made a fool of, so he conjured a story about how he saw the same traitorous actions in her mind too," he explained plainly.

It made Faythe sick. She had never seen him so detached and unreadable. She wanted to believe him—he had no reason to lie— but he was fae and a king's guard; she would be a fool to think he was any different to his companions when they were all tethered by the same leash. Her anger flared to a reckless rage, and before she could stop herself, she honed in on him—his mind—intending to take the information for herself to be sure.

She was met with a stone-hard black wall, as anticipated, but she threw herself into it and focused all her mental strength on pulling it down.

"Stop," he growled, his voice low in warning.

She didn't and kept trying until sweat trickled down her forehead and a headache formed from the effort. The woods disappeared into a faint blur as she hurled everything she had into the block on his mind. Her mind was a wrecking ball, slamming into his over and over while she pictured the wall's destruction that would grant her free access to his thoughts; his *memories*. She could feel it weakening, but not nearly enough for her to get inside.

"Faythe, stop. Now!" he barked louder this time.

When she didn't back down at his second command, he was upon her in a flash. Her feet were out from under her, and she was airborne for a split second before her back met the cool grass.

She breathed heavily as the mental contact severed, and she took in her surroundings again. He was on top of her, one knee applying light pressure to her chest, while his hand held hers locked above her head. Her eyes flashed, and she thrashed to get free, but his hold only tightened, and her eyes burned in frustration.

Giving up, Faythe went limp beneath him, squeezing her eyes closed to calm herself. One look in his eyes right now, and she knew she would erupt again. He made her feel like nothing when he enforced his strength, and she hated him for it.

"Don't try that again," Nik said in quiet, lethal caution. Then the pressure released completely, and he walked away from her.

She lay there a moment longer, gathering herself so she wouldn't lose control again—then she pounced to her feet and whirled to face him. "I don't need your help anymore. I'll figure it out for myself," she hissed coldly. She didn't wait for his response, twisting on her heel and marching straight out of the woods.

He didn't follow, and she didn't look back.

CHAPTER 30

S ITTING AT A workshop bench surrounded by open books she had no interest in actually reading, Faythe sighed. When she awoke that morning after her blowup with Nik, she instantly felt guilty for her outburst. Sure, he deserved some of her anger—he had kept information from her when he knew what it meant—but he didn't deserve her attempt to infiltrate his thoughts.

In hindsight, she was glad she hadn't been able to break through his firm mental barriers. He had looked quietly furious at her for trying, and she didn't blame him. She sulked because she felt like she had lost a friend. Not just a friend to practice her mind skills with; Faythe felt the loss much more than that, fearing Nik would never forgive her.

She had come to the blacksmiths since she had nowhere else to go with all her spare days and would be bouncing off the walls if she stayed in the hut. She'd told Marlowe about her dismissal from the bakery, and her friend had been more than welcoming—had even offered to teach her a thing or two about her trade.

Marlowe sat at another bench, still poring over the foreign note Faythe had long since given up caring about. However, the blacksmith was fascinated and spent a lot of her time trying to decipher it.

"I think I have it!" she exclaimed, making Faythe jump a little as they had been sitting in silence for some time. "Well, there are some words that don't make full sense yet, but I have most of it." She twisted in her seat and beckoned Faythe over with an eager wave.

Faythe welcomed the distraction and obliged, going to stand close to where she sat.

"It's worded like a poem, with stanzas and rhyming couplets, but it doesn't make sense really." Marlowe held out the new piece of paper she had scribbled her translated version onto.

Faythe took it with a frown and read:

Spirits of the Realm, there were three;
A balance of life, soul, and death.
And all together they would agree
To balance the world until their last breath.

One to guide the light,
Her temple stands tall,
In a wood that begins in fright.
A fear is the key, or thou shalt fall.

One to tame the dark,
Her temple sinks low.
In a black labyrinth stark,
Blood is the key to chase away foe.

One to connect the souls,
Her temple rises high.
A winding path not without ghouls,
A bond is the key to touch the sky.

Each hold power of mighty great,
But together they form one.
The Riscillius is needed to open each gate,
To retrieve the pieces and undo what was done.

Faythe's eyes widened as she finished, and she set the paper down, pointing to one word that sent a spear of ice through her. "Do you know what this is?"

Marlowe squinted. "Riscillius? That's what puzzled me too." She got up and went over to the stack of books.

Faythe trembled with anxiety though she hid it with clenched fists. It had to be a coincidence that it sounded like the name she'd heard through the temple doors. Her thoughts were a mess as her mind started putting together pieces that would fit.

The poem was a riddle and had something to do with the Spirits. She knew the temple she had visited must be the "light" the poem referred to. The location was a match. The woods had demanded she reveal her darkest fear, and upon getting it had let her pass. Nik had pointed out the symbol on the door—the circle with three overlapping lines—was of Aurialis, the Spirt of Life and Goddess of the Sun.

She felt dizzy and had to take Marlowe's vacant seat. The killer question that sent her reeling: Why was there such an ancient artifact in her mother's pocket watch?

Had she known about it?

Faythe shook herself at the thought. No—she couldn't have known anything about it; would never have been in the woods either.

"There are mentions of it in this book of old relics and such," Marlowe said, scrutinizing a new tome. "A 'cillius' is like a stone or glass, and 'riscus' means something like 'to look' or 'see.'" She looked up at Faythe as if she might understand it more.

A shrug was all she could muster, trying to keep her face impassive so she didn't give away the fact she knew what any of it meant.

"It's just an old romantic poem on the Spirits," she said, keeping her tone disinterested. She couldn't tell Marlowe about the temple for risk of her finding out other things.

Until Faythe could make any sense of it herself, there was no point anyway; she still had no way of getting inside. Besides, whatever the Riscillius was, there was no guarantee it was even in High Farrow.

"I've read of the Great Spirit Temples. These must be their locations," Marlowe pressed, coming over to examine her translation again.

"Who knows if they even still stand?" Faythe drawled. She kept her voice bored despite the racing thoughts that shook her to the core.

"They say it's the one place someone can make real contact with the Spirits," Marlowe continued, relaying her knowledge regardless.

Faythe scoffed. "And you believe that?"

"You don't have to be so pessimistic all the time, you know?"

"I just like to be *realistic.*"

Marlowe rolled her eyes, and her brow creased slightly. "I wonder what it was doing in your watch."

Faythe stood from the bench. "Probably just some old, forgotten tale written by a long-passed ancestor."

Marlowe didn't look convinced, but she didn't say anything else about it. "Are you ready for your fight tonight?" she asked instead.

Grateful for the change of topic, she grinned smugly. "Always am."

Marlowe answered with a wan smile, and Faythe felt a pang of guilt. She knew her friend hated keeping her deadly secret from Jakon even more than she did. Regardless, she helped by keeping him busy every time Faythe had a fight, usually inviting him to stay at her cottage overnight.

She put a hand on her friend's shoulder. "I haven't lost yet," she said by way of consolation. "And thanks for keeping Jakon…

occupied." She added a hint of suggestiveness to lighten the mood.

Marlowe gaped, and her cheeks turned bright. Faythe chuckled mischievously, moving around her to leave.

"See you tonight!" she sang before strutting out of the blacksmiths.

CHAPTER 31

T HAT EVENING, MARLOWE skipped through the door of the hut without knocking—as Faythe and Jakon had insisted a while back—and beamed at Faythe as she grabbed a meat pie for herself and joined her in the kitchen, where they both dug in.

"Keep your appetites. It's the shows tonight—there'll be plenty of stalls," Jakon said as he emerged from the bedroom where he'd gone to change out of his work clothes.

Faythe cursed internally. She'd forgotten all about the annual shows that took place in the square. They were a small dose of entertainment before the autumnal equinox outdoor ball at the end of the week and a tradition Jakon and Faythe attended every year. She loved watching the performances, and he knew it. Except this year, she had unknowingly double-booked. She had a far more unsavory activity planned for the night.

Faythe shot her gaze to Marlowe in a plea for help, but her look suggested she had no idea how to get her out of going. "I—I totally forgot. I'm not feeling too great tonight. Maybe you guys should go without me?" she said pathetically, unable to come up with a more convincing excuse.

Marlowe nodded in understanding, trying to help her cause, but Jakon frowned deeply.

"That's never stopped you missing the shows before," he accused.

Faythe wracked her brain, but nothing came up. He wouldn't buy that she was simply too ill to attend, so she mustered a weak smile.

"You're right. I guess I could come for a bit."

Jakon relaxed, and Marlowe disguised her worry with a wide grin.

"I'll just go change," Faythe said to excuse herself.

In the bedroom, she cursed again as she stripped down. She had to think of something to excuse herself early, but for now...

She climbed into her fighting suit and pulled on her boots before choosing a dark crimson gown and sliding into it over her leathers. It made her a little bulky, but not enough that Jakon would notice, especially not if she wore her black cloak over the top.

The bedroom door opened with a creak, and she jumped, but she relaxed when Marlowe's head poked around the frame.

"What are you going to do?" she whispered.

"I'll have to leave early." Faythe lifted her gown to show what she wore underneath.

Marlowe grinned in appreciation.

"Can you convince him to leave with you now? I'll need a minute to stash the other things."

Marlowe answered with a nod. "Good luck," she mumbled before closing the door again.

Faythe heard them chatting in the kitchen when she went into the washroom to braid back her hair and hoped Jakon wouldn't think anything of her hairstyle choice. She usually only pulled all her hair back when she went to practice swordplay or on particularity hot days.

When the door clicked shut, signaling their leave, she slung her cloak on and gathered her other fighting items without a wasted second.

Faythe walked hastily through the streets with her hood up. It was unusually busy with the shows going on, and she found herself having to weave and squeeze through small crowds on her way to the square. She concealed her other fighting items under her cloak, but no one paid her any attention.

Taking a long route down a backstreet she knew would be quiet, she ducked into Crow's Lane after checking the coast was clear. There, she found an old discarded crate and lifted it, placing her items down before covering them over with the wood. She added a few more that were laying around on top for extra measure —not that she expected anyone to be wandering down here. Satisfied, she left the way she came and merged with the flow of traffic on Main Street headed for the event.

When she got to the square, it was packed. A stage had been set up on the far side. Kids sat as close as they could get while the adults stood behind, tightly compacted together. She had no idea how to find her friends in the masses and cursed herself for not anticipating it.

An idea came to mind. Faythe darted around the corner. She had never tried to climb the roof in a dress, but she was wearing her suit underneath. She hoisted the skirts to her waist, and with free leg movement, she scaled the usual way up. Faythe lay on her stomach and peered over, careful no one would notice her. This was their hideout spot, and she didn't want to give away their vantage point.

It didn't take her long to scan through the heads before she spotted the familiar blonde and brunette couple near the edge of the crowd with drinks in hand. Location pinpointed, she quickly shimmied back down to the ground to join them. Weaving and nudging her way to her friends, she greeted them cheerfully over the clamor.

"We weren't sure if you would find us. Jakon was about to head back for you," Marlowe said.

"I have my ways." Faythe flashed him a grin, and his eyes instinctively flicked behind them and upward as if he would spot her still spying on them from the rooftops.

"Why do I ever doubt you?" He shook his head, sipping from his cup.

Marlowe held a glass out to her. "It's wine," she said with a hint of caution, and Faythe knew it was to make sure she didn't drink too much of it ahead of her other planned activity.

She nodded gratefully and took the glass but didn't drink straight away.

The lights that canopied the square went out, and the crowd reacted with increased noise and piqued attention. Faythe checked her watch. She had time to enjoy at least one show.

The curtains drew back, and a lady dressed in a magnificent ball gown appeared behind them along with a large harpsichord. The crowd gushed, and even Faythe gawked as the woman took a small bow and sat in front of the beautiful instrument. Her fingers graced the strings with a melody that weaved through the bodies, striking Faythe right where she stood. The whole world disappeared around her until she was completely transfixed. Then the woman began to sing, and a pleasant thrill rocked her to her core. It was a tale of the Spirits—their beginning and their purpose—and though Faythe didn't think she believed in such things, she drank every word and marveled over the graceful, poetic depiction. The lady's fingers plucked and stroked with such eloquence, the melody rising to the stars and beyond in a quickened tempo. Her body moved with each note like a wave in a storm as she poured her heart and soul over the strings.

Then she slowed, and Faythe swore she looked right at her as she sang her final verse:

The heir of souls will rise again,
Their fate lies in her palms.
With rings of gold and will of mind,
She'll save the lives of men.

A sudden loud disruption in the crowd jerked Faythe from her hypnotic state. She looked to Marlowe, who was beaming and clapping along. When Faythe returned her attention to the performer, the woman was standing, taking her last bow, and did not look in their direction again as she left the stage.

But Faythe was left with a strange, unsettling feeling.

Shaking it off, she reached in to check her pocket watch and realized she would be late if she didn't leave now. When no one was looking, she emptied her glass of wine to appear as if she had drunk it before turning to her friends.

"I'm really not feeling good. I think the wine had the opposite effect tonight," she said, putting on a drained face.

Jakon's brow furrowed. "We can go back—"

"Aw, but I'd like to stay," Marlowe cut in for her. "I don't usually come to these things. Faythe will be okay—won't you?" She turned to her.

Faythe played her part. "Of course. You guys stay. There's no point in us all sulking at home tonight. Enjoy the rest of the shows," she pleaded.

Jakon's forehead only creased deeper. She could tell he wanted to protest, but at Marlowe's sad look, he let it go with a sigh. "All right. Well, I'll see you at home then," he said a little reluctantly.

She gave them both a quick embrace before weaving her way back out of the mob. She was quick at making it to Crow's Lane in her hurried pace and soon beheld Ferris leaning casually against the wall, waiting for her as usual.

"A little overdressed, don't you think?" he remarked.

She didn't deign to respond and started pulling the crates down, discarding them quickly to get to her hidden items. Not waiting to see if Ferris would turn around since she was already dressed anyway, she started to untie the back of her gown and let it drop. He didn't flinch, but she knew he was disappointed she wasn't actually standing in her undergarments in the middle of the street.

It didn't take her long to be fully equipped with her sword on her back and her hood and scarf concealing her face—fully embodying the Gold-Eyed Shadow she'd come to be known as. She hid her dress just as she had with the other items. Then, not wasting a second as they were already pushed for time, they made haste indoors, refusing to stop for anyone when they stalked past.

They arrived in The Cave just as the pit master was announcing the victor of the previous fight. At the top of the pit entrance, Ferris took Faythe's cloak from her—as was their routine now—and when they announced the next fighters, she descended and let herself fall into her lethal calm. By the time she emerged into the great fighting ring, she was ready. The audience seemed to grow larger each time she was here, but she never let it rattle her focus.

When her competitor emerged, she had to hide her surprise. He was of a lot smaller build than she was used to being pitted against, standing only a few inches taller than her. While it might have been a relief to anyone else, Faythe still saw the opponent as the toughest she was yet to face. Her size wouldn't be of much advantage in this match. She would be wise to assume he could be equally as quick on his feet. But she gauged she might also be an equal match in strength—or at least close to it. That was all she needed.

The pit master announced the beginning of their combat, and they stalked each other with a tracker's eye. As anticipated, he was fast. Faythe dodged a lot of his advances, but he was smart and started to predict her moves.

She tried to feign right while going for an attack to the left, but he saw it coming, and she felt his elbow connect with her side, knocking the wind from her. She stumbled back and didn't have time to regain her composure before he kicked her stomach. She went flying backward, hitting the ground hard.

Pain stabbed her abdomen, but she rolled just as he went to bring his blade down and shot to her feet. For the first time, she was closely matched in stealth.

Their blades connected in a series of high-pitched symphonies as they parried back and forth. When they met in the middle, her opponent pushed his blade against hers, sending her backward. In the same breath, steel flashed before her eyes, and Faythe twisted—but not fast enough. She felt a sharp sting across the top of her arm where the edge of his blade had sliced.

Retreating but not losing focus, she gaped. She was losing.

As a reigning champion, she'd let herself get complacent; arrogant. Her flame of passion had dwindled into dying embers. Besting brute men never challenged her. But now, coming to this realization awoke something within Faythe, and she found herself on the edge of his mind without even trying. Everything was right there for her viewing pleasure, but she couldn't dive too deep or she wouldn't be present enough to fight.

His movements flashed through her. She deflected far faster than she ever had before, gliding like smoke around his swipes of steel. It was as easy as breathing when she gave herself over to the instincts of her mind, and she moved with graceful swiftness to avoid his advances and deliver her own counterattack—all while being careful not to dodge so fast it wouldn't look realistic. Though no one could ever suspect the advantage that dwelled within.

She had already cut him a few times, only to rouse the crowd and satisfy the onlookers' bloodlust. She let her smile reach her eyes under her mask, taunting him as his frustrations grew. He ditched any sort of strategy for a series of lazy, frenzied attacks. Finally bored, Faythe twisted around to avoid his final blow and kicked his feet out from under him, standing over him a heartbeat later with two hands braced to plunge her blade down through his chest.

The crowd roared as the man beneath her seethed with rage— a look she was eerily familiar with. She made a few supercilious bows, remaining in character for the revelers above, before swaggering to her exit, a victorious smile tugging at her lips.

CHAPTER 32

FAYTHE WAITED IN Crow's Lane for Ferris to appear. Her arm stung and still bled a little as she examined the full extent of the injury, having no idea how she would explain it to Jakon. The bruises no doubt forming on her side and ribs would be much easier to hide.

Ferris gave a low whistle. "I thought I was going to lose you there for a moment."

"So did I," she grumbled.

"But alas, you pulled through." He held out two pouches of coin—getting lighter each week, but still a generous amount.

She snatched them, then she took her cloak and slung it over herself.

"How are you feeling?" he asked.

Faythe gave him a flat look, ignoring the fatuous question. "I need more time to fight the fae. I won't stand a chance if I'm weakened in the slightest. Another two weeks."

He opened his mouth to protest, but she gave him a look that said it was reschedule or she would back out completely. Ferris nodded in agreement.

"There's already a lot of talk about it. It's going to be a packed night."

This wasn't exactly encouraging information. Grabbing her discarded gown, she made to leave, but Ferris grabbed her arm.

"Even if you lose, we'll still make good money. Don't worry about it too much," he said by way of comfort. When she answered with a small nod of thanks, he released her.

Becoming one with the shadows, Faythe made her way home.

Expecting Marlowe and Jakon to still be at the shows or her cottage, Faythe threw the hut door open and halted in shock at the sight of them in the open kitchen, seated at the table. While she gaped, Jakon got to his feet, his face a mask of rage and disappointment. Marlowe met her bewildered look and winced, her face wrinkling in apology.

"I'm sorry, Faythe. He knew something wasn't right. I had to tell him," she said quickly, silently begging her forgiveness.

Faythe looked at Jakon and swallowed hard, waiting for the shouting to begin.

"How long?" he asked quietly.

She would rather he shouted at her, if only so she wouldn't have to stare at his completely heartbroken face. "I... Jakon, I'm sorry. We needed the income, and I—I'm good at it," she stumbled, unable to justify going behind his back.

He laughed bitterly, barely able to look at her. "Clearly, if you've been lying to me for as long as I think you have." He shot an icy look at Marlowe. "Both of you."

The blacksmith recoiled at the comment, and Faythe stepped between them.

"It's me you're angry with, not her. I made her keep the secret. You would never have let me do it."

His eyes targeted her again. "It's not for me to *let* you do anything, but *lying* to me? And getting Marlowe to distract me—that's what you've been doing, isn't it? It's an all-time low for you," he seethed.

She winced at the words but regained her composure. "I lost my job at the stall—I didn't know what else to do. I wanted to earn my own money with a skill I happen to be really good at. It may not be up to your *standards,* but so far, I've done a pretty damned good job," she retorted, not bothering to specify she had started fighting long before she was let go from Marie's service.

His eyes flashed to her arm, and he scoffed. "Yeah, it seems so."

She pulled her cloak back over it to cover the tear in her suit and glared at him. "It's the first time I've even had a scratch, you prick." They stared off for a long moment, the tension growing thick.

"Please can you not fight?" Marlowe said quietly from behind them.

It was Faythe who conceded first. With a long sigh, her face turned apologetic. "Look, Jak, I'm sorry I lied to you. Even at the mention of it, you were jumping in to stop me. I chose to do this, and you don't have to like it, but I need you to accept it."

The look of distaste and disappointment didn't leave his face as he huffed in disbelief. He fired Marlowe the same look before turning on his heel and retreating to the bedroom without another word.

Faythe whirled to Marlowe who had tears forming in her eyes. Her shoulders sagged at the sight. This was all her fault. She'd caused friction and distrust between them all.

"Marlowe, I'm so sorry—" she began, but Marlowe waved a hand.

"I chose to help you. It's not all your fault." She cracked a weak smile that broke Faythe's heart.

"No. I've been so selfish and foolish to think we could have kept it up without him ever finding out. I didn't consider your relationship in this, and I'm sorry."

Marlowe stood from her seat and motioned for Faythe to take it without a word. She did, and Marlowe removed her cloak, waiting for Faythe to unzip her suit so she could examine her wound. Her heart fractured. She didn't deserve her tenderness—not now.

Faythe winced pulling her arm free but sat in her modest black undergarments while Marlowe filled a small basin with water and grabbed a cloth. Then she went to work, wordlessly cleaning Faythe's arm with loving softness, while Faythe clenched her teeth to keep from hissing at the stinging sensation.

"He was suspicious the moment you left tonight," Marlowe whispered. "He said nothing would make you miss the shows, and then he started to recall other times he thought your behavior was amiss. I couldn't persuade him otherwise when he insisted we come back here, and when you weren't home…it all came tumbling out. I'm so sorry, Faythe. I couldn't think of any excuse for where you might be." She sniffed, crying.

Faythe put a hand over the one that was brushing her arm, and Marlowe looked at her through teary eyes. "This is my doing, and his anger is with me. You have absolutely nothing to be sorry for. You're a better friend than I deserve sometimes." She smiled and reached to brush a stray tear from her friend's perfect porcelain cheek. "He won't stay mad for long," she said softly, trying to ease her own fears as much as Marlowe's.

"Maybe not, but I worry we've broken something that won't be so easily mended."

Faythe knew it too. It would take time before Jakon fully trusted either of them again, and her gut twisted. While one secret was now out in the open, an even deadlier one lay within her than was still unknown to either of them.

When Marlowe finished, she took a seat opposite Faythe.

"We should let him sleep on it. Nothing's going to be sorted tonight," Faythe said sadly.

Marlowe nodded and went to stand. "I think I should head home."

"I'll come with you." Faythe rose too. "If that's okay?"

Marlowe's answering smile was enough. Faythe pulled her suit back up and slung her cloak on, Marlowe doing the same, and they headed out without a goodbye. Jakon would know where they had gone and would appreciate the solitude. His last look had suggested he couldn't stand to be around them right now.

With a heavy heart, Faythe linked arms with Marlowe, and they took off down the cold, dark streets in somber silence.

CHAPTER 33

"H*AMMER*, F*AYTHE*?"

Marlowe's voice snapped her out of her wandering daydream. She glanced to her friend who stood holding a small dagger poised over an anvil expectantly.

"Sorry," she muttered, grabbing the requested tool and passing it over.

Marlowe took the item without looking and went to bring it down upon the blade but paused, examining it with a sigh. "I know we both have our minds elsewhere, but rawhide is not going to fare well against steel." She walked the few steps to swap her hammer without asking Faythe again. Probably wise. Faythe had failed to retain any of the information Marlowe tried to teach her about the blacksmithing trade.

She had been staying at her friend's cottage, borrowing Marlowe's clothes and following her to the workshop to distract herself from her aching heart. They were both suffering and had barely mustered any cheerful chatter in all their brooding. Faythe had decided to give Jakon as much space as he needed and would let him come to her—to *them*—but it had been three whole days since he discovered her unsavory nighttime antics, and each day, her heart cracked deeper.

It was the autumnal equinox outdoor ball on the hills tonight. Faythe couldn't even bring herself to be slightly excited and had even considered not attending for the first year ever. It was much like the summer solstice, with bonfires, dancing, and stalls, but revelers usually wore masks or dressed as animals as a tribute for a good harvest that would see them through the winter. Faythe and Marlowe had already been shopping for their outfits last week.

"How long do we give him?" Faythe pondered out loud.

Marlowe paused her work and gave her a sad look. "As long as it takes," she offered.

It didn't help the sinking feeling Faythe had that he might never forgive her—not fully. She had lied to him for over a month and put a wedge between him and Marlowe because of it. She was horrible and selfish and wondered why Marlowe didn't hate her too. She would deserve it, even accept it, if she did. But she was also incredibly grateful the blacksmith remained by her side. Marlowe was all she had to keep her from full self-destruction. She'd already pushed Nik away twice now, but missing Jakon was a deeper kind of empty void.

Faythe pushed off her perch by the tools and wandered aimlessly, eager to find something to take her mind off everything. She found herself by Marlowe's smaller workbench, where the translated paper still remained along with the original and a series of books, as if Marlowe had tried to look deeper into some of the meanings. She noticed a few scribbles and circled words on her translated version and picked it up in curiosity. Next to the first line, she had written the names of the three Spirits:

Aurialis, Dakodas, Marvellas.

A line was drawn from the second verse.

Fenstead: Silver Forests?
High Farrow: Eternal Woods?

Faythe froze, realizing that must be the name of the woods she and Nik frequented. But she didn't believe her friend would try to visit the woods that seemed like a living nightmare. No one tried to go in there.

She glanced at Marlowe still fully concentrating on her work. No—her friend was a picture of pure, delicate grace. She couldn't imagine her ever setting foot in a place like that and enduring the same horrors Faythe had. She went back to examining the paper and the line that was drawn from the second verse:

Dalrune: Mortus Mountains?
Rhyenelle: Niltain Isles?

The thought of another one of those temples being as close as the mountains bordering High Farrow made her uneasy. But they were just old, useless stone buildings. At least, that was what Faythe convinced herself to retain her sanity about *how* she came to discover the Light Temple and what other magickal tricks could surround any others.

The third verse only had one possible conclusion for where the temple might be located:

Lakelaria: Sky Caves.

Faythe felt slight relief. At least there was no chance of her coming across *that* one. Regardless, they were all just Marlowe's speculations; her obvious thirst for knowledge and ancient wonders coming into play. This was *fun* for her.

One word circled in the last verse made Faythe's heart jump. A line leading from it said:

The Riscillius—The Looking Glass?

Was this Marlowe's new translation of the word? Why had she not thought to share the information? Perhaps Faythe had done *too* good a job in appearing impassive to the whole thing.

"You've been busy," Faythe commented, waving the paper at her.

Marlowe looked up and shrugged. "Just something to pass the time. I find it interesting."

She didn't explain more, which Faythe found strange. Her friend was always enthusiastic about sharing her findings and going off on tangents about strange, wondrous things.

She didn't press further as the blacksmith quite literally threw herself back into her current piece, bringing the hammer down time and time again with a little more frustration in each swing.

The rest of the day passed agonizingly slow. Both women were headed out of the workshop for home when they froze in their tracks at the figure waiting before them.

"I have come to escort both of you ladies to the equinox ball tonight," Jakon said with a sheepish smile, fiddling with a plain black mask in his hands.

Faythe let out a small sound and ran for him, not bothering to worry if he was still too upset to accept her embrace. It all melted away when he caught her and returned her hug. The weight of the world lifted from her shoulders.

"I'm so sorry," she blurted.

He released her and gave her a sad look. "This doesn't mean I fully forgive you...yet."

She nodded, understanding it would take time to regain his trust but still overwhelmingly happy he was here. She had missed him more than she imagined.

His eyes darted to Marlowe still standing by the curtain, and Faythe stepped back. Jakon walked over to her and stopped a foot away.

"I'm sorry, Marlowe. I understand you only kept it from me to be a good friend to Faythe, and I can't fault you for that." He shot her a glance—because he would have done the same if she'd asked him.

Faythe's face fell. She hated being the reason they had any kind of divide and vowed to never use either of them like that again.

Marlowe's answer was a bone-crushing embrace, and at the sight, Faythe's relief flooded out of her. They had returned to some form of normalcy, though she had a long way to go to prove herself to Jakon.

In that moment, she decided her secrets would not drive a wedge between any of them again. She would find a way to tell them about her abilities, as ludicrous and impossible as they were, and she would pray her friends accepted her as the same person she still was—not view her as the weapon she could become.

CHAPTER 34

F AYTHE SMOOTHED DOWN the pleats of her skirts, anxiously awaiting Marlowe and Jakon's arrival so they could go to the celebrations together.

Her two friends had gone back to the cottage so Marlowe could change since Jakon had already come in his outfit for the ball. Faythe had returned to the hut and now stood in her white floating gown. Its bodice was layered with a feathery texture that matched her eye mask. She had chosen to imitate a swan tonight and had braided the sides of her hair back and added matching feathered white clips to further portray her animal of choice. She fiddled with the mask adorning her face, and then a thought crossed her mind, sending her heart into a gallop.

Would Nik be there tonight?

He had been assigned to patrol the summer solstice, so she imagined there was a good chance he could be at this large event also. It required more fae than usual in case anything got out of hand, what with the streets being filled and foreign vendors stopping in town to sell their wares.

The thought made her suddenly giddy to leave, and she paced to curb her anxiety while she waited for her friends. The last time she saw the fae guard, they hadn't left on good terms. In fact, that was a light way of putting it. She'd tried to force herself into his thoughts against his will and as good as declared she never wanted to see him again.

Faythe had been wanting to make amends for that night since it happened but was too cowardly to infiltrate his mind at night. The celebrations would offer the perfect opportunity to *accidentally* run into him, and she would tell him she was sorry and hope for his forgiveness—something she was gaining the habit of doing to everyone around her.

She could live with it if he decided she'd crossed a line and never wanted to speak to her again. She could, but she cursed the stab in her heart at the thought.

The door swung open, and Faythe leaped in excitement as she beheld her friends. Marlowe looked stunning in her turquoise and royal blue gown that matched her mask. She had chosen a peacock and simply glowed as she embodied the creature. Jakon was dressed in mostly black. His sleek mask had a slight point to its nose. A crow. Simple, but he too looked the picture of elegance.

"Look at us!" Marlowe cried cheerfully, glancing between them all.

Faythe grinned, bounding over to loop her arm through Marlowe's, and they left the hut, emerging onto the bustling streets already thick with revelers in an array of different masks and costumes. Laughter and chatter floated through the air as well as the smells of bonfire and various delicious foods. They stopped to purchase some chocolates and wine before making their way up to the grassy hills where the main entertainment would be.

In the dark of the autumn night, the hills were alight, diffusing the sky with hues of yellow and orange from the tall stakes that burned with passion and fury. People moved around them, some throwing their own sculptures of wood or bits of cloth into the inferno with an added prayer to the Spirits.

Faythe had been subtly scanning the crowds everywhere they

went for a certain fae guard but had so far had no luck and was beginning to think her efforts were futile with the amount of people and fae patrol out tonight. Though the fae did stand out as the only ones who were unmasked and in uniform.

They made their way over to a large gathering that had formed around some fire breathers performing dangerous tricks that had everyone transfixed.

"I've always wondered how they do that," Marlowe commented.

Faythe only hummed in agreement. She watched for a while longer before she felt compelled to scan the masses again. Colorful masks were everywhere. Couples danced, children played, women chatted, and then…

She sucked in a breath as her eyes met with a familiar emerald green pair.

He wore a black mask and had his hood up on his cloak, but there was no mistaking him—Nik stared right at her on the edge of the audience to her left. He angled his head, beckoning for her to follow, and then he turned to leave the spectacle.

Faythe looked to her friends who were still immersed in the show. Jakon had his arm lazily draped around Marlowe's waist.

"I'm going to get more wine. Do you want anything?" she asked.

Marlowe tore her eyes away to answer, "No, I'm good. Meet us right back here?"

She nodded and didn't hesitate as she turned and pushed her way out of the growing cluster of people. When she was in a more open space, she stopped to scan the mob again but couldn't see Nik.

"Up the hills."

From his voice in her head, she knew he had to be close and watching her to be able to project the thought. She twisted her head around, and sure enough, he was standing at the top of the hills. Once she spotted him, he turned and kept walking farther toward the woods. Faythe hastened her pace to catch up, weaving her way past scattered bodies and dodging children who ran through her path. They continued until the clamor was faint and there were no people this far back.

Nik stopped at the tree line and leaned against one, casually folding his arms. "You look very eager to find someone tonight," he said in greeting when she caught up.

She scoffed. "Don't flatter yourself." Her cheeks flamed, and he gave her a knowing smirk. Desperate to change the subject, she asked, "You're not on duty tonight?" as she noted his casual attire beneath his cloak. He didn't plan to stay long.

Nik didn't respond straight away. His eyes grazed over her. "No, I am not," he said at last.

Thinning her lips, she was about to cower out, but she blurted, "I'm sorry." At his surprised look, she continued. "I tried to push into your mind, and I crossed a line. So I'm sorry," she finished awkwardly, adjusting her mask as her skin grew clammy beneath it.

He laughed, and she gaped at him. "How much sleep have you lost over that?" he teased.

"None! I just thought it would be polite to apologize, you prick." She turned on her heel to leave but was stopped by his call.

"Wait."

She paused with her back to him.

"You did try to cross a line, but you didn't succeed. I understand why you wanted to, but I promise you, Faythe, I had nothing to do with that woman's death, and I would have stopped it if I could have," he said sincerely.

She slowly turned to him. She thought she would be the one doing all the apologizing, so she couldn't hide her surprise at this turn of events. His face spoke volumes too. He *was* sorry. And all this time, she had tormented herself over what *she'd* done and would need to atone for.

"You're different, Nik, from the rest of them," she said quietly.

His lips curled up. "I don't know if that's entirely true."

"I do."

He looked at her with an intensity that made her pulse race.

Averting her eyes, she cleared her throat. "What are you doing here tonight?" It was the first diversion that came to mind.

"Am I not allowed to enjoy the celebrations like everyone else?"

She didn't want to point out that his casual clothing, aside from the mask, suggested he wasn't here as just another reveler.

"If you came all this way to apologize, consider me flattered."

His eyes danced beneath his mask. "Maybe I did." He paused, looking her over again with deliberate slowness, and Spirits be *dammed*, it set off all kinds of scandalous thoughts. "Or maybe I came to see just what great spectacles the outer town had to offer."

She didn't balk at his gaze, lifting her chin. "And how do they fare in comparison to your fancy inner city?"

His smile widened, and his eyes flashed. He straightened and stalked over to her, coming so close she could take one last daring step and close the gap between their bodies. Leaning his head in close, his warm breath on her neck sent ripples of desire down her spine to pool at her core.

"I think I much prefer the sights to behold here," he said, each word vibrating wonderfully over her skin. She had to suck in a breath when she felt his fingers graze slowly over the feathers of her bodice, trailing right between her breasts to finish at her navel. "How fitting," he mumbled quietly.

She didn't know what he meant by it—or really care in that moment as his lips hovered below her ear. The whisper of a kiss lay there, and she wanted him to make contact so desperately she thought she would come apart.

Then he stepped back swiftly with a wicked smile.

She must have looked as dazed as she felt. He slid his hands into his pockets, amused, while he watched her try to clear her head and calm her frenzied heartbeat.

"Your friends will be wondering where you are by now," he said innocently.

Her mouth popped open, trying to form a retort, but when nothing came, all she could mutter was, "Prick." She turned on her heel to stalk back down the hills while the echoes of his laughter followed her.

Faythe stopped by a stall selling wine and purchased a cup before heading back to where she'd left her friends. Jakon and Marlowe were at the edge of the fire show, out from the crowd, laughing with each other. She almost didn't want to interrupt their moment of carefree joy.

Still, she approached in a haste. "Sorry—the queue was long," she said. Her breathlessness wasn't fake, however.

"You didn't miss much. We were going to go watch the magicians next." Marlowe beamed.

Faythe rolled her eyes. "You know it's not real magick, right?" she teased. Only the fae possessed magick, and it was usually confined to one form. These "magicians" were merely cunning human tricksters.

"Don't be such a killjoy," Marlowe grumbled, grabbing her arm and dragging her in that direction anyway.

They stayed for another hour, trailing around and visiting different stalls and entertainers until they started to get tired of all the flamboyance. They removed their masks as they left the greenery, and Faythe moaned at the fresh air that cooled her face where the material had clung to her eyes and nose.

The streets were quieter as they strolled back to the hut. They were about to turn the last corner when four figures came into view like dark, looming shadows. Faythe didn't even have a second to react before the largest grabbed her and started to drag her down the dark alley opposite where they stood. His hand clamped over her mouth, and to her horror, she caught sight of another brute grabbing Marlowe the same while the other two tackled a thrashing Jakon.

Once they were all out of sight down the alley, she was thrown against the wall. The impact ricocheted down her spine, and stars danced across her eyes from the blow to her head. When her vision returned, she recognized every one of them, to her absolute terror: the men she'd fought and beat in The Cave. They had figured out who she really was and were now seeking revenge for their humiliation and disgrace at her hand. And her friends would suffer for it too.

The one she'd bested on her first night held her. "You think we wouldn't find you, *Gold-Eyed Shadow?*" His breath reeked from the closeness while he spat the words in her face.

She had no weapons on her tonight—none of them did—and she could see no way out of their compromised position. At least, not with her companions. They would be able to kill her right here, and no one would stop them. But Faythe wasn't afraid for herself as she looked to her friends in cold panic.

"Your fight is with me. Let them go." She seethed through her teeth.

Marlowe was crying and near hysteric under the grip of the tall, built man—her second combatant—and Jakon was so frantic in his struggle that the other two had already hit him several times in an attempt to silence him. His lip bled, and there was a cut above his eyebrow.

Faythe saw red and snapped her eyes back to the crook who held her. "Hurts even more now you see the *girl* who beat you beneath the mask, huh?" she taunted. Anything to get their attention off Marlowe and Jakon. "It gave me great delight to take you all down." She laughed haughtily. "You can't handle that I stripped back your guise and exposed you for what you really are—a coward."

His face contorted with inhuman rage, and he slammed her against the wall again before sending his fist into her gut. The breath was knocked from her, but before she could double over in pain, he grabbed her by the throat, his grip tightening.

"Not so brave now," he sneered. "You're nothing without your fancy sword tricks."

Faythe clawed at his arms as he began to close off her airway. Her throat burned from the restricted breath, and a loud pounding filled her ears. She barely heard the commotion of Jakon fighting the others, but then Marlowe's bloodcurdling scream sent a wave of wild panic through her.

She was completely and utterly helpless under the strength of his grip. She would die right here, under his hands, in a few short minutes. She had failed them...

Air flooded down her throat all at once, and she spluttered as the brute was suddenly ripped away from her. Faythe fell to her hands and knees, gasping for her lungs to fill with oxygen once again. She allowed herself all of a few seconds to let the dizziness pass and her vision to clear before she looked up in time to see a familiar dark-haired fae take out the final man. They all lay unconscious—or dead—where they had stood just a moment ago.

She couldn't even begin to wonder how Nik got here or managed to find her just in time. Marlowe's hysteric cries rang through her, and her eyes returned to the alley floor, where she saw her leaning over Jakon.

Then she beheld the dagger protruding from his abdomen, and the world stopped.

She stared in wide-eyed horror for a second before she scrambled to her feet, falling back to her knees beside him in bone-trembling shock. His breathing was severely weak and labored, but he was still conscious, and when his eyes met hers, they held nothing but blind dread. She couldn't speak, couldn't move, and didn't know what to do.

It was Nik who spoke finally. "We need to get him inside. Do you live far?" His voice was calm, calculating, like a warrior on a battlefield to his comrades.

She mustered a vacant shake of her head in response.

Rough hands grabbed her by the arms, pulling her to her feet. She went to protest and fall to Jakon's side again, but Nik was already there, sliding an arm under his back and helping him to stand.

"Do not remove that blade," he said firmly.

Jakon held his stomach where the blade was fully submerged. Faythe could only stare, paralyzed by emotion, while Marlowe's hysteria was barely audible.

"Faythe, we need to go *now*," Nik growled.

She snapped back into herself. They needed to act fast, or it would be Jakon's life. Every second counted. She nodded sharply and rushed out of the alley, checking it was clear before motioning for them to follow. Nik carried Jakon's whole weight—one arm braced around his waist, the other holding Jakon's arm over his shoulder—but her friend was so pale and limp Faythe almost collapsed at the sight. She had to keep her calm—at least until they were inside and could tend to the wound.

Mercifully, they made the short journey without meeting another soul on the streets. They burst through the wooden door, and Nik set Jakon down on the kitchen table. Marlowe began immediately crashing through the kitchen for towels and a basin of water.

Faythe tore Jakon's shirt without thinking to get a better look at the wound. She recoiled. There was so much blood. Too much. Blind terror consumed her. He wouldn't live much longer if they couldn't stop it. And if they could, they would have to pray to the Spirits the dagger hadn't hit anything major inside. She met eyes with Nik, but she didn't have to read his mind to know he was thinking the same thing: The odds were incredibly grim.

Marlowe arrived next to her and began to press towels around the blade. Then she put her hand around the hilt to pull it out. When Nik's hand caught her wrist, the blacksmith could have killed him with the look she shot.

"He'll start bleeding uncontrollably as soon as you remove that," Nik explained.

"We can't leave it in there!" she cried.

Jakon was too quiet. Faythe looked at him. He was so pale she would have mistaken him for dead if his eyes didn't flutter. He released a moan of pain.

"You are not going to die tonight, Jakon Kilnight. Do you hear me?" she said firmly.

He didn't respond, and her panic surged. She looked to Nik for command as if he'd know what to do, but his face was grave. He knew there was no coming back from a wound like this on a mortal man, and the dawning of that realization snapped something in her.

"Do something!" she shouted.

"Faythe, I..." He didn't finish what she knew he was going to say.

There was nothing to be done.

Just then, a faint beacon of hope lit from a flash of memory. Faythe's eyes widened, and her head whipped up. She turned to Marlowe.

"Listen to me. You keep him alive. Keep him awake and stifle the bleeding as much as you can until I come back," she spoke with controlled calm.

Marlowe nodded with a sob and fixed herself over Jakon, pressing more towels to his wound. Faythe didn't waste a breath, whirling to the cabinets behind her and throwing everything out of her way until she found what she was looking for.

"Faythe, what are you doing?" Nik asked.

She didn't pay him any attention, couldn't waste a single second, as she grabbed the small bottle and hurled herself out of the hut and into the streets without another word. She didn't care that her white dress was now stained crimson or what the occasional passerby would make of the ghastly sight as she raced past. She hauled her skirts up to mid-thigh and sprinted as fast as her legs could carry her, the burning in her lungs disappearing in her targeted focus.

Faythe took a route she knew would have the least stragglers from the celebrations and flew up the hills. She didn't pause for a single second when she reached the woods. Branches clawed at her ankles as she darted through it, but she never registered any pain. When the waterfall clearing came into view, she breathed a sigh of relief and fell to her knees at the water's edge.

It was a huge gamble and one that could cost her the last moments at her best friend's side, but she *had* to try—even though Nik's words haunted her the whole way.

"They say they can heal any mortal wound, but I've never been able to bottle them."

She prayed to every Spirit and God in the realm and promised to worship them for the rest of her miserable life as she uncorked the bottle and plunged it into the lake. Ice doused her when she pulled the bottle out. It was just plain, clear water...no glowing yucolites. She tried again and again, but still, the container collected none.

"Please!" she cried skyward. She began to sob as she kept sinking the bottle in, trying to catch them, but they mocked her by darting away every time.

"Faythe."

A woman's voice, like an echo from a shadow, sounded around her. She turned and beheld the mighty white stag at her side. Instead of being struck with fear, she whimpered in frustration. She didn't need another stupid tour to the temple; she needed the yucolites.

But the stag did not beckon her this time and instead walked closer—so close Faythe got to her feet in fright that she was about to be trampled.

"What is it you come for?"

It seemed to say the words as she looked into its eyes. She blinked for a second, and in her desperation, she replied, "My friend—he's dying. I need...I need these." She pointed to the glowing orbs in the lake.

"*There is no give without take, Faythe.*"

"I'll give you anything you want."

"*Be careful what you say.*"

"*Please!*" was all she could cry. She had no time to play this game.

"*You will have to return something that was once stolen from here,*" it said. "*It dwells now within the palace of High Farrow. The Light Temple ruin.*"

Faythe didn't have a second to spare or she would have laughed at the impossible task. "I will."

"*If you do not, your soul will belong to my woods for all eternity.*"

"I said I'll do it!" she yelled. Every second that passed was a second closer to Jakon's heart stopping.

"*Then the bargain is struck.*"

She couldn't contain her gasp as she felt a sharp tug within her —a chain that anchored her to this place and would remain until she fulfilled her end of the deal.

Not wasting another breath, Faythe dropped to her knees and dunked her bottle into the water once more. When she pulled it back out, a whimper of relief came from her at the dozens of yucolites that now floated within.

"Thank you." She pushed to her feet and began sprinting back the way she came. She thought she heard faintly, just as she met the tree line...

"*I shall see you again soon, Heir of Marvellas.*"

CHAPTER 35

F AYTHE EXPLODED THROUGH the hut door, nearly taking it off
its hinges. She was panting raggedly from her flat-out round-
trip sprint but didn't let the pain in her throat register as she rushed
over to Jakon's side. He was still breathing—barely, but it was
enough.

"You caught them?" Nik said in disbelief.

She ignored him. "When I say I want you to pull the dagger
out…" she commanded Marlowe, who sobbed but nodded, bracing
her hands around the blade. "Nik, I need you to be ready to apply
pressure with a towel immediately," Faythe ordered.

He didn't say anything and braced himself with a cloth, ready
to tame the immediate blood flow.

She felt a hand weakly curl around her wrist, and her eyes met
Jakon's tired gaze. Pain laced his eyes, but she couldn't let it break
her in that moment. He needed her.

She cupped his face and leaned down to say, "You're going to
be okay, but this is going to hurt."

He managed a slight nod, and then his head went limp to the
side, eyes closing, as his fingers left her wrist to dangle over the
table.

Faythe went cold. "Now, Marlowe!"

To her credit, Marlowe didn't hesitate for a second, and Nik was right there applying the necessary pressure when blood started to pour. Faythe couldn't be too late. She yanked the cork off the bottle and, as precisely as she could with her trembling hand, poured the liquid over the deep gash.

Straight away, the yucolites came together as one over the wound and formed a glowing seal. The blood dramatically ceased but still fell slightly while the light magick did its healing work.

The three of them stepped back to watch in awe, but then Faythe lunged forward to examine Jakon's face. She felt for a pulse and recoiled in world-shattering horror when she couldn't find one. Marlowe sobbed loudly again and fell back against the cabinets as Faythe went rigid in shock.

"Give it a moment to work," Nik said softly.

Faythe met his eyes as if it would calm her, and it did. His waves of comfort smoothed the edges of her sharp panic. It relaxed her enough that she was able to go back to Jakon. She grabbed his limp hand in hers and stroked his hair while she waited in painstaking agony for him to take a breath.

The seconds felt like hours, and she focused on his mind as best she could without his eyes to open the doors, coaxing him to come back.

"You can't leave me, Jakon. I won't survive it," she said into his empty mind.

Silent tears fell down her cheeks when she didn't hear anything in there. It was dark and hollow. She was too late, and now she would pay the ultimate price. Her worst fear was coming true: Not only could she not protect those she loved, but she was responsible for bringing perilous danger right to them.

Just as she began to spiral into a bottomless pit of guilt and grief, she caught the echoes of a faint voice.

"I won't ever leave you, Faythe."

She sucked in a sharp breath at Jakon's mental response—so

quiet she thought she imagined it in her desperation. But his chest started a low rise and fall again. She let go of that breath in relief.

Marlowe shot over. "Thank the Spirits," she sobbed.

After a few more tense seconds, Jakon groaned. His eyes flickered open. He blinked a few times before he turned to look at Faythe, and a small noise came from her.

"You can't get rid of me that easily." He gave her hand a weak squeeze.

"It seems not," she said quietly, a smile tugging at her lips.

Marlowe came up beside her, and she smiled at her friend, moving out of the way so she could take the spot. The deep wound on Jakon's stomach still glowed, and she had no idea how long it would take for the yucolites to fully heal him—if they could.

She ran her hands over her face and breathed her first relaxed breath in what felt like a lifetime. Nik was right in front of her, and she couldn't stop herself as she fell into him, wrapping her arms around his waist. He held her tightly. She closed her eyes in silent solace as the events and reality finally caught up with her.

None of them would have made it out of that alley alive if Nik hadn't showed. He'd taken out all four men in less than a minute. They wouldn't have got Jakon here if it weren't for Nik either. He grounded them—was the calming source—when it mattered most.

"Thank you."

She projected the words to him and hoped he heard through his walls.

"There's nothing to thank me for, Faythe. You saved him."

"I'm also the reason he almost died."

Something in her cracked at the truth. This was all her fault.

Nik's arms gripped her shoulders, pulling her back to look at him.

"Walk with me?"

She looked at her friends. Marlowe stood over Jakon, gently stroking his hair while he fell asleep. Faythe's eyes darted to his chest in a spear of panic, but it eased when she noted the steady rise and fall.

Walking over, she put an arm around Marlowe in quiet comfort. "I won't be gone long," she said quietly.

Marlowe looked at her and then at Nik and gave a small nod, returning her focus to Jakon wordlessly.

Faythe looked down at herself. Her white gown was stained with Jakon's blood, and it turned her stomach. She excused herself to quickly change and then went to the washroom to scrub her hands at least. A full-body wash would have to wait.

She threw on her black cloak and emerged, checking Jakon over one final time. Assessing that he was in good hands, with the yucolites still working their magick, she followed Nik out into the night.

They walked in silence for a few streets until they turned into a narrow, dimly lit alley.

Nik stopped to turn to her. When he didn't immediately speak, she did.

"How did you know where to find me tonight?"

It wasn't an accusatory question, but she noted he had a good sense of where and when to find her and rarely offered any explanation. Though he was at the equinox ball, it was too much of a coincidence for him to be passing in their moment of dire need when she'd left him long before the fatal confrontation.

He stayed quiet for a moment, brow creasing in deliberation. "I've been keeping an eye on you ever since you started fighting in The Cave," he spoke at last.

Her mouth opened in shock. She was about to ask how he knew about it, but he continued.

"I looked into that foul beast's mind that first night. I saw the look he gave you, and my assumptions were right. He was never going to let it go."

Faythe stayed silent—out of bewilderment or awe, she wasn't sure.

"The more men you fought... *Gods*, Faythe, you were only adding more to his army each time. He didn't know who you were —not really. I still don't know how he figured it out. None of them knew, and I've been tracking them since in case they did."

Faythe was in disbelief. All this time, he had been protecting her, and she hadn't realized. She'd been so caught up in the money and victory she was ignorant to the growing danger she'd amounted against herself, which ultimately fell on her friends too.

"Why?" was all she could muster in response.

She didn't deserve it. Her friends, Nik—everyone was hurt because of her, and her worst fear was coming true. She couldn't protect anyone, and instead could only rain danger upon them.

He stepped closer, and she angrily swiped a stray tear that fell. She gritted her teeth. She didn't want to cry anymore and felt her rage and guilt rising to the surface in that self-destructing way it always did. As if sensing it, Nik's rough fingers curled tenderly under her chin, and he gently guided her head up to meet his eye.

"This is not your fault, Faythe. It was spiteful, vengeful human men who have nothing else to live for. You won against them, fair and square," he said fiercely. "And you put on quite an impressive show, by the way." He gave her a weak smile in an attempt to lift her spirits, and *damn him*, she could love him for trying.

They stared at each other in earnest silence for a long moment, and then he released her. She almost whimpered at the absence of his touch, but he didn't step back.

"You've been in my head enough times. I think it's only fair you let me in yours just this once," he said quietly; carefully.

Her heart skipped a beat. "I'm thinking..." She swore internally. Then she cursed the world, cursed the Spirits, cursed everything that made them such an unsuitable match in every way. "Screw the damn consequences." She pushed up on her toes, hands going to the back of his neck. Then his mouth met hers, and the stars awoke, chasing away the darkness that had started to engulf her.

Nik's hands glided across her waist in response, leaving trails of fire where he touched. She was about to pull back, only needing to kiss him once to know she wasn't alone in her feelings, but his grip tightened, pulling her flush against his body as if he knew her intention. She didn't object. Instead, she leaned in further, arching her back and feeling like she could never be close enough to him. Their lips moved together passionately, almost desperately, every impulse and desire that had been mounting since the day they met pouring out of her and into that kiss. Her fingers wove through the silk of his jet-black hair, savoring the luxurious feel. She was all too aware of his own hands exploring her waist and back, making her body ripple with impulsive lust.

Faythe didn't realize they had moved until her back met the coolness of the wall behind. He leaned into her this time, trapping her between two forces of safety. His hands left her waist to cup her face, and she whimpered at the loving tenderness of his hold.

Then, just as she thought she might explode with ecstasy, he pulled out of the kiss. She almost cried. But he stayed close, resting his forehead against hers, and for the first time, Nik looked almost as short of breath as she was.

Faythe chuckled softly, and he brought his head back to look at her.

"Should I ask what amuses you?"

Her eyes danced with delight. "I guess it doesn't take much to make you breathless after all."

He huffed a laugh, and Faythe's heart fluttered at the sight of him. He looked *happy* in a way she'd not seen him before. It lit a small beacon in her among all the negative emotions. Knowing she could make him happy—it might just be her salvation.

CHAPTER 36

J AKON WAS STILL pale and clammy, but he was breathing, and it
was a steady, even rhythm as Faythe monitored each rise and
fall of his chest from her seat beside him. Marlowe tenderly
cleaned the wound that still glowed from the magick of the yucolites. She had not asked Faythe about them, and Faythe wasn't sure
how she would explain it or their unexpected savior in the form of
a fae guard.

Nik had left her at Jakon's side an hour ago. He had no reason
to be here when he woke up, and Faythe wasn't ready to explain
him to her friends yet.

When Jakon stirred, Faythe was on her feet in an instant, scanning his face. With a weak tilt, he turned his head, and his eyes fluttered open. After a few blinks, he went to sit up, but Faythe held his
shoulder.

"Just a bit longer," she said quietly.

He looked at her then, brow creasing in confusion. It took a
moment, but she knew the events of the night had caught up with
him when his eyes widened in horror.

"Are you hurt?" His voice was hoarse. He studied her over, and
then Marlowe.

"No, but…you were, Jak. I'm so sorry." Faythe's lip wobbled.

He propped himself on his elbows against Faythe's protests and beheld the glowing line on his abdomen. It was clean of blood and had almost finished sealing as the yucolites began to dim.

His eyes were wide as saucers. "How?" was all he managed.

"I'll explain everything."

She would have to. It scared the rutting damn out of her, but there would be no more secrets between any of them. She would find a way to live with their judgment of what she was and what she had kept from them these past months because her friends deserved to know. She had endangered their lives with her secrets and would rather face eternity alone than let them risk their lives in her web of lies again.

"Can you move? I think we should all try to get some sleep," Faythe said, exhausted both mentally and physically.

He nodded, and with Marlowe and Faythe's help, they managed to shuffle into the bedroom and set him down in his bed.

Faythe loaned Marlowe some nightclothes when she insisted she wasn't going anywhere while Jakon was still in recovery. The two women squeezed themselves into the cot beside him, and Faythe let herself fall into beckoning oblivion knowing she and her friends were safely asleep.

Faythe stood in the gold-and-white shimmers of her mind as she flicked through memories of her longest best friend. The thought of nearly losing him had haunted her on her way to sleep, and she found herself immediately needing the comfort of his presence.

Happy memories. She smiled and even laughed at some of their earlier antics. Reflecting on their younger selves made her heart hurt. They had been so innocent and oblivious to the world around them. Even though they had never had any luxuries and struggled to keep fed, their childhood years had been blissful; the most carefree and joyous.

She felt Nik's gentle nudge on the edge of her mind before she allowed him to enter, but then his full presence surrounded her. She didn't turn to look at him as she continued to watch the memories unfold in front of her like a motion picture.

"I can leave. I just wanted to check you were okay," he said carefully.

She shot him a grateful smile over her shoulder, then she held her hand out, inviting him to come closer. He obliged, coming up behind and resting a hand across her lower back. His touch, even in her mind, soothed every aching feeling.

"He's almost fully healed. It's a miracle," she said, turning to look at her friend's face as she recalled the memories to display in front of them.

"You look happy with him," he observed.

Faythe detected the slight hint of a question in his words. Everyone had wondered it at one point or another—why she and Jakon had never become a romantic couple.

"We were... Still are," she corrected. Noting the slight stiffening of his hand on her, she continued, "I love him, but not in the way everyone expects. He's not a lover. He's not just a friend or a brother either... I can't explain it." She twisted to face him, her hands coming up to rest on his chest. "But you should know, I've never felt *this* way for him." She reached up to brush her mouth against his, and he responded by pulling her gently closer so no air could move between them. The kiss was short but needed.

When they pulled back to look at each other, his eyes sparkled. He smiled down at her, and it made her heart flutter wonderfully. It felt right with Nik. She hated that she had ever denied herself before. They would figure it out, keep it secret to whatever end if they had to, and only meet in here or the woods if necessary, because any time she could get with him would be better than nothing at all.

He leaned down and kissed her again, harder this time, as if in silent agreement with her thoughts.

She sighed contentedly and turned to her memories again just as the scene switched.

A much more recent memory: the day of the summer solstice when Jakon had just arrived home, about to present her with the sword she'd come to call Lumarias. She tuned in to hear the excitement in his voice when he gave her the one thing she'd wanted most—now her dearest possession. Faythe closely examined it while Jakon explained its craftsmanship. She grinned at the recollection as she had yet to know the brilliant mind behind the sword and how close she would become to the blacksmith.

"The blacksmith kindly offered the stone with no charge. Called it The Looking Glass—some ancient stone that's supposed to bring good fortune and all that."

Faythe sucked in a sharp breath, and her mouth popped open. She couldn't have heard it right. She rewound the memory, convinced her mind was possibly mixing up words from another event. But then she heard it again, unmistakably:

"The Looking Glass."

She froze, and Nik noted her stiffness. "What is it?" he asked in concern.

How could she not have made the connection earlier? If Marlowe had indeed translated the word correctly, it meant the Riscillius required to open the temple...

Looking over the blade in her memory again, Faythe was astonished she'd never paid heed to the markings etched on the guard of her own sword before: three similar symbols in a vertical line. Blended in with the tone of the metal, it would take a keen eye to distinguish them, but when she did, a cold chill went through her as she identified the top one to be the mark of Aurialis.

Why would the blacksmith put such a thing on her sword? She knew her friend had a guilty pleasure for the Spirits and other mythical lore, but it made no sense to incorporate it into her work.

Faythe felt shaken with dread at the recurring sight of that damned symbol. She cursed herself for her own slowness in not making the connection sooner. But had she really held the real thing in her sword this whole time? Her stomach fell slightly. There was a good chance it was only a replica from some nonsense merchant trying to get more coin. A simple rock with no abilities whatsoever.

There would only be one way to find out. But...did she really want to discover what dwelled inside the temple? Perhaps there was a damned good reason it was sealed and could only be opened with one very specific, very ancient stone. She might risk awakening something that had been asleep for centuries.

"Faythe, what's wrong?" Nik pressed again.

She twisted to him. "Nothing," she said sweetly, though her mind was reeling. If there was danger behind those doors, she didn't need to risk anyone else finding out the hard—possibly deadly—way. "I think I'm going to get some sleep. It's been a whirl of a night."

He gave her a smile of understanding and ran the back of his hand down her cheek. His fingers settled under her chin, angling her face up to kiss him again. She would never get tired of the feeling it gave her and the light it brightened inside of her.

"I'll see you soon," he promised when he pulled back.

She answered with a nod and then watched as he faded into her swirls of gold mist before disappearing altogether.

When she could no longer feel his presence, she forced herself awake.

CHAPTER 37

FAYTHE'S EYES SNAPPED open, adjusting to the darkness of the small bedroom. She didn't have to glance at Jakon to know he was asleep from the familiar sound of his light snoring. She cautiously tilted her head to the blonde beside her—also sound asleep.

She slowly rose from the bed and tiptoed out of the bedroom in a deliberate pattern to avoid the uneven spots on the floorboards that creaked loudly. In the main room, she didn't dare move or breathe too loudly while she maneuvered the space with stealth, swinging on her cloak and snatching Lumarias. Then Faythe misted into the night, giddy with an adventurer's thrill.

Logical reasoning didn't come into play as she darted in and out of shadowed streets before scaling the hills to the eternal woods. If she really held the key to those doors, the *Riscillius,* all this time…

It could just be a simple rock. Then I can let go of my fixation on the damned thing.

But the reckless, dark side of her hoped The Looking Glass needed to open the temple was indeed within her grasp. Her fingers flexed tighter around the hilt of her sword in adrenaline-fueled anticipation while she marched through the trees to the waterfall clearing.

She halted abruptly when she emerged, her heart skipping a beat as she stared incredulously across the open space. The mighty white stag stood in wait as if it knew her intentions. She didn't let the thought rattle her nerves and pressed forward, following the beast for the third—and hopefully final—time. She would either come to find what it so eagerly wanted to guide her to, or she was foolishly trailing behind the Grim Reaper incarnate, happily escorting her to a sure death beyond those doors, ready to claim her soul that was still bound to the cursed woodland.

The temple glade unfolded in front of her, and the loud pounding of her pulse thrummed in her ears as she watched the stag float up the steps and disappear through the stone doors once again. Realizing this time, she might truly hold the key to follow it all the way, Faythe pulled her sword free from its scabbard without looking, taking slow steps toward the looming structure. The cry of steel awoke her senses, turning her attention to the rational thoughts that screamed the danger of what she was about to do.

There was only one glaring problem: How to use the Riscillius?

She held up the hilt of Lumarias and squinted at it. There was no obvious lock on the door, and even if there were, the thought of having to ruin Marlowe's perfect craftsmanship to remove the stone pained her. Her sword was more than just a key. It was strange to think she could be bonded to an item, but her attachment to Lumarias was strong.

She stalked up the portico and held out the rock, pressing it against the door at all angles and feeling over the rough surface for any unusual marks or dips that could indicate a slot for the Riscillius. Nothing revealed itself, and Faythe's frustrations grew.

Why lead me here and not offer a clue to get inside?

In her moment of anguish, she growled loudly and slammed a palm against the hard stone. It did nothing but sting her skin and send a hideous jolt of pain up her arm. She rested her forehead against the cold stone door, about to cry out to no one in particular, when a soft female voice made her whirl around.

"It's a lens."

When Faythe's eyes landed on a familiar blonde head, all she could do was gawk in absolute shock at the sight of Marlowe at the bottom of the steps. She couldn't speak for a moment and blinked hard a few times to be sure she wasn't just another illusion conjured by the eternal woods.

"What?" was all Faythe could breathe in response, still not believing her friend was really there.

Marlowe nodded to the sword in her hand. "The Riscillius— The Looking Glass. It also means 'to see what is not there.' It's to be used as a lens to open the temple." Her voice was different and her expression conflicted. It looked out of place on the blacksmith's usually bright face.

Then her words registered, and Faythe too glanced down at Lumarias. "How would you know that?" she asked shakily.

Marlowe didn't answer immediately. Instead, she climbed the few steps to level with Faythe and held her hand out. Faythe passed her the sword, too stunned to object or force any explanation from her. The blacksmith gave a small smile—which was a slight relief at least—and then she held up the pommel to her eye.

Faythe watched silently as her friend reached into her pocket and pulled something out. Chalk.

"I saw it…in a dream," Marlowe spoke quietly. Stepping up to the doors, she began to draw steady lines across one side. "You wouldn't have believed me before, and it was not for me to tell you either." She carried on tracing, not meeting Faythe's eye as she pondered her deep thoughts out loud. "You needed to figure it out on your own. Everything has an order. Disrupt it, and you can throw it all out of balance. One small alteration to the chain of events…can change the fate of the world."

Faythe's heart hammered in her chest. It was Marlowe's voice, yet the words shook right through her very bones, so she couldn't be sure if they were entirely of her friend's making.

"Did you follow me here?"

The blacksmith cast her a smile in answer. What it meant, Faythe wasn't certain. She raised the stone to her eye once again before switching sides, continuing her delicate tracing across the gray stone. Then she held the sword back to Faythe.

She dared to bring it to her eye with a shaky hand and gasped as she saw the markings glowing bright gold under her friend's white chalk drawings.

"The temple is warded by a memory spell," Marlowe explained. "You won't remember the markings to enter in a few minutes. You'll need the Riscillius each time as they will fade from the doors once they are sealed again."

Did her friend know this all along?

Faythe looked at Marlowe through new eyes, caught between heartbreak and admiration that she had kept such knowledge from Faythe throughout their friendship. But she decided she had no right to be angry for the deception when she harbored a deadly secret of her own.

Then another thought froze her still, and she stared at her friend.

Did Marlowe know about her abilities too?

It would be impossible. Her ability wasn't something the blacksmith could pick up from a book—not connected to Faythe specifically. Though this didn't ease her nerves. She was an anomaly that shouldn't exist in the world; a *human* with an unexplainable gift...

Was the quiet, book-loving blonde one of her kind too?

Faythe trembled, unable to reel in her racing thoughts and wild, outlandish conclusions about her friend's knowledge. It seemed too vast, too *perfect*, and Marlowe always held the answers as if she knew exactly when they would be needed. But Faythe couldn't bring herself to outright ask or accuse her. Before she could send herself into a frenzy of possible explanations, Marlowe finished her artwork on the temple doors and stepped back. Faythe copied the movement in nervous anticipation. After a moment of deafening silence, the doors groaned loudly, caving inward a fraction.

Faythe was stunned. Quite literally. She stood with her mouth agape and couldn't peel her eyes from the slither of darkness that opened into the temple. Her hands shook violently, and she gripped Lumarias so hard it hurt.

When no danger immediately presented itself, Faythe cast a look to Marlowe. The blacksmith beamed enthusiastically.

"Shall we?" She didn't wait for Faythe to join her as she walked the few paces to brace her splayed palms against the door.

Faythe watched her strain for a second, still dumbfounded by the events, and then she moved to help. Together, they pushed against the heavy door. External light flooded in to illuminate the interior of the temple. Marlowe moved to enter first, unfaltering, unflinching, while Faythe remained on the edge of caution, eyes darting to scan every inch of the place as she took her first wary steps inside. She kept her sword poised.

But it was not at all what Faythe was expecting. There were no rows of benches or any sign this was ever intended as a place of worship. Instead, the great hall was surprisingly empty. The first thing that caught her eye was the symbol engraved into the center of the ground—the mark of Aurialis, identical to the one on the door. It became the focal point of the room, shimmering gold under the light emanating from a dome in the roof that allowed the eternal sun to penetrate a perfect circle.

The walls were lined with rows of sunken alcoves, each holding various old books and artifacts. Marlowe found herself at home with the treasure trove of knowledge, already scanning the pages of a thick volume. A deep frown creased her perfect skin. Luckily, no threats were triggered in her boldness to tamper with the long-forgotten items.

Despite its abandonment, the temple didn't choke Faythe's lungs with dust or sting her nose with damp stone rot. The air was surprisingly clear and bright. She breathed deeply to calm her racing heart and allowed herself to admire the beauty of it now it was clear no foul creatures or deathly traps lay inside. Though the latter still kept her slightly vigilant. Nothing was certain with ancient magickal dwellings.

Spying a podium past the circle of light, Faythe stalked for it. As she stepped over Aurialis's crest, Marlowe called out.

"Wait!"

Faythe halted on command, bringing her sword up in a spike of fear. But when she did, what startled her was the laser beam of light that shot out from the pommel—from the *Riscillius.* Marlowe stared at it wide-eyed too, an indication her friend didn't hold the answers this time. Faythe's eyes followed the line of white light, but it struck nothing except the gray stone of the wall near the exit. When she moved her sword, the beam moved with it, always channeling through The Looking Glass.

Then she saw it.

Right above the stone doors, she spotted a protruding sculpture in the shape of an eye. And within it...a stone identical to the one she held.

She didn't need Marlowe to conclude the obvious. Without overthinking it, Faythe took a firm stance and braced Lumarias in both palms, blade pointing to the ground. The laser wavered slightly, and she gripped the hilt tighter to steady her trembling hands. She didn't look to Marlowe again, and the blacksmith made no call to stop her as she began to guide the light to connect it to the crystal above. She tuned in to the sound of her own heartbeat, cast out all thoughts of reservation, and then, when the light met its destination...

All went blindingly white.

Marlowe no longer stood beside her as she was encased in an impenetrable veil of the brightest white light. She dropped her hands, keeping her blade poised, and twisted to look for any sign of the grim stone walls that were around her a second ago. She looked to the floor, relieved when it confirmed she was indeed still inside the temple. The symbol of Aurialis remained under her feet, now glowing brightly.

She called out to Marlowe, but her name only echoed off the phantom walls, and her panic surged. She was about to reach out and touch the white sheet that surrounded her when a voice spoke.

"Hello, Faythe."

She whirled to meet a tall, slender woman. Only, she wasn't fully there. The figure appeared slightly opaque and glowed around the edges. Despite this, Faythe's breath left her as she stared at the ethereal beauty. Her hair was moon-white and poker-straight down her long, slim face. A silver ornate band adorned the top of her head, over her forehead, and she wore a gown of layered, flowing white.

"Who are you?" Faythe managed to get out, though her throat had turned paper-dry.

"My name is Aurialis. Your people call me the Spirit of Life and Goddess of the Sun," she answered, her voice like a melody.

Faythe's face blanched. She was convinced the form in front of her was nothing but a mind trick triggered by the stones.

"We don't have long. The veil can only be opened for a few minutes at a time," Aurialis continued softly.

"How do you know my name?"

"I have been watching you and your companions for a long time. Nothing is chance; nothing is coincidence. Your destiny has led you here, and you must trust your instincts and the people around you to guide you."

Faythe shook her head. "I think you're mistaken—" Her objection was interrupted as the Spirit continued.

"No, Heir of Marvellas. You are exactly where you are meant to be."

"Why do you call me that?" she snapped. It was not the first time she had heard the name in these woods.

"Because it is what you are, golden-eyed child. Your power is what the land has been waiting for."

Faythe's eyes narrowed. "What do you know of my *power?*"

"Those with abilities of the mind among the fae are bloodline-blessed by Marvellas, the Spirit of Souls, from her time as a Spirit of your world. When she joined you, her direct human descendants also inherited powerful forms of her gift," she explained, her tone and expression unchanging. The Spirit's eyes were the lightest shade of blue, almost white, and Faythe's gold eyes were transfixed.

Faythe could almost laugh at the absurdity of the story, but it didn't feel appropriate. Instead, she gathered herself enough to say, "My mother?"

"Also a descendant of Marvellas. She thought she could be the one to fulfil the prophecy, but she did not have the same power as you, Faythe. I have waited centuries for you."

Faythe felt sick. Her mother had known about all this? The watch, the temple, their abilities…

"Did she know…about me?" She wasn't sure she could handle the answer.

"Yes. And she tried to take your place, but it could never be."

Faythe breathed sharp air. "She was here?"

"She knew of a prophecy—that one conceived from both a bloodline-blessed and direct descendant of Marvellas would hold enough power in their blood to wield the Tripartite Ruin and rid Ungardia of the evil that grows. She came to me when she learned of your conception."

Her head pounded trying to take in the crushing new revelation. "My father?" she asked in barely more than a whisper.

"A bloodline-blessed."

Which only confirmed one other thing that brought the world down on Faythe. Her father was a Nightwalker—and a fae.

"I think you have it wrong. I can't be—"

"I don't have much longer, Faythe. This is the only way I can speak to you directly for now, but I still have ways of communicating with your world. It is not by chance you come to me tonight. I have been working through your companion to help guide you here when the time was right."

Dawning flooded over Faythe. "Marlowe?"

The Spirit raised her chin, and Faythe braced herself for what she was about to be told.

"She is an oracle. She has the gift of foresight through the Spirits. She is your knowledge."

The word repeated over and over in Faythe's mind, and she swayed with the weight of it. *Oracle.* She didn't believe such a thing existed—not in this realm, and certainly not in the form of a harmless, beautifully natured *human.* Was anything legend anymore? Or had every inconceivable myth once derived from some distorted truth? Faythe herself was living proof of the defied odds, and Marlowe...

Gods above.

"The Riscillius was cast into your sword by Marlowe with my influence," Aurialis explained. "Long ago, your mother sold the stone when I told her what you were destined for, hoping you would never come to find me. What she didn't know was that The Looking Glass would sit idle in the blacksmiths until a curious young woman would stumble upon it in her father's workshop. One who would cross your path and forge a great bond. When you learned of your ability, it was time to set the rest in motion. The making of your blade was not the first encounter between your two friends."

Faythe gasped at the knowledge Jakon was involved too. This couldn't be true...

"Their paths briefly crossed before, and in friendship, Marlowe offered Jakon a price that would allow him to afford the weapon. Lumarias—*The Key.* Even the oracle remains in the dark about the extent of her ability, but in time, she will understand. As will you, Faythe."

The world shifted from under her. Faythe fell to her knees, her sword clattering to the ground, unable to trust she wouldn't pass out from standing. Her thoughts screamed louder than any words, the tornado of emotion at the revelation about herself and her female companion threatening to shatter her completely.

"I am no one," she whispered.

"You are the last hope."

"Hope for what?" she snapped a little nastier than intended.

The Spirit remained impassive. "There is much for you to discover, but you are on the right path. You have already befriended knowledge, courage, and wisdom… Resilience, strength, light, and darkness will find you soon, and together with your power, you will see the world righted." Aurialis started to fade, and Faythe shot to her feet.

"Wait! You've left me with more questions than answers," she called.

"We have no more time right now, but we will see each other again soon. The stones require twenty-eight suns to charge and be strong enough to pierce the veil. Do not be fearful, Faythe, and be wary of colorless eyes."

With those last words, the Spirit Aurialis faded completely.

Faythe remained in the circle of light a moment longer until, suddenly, it dropped, and she had to blink rapidly as her eyes stung at the sudden dullness. She met Marlowe's ocean-blue orbs, and they both stood, silently staring at each other in bewilderment.

The blacksmith, the timid bookworm, her closest female companion…*an oracle.* Faythe didn't know what Marlowe already knew about herself—whether she knew the term for her gift that put so many things into clarity—but it was time for Faythe to reveal her own secrets to her.

Or, more importantly, to find out what the blacksmith already knew.

CHAPTER 38

NEITHER WOMAN SPOKE as they sat on the stone steps of the temple. Faythe tuned in to the serenity of the woodland around them to organize her thoughts, dizzy with where to start on her storm of questions and explanations. The silence also allowed her to calm the raging emotions that put her on the edge of eruption. Though she feared her composure would be short-lived when the inevitable conversation with the blacksmith would lash her with harsh truths and inconceivable answers.

The temple had sealed itself once again. The marks Marlowe drew had indeed faded away and erased themselves from memory.

All this time, her friend had been cradling her own unexplainable ability… Above everything else, Faythe felt *guilty* for being too consumed by her own problems to see that Marlowe too was suffering in silence, unaware of what her knowledge and foresight truly meant.

Marlowe dared to speak first. "You saw Aurialis, didn't you?" It was a statement rather than a question; Faythe didn't need to confirm what the blacksmith already knew. Her blue eyes bore into her gold ones, but she didn't balk at their intensity.

"You knew I would come here tonight." Faythe didn't leave the fact open to denial.

Marlowe looked away from her then and wrung her hands together nervously. Faythe kept her focus on steadying her heart rate, which had picked up an uneven tempo in anticipation of the difficult conversation ahead.

"I've known a lot of things," Marlowe began quietly. "Some things, I have no explanation for. I see visions—mostly in my dreams, but sometimes in the day too. I can't always be sure what they mean until events happen that put them into context and I know exactly what to expect next." Her face crinkled in deep concentration as she tried to verbalize that which she couldn't make full sense of yet.

"Do you know what you are?" Faythe asked in little more than a whisper.

Marlowe turned to look at her and gave a helpless shake of her head in response. The terrified glint in her eye cracked Faythe's heart. She had the answer to the blacksmith's burning question. Aurialis had told her, and she felt grateful to be the one to relieve her of the most terrifying feeling of all...

Not knowing your own self.

Faythe was all too familiar with the once overwhelming daunting notion. She had found solace and guidance in the form of a fae guard. In the form of Nik.

She took her friend's hand, and Marlowe's shoulders loosened slightly as she flashed a weak smile. "Your knowledge far surpasses the books you read." Faythe huffed a laugh in awe as she saw Marlowe in a whole new perspective. "You have a gift, and I can't believe I'm about to say this, but Aurialis told me..." Faythe paused to take a deep breath, and the blacksmith's hand tightened in her grip, her eyes widening a fraction. "She told me...you're an oracle, Marlowe. As insane as it sounds, I'm not surprised by the concept —not with you."

The blacksmith was quietly stunned. Mouth popping open, she

averted her gaze from Faythe as she mulled over the revelation. She didn't look horrified or fearful or worried. Rather, she looked...*content*. Faythe could almost see the internal cogs at work as Marlowe pieced together loose ends to explain her visions. She could only imagine how frustrating it must be for her friend to see so much, *know* so much, and not be able to make any sense of it.

Finally, the blacksmith inhaled a long breath, straightening as she let it out through her nose. Her face brightened in *liberation* at the light shed on her gift; the *purpose* she now had for it.

"I think a part of me always knew I was different, yet I didn't want to believe it. I've read many, many things—myths, legends, histories—but I could never comprehend that any of it might apply to *me*. I'm just... I'm just..."

"Incredible," Faythe finished for her, beaming in admiration.

Marlowe gave a timid smile, but then a sad frown creased her forehead. "I haven't been entirely truthful with you, Faythe. I knew about the Riscillius—what it really was—from the moment I translated its mundane name, The Looking Glass. And I knew exactly where it was. I *cast* it into your sword, though I didn't know at the time what it would come to be used for. I didn't know about *you.*" Marlowe fidgeted with the folds of her tunic, still unable to meet her eye as she told the story.

Faythe stayed silent, absorbing every word.

"Then, after that day you came to me at the compound, the visions started to get more frequent. But they came in riddles." Marlowe nodded her head to where Lumarias lay across the step below them. "I cast the marks of the three Spirits into that sword before I even knew you would be its wielder. Then, when we met... I can't explain it, Faythe, but I knew it was important you learned about the Spirits. You needed to *believe.*"

"Why didn't you tell me?" She couldn't hide the hurt in her voice as it cracked slightly.

A pained look flashed across the ocean of Marlowe's eyes. "It wasn't for me to tell you; only to guide you. As I've said, everything has an order, and there are far bigger fates at stake than just ours. I can only interpret the visions and offer guidance in the right direction. I'm sorry I lied to you. I'm sorry I kept it from you, everything I truly knew, but I hope you can forgive me...and trust me." The blacksmith went rigid under her touch, bracing for Faythe's possible rejection.

Faythe felt the need to squeeze her hand in reassurance and consolation but didn't respond with words to confirm *nothing* could make her turn her back on her. Something was burning a hole through her chest that she had to get out first.

"Do you know...do you know about...about my—?"

"Your abilities?" Marlowe said, and Faythe recoiled in wide-eyed shock. Before she could say anything, the blacksmith continued. "Not at first. Not for a long time, actually. Then one day, I felt compelled to read an ancient text about prophecies and mythical abilities. It was fascinating, but I thought nothing more of it. Then a few days went by, and you showed up at the compound...asking about the one thing I couldn't get off my mind: the Nightwalkers' *higher* power. That was when it clicked. I'd once read a story about the Heirs of Marvellas—the *gold-eyed children.* Humans with a unique talent: control of the mind, both conscious and unconscious." Marlowe's eyes twinkled in disbelief, and Faythe shifted nervously. *"By the Spirits,* Faythe. I couldn't believe it at first. It's still hard to wrap my head around. You're a miracle."

Her cheeks flushed crimson, and she had to avert her eyes. "At least I'm not the only one. I knew you were a lover of books and wonders, Marlowe, but you had to blow all expectations out of the water and be an *oracle?* It's a tad overdramatic, don't you think?"

Marlowe laughed—a genuine, humble laugh that lifted the heavy weight in the air that threatened to suffocate Faythe if they stayed so somber. It elated her to see the wide grin on the blacksmith's face, and she knew they didn't need verbal acceptances then; their souls were fused. Faythe could see it now clearer than ever. They'd both defied the odds to exist. It was a relief Marlowe already knew about her abilities. Faythe didn't feel like such a freak of nature. She would find a way to tell Jakon about them too—about both of them. After everything he had gone through, everything he had sacrificed for them, he deserved to know.

One final question battered her mind restlessly, almost painfully, as she fought against forming the words. She didn't know if she could handle the answer or even *want* to know it. But the only other person who might possibly be able to give it to her—other than Aurialis—was Marlowe with her gift.

When the silence settled, she lost the fight and blurted, "Do you know who my father is?"

Marlowe gave her a grim look. Faythe's blood pounded in her ears as if trying to block her from hearing the blacksmith's response. When her friend shook her head, Faythe's stomach dropped. She couldn't be sure what was more crippling: the disappointment, or the relief. A part of her longed to discover her true heritage; her *fae* heritage. But an even bigger part, she realized, wanted to remain blissfully ignorant for a while longer.

Marlowe spoke. "I don't know who he is, but I do believe it's not yet the time for you to find out. You have to trust in the order."

Screw the dammed order!

It suddenly made her anger boil that perhaps nothing was in her control anymore. It twisted her gut to feel like she wasn't dealing the cards in her own life. She may be an Heir of Marvellas, whatever that truly meant, but she also felt the tether to another ethereal being—to Aurialis. She had tied herself to the very roots of this woodland in her desperation to gain the yucolites and save her friend. It had been a trap, and she now felt in a tug-of-war between two all-powerful beings.

"I need to gain access to the castle," Faythe said, her tone turning dark.

Marlowe's brow furrowed.

She raised her chin in a flare of determination, staring out over the vibrant, glittering woodland. Despite its beauty, she was intent on freeing her soul from its prison.

"I made a bargain to get the yucolites that saved Jakon. I need to return Aurialis's ruin to her temple…and it's within the castle." She dared a look at her friend, though she didn't seem at all surprised by the foolhardy errand. Faythe's brow relaxed and rose in realization. "But you already know that, don't you?"

Marlowe smiled sheepishly. "I knew your path would lead you to the royal household. That is all," she admitted.

Faythe huffed a laugh. Her friend would always be one step ahead of them all, solving conflicts that were yet to arise.

"There's one person we both know who is cunning enough to know of a route in. Who happens to work for a high household that has unsavory dealings with the fae beyond the wall?"

A light switched on, and Faythe slowly turned her head away, reluctantly grumbling, "Ferris Archer."

"My girlfriend is a *what?* And my best friend… *Gods above.*"

Perhaps it wasn't the best idea to open up to Jakon while he was still in recovery. Sitting across the table from the two women, he looked even paler than he did in death. But he had been insistent, and they didn't want to delay the inevitable any longer.

Faythe's thigh hurt from gripping it so tight in her nerves, anxious about Jakon's reaction to the unveiling of her ability—then of Marlowe's. The double dose of shock made his emotions too hard to read. Faythe felt as if she were teetering on the edge of a cliff, waiting for confirmation he didn't think of her any differently, didn't hate her for keeping it from him, and didn't fear her for what she was.

It was selfish of her to only think of herself in the painfully tense wait, but Marlowe being an oracle with the gift of foresight was far less intrusive and deadly compared to what dwelled under her own skin.

"So you really went all this time without realizing what you were?" Jakon asked at last, looking directly at her. She supposed, above Marlowe's gift, it was even harder for him to believe the woman he had spent a decade living with had turned out to harbor such a lethal ability. She could only imagine the shock of it. But he remained curious, and it was a relief he wasn't displaying any distaste or horror toward her.

She shook her head sheepishly. "Once Nik explained it, you can imagine my reaction. It didn't make sense, but at the same time…it did."

Jakon shifted, his face turning defensive, and she knew exactly what triggered it before he spoke. "So you and this *fae guard…*" He trailed off with a hint of wariness.

Faythe sighed. "His name is Nik. And I didn't intend for anything to happen between us, but it did." Her eyes turned pleading. "I don't expect you to like it, but it's my choice."

His face softened, and he nodded. "Whatever makes you happy, Faythe. But he should know, fae or not…I'll kick his ass if he hurts you."

Faythe stifled a laugh at the ridiculous image of Jakon and Nik having it out with each other on a sparring field. She had no doubt Nik would be the victor, but with Jakon's courage and determination, it would at least be worthy entertainment.

"Have you ever…you know, read my mind?" he asked with a wince.

Faythe's face fell. "Once," she admitted, recalling the day she infringed upon both their thoughts. "When I came home late a couple of weeks ago… What you said about me being selfish, Jak— I only wanted to know if you truly meant it. So I looked into both of you, only on the surface." A sad look passed his face. "But never again since. I won't ever do it without your permission, I promise," she said firmly.

Both friends gave her a grateful nod though she didn't feel deserving of it.

"So you have complete control then? You don't just bounce around minds and hear things in passing?" Jakon queried further.

"I can hear things if they're projected loudly enough, when a person doesn't realize just how loud their thoughts are. But mostly, I have to sort of…reach in." She cringed at the notion.

Faythe went on to explain about mental barriers and how she got Nik to teach her how to protect her mind—from herself, but mostly from other Nightwalkers. She struggled to put her ability into comprehendible words and had to admit there was a lot she was still figuring out.

When they settled into silence, Faythe rose to her feet. "There's something I have to do," she said, going for her cloak.

"We'll come with you," Jakon responded immediately. He went to stand but winced, clutching his middle.

Faythe gave him a scolding look. "I don't think so." Then she looked down at Marlowe, offering an encouraging smile. "I think you two have a lot to talk about."

The blacksmith nodded in appreciation for the opportunity to explain what she knew of her oracle gift. She glanced at Jakon, and his face also smoothed out in realization of the time they needed alone as a couple.

"Where are you going?" he asked in concern. He had every reason to be anxious with the trauma of the thugs' ambush still fresh. Nik had assured her he'd take care of them, but she didn't have the stomach to ask what he meant by that. She'd told Jakon as much, but if the tables were turned, she'd be sick with worry too.

"I'm not putting you in any more danger than I already have. I'm going to tell Ferris I'm done."

CHAPTER 39

S TEPPING UP TO the large white house, Faythe felt confident
when she rapped on the door and took a step back. To her
relief, Ferris's mop of wavy red hair came into view, and he grinned
at her.

"How are the preparations for your big fight at the end of the
week?" he asked in greeting.

She didn't match his dark delight. "I'm out, Ferris."

His face fell instantly, and he stepped outside, closing the door
behind him. "What do you mean, *you're out?*" he hissed.

She didn't balk at his switch in tone. "I mean exactly what I
said." She went to turn on her heel, but he grabbed her elbow. Her
head snapped around to snarl at him.

"You can't back out now—not for this one," he said with a hint
of trepidation that alarmed her. In all her years of knowing him,
she had never seen him cower from anything. But right now, there
was genuine dread in his eyes.

"What have you done, Ferris?" she asked calmly, though her
heartbeat quickened in anticipation.

He let her arm go to run his hand through his rugged hair and
began a short pace. "I didn't *do* anything except what we agreed,"

he shot defensively. "But the fae—he's expecting you, and it's *my* head if you don't show," he said through his teeth.

Her frown deepened. "Just tell them I'm no longer interested."

"Did you not hear me?" He halted in front of her, his face grave as he said, "It's not about the money, the glory, or any of that anymore. If you don't show, he said he would *kill* me."

She paled. "It's just a stupid fear tactic—"

"No, Faythe," he interjected. "He was *deadly* serious. He's one of them—you know he can get away with it."

Horror clung to her like a frozen blanket. "I was attacked last night, Ferris. Jakon was stabbed by one of those vengeful monsters I fought in The Cave, and he almost *died* because of it! Do you understand? I won't risk his safety again for others' *entertainment,*" she tried to keep her voice low, conscious of the occupants in the household behind them.

Now it was Ferris who blanched chalk-white. "I—I didn't know…"

Faythe shook her head in disbelief, turning to walk away again.

"You don't have to win! Just be fast enough to dodge until he can get you to submit," he said desperately.

She huffed a humorless laugh. "Is that all? And what if he decides he wants to *kill* me?" Faythe wanted to shout and rage at him—it was his crazy plan to challenge a fae in the first place—but, frustratingly, she realized she couldn't. This was just as much her mess for being so foolishly naive to agree to it.

"I'll make sure there are men in place to intervene," he said, though even he knew it was little consolation.

She wanted to laugh in his face at the completely futile offer of protection. If a fae wanted it, she'd be dead before another man could take one step. Her hand was forced. It was either risk her life or forfeit Ferris's. While she didn't particularly hold the strongest love for him at the best of times, he was still a friend, and she'd be damned if she let anyone else get hurt when she had a chance to prevent it.

"If I save your ass now to die in that cave, you'd best believe I'll be seeing you in pits of the Netherworld when Jakon gets a hold of you."

"Don't I know it," he muttered.

She didn't plan to ask Ferris for his help in gaining access beyond the wall yet. Admittedly, she wanted to hold off just a little longer in fear of the daunting task. But it seemed like the perfect—and perhaps the only—opportunity she would get since he owed her for risking her life in The Cave.

"I need something in return," she blurted.

Ferris cocked an eyebrow, folding his arms inquisitively. "Whatever you need, it's yours."

She exhaled a long breath, closing her eyes for a moment, not quite believing she was about to ask such a foolish request. "I need a route into the inner city...then to the castle," she got out quickly. When Ferris didn't immediately respond, she squinted one eye open to check his reaction. It remained the same: unflinching, deliberating.

"When?" he asked at last.

Relieved he wasn't reprimanding her for the obvious recklessness of such a plan, she straightened. "Soon," was all she answered. She had to get through this fight first and couldn't let the thought of her impending fool's mission distract her.

Unless I die in that cave. Then Aurialis will be free to torment my soul with my failure for eternity in those woods.

"You may want to listen carefully then. It will not be an easy task."

No—nothing ever was. But it had never stopped her from trying before. She tuned in carefully to Ferris's instruction, all the while trying to tame her leaping heart, which was close to eruption now.

CHAPTER 40

"ABSOLUTELY NO WAY in rutting *damn!*"

Though she expected Jakon to blow up at the news of her fight with the fae, Faythe winced at the outburst. "They threatened his life—I have to at least *try,*" she argued.

Jakon's eyes were livid, and she would be lying if she said it didn't scare her a little. "Better his life than yours," he growled.

She gave him a flat look. "I'm not going to try to win. I only have to be fast enough to dodge and let the fae beat me—safely," she added quickly.

He scoffed. "You're good in combat, Faythe, I'll give you that, but you're not *that* good to outrun a *fae!*"

"You're right—no mortal is. But you forget I have other… advantages," she countered with a cunning smile.

He caught on to her meaning but shook his head. "They're still too quick."

Faythe explained how she had been training with Nik to reach in and glean her opponents' maneuvers before they physically made them, and how she'd succeed to some extent against the fae guard. Surprisingly, Jakon looked impressed, and his anger even cooled—slightly.

"That damned rutting *bastard*. I swear, when I next see him—"

"You'll do nothing," Faythe cut in. "I agreed to it. If I can just get past this one last fight, I promise there will be no more." She held his stare, and she could see he was fighting against the will to protest further. But he conceded with a reluctant nod.

Marlowe had gone back to her cottage for the night after much persuasion from Jakon that he was almost in full health and didn't need coddling. Her two friends had worked over everything, and it was an immense consolation to know nothing had changed between them because of what Marlowe was. Jakon always had a heart of gold, and Faythe felt horribly guilty she ever doubted his acceptance of either of them.

She was relieved when the blacksmith hesitantly agreed to stay at home for the night. Faythe's cot was much too small for the two women to get a comfortable sleep, and she had been dealing with a stiff neck and back all day from the previous night. It was also liberating that Faythe could tell Jakon about her plans to meet with Nik. Although she didn't need to sneak out anymore, Nik still insisted they meet after midnight. She didn't press the reasons why but hated the uneasy feeling he wasn't being entirely open about his assignments in the guard beyond the wall. He still never spoke of it.

She quickly dismissed any thoughts of suspicion. He had given her no reason to be paranoid or distrust him. She swallowed the feelings of caution and passed them off as nerves for what was blooming between them. She had yet to fully understand what it was.

Jakon retired for the night after a long lecture on being safe and careful, throwing in a few threats to Nik should anything happen to her. Faythe rolled her eyes the whole time at his overprotective nonsense—the irritating downside to him knowing everything.

She envied his soft snoring she could hear from the kitchen, where she stood cloaked and ready to leave. She was mentally exhausted from the beating of emotions she'd taken after her confession to Jakon and confrontation with Ferris, both piled on top of an abundance of new information she'd received from a Spirit she'd long believed to be a myth. Faythe was surprised she was still sane, and she craved a long, restful sleep to keep it that way.

But she longed even more to see Nik, she realized, and it made her giddy with excitement. She forced everything else she had to deal with to the back of her mind. She had to find a way to ask him if he'd agree to meet her every night this week for practice. She only had five nights left before she would face off with a fae opponent in The Cave, and she needed every second of learning to tune in to her abilities if she were to even stand a chance of not being annihilated. She only hoped she wouldn't have to tell him exactly *why* she was so eager to exercise her mind so much. She feared his reaction would be far worse than Jakon's.

When the hands of her watch hit midnight, she left the cottage quietly to not disturb her friend and made off down the streets, stealthy under the cover of the shadows. In the woods, she made out Nik's figure with his back to her as the clearing drew close, and her heart leapt with a thrill at the sight of him. He turned to her when she emerged past the tree line, and his greeting smile was enough to make her breathless. He took a few steps forward to meet her, and they stopped within arm's reach.

"How are your friends?" he asked quietly, his emerald eyes sparkling as he looked down at her.

"I don't think I want to talk about them right now," she said, taking the last step to close the space between their bodies. Her hands reached up, fingers curling in the back of his hair, as she pushed up on her toes to kiss him. She could never get enough of how it made her feel; how being *close* to him sent her into a whole new world of blissful freedom from any of her fears or worries. He kissed her back fiercely, and she felt the longing in him too.

When they broke apart, neither stepped back. Nik traced his fingers along the side of her face, and she leaned into the touch.

"I've been waiting quite a while to do this," he mumbled softly.

Her eyes bore into his, telling him she had long desired it too.

She kissed his palm at her cheek and then abruptly stepped back, out of his hold. At his look of protest, she chuckled in amusement.

"As much as I'd love to do that all night, I need your help."

He didn't answer, instead folding his arms and tilting his head inquisitively.

She nervously shifted her weight. "I need to work on my mind abilities in combat. Will you go back to being my test subject?"

He curved an eyebrow. "I'm sure we could dedicate a couple of nights to—"

"Every night?" she blurted before she could stop herself. His face fell into a frown, and she cursed inwardly. "I mean, the sooner I get acquainted with what I already know I can do, the better I can get at exploring other things," she recovered quickly.

Faythe knew she'd ruined it when his eyes narrowed a fraction.

"Why so eager for it to be in combat?" he questioned accusingly.

She cursed herself again and wracked her brain for an excuse, but nothing came that would withhold the inevitable reveal of her foolish mission.

His frown deepened at her floundering silence. "What aren't you telling me?" A look of hurt crossed his eyes—that she would attempt to hide something from him.

She sighed in defeat. "Promise me you won't blow up about it?"

He gave her a look that said he could make no such guarantee.

"Promise me," she repeated, a plea in her voice.

His only reply was a small nod, and she scowled at him. Taking a deep breath, she rambled through the deal with Ferris and why she couldn't back out of it. When she finished, she dared to look at him through one eye. His face was a mask of calm, dark rage, and it shook her far more than Jakon's outburst.

"You are *not* going to that fight," he said in a lethal quiet that would send most men running.

"Didn't you hear? I don't have a choice—"

He was a foot in front of her in an instant, his green eyes much darker than they were moments before. They burned holes straight through her.

"I don't think you quite understand what you've naïvely signed yourself up for. It'll be your death warrant, Faythe. Win or lose."

"I can do this," she argued, her own anger simmering. She was sick of everyone believing they knew what was best for her and what she was capable of. Sick of being treated like some delicate *girl* to be protected.

His eyes flashed. "The fae don't go easy. They don't give in— especially not to a *human*. They won't hesitate to kill you given the opportunity, and you're offering yourself on a damned silver platter." He seethed, walking away.

"If you won't help me, I'll damn well teach myself. But you can't stop me."

He whirled back around, and there was nothing kind in his face at her defiance. They stared off for a moment, neither backing down, until Nik sucked in a long breath and ran a hand over his face.

"Your heroism is not admirable; it's reckless," he said, but she didn't respond to the remark. He sighed. "If you can't best me by the time this fight comes around, I don't care if I have to tie you to a gods-damned tree—you will *not* be going."

A compromise, she supposed, and a challenge.

She straightened, a smile tugging at her lips. "Deal."

His face fell, and she knew he was struggling internally not to screw the deal and be sure she never made it back to The Cave regardless. She knew he could by brute force alone, so it was a small relief when he agreed to at least give her a chance to prove herself.

"This friend of yours means nothing to me, but you..." He trailed off as if unable to finish the sentence. He didn't have to say anything more; his face was laced with fear that something could happen to her down there. She was as fragile as an insect compared to him.

She closed the distance between them and held a hand to his face. "I know," was all she said, and he loosened under her touch. Faythe kissed him once—in promise that she would walk out of that cave alive. Though she knew it was not a promise entirely in her power to make, it was all she could do to curb his worry.

She stepped back and walked a few paces away. Drawing her sword, she turned to him with a goading smile.

"Shall we begin?"

His answering look was weak, but Nik obliged, unsheathing the blade at his side and coming to stand off against her.

Her eyes locked on his. "As always, don't hold back."

CHAPTER 41

"ARE YOU EVEN *trying?*"
Faythe ducked as she narrowly missed yet another of Nik's inhumanly fast swipes. Without giving her a second to respond, she saw his next move and jumped before he could knock her feet out from under her. She wanted to scowl, but she knew better than to listen to his taunts by now. He had been using them as a distraction tactic, and it had taken her a while to catch on before she started to block his words out completely.

"Honestly, I think you should just give up," he drawled, bored and not in the slightest bit out of breath. But he didn't stop, or even slow for that matter, as she parried against his brutal onslaught of attacks.

She was sweating and had not once broken eye contact, using all her mental focus to foresee his next anticipated move. It was the last night they had before her fight tomorrow, and she had gotten better. A lot better. But it still took an incredible physical and mental toll on her, and she took every moment she could get when she wasn't training to fall into a dark, restful sleep and regain her strength.

The thoughts had started to come to her quicker, and now, she was able to dodge more swiftly through practice. She found that although she could remain in his mind without maintaining eye contact, the information came a lot quicker if she held it. Nik had opened his mind enough to let her in for those immediate thoughts only. She didn't dare try to go beyond, though she was sure he would be guarded in case she tried anyway.

No one liked to have their personal thoughts raided, and it wasn't the way she wanted to find out more about him.

After a couple more dodges and clashing swords, she twisted away from his next move before he made it and held the point of her sword to his back. She let out a breathy laugh of victory and began to lower her blade, but the moment she let her guard down, he twirled, taking her feet out from under her. In the same breath, Nik held her as they twisted so she fell on top of him instead of the hard ground. It wasn't much better; he was almost as solid as stone, and the air was knocked from her despite his chivalry.

He rumbled in laughter beneath her as she scowled, rolling off him to lie on the ground.

"You don't take your mind off him for one second, not even once it's over. You keep focused until you can clear the ring." His voice dropped into stern command. "Even if you think you can, you don't win. It will only put a much deadlier target on your back." He propped himself up and leaned sideways so he half-hovered over her. He looked into her eyes, and her guilt rose at the pain on his face.

She reached out to touch it. "I'm going to be okay, Nik," she assured him with all the confidence she could muster.

It was hard to comfort those around her when she had her own fears and doubts about how she would fare in The Cave. But she would wear the mask of bravery and resilience for her friends and for Nik.

He leaned down and brushed his lips against hers before kissing her fully. Slowly and tenderly at first, but then she felt his tongue in silent invitation to deepen the kiss. Her mouth opened, and he didn't hesitate to heat the moment between them.

They had barely been able to keep their hands off each other over the course of the week. They'd spent every night together, but Faythe always held back the full extent of her desire that pulsed every time she was near him. She couldn't allow herself to get too distracted from her task.

But now, with the threat of tomorrow looming and her days not promised, she felt the overwhelming urge to be close to him and show him just how much he mattered to her.

She ran her hands through his hair, savoring the feel of the silk entwined with her fingertips, and arched her back in her longing to be closer. He moved, coming to hover over her completely between her legs, but while his body pressed against hers, he remained utterly weightless above her. Heat flushed her skin, awakening every sense and impulse, while his hands roamed over her waist and bare stomach where her shirt had lifted, leaving trails of fire everywhere his fingers caressed. A part of her screamed for his hand to travel higher—or lower. Her hands left his hair to feel the powerful contours of his back, and to her delight, she found his shirt untucked. When her fingers brushed the wonderfully smooth skin around his waist, he buckled slightly, the movement enough to frenzy the lust at her core.

His mouth left hers. She was about to cry in protest, but his lips found her neck, and she sucked a sharp breath, tilting her head back in invitation. She felt him smile against her throat as he trailed teasingly downward. The sensation filled her with new waves of pleasure.

"Nik," she breathed.

He stiffened at the sound, and his eyes met hers with a flash of hunger and desire.

She was breathless, but the pause was enough for her to gather her thoughts. She recoiled slightly in realization of what her lust-clouded mind wanted from him, right there on the woodland floor.

He must have seen the hesitation in her eyes as he gave her an understanding smile. Kissing her mouth once more, he twisted so he was back to leaning on his side next to her.

Her cheeks heated. "I don't want to go too fast," she admitted.

He brushed a stray piece of hair from her face and leaned in to kiss her again, his breath caressing her neck as he spoke. "We can take all the time we want." He left one last whisper of a kiss on her collarbone, and it would have set her off again if he didn't immediately jump to his feet afterward, leaving her dazed and frustrated, still lying on the grass.

"That's enough rest," Nik called from his position behind her.

She groaned and didn't move. "We've been at it for hours already!" she complained.

"And another one might just be the difference between you walking out of that cave with one arm or two."

Her lips thinned. She was about to retort back when rough hands grabbed hers, hauling her to her feet. She never even heard him approach, and the sudden movement made her head spin, but Nik only grinned wickedly.

She narrowed her eyes. "Stupid fae prick," she grumbled under her breath.

His smile widened in response as he held her sword out to her. She took it begrudgingly, and he didn't give her even a minute to brace herself before he was making her retreat through a series of ruthless attacks that sent the *clank* of joining steel echoing through the clearing once more.

Nik was relentless in his assaults over the next hour, and Faythe was more drained than she had been after any of their previous sessions. She knew it was because it was their last before tomorrow night and he was overcompensating to cram in what would likely have taken months for her to grasp. She wasn't perfect, and he had still managed to theoretically kill her on many occasions, which made Nik *very* wary about letting her go through with it. But she had also managed to best him a handful of times—or at least dodge long enough that she could concede in a safe position.

Like Nik had said, she wasn't out to win anyway, or it would most definitely be her head.

"I won't be able to be there tomorrow night," Nik said quietly.

Faythe's stomach dropped. "Why?"

They hadn't discussed it before, but he had been secretly watching her for every other match, so it disappointed her to know he wouldn't be there when it mattered most. If only because he was probably the only one capable of intervening on her behalf should things take a turn for the worse.

A conflicted expression flashed across his face, but it was gone when he looked at her. "I'm not supposed to be out of the city walls. If there are other fae there...I can't be seen," he said.

Faythe crossed her arms. "You've been beyond city walls before. You were on patrol at summer solstice," she argued.

A day that seemed like a lifetime ago. So much had changed. *She* had changed. Her life was completely different to the girl who had danced around bonfires on the solstice. Faythe didn't know if it made her sad or grateful. Her life before was safe—carefree, even —but it was also a lie that had held her back from discovering who she truly was.

"That was...an exception," he said carefully.

She knew there was something he was holding back from her, and she wanted to push. Maybe it was her nerves for the fight tomorrow or anger that he would abandon her when danger was imminent, but she realized how little she really knew about the fae guard she spent so much time with and had come to care deeply for.

"What do you really do behind those walls, Nik?"

A dark look flashed across his face so fast she could have missed it. He didn't reply.

She huffed a humorless laugh. "Right, of course. Not something you could share with a lowly *human.*" She sheathed her sword and grabbed her cloak, fastening it around herself and making to leave.

His hand caught her elbow. "Don't leave like this," he begged, his face desolate.

She whirled around to face him. His eyes were pleading, but she was too angry to feel bad for him. He knew everything about her and wouldn't share anything about himself. Perhaps he had a gag order from the king to not speak of his affairs in the city or the castle, but it still hurt that he didn't trust her enough. It would remain solely between them, whatever information he shared about his personal life.

"I have to rest to have all the strength I can for tomorrow. I guess I'll let you know how it pans out—or not, since it doesn't seem to be to your interest." She knew it was a low blow. He had been on edge all week and had to refrain from outright banning her from going. Yet she couldn't stop the nastiness that came from her.

His grip on her arm tightened slightly. "I won't be there, but I've made sure other guards will be. Whoever you fight tomorrow will not get the chance to seriously hurt you, certainly not kill you, before they have orders to intervene." His voice was low and stern.

Her brow furrowed. "Orders from who?"

His jaw twitched. "Let's just say, I have influence," he said in a way that told her the conversation was over.

She was wise enough to note it and gave him a small nod in understanding.

His face softened then, and he sighed, twisting her around fully and pulling her to him. She embraced him around the waist, inhaling his comforting scent when he wrapped his arms around her shoulders and rested his chin over her head. Just like that, all her negative feelings melted away.

"You mean a great deal to me now, Faythe. I won't let anyone harm you," he said, his words so hushed they tugged at her heart.

She pulled her head back to look him in the eye. "You mean a great deal to me too, Nik."

His hand held her chin as he kissed her one last time.

CHAPTER 42

D AYLIGHT FELL TO welcome twilight, and Faythe watched the hues of pink and orange diffuse the sky from her position on the rooftop. It was serene and could almost distract her from the fight of her life that would take place in just a few hours.

She looked all the way out, past the harbor and over the unwavering line of the horizon, where the water shimmered confidently under the last fleeting rays of the bold descending sun. The air was clear and the streets below silent as the town settled before dusk chased away the last drops of the day.

She was already dressed in her black suit, which had been mended by Marlowe the day after her last appearance in The Cave. Her cloak billowed behind her slightly in the cool night breeze, but she never registered the cold. She had told Jakon she wanted a moment alone and came up here in the hope the tranquil air would help to sedate her nerves. And it did, to an extent, while she reflected on everything she had learned with Nik and his assurance the fight could not get out of hand thanks to his friends in the guard.

Now she'd had time to calm, she was glad Nik would not be there. She would likely take a beating of some sort, and she knew firsthand the pain of seeing a close companion hurt. If it were the other way around... *Gods,* she wouldn't be of much help, but she would damn well *try* to intervene. Against man, against fae, against the damned Spirits if need be—she would fight for those she loved.

With a final breath, Faythe left the rooftop.

"Are you *sure* you have everything you need?" Jakon fussed for the third time.

Faythe rolled her eyes and made a show of patting herself to check. Though, aside from her clothing, all she had was Lumarias sheathed to her back.

"Armed and ready." She saluted him in an attempt at light humor. He was growing more antsy by the minute, and it was seriously damaging the calm Faythe had been reeling herself into for the past few hours.

He was about to scold her when Marlowe walked through the front door of the hut. As much as she had tried to persuade them to stay home, both her friends were firm on the fact they were going to attend tonight. Ferris was going to meet them here to get Jakon and Marlowe in, while Faythe would arrive alone a short while later. She didn't want to be seen entering with them as the "Gold-Eyed Shadow" in case anyone looked closely enough to make the connection.

"I made this for you," Marlowe said as she approached Faythe, holding something in her palms. When she removed the small piece of cloth concealing the item, Faythe gasped at the beautiful jeweled long dagger beneath. "For good luck." Marlowe smiled weakly.

Faythe was deeply humbled by the kind gesture and took the dagger from her, marveling at it for a moment before embracing her friend tightly. "I love it. Thank you. It means a lot," she said in all sincerity. She would have a piece from both of them on her

tonight, and that symbol alone lit a new fire of strength and determination within.

A moment later, a light rapping sounded at the door, signaling
the arrival of Ferris. She looked to her friends and straightened
with every ounce of mustered courage, more to ease their concerns
than in genuine confidence.

"Let's get this over with, shall we?"

Standing as the same immovable force, the guards on either side of
The Cave entrance didn't balk or hesitate to open the thick iron
doors as she swaggered toward them, concealed under her hood
and mask. She didn't let herself flinch either upon noticing the
crowd of people reached all the way to those doors. They parted
hastily when she approached.

The whole venue—if that was what it could be called—was
packed to full capacity, and as much as she tried to ignore it, she
would be lying if she said it didn't rattle her nerves. She was used to
large audiences, but *this?*

She weaved through them like a black wraith, and they
moved out of her way where there was small space to do so.
People turned to each other and whispered as she passed, but
she kept her eyes focused on getting to her usual entrance to the
pit. She couldn't see her friends in these masses and didn't
want to try looking.

When she got to the other side, Ferris was already waiting for
her, biting his fingers as he scanned the balconies. His eyes fell on
her, and he visibly relaxed as if he thought she might not actually
show up after all.

"How are you feeling?" he asked.

She gave him a dead look, not deigning to respond to his
ridiculous question.

He winced and nodded his understanding. "Well, they should

be ready any moment now you've arrived," he said quickly, taking her cloak like he always did.

She should have expected it, but for some reason, it unnerved her that her fae competitor was already in the same vicinity and had been waiting for *her.* She didn't dare scan the mobs to find out if they were watching her at this very moment. The place was packed mostly with humans, but she hadn't failed to notice the few pointed ears standing on the front line of the balcony. Humans left space around them, not bold enough to stand too close.

"One last time, Faythe. And thank you, truly. You're the bravest person I know," Ferris said, putting his hand on her shoulder.

If there weren't so many eyes on her, she would have embraced the bastard, if only as one last comfort before she went down there, and to show her appreciation at the comment.

"We bring you the fight of the decade!" the pit master bellowed from below.

Faythe stiffened, and Ferris noted her surge of nerves at the announcement. He braced his hands on both her shoulders and forced her to keep looking at him.

"It'll be over quick. You won't be harmed too badly. I've seen fae guards posted down below."

Faythe sagged in relief a little. Not that she doubted Nik's word, but it was reassuring to know they'd be so close and were already stationed down there.

"I introduce the notorious Gold-Eyed Shadow!"

The revelers roared at her mention, and she breathed consciously, willing her heart to slow as she did before every fight. Ferris muttered a brief, "Good luck," as she turned to walk down the stone stairs, right into the lion's den.

She descended with deliberate slowness, letting the jeering sounds of the crowd above fade, then tuned out completely with each step down she took. She plunged herself deep into the well of calm that would allow her to focus solely on her target and the sword she would wield. Faythe called on Nik's teachings, Jakon's courage, and Marlowe's confidence and set fire to the embers of her own determination to succeed. She closed her eyes, steadying her heart rate to still her trembling hands. By the time she reached the bottom, she'd opened them, completely embodying the ego of the Gold-Eyed Shadow one last time…

She didn't look up and risk her nerve, especially if she were to spot her undoubtedly anxious friends. Instead, she took in the familiar surroundings of gruesome, bloodstained stone walls and the entrance where her opponent would appear.

The pit master stood in the middle looking more shaken than usual. She supposed it had something to do with the presence of the three fae guards who were evenly spaced around the circular arena, each looking rather bored but standing straight with their hands over their swords should they be needed. She swallowed hard to moisten her paper-dry throat. Was her opposer *that* dangerous? She knew the fae were fast and strong, but even this seemed a little excessive for one being.

"And now, I present the challenger." The pit master's voice faltered a little as he paused, already taking a step toward his exit. "Captain Varis of the Royal Guard!"

Everything around Faythe stopped the moment she heard the words. She recoiled in cold horror when the captain emerged from the entrance, his face taunting in malice as he stared directly at her with his first steps into the ring. His wicked scar gleamed under the lights of the pit, making him look all the more terrifying.

She had to remember to breathe. She couldn't lose her valor now, or the fight would be over before it even started.

Then she recalled something about the captain Nik had warned her about so long ago. It was almost her undoing…

He's one of the king's most talented Nightwalkers. Don't ever underestimate him.

It shot a spear of ice-cold dread down her spine, threatening her sedated composure. All of her practice and training could be for nothing if he had mental barriers like Nik's. Her one advantage was her ability, and it was the only thing that stood between her and being able to last even one minute in this fight. Without it…

She didn't even allow herself to wreck her emotions with the thought.

It wasn't humiliation she was afraid of; it was the look in the captain's eye that told her he wasn't going to end it that quickly. No —he wanted to make her suffer, and no one would stop him since that wasn't against the rules. She was only protected against excessive brutality and a death strike, but she knew he'd be smart and would play it to look as if every hit he dealt her was fair game.

The pit master called for them to draw their weapons and take stance. She was running out of time, and as she unsheathed her blade, she held his black stare and gently pushed into his mind in case he could feel her.

She almost buckled in panic when she met a similar black barrier wall, but then…

Cracks!

There were gaps in his mental barrier, unlike Nik's. She could only assume that by some small mercy of the Spirits, Captain Varis hadn't reinforced his mental shields in the daytime—because he wouldn't expect to need to guard himself against someone like her. A slight relief, but she knew it would be twice as difficult to see his movements through the tight spaces in the wall.

The pit master had already retreated to the stairwell as the captain approached her with a predatory grin. Inside, she trembled violently like feeble pray, but her exterior embodied the laser-focused combatant she needed to be to make it out alive.

He began to circle with his blade angled, stalking her, and she kept her complete focus on him as she mirrored his movements. Before the announcement could be made for the fight to begin, she saw his intention to strike and spun to narrowly avoid the swing of his sword. He had no plans to wait for a formal invitation.

His eyes flashed at her unexpected swiftness, but he composed himself and sized her up again. She tracked him. She could see his movements, but not nearly as fast as she'd come to read them in Nik's open mind. She would have to make it work—at least long enough to give them a show and surrender herself.

His next attack flashed through her, and she brought her sword up to meet his in the nick of time. Her heart rose in her throat, and she hissed through clenched teeth, putting her whole weight into holding off his blade. He was too strong, however, and in her efforts, her concentration faltered. Varis pushed roughly, causing her to stumble back, and with the same breath, his fist connected with the side of her face.

Pain shot through her jaw. She slammed, palms splayed, against the ground with a loud smack. Her eyes blackened for a second before she pushed herself to her feet, swaying a little from the disorientation. A copper tang filled her mouth. Blood. She leaned forward, pulling the scarf down quickly to spit the blood that pooled on her lip. Adjusting her face cover again, her head snapped back up to him. Faythe's rage was immeasurable, and it threatened to blind her into recklessness rather than focus her into stealth. She took slow, concise breaths to reel in the all-consuming emotion.

The captain's eyes were wholly black and sparkled with sadistic pleasure at the sight of her blood. She rolled her shoulders back and focused on the dark orbs once again.

He lunged at her with an onslaught of attacks, which she danced around the ring in answer to, not raising her sword to meet his again. Her head throbbed with concentration to see each maneuver before he could land a blow, and when she faltered slightly, she was sent sprawling to the floor again from a punch to her stomach.

She gasped for breath on all fours at the force of it, but he was next to her again before she could regain any composure and kicked her stomach right were the last hit was. The pain was excruciating as she was thrown onto her back and her head ricocheted off the stone floor. She couldn't do it—couldn't last against the unhinged beast. Her anger diffused and welcomed despair. She wanted to dissolve into the hard ground beneath her. Was she underwater? The roars of the crowd were distant…distorted, and the lights blurred and dimmed.

I'm sorry, Jak. I'm sorry, Marlowe. I'm sorry, Nik. I tried.

"Get up," the wicked voice spat.

She couldn't. She was ready to succumb to the darkness that offered relief from the pain and failure. She wanted to sleep and drift away from all the roaring chaos of the crowd and the stabs that laced her abdomen and head. But then rough hands grabbed her, yanking her to her feet and forcing her to stare into depthless black holes.

"You call that a fight? I said, *get up!*" The captain seethed in her face. He let her go, and she was surprised when she stumbled back but remained upright, her sword still clutched with an iron grip in her hand. She looked down at it.

Lumarias. The Key. I will not cower.

She blinked a few times, and her vision focused. She had to keep going. Her body groaned in protest as she straightened, rolling back her shoulders and fixing her eyes on the captain again.

Pushing through the pain, she continued to deflect with her sword in both hands as their connecting steel sang together, slicing through the bustle of the audience above. She didn't let her blade meet his for long enough that he could use his strength against her again.

His blade caught her leg at one point, and she was forced to retreat when fire ripped up her thigh. Still, he stalked her with predatory slowness, relishing in her pain as he played with her. He didn't give her long to recover, and their swords crossed once again. She was fast—but he was faster, and his stamina never faltered in the slightest, whereas hers was on the verge of full depletion. He landed another sharp jab with his elbow to her side. Faythe was a mere second from missing it completely. While it winded her, she stood her ground.

After another round of quick parry, she failed to see his next move, and his fist connected with her sword hand, sending Lumarias flying from her grip. In the same breath, he lunged for her—the killing blow. Not even the fae standing close by would be fast enough to stop it.

Time slowed as she tracked the blade that promised her death rising above her head.

But the image of his intention flashed in her mind a second earlier than he acted. Right before he could bring his sword down fully, she took one step forward to meet him, pulling Marlowe's gifted dagger from her side.

Then everything went quiet.

He halted, his sword mere inches from her neck…as she held the point of her dagger under his chin.

A mutual defeat.

The crowd fell mute.

Her breathing was ragged, her pulse erratic. She held the captain's stare as his nostrils flared and his eyes turned wild. It should have been over, but she saw something snap in him.

He was so close she never stood a chance to react when he grabbed the wrist that held her dagger so hard she dropped it. He let go of his own blade as both his hands curled tightly around her throat, lifting her to her toes, and he leaned into her.

"You think I don't know who you are, *girl?*" he hissed in her ear.

Faythe choked against the viselike grip of his hands, which squeezed harder to restrict her airway.

"Captain Varis, the fight is won," she heard one of the guards call as they all took a step closer.

Faythe clawed at his hands that didn't loosen off at the warning. It would take minimal effort to crush her throat in a second.

"Who do you think sent those men after you? Foolish girl. You can hide everything but your eyes and that damned sword of yours," he spat. "Only a fool would believe a weak, pathetic *human* girl could best a man, and especially not a *fae.*"

"Captain Varis!" a guard called again in final warning.

She gasped for air as blackness started to cloud her vision.

"You're hiding something, *Faythe,* and I'm going to find out exactly what it is. You made the biggest mistake of your miserable life tonight." He released her with a forceful shove, and she collapsed to the ground, sputtering for air in agony under her mask. Varis crouched down to retrieve his sword and leaned in close again. "I'll be seeing you soon, Faythe, but maybe not in the way you think." His last words were a playful taunt before he sauntered out of the pit.

Faythe remained on all fours for a moment to return her breathing to normal, but when she was conscious enough to think, her blood went cold.

What had she done?

CHAPTER 43

"**H**E KNOWS."

They were the first words Faythe had uttered since they met back at the hut nearly an hour ago. She'd been too consumed by panic to speak. Jakon hadn't stopped pacing, trying to coax something out of her, while she sat at the table in a pair of sleep shorts and a crop top letting Marlowe tend to her wounds.

Faythe could barely register the pain as her friend cleaned and dressed the deep gash on her thigh and bandaged her bruised ribs. She knew there would also be a harsh purple mark along her cheekbone and that her lip would be swollen with a nasty cut. But none of that mattered as she was soon to be caught and executed anyway.

"Or at least, he will as soon as I fall asleep," she added quietly in her state of shock.

It was the hint the captain had given her in his last words: *"Maybe not in the way you think."* They had been replaying in her mind, filling her with cold dread, the whole time since.

"Does someone want to explain this to me? It's over—why is everyone so worried?" Ferris said from his spot in the corner.

Faythe had forgotten he'd followed them back here to make sure she was okay and give her the money she was owed from tonight. She didn't want it. She wanted to give it all back and to have never set a single foot inside that cave. Everything since that moment had been a slow descent into a deadly fate she couldn't escape.

Before she could reply, Jakon halted his pacing and stared at Ferris with an inhuman rage. In two strides, he had Ferris pinned to the wall by his collar.

"You piece of *shit.* This was all your fault!" He seethed into his face.

"Jak," Faythe muttered.

He didn't respond and continued his stare down as if deciding whether he should swing.

"Jakon," she repeated in warning.

Reluctantly, he released Ferris with a rough shove and stalked back over to the table. "What do you mean, 'he knows'?" His anger boiled but not toward her.

She took a slow breath. "He knows I'm hiding something, and he intends to find it out." She trembled as if the cold air was just now catching up to her where she sat half-dressed.

Marlowe draped a blanket gently over her shoulders, and Faythe smiled gratefully as she dropped into the seat next to her, satisfied her injuries were the best she could make them. Jakon cursed—a lot—and she watched the wheels turn in his head as he tried to figure out what to do. It pained her, but she wouldn't have any of them dragged into her mess.

An idea came to her. "I...I have a tonic. Nik gave it to me when I was still learning to control my ability. It will stifle it when I sleep and also protect me from...others." She winced, not able to say the captain's name without seeing the vicious scar and malice that laced his face. It was a temporary solution. She only had two nights left of the tonic at best, and Nik had said it could have fatal consequences if used for long periods. "It'll give me two days at least." She couldn't bring herself to think of what she would do after.

"Then what?" Jakon pressed.

Faythe knew what she would have to do to keep herself and them safe. The thought of stowing away in a barrel like her friend Reuben made her stomach turn, and she had to cover her face with her hands and breathe for a moment. She had never left High Farrow. This was her home, and she would have to abandon the kingdom and, worst of all, her friends. What crushed her spirit was that she would never get to sever the tie the cursed eternal woods held on her soul. She had failed in that too, and her bargain would forever remain unfulfilled. She would never get to join her friends when the Afterlife claimed her. It was a crippling, damning feeling.

"I failed you all, and I'm sorry," she whispered.

Marlowe's arm went around her shoulder, pulling Faythe into her warmth. "We're going to figure this out together," she said, her voice calm and soothing.

"Again, anyone want to fill me in?" Ferris said.

Jakon whirled to him, and Ferris wisely flinched into a defensive position, but Jakon never moved. If looks alone could kill, he'd have already turned to cinders.

Seeing no reason to keep her secret any longer, Faythe reluctantly rattled through the basics so Ferris would understand their urgency and the cause of the thick tension in the room. It felt strange but also liberating to be able to talk about it so openly.

"Bullshit," was his first response to the reveal of her abilities. "Prove it."

Faythe scowled at him. "I don't have to prove anything to you, prick."

His eyes narrowed as his face turned contemplative. "Well, if what you say is true, we need to get you out of here."

Jakon looked to her immediately. "I'll come with you."

She shook her head. "Absolutely not. This is my problem, and none of you are getting dragged into it."

"We would never leave you to face it alone. We all go," Marlowe added softly.

Faythe snapped her head to the blacksmith and leaned out of her embrace. "Not a chance in—"

"You don't get to decide for us," Marlowe cut in. "We are in this just as much as you are, like it or not." Her tone was firm— something Faythe wasn't used to from the softly spoken blonde. But she would be wise not to argue with an oracle connected to the Spirits.

"I can get you safe passage," Ferris cut in before Faythe could argue further. He looked between them. "For all of you. I could get you to Rhyenelle. You're not traitors. You could stand a chance of being let in as citizens. Marlowe has a trade skill that could be useful to them, Jakon is a farmer, and, well…dance a little with your sword, Faythe, and they might see use for you."

Faythe bit back her retort since the offer was exactly what she needed, but her heart dropped at the inclusion of her friends. "I can't ask you to give up your lives here," she pleaded.

Jakon's face softened, and he took a seat in front of her, reaching a hand over to take hers. "You don't have to ask. Wherever you go, I go."

Marlowe nodded in fierce agreement.

They were willing to sacrifice everything they had built here to follow her on a road of uncertainty, and it was a debt Faythe would spend the rest of her life—however short or long—repaying.

"I'll make the arrangements for two days' time. This should be enough, with the rest of your earnings, to get you all by for a while on the road and help you settle in when you arrive." Ferris came over to the table, careful not to be within Jakon's reach as he still glared menacingly at him, and dropped a heavy pouch of coin in front of them. His portion from tonight, Faythe realized.

She was about to protest, but he gave her a look that told her not to bother.

"You earned every penny." He stared at her in curiosity for a moment and then huffed a laugh. "Who would have thought? Faythe, a human mind reader."

She smiled sheepishly, and he flashed her a sad smile back.

"It's a shame it turned out this way. And for my part, I'm sorry."

She gave him a small nod of understanding and forgiveness. He returned it and then spun on his heel toward the door.

"I'll see you all by Westland Forest at nightfall in two days," he said as he left. Then the door closed behind him, and the three companions were alone in solemn silence.

A knock sounded at the door a short moment later, and they all looked to each other expectantly.

"I won't hesitate to strangle him this time if he's come back," Jakon muttered as he stood to answer it.

Faythe's eyes widened at the tall cloaked figure who floated in seconds later. Nik's brute statue made their small hut seem even more feeble.

When they simply stared at each other and no one spoke, Marlowe stood from the bench. "Jakon, will you walk me home?" she asked sweetly, and Faythe could have hugged her for it.

She didn't think she could handle explaining the events of tonight—specifically, what it meant for her and Nik as a result— while her friends were in the same room. It only now dawned on her that this was likely the last time she would ever get to see the fae guard, and it shattered her heart into pieces where she sat.

Jakon nodded to her, understanding she would need this time alone to say goodbye, and the couple left without another word.

When she heard the door click, Faythe stood, coming around the table to where Nik had yet to make a move. His jaw flexed as he silently scanned over her face, taking in her injuries. She held the blanket around her to conceal her ribs, but it still exposed her bare thigh and the large bandage the wound was bleeding through a little.

"I had to make sure you were all right," he said, his voice achingly quiet in an attempt to contain his anger at the state of her.

"It was Captain Varis," she blurted, not able to delay the inevitable heart-wrenching news that she was leaving.

His eyes flashed in a rage like nothing she'd seen before, and he straightened. "And you let him win, didn't you?" he asked, his voice like a knife's edge.

She winced at the dark look on his face. "Kind of," she said, and she noted the slight tremble of his tightly clenched fists. "He was going to kill me—I *saw* it. None of your guards would have been fast enough to stop him. So we came to a mutual defeat."

Nik let out a humorless laugh, running a hand down his face. Before he could reprimand her for not being smarter somehow, she continued.

"It wasn't a coincidence. He knew who I was, and he knows I'm hiding something," she explained quickly. She didn't have to go further as realization immediately clouded his face, and his rage turned to horror. Her next words came out in a choked whisper. "I have to leave, Nik." Tears burned the backs of her eyes at his look of pain, and she blinked hard to force them away.

He walked the few steps over to her and took her face gently in his hands, wary of her bruised cheek. "I'll take care of it," he said, but she saw his determination falter. It was too far out of his control this time.

She shook her head. "I leave for Rhyenelle in two days. Jakon and Marlowe will be coming with me."

He rested his forehead against hers. "Faythe," he breathed, but no other words came. They both knew it was her only chance at safety.

She let the blanket fall to wrap her arms around his neck, and he held her tightly. Her silent tears fell then. It wasn't fair. They were being ripped apart because of some monster and his need for dominance and violence. She allowed herself to believe she could have had something with Nik. An unorthodox, complicated relationship for sure, but she would have accepted it, and the risks that came with it, for a chance to be with him.

His hands trailed over her bare waist below her bandages, and his touch soothed the pain in her heart just for a moment. When she leaned back to look at him, she traced the contours of his face with her fingers. Over his jaw, then his nose, then his mouth, trying to memorize every detail if this was the last time she would ever see him.

She leaned up to kiss him fiercely, and he responded with aching tenderness. Her body caught fire everywhere he touched as his hands roamed her exposed skin, painfully delicate to be cautious of her injuries. But she didn't want gentle and didn't care if her body protested as she pressed herself to him. A quiet sound came from her, and he leaned down, hooking his hands under her thighs and lifting her so she didn't have to strain on her toes to kiss him. She wrapped her legs around his waist and could have exploded from the new angle, which offered her better access to his mouth. His hands at the tops of her thighs made her wild with desire. While she wanted him—all of him—she knew giving over to her desperate impulse would only make their parting all the more gut-wrenching.

Before things could get too heated, the kiss slowed, turning devastatingly tender. His lips left hers, and he kissed her neck—sweetly, not lustfully. He seemed to be savoring the smell and feel of her. Then he set her gently back on her feet and stared at her while he stroked her bruised cheek.

"I'm going to miss you," Faythe whispered, not trusting her voice to sound steady.

He gave her a sad smile. "There will never be another like you, Faythe. Human, fae, highborn, commoner... Never another soul like yours."

She knew the comment had nothing to do with their personal relationship, and the words broke and fixed her at the same time. She didn't have the expression to respond, so she only leaned into him once more, suddenly aware of the cold draft around the hut as his warmth encased her in its net of safety.

They held each other for the last time. Neither had it in them to say a formal goodbye, so, with a final lingering kiss, Nik left without glancing back.

Faythe fell apart the moment the door clicked shut behind him.

CHAPTER 44

T HEY SPENT THE following day gathering provisions for their journey. Only what was necessary—the rest they could buy on the road and once they got to safety in Rhyenelle.

Jakon had been on edge all day, re-checking everything and going over every detail of the plan more than four times already. It hurt Faythe to see him so worked up, but there was nothing she could do to persuade him to change his mind.

Marlowe had been at her cottage all day, assembling what she needed and spending the last of her time with her father. The fact she would be leaving *family* behind pained Faythe the most, but, like Jakon, Marlowe was adamant she would be joining them.

Faythe spent the whole day in a quiet pit of despair at what she would be leaving—*who* she would be leaving. She would not get to see Nik again, not in her mind or his, before she left since the drops had done their work last night and sent her straight into a dark sleep without even a flash of her gold mist. They would do the same tonight also.

Jakon had left her to her brooding, figuring she wouldn't be much help in the planning of things anyway. She had sat in her bed most of the day, reflecting on her life in High Farrow that was about to come to an end.

She was watching the dusk fall through the small square window when Jakon finally joined her in the bedroom. He sighed sadly upon seeing her.

"You've always longed for adventure. Try to see the bright side." He offered a comforting smile.

But she couldn't bring herself to even force one back. He was right: it would be a new beginning and offered an opportunity for them to see more of Ungardia. Who knew what she might discover in Rhyenelle? She only hoped it would be completely mundane, and her dealings with the Spirits and malicious fae captains would be over.

She shuddered when the encounter with Aurialis crossed her mind. She would never get to see the Goddess again. Whatever she thought Faythe was needed for, she'd have to find another suitor, and the answers to Faythe's burning questions about her heritage might forever remain lost.

She reached over to the table to grab the last of the drops, eager to get the final night over with and start their journey by twilight tomorrow.

A loud banging out front made her jolt, and she almost knocked the glass bottle right off the nightstand.

Jakon frowned, turning to leave the bedroom. Faythe shot up too as the frantic banging continued and her heart started to race. She grabbed Jakon's elbow.

"What if it's him?" she whispered in cold panic.

She didn't have to say his name for Jakon to gather she meant Captain Varis. His eyes widened at the possibility, and he scanned the hut wildly for a plan, but they both knew the only way out was the front door.

She was about to scramble to find a hiding spot when a voice called through the wood.

"It's me, Jakon, *please!*"

Faythe recognized the voice but couldn't put a face to it. Jakon, on the other hand, went wide-eyed in fear as he ran the few paces to the door, swinging it open. Dalton came into view, and Jakon quickly scanned behind him before nodding him inside.

"Where's Marlowe?" he asked desperately.

Dalton panted heavily. He was unfit at the best of times and appeared as if he had more or less run the distance across town to be here. Faythe began to tremble in anticipation.

"She—they…came…and—" The man could barely get out the words.

Jakon grabbed him by the collar to keep him upright as he gasped for air. "Where is she, Dalton?" he pressed urgently. Faythe had never heard such dread in her friend's voice, and it made her sway in dizzy suspense.

Dalton finally caught enough breath, and his next words brought the world down on her. "Guards took her, said it was for treason, but she would never—"

Jakon released him and took a step back in horror. He looked to Faythe.

"It's a message," she choked out. "He couldn't find me through my head, so he went for hers." The final dawning came out in hushed terror. "He took her because he found out it would hurt more than anything he could do to me physically."

The realization crippled her. She looked between the two horrified men, completely at a loss for what to do. Captain Varis would have taken Marlowe to where all those detained for judgment ended up: the castle prison. She refused to accept there was no saving her friend, and Faythe knew exactly how she would gain access past the wall to pledge for her life.

She had already been briefed by Ferris on a sure path through. It was unpatrolled; a secret labyrinth that tunneled through the inner city. The redheaded deviant was many distasteful things, but she thanked the Spirits for his cunning brilliance in that moment.

This was a route used by very few in the know to smuggle unsavory and often unlawful items into the city, right under the king's nose.

Faythe twisted, heading into the bedroom without another word. Everything around her went still as she fell into a cool, calculating calm. Her eyes flashed to her empty cot, and she contemplated contacting Nik. He was in the royal guard and could at least ensure Marlowe stayed alive long enough for Faythe to infiltrate the castle and gain an audience with the king to beg for her release. But she had nothing to send her into a quick sleep that would awaken her Nightwalking ability, and there was no guarantee Nik was even asleep himself. The night was still young. Every minute that ticked by was too precious to risk.

No—she didn't have time to attempt a message to him that way. Her rage was a storm of fire and ice under her skin. If the captain wanted Faythe, he would damn well get her.

And my dagger won't halt before slitting his throat if given a second chance.

She stripped down, changing swiftly into her suit as it would allow for the best movement in her task. She tried to make herself numb to the painful aches of her body from the brutal beating yesterday, but she had to clench her teeth to keep from hissing at the sharp stabbing in her ribs and thigh especially. Jakon's presence behind her was noted, but she paid him no attention. She was fully changed and braiding her hair back in record speed.

"What are you doing?" he demanded.

She strapped Lumarias around her hips and equipped her dagger in a few swift movements, charging back out of the bedroom. "I'm going to get her out." Faythe swung her cloak on and was pulling up her hood when Jakon caught her elbow. She almost snarled at his move to delay her. Every ounce of kindness and mercy had left her moments ago.

"And how exactly do you plan to do that?" he hissed.

"There's a way into the city—underground," she said quickly. "I would ask you to stay, but I know you're not going to, so don't slow me down." She ripped her arm from his grasp and didn't wait for his response or for him to equip his own sword and cloak.

Faythe glided back into the main room and stopped just for a second to rest a hand on Dalton's shoulder. "Go home. We'll bring her back, I promise," Faythe said as confidently as she could though her own uncertainties threatened her calm demeanor.

Then she left the hut, intending to walk straight into the trap the captain had laid and bring the hunter down with her.

CHAPTER 45

WAVES THRASHED VIOLENTLY against the jagged rocks Faythe and Jakon clung to in desperation. The entrance to the tunnels was far away from the town dwellings, on the opposite side of the great inner-city wall, at the edge of the kingdom by the wicked Black Sea.

There was a far easier way into the large cave that began the underground labyrinth into the city, other than the completely insane route Faythe had taken them on that had them putting their lives at risk. But when they stopped to scan the footpath Ferris had pinpointed, she immediately spotted the fae halfway down the road and was forced to retreat. They weren't uniformed guards; they appeared to be some of the rookies Ferris had warned her about.

The only alternative route had been to scale the deadly, steep, and nauseatingly high coastline. Any other day, Faythe would have shut down the impossible idea, but with Marlowe's life on the line, all logical thought had left her.

Clawing over the next uneven bulge in the wall, her gloved fingers ached hideously with the iron grip she held at all times. She cautiously shuffled her way across the next relatively flat side. It was made all the more difficult by her already injured body, but the bitter-cold wind helped to numb the stabbing in her chest with every movement. More than once, her foot or hand slipped slightly against the slime and dampness of the sea-battered rocks, and each time, her heart leapt in her throat. Adrenaline kept her moving. To let clumsy, misjudged footing end her life to the monstrous sea below would be embarrassingly tragic now.

Finally, Faythe hauled herself high enough that she was able to peek over the edge and check the entrance straight ahead.

Clear! Thank the Spirits.

No fae lingered around the mouth of the cave. She whipped her head down in a surge of panic but let it go the moment she spied Jakon—as safe as he could be with the waves that crashed higher each time as if desperate to claim his body in their black waters. She shuddered violently at the thought.

Taking the final stretch upward to level with her, Jakon also halted to investigate the area of solid ground. "How the Nether-damned did you find this?" His voice was barely audible against the howling wind and storm below.

Knowing Ferris's name had become something of a trigger for Jakon's violence, Faythe didn't answer. Instead, she steadily maneuvered her footing, bracing her arms and pulling herself up and over to lie flat against the oddly comforting firm ground. Jakon copied her, and they both stayed down, her heart galloping now they were semi-exposed and at greater risk of being caught. They still had bush cover, but in the autumn they had shed their leaves and offered little hiding.

Faythe commando-crawled forward on her forearms until she came to the edge of the bushes. When no lingering fae came into view, she sagged a little in relief.

A torch flickered in its hold outside the cave, burning a vibrant *blue* instead of amber. She didn't have time to admire the wonders of the magick that made it so, only noted it as an indication that the labyrinth was indeed in use tonight.

They would have to be vigilant inside.

She jumped into a crouch, every sense on high alert, before slowly rising to her full height. She was terrified as she stared into the black void of the cave mouth. The unknown dwelled inside. They had no map other than Ferris's vague description of what to expect and where to turn. She only prayed her recall of his directions wouldn't turn up blank when it mattered most.

Faythe felt a hand graze her lower back and jerked hard in fear, her hand shooting to her side for Lumarias. Her eyes fell on Jakon, and she winced, muttering an apology when he recoiled.

"Are you sure you want to do this?" he asked worriedly. She knew he wouldn't hold any judgement if she cowered out. In fact, he would likely be relieved more than anything if she decided against the brash plan.

"I don't have a choice," she muttered. The captain's fight was with her, and she'd be damned if she let Marlowe's life end as collateral in the battle between them.

Jakon gave her a weak smile in understanding, and she couldn't help but fall into his arms at his look of sadness and uncertainty. He held her tight, and she let all her fear and crippling worry go numb in his embrace, absorbing his fierce courage instead for the dangerous path ahead.

When they released each other, they exchanged one last look of affirmation. Then they turned and didn't falter a step as they stalked to the entrance of the cave.

Jakon swiped the torch outside—smart, as they would have little chance of finding their way in the pitch-black inside. Without the bitter, whistling wind, only two sounds remained: the thrum of her own heart, and the slight shuffling of their boots against the grain of the cave floor. Not even the glowing blue flame uttered a single crackle. It allowed Faythe to tune her hearing in to anything outside of those two noises.

They followed a long, straight path for a minute, and she felt the walls closing in as the passage narrowed the farther they ventured into the belly of the cave. It made her breathing turn ragged; arose her fear of confinement in the underground space. She flexed her fists to distract herself.

After another painstaking stretch of passage, they came to a junction. It was time for Faythe to wrack her brain for Ferris's instructions, but in her wild frenzy of thoughts and emotions, the sequence of left and right paths they had to take to end up at the castle became a disarray of blurred lines.

"I think it's that one," she said shakily, pointing to the right. She wouldn't tell Jakon she wasn't entirely sure but was rather following her gut.

He didn't seem inclined to question it, which dropped guilt in her stomach that he was blindly putting his trust in her to guide them through the maze of mud and stone.

Hopefully, there aren't any ghoulish creatures lurking that Ferris failed to mention...

A sharp tremor rattled down her spine. Jakon pressed forward, and with a deep inhale to soothe her rising doubts, she followed after him. Faythe walked close to his side, almost glued to him, as if he might be snatched away from her by the shadows—or she from him. She was selfishly glad for her friend's presence; her fear might very well consume her if she attempted the venture alone.

They walked straight for a few more arduous minutes, and Faythe knew the prestigious inner city would be alive above them by now. She tried not to dwell on the nerve-wracking fact. They came to two more crossroads. Each time, Faythe chose on impulse which path to take, not allowing herself time to debate her decisions. But it wasn't her strained hearing that was alerted first; it was her sight, picking up a faint glow in the far distance.

Could it be a way out?

Her hope was short-lived when the light expanded, revealing an intersection at the bottom of the passage. Her hand lashed out to grab Jakon's arm, and they both halted in cold horror.

They weren't alone.

Jakon looked to her, wide-eyed, and it was the last thing she saw before he threw the torch to the ground and tried to snuff out the blue flame. No matter how much dirt he shuffled over it, however, the fire still burned bright.

Faythe's pulse turned erratic when she picked up on voices growing louder with each passing second. The blue flame had been conjured from magick; it was logical to assume it could only be extinguished by it too. Gripping Jakon harder, she pulled him with her as she silently jogged back into the pitch-blackness, away from the torch light.

Their company was too close for them to retreat the whole way back without making a noise. They would have to hope they could hold the element of surprise long enough to attempt an ambush. Faythe stayed deathly still, pressing her whole form hard against the freezing wall as if it could swallow her whole and save her from the impending confrontation. She freed Lumarias—slowly, silently. Jakon stood against the opposite wall.

More than one voice echoed, louder now. They would need both angles to stand a chance. Though if the oncoming voices belonged to the fae, Faythe doubted any weapon, attack, or position could save them.

She didn't let the fact cripple her internally. They couldn't fail —not when they hadn't even made it to the city streets above.

She turned her head to watch the shadowed forms grow larger, their distorted bodies like wraiths filling the bottom of the intersection. Unable to balance her breathing with the racing of her heart, Faythe felt dizzy under the weight of danger.

Then shadows were made flesh when the figures rounded the corner toward them. They each held a torch of blazing amber. With their faces illuminated, the first thing Faythe identified almost made her sigh out loud in shock and relief.

Humans!

"That pompous bastard! Making us trek all the way here and not show!" one man cried. He had a short, lanky stature. Faythe had already picked him for herself as he was conveniently on her side anyway.

The other, a bit taller and packing muscle in comparison, grumbled in agreement. "I think we may have to find another fae for dealings on the inside. Lord Hellias may be compromised," he said roughly.

Faythe flashed Jakon a look, barely visible under the cloak of darkness, and he gave a short nod. They didn't need words to confirm their plan of action in that moment. Over their decade of friendship, they had developed their own unspoken alignment of thought.

"That's strange," the lanky man mumbled, brow creasing when he caught sight of their discarded torch still glowing a few meters away from where they lay in wait. While the smaller man bent down to investigate it, his companion wisely drew his sword, scanning the area—but, foolishly, he advanced with caution toward them.

Just a little closer…

Before he had a chance to distinguish their bulging forms against the flat wall, Jakon lunged, and Faythe didn't hesitate to follow his lead. The larger man clashed swords with Jakon, and she only hoped he was winning as she darted for his friend, still crouched, and heaved her foot against his chest. He went flying backward, splaying across the ground in terrified bewilderment. Then she was above him, sword poised over his heart.

She breathed hard, letting go of her pent-up suspense. The cries of steel added anguish to the shadows, but Faythe couldn't take her eyes off the man under her blade to check if Jakon was leading the fight.

There was a loud clattering of steel against stone. *Someone's disarmed.* Her heart thundered at the thought of it being Jakon. Then she heard a quick-step commotion.

Come on, Jak…

Finally, a loud thud as a body hit the ground. She froze.

Please, please, please...

When a figure caught the corner of her eye, she didn't hide her long breath of relief at the friendly face.

Jakon smirked. "Did you really doubt me?" he said with mock hurt.

She scowled in response before they both turned their attention to the man staring back fearfully.

"Which path takes us inside the castle?" Faythe asked with malice in her tone.

The weasel of a man scoffed, flaring Faythe's anger. She pressed the sharp point into his chest, and he hissed, recoiling further back into the ground.

"Which path?" she repeated through her teeth.

His eyes narrowed and nostrils flared. She raised her elbows to add more pressure through her blade.

"Left!" he said quickly, before she could break the skin under his tunic. "You'll want to go left, then take the next two rights. There'll be a ladder to an exit chamber—it leads to an alley just outside the castle gates. You're on your own from there," he told her reluctantly.

With the information she needed and not wanting to waste any more time, Faythe looked to Jakon. He gave her a quick nod, and she knew what he was about to do. He lifted his foot, and Faythe turned her head to avoid the brutal sight. But the sickening crack as he knocked the man unconscious still made her wince.

She didn't look down at him while she straightened then pressed forward once again, swiping their eternally flamed torch.

Their pace quickened with the new certain route—and in fear that the men they'd left to the bitter, dark cold might not be alone down here. They scurried like rodents through the next couple of passages.

He'd spoken true, and Faythe sagged in relief at the circle of light she spotted in the roof ahead. She didn't give Jakon a chance to be annoyingly chivalrous and insist he go first up the ladder; she subtly overtook him, curling her fingers around the iron bar, and started the climb. She heard his mumbles of protest but didn't acknowledge them. At the top, she braced her splayed palms against the thick metal, straining as she pushed it open a fraction to glance through the smallest gap she could.

It wasn't as dark as she expected. In fact, the gray stone ground sparkled a little. She used her shoulder to lift the hatch higher. Then the heavy weight of it was suddenly relieved from her completely.

Her shock and horror didn't have a moment to settle as, in one blinding movement, bright light encased her, and she was flying. Or, rather, was being hauled out of the underground dwelling with immortal swiftness. It took her a second longer than it should have in her bewilderment to refocus, and when she did, the world fell from under her at the sight of the four fae guards surrounding her. She had been tricked.

That lying sewer-rat bastard!

"Well, well," one of the fae drawled in amusement. "What a night this has turned out to be."

She took in her surroundings then, and her anger toward the trickster switched to cold, trembling fear. She stared directly ahead, down the long garden path beyond the iron gates, craning her neck in awe and horror at the dauntingly tall white stone castle. She had naïvely believed the spineless coward's directions, and he'd led her right to the wolves guarding the castle perimeter.

"You're not the first to have tried to gain unpermitted access into the city, though you're certainly the most foolish," another guard sniped.

She didn't have it in her to respond with words or facial expressions. She could only surrender to her shock and disbelief that it was over. She had been caught and would be taken straight to…

Straight to the castle!

It was exactly where she needed to be. *They* would be the fools for escorting her directly to her intended destination.

Then, in a spear of panic, she remembered she hadn't come here alone.

Faythe didn't dare glance back at the hole she'd been pulled from and risk arousing their suspicions. Jakon was smart—he would have seen her being grabbed and wouldn't be foolish enough to expose himself too. There would be no plausible reason to doom himself; he had to stay below and find another way in or out. Though the latter, she had painful doubts about. He wouldn't leave her or Marlowe, who was already beyond the royal fortification.

Mercifully, he didn't emerge from the dwelling behind her, and after a quick glance down, the fae guards seemed satisfied enough to seal the hole back over.

Faythe didn't fight when a guard approached and grabbed her arm. She began walking when he tugged, not even offering a scowl of defiance. The weaker she appeared, the less of a threat they would consider her. Not that she thought four fae would ever consider her such if she did resist. But it worked. She was let go and allowed to walk of her own accord toward the castle gates.

They opened as they approached, and she noted only one fae guard accompanied her through while the others went back to their stations around the perimeter.

How hard would it be to elude one guard?

She didn't think it would be easy, but she rattled her mind for ideas of how to escape once she was within the castle walls. The fae took her through the main entrance, and she felt oddly out of place stepping up such pristine white steps and through the ornate, dauntingly tall iron doors that were also hauled open upon their arrival.

In better circumstances, she would have stopped to admire the grand, brightly lit reception hall. Everything glittered in stark contrast to the night outside. She had to blink rapidly to curb the slight sting in her eye.

It was an ocean of white and royal blue as he led her through a series of long, wide hallways. The griffin crest of High Farrow adorned the tapestries, and elegant sculptures stood intermittently. She shook her head and focused. She couldn't afford to get distracted by marvelous decor. Any turn now, and she would likely descend from the beauty, right into the grim pits of the dungeons.

Another figure rounded the corner down the hall.

A female fae!

Faythe had to refrain from gawking. She had very rarely seen a female as the outer town was too dull and dirty to appeal to the elegant, immortally beautiful race. The one before her was exactly that—and far more. She was slender, with rich, light brown skin, perfectly poised as she almost floated toward them. The waves of her gown caught on the wind behind her. Then her eyes fixed on Faythe, and she almost flinched at the attention. But it wasn't fear Faythe was struck with; it was reckless adrenaline.

She flashed her eyes at the guard who wasn't on the right side to be between her and the female drawing closer. While his hand rested on the hilt of his sword, he marched at almost an arm's reach from her, thinking there wasn't any chance of a mere human girl being able to escape him. A fool. She was quick, and her plan didn't require her to be able to maneuver far.

Perhaps she had gone completely and utterly insane in her desperation to save her friend. Faythe subtly reached for her dagger under her cloak, slowly sliding it free with no sound. Then she braced herself, counting her heartbeats with each step to steady her trembling hands. She would have one second, one chance, and no room for error.

When the female came to pass, Faythe lunged forward, twisted on her toes, and halted in position behind her. She breathed hard as she faced the guard, who stared back in wide-eyed fury—not at her face, but at the dagger she held poised over her captive's throat.

CHAPTER 46

"I NEED AN audience with the king."

Faythe spoke the words calmly; confidently. She stood behind the female fae with her arm wrapped around her shoulder, dagger pressed into her throat to slit it clean in one movement should the guard get any ideas. The female, to her credit, didn't whimper or tremble at all beneath her.

The guard assessed the situation with his sword drawn, eyes calculating everything, like a male in combat. Upon concluding there was no maneuver he could make quicker than she could cut, he nodded.

She didn't let her relief show.

Faythe knew there would be no coming back from harming or threatening a fae, especially not within the *castle*. It was a sure death sentence but her only ticket into the throne room to plead the case for her friend's life. It was an ill-conceived plan and perhaps a fool's hope, but it was all she could come up with in the heat of the moment as every echo of the phantom clock struck an over-whelming fear that she would be too late to save her friend. All logic and reasoning had left her long ago.

"This way," the guard said—not in anger or worry, much to her displeasure. Yet she knew if she let her guard down for a split second, she would be disarmed and detained before she could take a breath. So she focused on her surroundings as she followed the fae guard down the hall to her doom.

They walked through a short maze of passageways and bright, open halls. Faythe kept her hold on the female firm, ears straining for sound, and an eye on every corner should another guard appear. The halls were surprisingly quiet, and she thanked the Spirits for that small mercy. Any more of them, and she would risk losing her hostage before she could make it to her destination.

It wasn't long before a set of very large double doors came into view down the hall, and Faythe's heart became a wild beast rattling in her chest. It definitely wasn't the best way to get the king's attention, but she could only hope her hostage was valuable enough to get him to listen.

The two guards posted outside the ornate wooden doors drew their swords the second they laid eyes on them. The female's companion held up a hand, and they lowered their blades slightly, still remaining rigid.

"Open the doors," the guard commanded.

Their eyes looked her over, assessing if there was anything they could do to save the female and prevent Faythe from gaining access to the throne room. With anger and reluctance, they grabbed a handle each and hauled the doors open.

"All of you inside first," Faythe ordered. She wasn't foolish enough to leave her back exposed so they could grab her before she could inflict harm on her captive.

They did as she asked, and once they were all past the doors, she allowed herself one second to breathe and release all her nerves before following. She only had one task—to free Marlowe—and then she would accept her fate in whatever form they chose. She would give herself up gladly if it meant the safety of her friends.

She paused for a moment in the doorway, assessing her

surroundings in case the guards had a plan of ambush the moment she stepped inside.

The great hall was almost as she expected it to look, but she'd never had a room make her feel so *dwarfed*. Colonnades ran parallel down each side, holding up a balcony that encased the perimeter. A true masterpiece of a chandelier hung low, illuminating the royal crest that was painted into the center of the large white marble floor space. Beyond the crest was a long dais that held three thrones: one prominent center seat cushioned in royal blue fabric with gold embellishments, and two smaller ones featuring silver instead.

Then she beheld the cluster of males gathered in a lazy circle at the far end to the side of the dais. Every pair of fae eyes was now locked on her.

Noting the guards still poised to strike just past the door, she motioned with her head for them to keep walking. They hesitated for a second, glancing between each other as if deliberating a strategy. Faythe pressed the dagger a little harder, and the female hissed. She wanted to apologize—she was merely collateral damage—but it did the trick as the three guards started to walk further down the hall, keeping their eyes firmly on her.

She didn't fail to notice another four of them under the balconies, two on each side. The whistle of steel echoed through the open space as they all became armed, alert to the danger that had infiltrated their castle.

Faythe wanted to laugh at the absurdity of the situation: seven fae guards and a handful of other powerful fae at the mercy of a human girl. Not even the bards could make this story believable through song.

"What is this?" a voice boomed from across the hall.

She saw him then. There was no mistaking the figure who trumped the whole room through manner and stature alone: King Orlon Silvergriff of High Farrow. Aside from the obvious gold crown that adorned his short black hair, he wore the royal coat of arms and a deep blue shoulder cloak over his impeccably tailored black jacket with gold buttons. He stood as the tallest male in the room and looked to be at least in his forties, if Faythe were to compare him to a human man.

She tried not to let her confidence falter as the king stormed closer, his face livid at the commotion. But she trembled slightly at his intimidating presence. Though her breathing was steady, her heart was erratic.

"I apologize for the dramatics, Your Majesty," she began, surprised the words came through her ridiculously dry throat, "but I need an audience with you. Your guards have wrongly imprisoned a girl tonight."

The king's eyes blazed at the sight of her. She wasn't sure if she had gotten lucky with her target who could be important to him or if the fact a human girl had managed to even get this far was what enraged him the most.

"I'll have your head for your insolence, *human!*" He spat the last word. "Guards!" He called them to seize her.

"Not until you hear what I have to say. I can slit her throat faster than your guards can stop me," she warned.

She watched the cogs turn in his head as he concluded as much. Whoever she had in her grasp was important enough at least that they wouldn't risk her life. Faythe looked into his eyes then— eyes of the purest black she'd only seen the likeness of once before, in Captain Varis. But he was not present in the room, which was a slight relief.

The king was silently seething behind those eyes, but he let her continue.

"Her name is Marlowe Connaise. She is the blacksmith's daughter, and she was wrongly taken from her home tonight. I want you to set her free." She spoke a lot calmer than she felt.

The king laughed haughtily. "You do not make demands, girl."

Faythe pressed the dagger further until it made a shallow cut, enough to draw a trickle of blood. She heard all the guards shift, but the king held up a hand to halt them. His eyes locked on hers, and if looks could kill, she would most certainly have turned to ash where she stood.

"Bring in whomever she speaks of," he commanded in a deadly quiet tone.

Faythe never dropped focus on every fae around her, noting one of them leaving through a side entrance in a hurry.

"You've made a grave mistake tonight," the king said to her.

"I only needed you to hear me and let her go—then I will accept my punishment."

His answering laugh was dark. "I don't bargain with my human subjects."

"Your Captain of the Guard wants me. He only took her to get me here," she said, hoping to anchor him to her fast-sinking ship.

The king arched an eyebrow. "Did he now? A bold accusation."

"It's the truth."

His eyes narrowed on hers for a second as he took her in. The gaze made her uneasy, but she didn't balk.

"Where is my captain?" he asked his guards casually.

A few shuffled, and another left the room—she could only assume to locate Captain Varis and bring him here. She couldn't let her fear show. Not until she achieved what she'd recklessly barged her way in for.

There was commotion from the side entrance where the first guard had left, and when two came back through, it took everything in Faythe not to loosen her grip in horror. She tried to focus her mind as she watched Marlowe get dragged in...closely followed by Jakon.

"I send you out for one, and you come back with two. How interesting," the king admired when he turned to them.

"This one was apprehended in the city, trying to get through the castle gates," the guard said.

Faythe commended Jakon for even getting that close when their plan had turned nether-damned. But as her eyes fell on the blacksmith beside him, her heart broke. Marlowe had been crying hard —she could tell from the streaks on her usually perfect face and her red, puffy eyes. Her hair was disheveled, and it lit Faythe's anger that on top of everything else, she appeared to have been mistreated.

Jakon was like a wild animal as he thrashed between the two fae guards holding him. His courage remained strong even in the hopeless odds against a species too superior in agility to be beaten.

The king looked back at her. "Another friend of yours, I assume?"

Faythe said nothing, and a cruel smile spread across his cheeks.

"Two for the price of one doesn't seem like a fair trade now, does it?" he taunted.

"They've done nothing wrong," she flared.

"That's not a verdict you can pass."

Just then, a door to the back of the room was flung open, and Captain Varis swaggered in, a dark force that made everyone around him recoil. Faythe didn't flinch even as he fixed his eyes on her with the same predatory gleam. He came to a stop near the king and gave him his attention, bowing low.

"Do you know this woman?" the king asked.

The captain's eyes went from the king to lazily graze over her. "This one in particular? I can't say I do, Your Majesty." He shrugged casually.

Faythe's nostrils flared. "He's *lying.*"

"Tell me, Captain, how this human girl came to elude your guards and capture my ward." The king spoke calmly, pacing back over to him.

Captain Varis stood straight, hands clasped behind his back. "It seems I'll have to make some necessary cuts and replacements."

The guards around them shifted, and the king looked over them all.

Faythe had the king's *ward* under her knife? She was as good as a daughter in some respects.

340

The king hummed in response as he finished his scan of the room. "I want everyone out except the guards," he announced to the hall. In a second, all the fae behind him, with whom he had been in conversation before her interruption, shuffled out the back immediately, and the guards repositioned themselves. "And bring me my son. He should see what they are capable of if left unchecked and what will be done to human traitors. I fear his heart has grown too soft for them."

"You will let them go. I'm the only one who has committed a crime," Faythe said, holding her position firm and jerking her head toward her friends, who wisely stayed quiet. Jakon had stopped fighting.

The king rolled his shoulders back. "Captain Varis, what is it the woman stands accused of?" he asked, gesturing to Marlowe without looking over.

"Treason, Your Majesty. I have seen it." As he said it, his eyes fell on her with vicious delight.

Faythe's stomach dropped in realization. He could make up any story he wanted, and Faythe's word would be nothing against it. He was one of the king's most powerful Nightwalkers, his trusted advisor, and Captain of the Royal Guard. It didn't matter what Faythe pleaded.

"Lying bastard!" Jakon spat from the side of the hall.

Faythe couldn't hold in her wince as one of the two guards punched him hard in the stomach and he fell to his knees. Then the other one hit him across the face, and she almost broke her position to lunge for them.

The captain's mouth twitched a little in amusement, and Faythe's anger flared wildly.

"Check his mind," she blurted, knowing it was a step out of line. But she had already danced and skipped over the gods-damned line so much it was blurred beyond existence now. "You have other Nightwalkers in your service."

The king's eyes snapped to her. "You dare to ask such a thing?"

He stalked over to her, and she adjusted the blade. Orlon stopped a few feet away. "Captain Varis is a skilled Nightwalker and has served me loyally. You are but a desperate human fool who will say anything to save a friend." His head tilted in curiosity. "Though I do admire your cunning bravery in getting yourself this far. It would be a pity kill you. Such a waste."

"You can't execute people on the word of one male."

His eyes narrowed on her. "You forget who you speak to, *girl.*" Then his eyes turned upward, to the main doors she had entered through, and a satisfied grin spread across his face. "Ah, my son, I'm glad you could join us."

Faythe was about to turn in case the prince thought to try anything smart. But instead, she gripped her hostage tighter and cast a glance to her friends, who went absolutely chalk-white and wide-eyed as they stared. Faythe's own panic rose at their reaction, and she braced herself.

When she felt the prince at her side, everything slowed. He stepped around her and came to stand a few feet in front of her.

She stopped hearing, stopped feeling, stopped seeing anything but him.

Noticing her slackened hold on the ward, the prince's eyes left hers for a split second, and he gave a quick nod to the guards she hadn't even realized had snuck up behind her. With a few quick movements, she was disarmed and detained, and the female was ushered away.

Faythe didn't fight; didn't struggle. All she could do was stare and stare, rooted to the spot in a state of frozen shock. Her heart shattered, and the world tilted as she looked straight into the expressionless eyes…of Nik.

CHAPTER 47

"WELL DONE, NIKALIAS."

The king's voice was faint, but when she heard it and whom he spoke of, Faythe snapped. The guards had a hold of her upper arms loosely as they no longer considered her a threat. As quick as a fae in her blind rage, Faythe reached to her side, drew her sword, and lunged for the prince.

She barely made it a step before she was tackled. Her face hit the cold stone floor, sword clattering out of her hand as a weight pressed on her back. Her vision blacked out from the force of the blow to her head, and her already injured ribs stabbed excruciatingly.

She swayed a little when they pulled her up to stand again and blinked slowly, waiting for the dizziness to pass. When it did, her eyes met the familiar emerald-green stare, and she fell apart inside.

He kept his face neutral, no hint of the kind, tender male she had come to know—even started to love. The male looking at her now held no warmth and no recognition. She glanced to the silver-banded crown over his sleek black hair in utter disbelief.

All this time, he had played her for a fool, and she had been stupid enough to walk right into his deception.

Had his plan all along been to discover the true extent of her abilities and offer her as a prize to his father? It made sense. He was always pushing her; always curious to know more. And she had confided everything in him like a damn naïve *child*. She should have trusted her instincts. She was no better than chattel to the fae, and she had led herself right into the abattoir.

Her heartbreak was overshadowed by cold, simmering fury. She wanted to make him suffer.

"I'm growing bored of the theatrics. Bring them all to me," the king said, strolling toward the dais.

Nik turned and followed. With a rough pull, Faythe was dragged along too.

The king stepped up onto the dais but never took a seat on his throne. Nik stayed below the platform and turned to face forward again, but he did not meet her eyes this time.

Faythe was forced to her knees before the king, and her friends joined her on either side. She didn't look at them for fear it would break her. She kept her eyes down on the white marble floor as her mind rattled through ideas that could still save them.

"What is your name, girl?" the king spoke.

She said nothing—an act of defiance that didn't sit well with him. A second later, a guard grabbed the back of her head, forcing it up to lock eyes with the king. She clenched her teeth to prevent the hiss of pain, not wanting to give any of them the satisfaction. Her gaze darted to the side, where they met with the black holes of Captain Varis. She wanted to tear him limb from limb at the look of victory and amusement on his face. He had gotten exactly what he wanted—more, even—to see her go down with those who were most precious to her.

"I won't ask again," the king warned.

When she kept her mouth clamped shut, the king gave a quick nod to the captain, who smiled in wicked delight as he drew his sword and stalked to Marlowe on her left.

Faythe's eyes widened in horror. "Faythe!" she shouted, then she snapped her head to look the king in the eye. "My name is Faythe," she hissed through her teeth.

"Resistance is not bravery, Faythe; it's foolish."

She bit back her retort, quickly realizing an argument with the King of High Farrow would not end well for anyone in the room. She was running out of options.

"Please," she begged. "Please, spare my friends. They have done nothing wrong." She had no other way out of this. They couldn't fight, and even if they managed to escape by some miracle, they would not get far before the king found them and executed them on sight.

"And here I thought begging would be beneath you," he commented. "I'm a little disappointed." He looked them all over for a moment, contemplating, and then he sighed with feigned sympathy. "I'm afraid I cannot let this go unpunished. You and your accomplices have been found guilty of armed infiltration of the castle with criminal intent against the crown. For your acts of treason, my sentencing is death—for all of you." He looked at the captain and gave him another nod to proceed.

The ground trembled beneath her as she watched Varis stalk toward Marlowe once more, his eyes dancing with an executioner's delight.

"*Don't you touch her!*" Jakon's voice was animalistic beside her. She heard the commotion of his struggle as he was roughly detained but couldn't look at him; she could only stare, numb with horror, at the dark beast who promised death with each stride.

"Please! *Please!*" she cried, desperate, staring into the king's eyes. But there was no mercy in them. She snapped her eyes to Nik instead. He could stop this; he could talk to his father and save her friend.

He didn't meet her desperate look. He also had his eyes fixed on the captain with an unreadable expression. His jaw twitched, but he made no movement and said nothing as he watched Marlowe's death loom closer.

Her friend was hysterical beside her as two guards grabbed her arms and shoved her forward in a firm position to be beheaded. A brutal, messy death as a spectacle for Faythe; an extra punishment for her to watch for making a fool out of his guards and capturing his ward.

She couldn't hear the sobs, couldn't hear anything, as she scanned everywhere trying to think of something, *anything*, that might offer salvation. Her golden eyes settled on the captain who lifted his sword skyward. Her whole body shook, numb and ice-cold, and a high-pitched ringing filled her ears. When his eyes met hers, a cruel smile appeared in the corner of his mouth. He wanted to delight in her reaction at the exact moment he took her friend's life.

The steel glinted in the light as he poised to bring it down in one clean motion. And as it started to fall, with her eyes connected to his, Faythe screamed.

CHAPTER 48

F AYTHE MET THE oily black wall of the captain's mind—and
shattered clean through it. She heard him choke slightly as
she instinctively seized control, and his hands halted the mighty
blade in the air above Marlowe's head.

"Captain," the king demanded at his paused execution.

She didn't know how she was doing it, but in her moment of
terror and desperation, she had latched herself to the part of his
mind that could command movement. As easy as if she were telling
her own body, she ordered him to step back and drop his sword to
the ground. She could see his physical resistance as he strained
against her influence, but, reluctantly, his feet moved, and the loud
clash of metal against polished marble ricocheted through the great
hall.

"Explain yourself!" the king bellowed in outrage.

"I...I can't—" the captain tried, but she could take away his
speech too.

His eyes remained on hers as disbelief and *fear* crossed his face.
A sly smile tugged at the corners of her lips, and the realization
made his eyes bulge when he finally fit the pieces together to
discover *she* was the one in his head.

"You made the biggest mistake of your miserable life when you decided to go after my friend," she said into his mind, bringing the captain to his knees.

The king's voice boomed again. "Captain Varis, you will stand at once!"

But he couldn't take his eyes off Faythe even if he wanted to. She held them fixed on her. Everything inside his mind felt *wrong*. So much malice and hatred in his thoughts. He relished in pain, and his anger surged through her. He wanted to kill her—that thought was loud and clear above the rest—and while she was in there, she realized she could kill *him*. She could shatter his mind or command a sharp enough twist to snap his neck. With his rage and thirst for violence pulsing through her and mixing with her own emotions, it took everything in Faythe to keep herself separate and remember who she was. She would gladly rid the world of such an evil and not think twice about it, but her logical mind sang through, and she knew it would not win favor with the king if she killed his captain.

But she could at least hurt him a little.

Reaching in to grab his deepest fears, she turned his internal monsters into a vivid vision. The captain began shouting in terror and thrashed wildly from his position on the floor, fighting off foes that were not visible to anyone else in the room.

The guards around him shifted in bemusement, angling their swords to strike the phantom danger.

"Enough of this! Seize the girl!"

Faythe felt rough hands haul her to her feet, but she remained focused on the captain for as long as she could, relishing in his fear just as he had hers—until another calloused set of hands gripped her chin with painful force, and her eyes met the black depths of the king's. As he seethed in her face, she heard the captain gasp for air. Her connection to his mind severed, and Faythe too returned to herself, her physical surroundings coming back into full clarity.

"What is this trickery?" The king let go of her roughly and

stepped back again, but he was reeling. His eyes narrowed on hers, and she lifted her chin. *"You?"* he said, incredulous. "Impossible."

Exposing herself had been the only way to save Marlowe, and she would find a way to hold the minds of everyone in this damned room if she had to. She cast a glance toward Nik and found him already staring at her, though he remained impassive to her display.

Faythe kept silent but didn't balk at his look, her eyes blazing at the sight of him.

"It's true." For the first time since he'd entered the hall, Nik spoke.

At the sound of his voice, her heart broke, and anger flared at the same time. Here it was: the great unveiling of everything he'd learned about her to send her to her doom. She glared at him, but his eyes left her to fall on the king—his *father.* The thought was still inconceivable.

"I've been watching her for some time now, gathering what I could to bring her to you. She is more gifted than I or any other Nightwalker, Your Majesty. She can enter the conscious mind," he said plainly, as if relaying battle information.

It made Faythe sick. She couldn't bear to look at his face, for all she could see was months of lies and deception. Every feeling had been so real for her when it had only been a trap to him. She focused her gaze on the king instead, whose eyes widened a little in bewilderment.

He took a cautious step toward her, sizing her up and down and making her feel horribly exposed. "What an interesting night this has turned out to be." He chuckled, though it lacked real humor. "A human with gifts more powerful than yours, you say?" He cast a glance to Nik, who said nothing. "And your friends?"

"It's just me," Faythe said quickly.

"What else do you know, Nikalias?"

She had to close her eyes for a moment to brace herself.

Nik angled his head. "Faythe Aklin. Mother—human, deceased. Father—unknown. She lives a simple life in Farrowhold, though her swordsmanship is quite impressive. No criminal or violent history. Her ability is an anomaly without any indication of where it derived from." His voice was smooth; factual.

She found the bravery to look up, but he was already focused on her. Anger and heartbreak fought to be her commanding emotion, but in the end, pain took over. There was no hint of kindness; no sign of remorse. He spoke of her as if she were no more than a rare find—an object—as he laid out the brief summary of her life to the king.

Faythe shook her head in disbelief and switched her gaze to the king. "Now you know everything," she said calmly, and then she straightened with confidence. "My friends played no willing part in any of it; I used them through my ability. They were unwitting bystanders in my plan to get here. They're innocent."

The king cocked an eyebrow in surprise at her confession. "And what exactly was your plan?"

"To avenge my mother. You had her executed," she lied easily.

"Faythe, no—" Jakon's voice sounded from behind, and it took everything in her not to turn to him when she heard him struggle against the guards.

"Their minds are not completely their own," Faythe said, dismissing Jakon's plea.

"Sounds like a fool's desperate hope to save her friends."

Faythe's nostrils flared. "I think we've all seen the extent of my reach." She cast a wicked smile to the captain, whose face contorted in savage fury.

The king also looked to him. "Indeed," he drawled, stalking back up onto the dais and taking a seat on his grand throne at last. He propped one elbow on the arm of the chair to hold his strong, angled chin as he pondered her fate. "Now, what to do with you? We do not know what you are capable of if left untested, untrained…" He cast another glance over to Captain Varis, who had regained his composure and stood livid, anticipating the call to end her life. "Powerful for sure, to bring a fae to his knees and whatever else you implicated on his mind." The captain's face twitched in humiliation. "You pose a threat to us all."

"You can do whatever you like with me if you let them go."

The king huffed a laugh. "Noble of you." He took a long breath in as if only now finding himself bored of the events. "Take them all to the cells. Separate Faythe," he said with a dismissive wave of his hand.

Faythe could have sobbed in defeat. He wouldn't listen to her, and they would all die here in this castle. She didn't fight when her friends were both pulled to their feet and they were all escorted from the hall. She dared one last look at Nik, but he never met her eyes. *Damned spineless coward!* She wanted to shout the words at him, but Faythe had become too tired for her anger to rise. She had failed, and her friends would pay the ultimate price. There were no more cards to play; there was no saving grace. She fell into a hollow pit of despair and let her hope fade to nothing.

CHAPTER 49

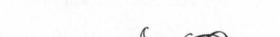

T HE PRINCE STARED after Faythe and her friends in cold trepidation but kept his face placid. His father could not know about his connection to Faythe and what he'd been doing these past months. *Gods,* if his father knew what she meant to him, he would kill her in an instant. It was one thing to feel sympathy and compassion for the humans, but to *love* one…

The king could never find out. He would end her life as a brutal lesson for him alone.

His mind was still reeling from seeing her, dagger poised over Tauria's throat, when he was summoned to the throne room. It took every restraint in him not to grab her and flee from his father right then. As much as it pained Nik to see the look on her face— the look of betrayal at learning who he really was—he had to be smart so he wouldn't get them both implicated. He only prayed Faythe would remain impassive about knowing him too.

She had played that part *too* well, and he knew her anger and loathing were not a front. There was no friendliness or love in her eyes when she glared right through him, and he had achingly tried to refrain from looking at her or his face would have begged her to hold off judgement until he could explain.

"Tell me what else you know of this...*Faythe,*" his father demanded as soon as they were alone again.

He shrugged nonchalantly. "Her powers are strong, as you already saw for yourself. But I think she is capable of a lot more."

"Do you think I should put her down before she becomes a threat?"

A test—his father was always one to feel him out on sensitive matters such as executions. He claimed his son's heart was too soft to one day be the ruler of High Farrow.

"Yes. The kingdom has no room for such an unhinged, traitorous thing." The words burned like acid in his throat when he thought of who he was forcing himself to speak such words about. But his father liked agreement and ruthlessness. After a pause to let his satisfactory answer settle in, he continued. "But then again... she could prove to be a useful *weapon.*"

The king raised an eyebrow in surprise. "Oh?"

He didn't let himself back out of the horrible fate he was about to propose. "As you said, the Nightwalking ability has *limits.* Faythe does not. She can know everything with a single glance into a conscious mind, right in the moment. She is powerful. With our training, she could bring your enemies to their knees before you. Best of all, no one would expect her to exist, least of all as a *human.*" He stepped up onto the dais to look down on his father still sitting on the throne.

Nik knew Faythe would detest the idea; would quite likely rather die than serve the king in such a manner, invading people's unwitting thoughts—even strangers—even if it would save her life. But it wasn't her own life Nik was counting on her being desperate enough to save.

"You are wise indeed, my son," his father commented, and he could see he was deliberating.

"I, for one, quite like her spirit." Tauria's voice bounced through the room. She dabbed a small cloth over her neck where Faythe had drawn blood, the wound already sealed over.

Nik raised an eyebrow, suppressing a crooked smile.

"What? It's not often you see a female with such fire." Her eyes twinkled mischievously.

He supposed he should have seen it sooner—that Faythe and Tauria matched in strong-willed spirits—but it made him nervous for the world if they were to ever meet. Without one holding the other as a hostage, that is.

"I shall think on it. And what of the other two?" the king asked the counsel.

Nik turned to him again. "It would be unwise to kill them. She won't make a cooperative ally if you kill her friends, and you can't force her ability out of her."

"If we let treason go unpunished, it puts the kingdom at risk and makes us look weak."

"I believe there has been no treason committed, Your Majesty. As I've been watching Faythe, I have also been tracking her friends to see what information they hold, and I have suspected nothing."

A small lie, but if Marlowe or Jakon were to die here—*Gods*, she'd bring the might of the Netherworld to their doors. While he had not really seen inside Marlowe's head for himself, he knew the captain had lied to get to Faythe.

Nik decided he would find some way to have Varis removed—and not just from his position.

"You say Captain Varis has lied. What reasons would he have?"

"There are rumors of his *unsavory* activities in the human towns. Perhaps he held a grudge against someone else, and the girl was collateral."

The king hummed and rose from his throne. "I will think on your proposition for this *Faythe* girl. To award a criminal with a high position in my court—a *human*... It has never been done before."

Nik could only pray to the Spirits his father would see her usefulness outweighed her brazenness, because the alternative... He couldn't bear to think of it.

CHAPTER 50

FAYTHE SAT HOLLOW against the cold, uneven wall of her cell, the ground chillingly damp beneath her. She would have registered the bitter nip of the icy stone if she were capable of feeling anything at all in her numb state. They had taken her weapons and even her cloak, then chained her to the back wall of the cell as if they were afraid anyone who came too close to the iron bars might fall under her mind's grasp if she had free movement.

The thought humored Faythe slightly. How the mighty fae people could be fearful of her... She didn't know if she could do it again—seize control of a mind like she did with Varis. She had acted purely on instinct and desperation and had no recollection of how to replicate it.

The harsh scrape of iron bit at her wrists. They were already red and swollen from her futile attempts to maneuver them free. The steady drip of a leak somewhere nearby had been the only sound for a while now, and she had no concept of how many hours had passed. She had been ripped away from her friends the moment they came down here, and she didn't know where they had been taken as she was alone in the block of dark, empty cells that reeked of neglect and death.

Jakon fought valiantly, but it had been wasted energy. Marlowe only cried, and Faythe was too broken to do anything but watch helplessly as they were separated without a chance of saying good-bye. Faythe wasn't even sure if they were still alive or had been executed the minute she was not there to stop it. So she lay down, the sound of her chains echoing through the loneliness, and slept for a temporary escape from her crippling pain and grief.

When she awoke again, it was to the screeching cry of a door opening and rough boots shuffling against gravel. She groggily propped herself up to lay her head back against the wall and brought her knees up in a casual position to greet her guest.

Captain Varis came into view, and Faythe huffed a laugh, all fear she had of the male gone. When his eyes flashed in rage, she laughed harder until she was clutching her stomach while the space echoed eerily with the sound. Recalling the look of helplessness on his face and the sight of him thrashing in terror made the laughter rumble through her in her state of delirium. But there was no humor, and she simply relished in making him angry. If these were to be her last days—last hours—she had nothing else to live for now. He had taken everything from her.

The captain slammed his palms against the bars, and the loud clash of rattling metal cut through her chuckles. She slowed her giggling to a stop but kept her wide smile. She was surprised he still remained outside the cell and had not entered to beat her to oblivion as his look told her he desperately wanted to.

"You'll find you won't get into my mind so easily next time." He seethed.

"Want to come closer, and we'll find out?" Her eyes danced in challenge.

His nostrils flared. She could see he was deliberating. The darkness put a dampener on her even being able to *try* to make the initial connection into his mind from where she sat. When she locked eyes with Varis in the throne room, she had felt everything through him, and the sensation of being in such a wicked mind still made her sick to her stomach. Mixing her thoughts and feelings with his was a dangerous gamble. If she dove too deep, she could have lost herself completely and done things there would be no coming back from.

"How you managed to deceive so many people in that cave… It's fitting it was your own foolishness and arrogance that brought you here. To think you could best *me.*"

"If I remember correctly, you failed to best me also. Not as sharp as you thought you were, it seems."

"I could have crushed your throat without any feat of strength."

"After I held a dagger under yours. But if it helps you rest easy at night to see that as a win, by all means."

She was really just trying to rouse him enough to get him to break through the bars so she could have a second chance to end him. She had no reason to hold back this time; the king had already cast his verdict on them all.

"I've seen your darkest fears, Varis. You are nothing more than a sheep in wolf's skin. You can drop the façade. It must be exhausting."

She watched in delight as his fingers flexed tighter around the cell bars, using all his restraint not to pull them clean from the wall and storm right in to kill her with his bare hands. He had more control than she gave him credit for as, instead, he lifted his chin after taking a moment to calm.

"Your life will be short, girl. I'll make sure I'm the one to end it for you. Consider it a parting gift…just like I gave your friends."

The air turned ice-cold, and Faythe lunged for him. The chains stung her wrists, but she bit back the pain and snarled. She strained furiously to get a line into his mind, but he was too far away, and his black eyes were barely distinguishable in the grim darkness.

"I'm going to *kill* you," she promised.

It was his chuckling that now filled the silence, and Faythe jolted again.

"You probably should have when you had the chance," he sang as he walked off.

The main door opened, and when it slammed shut, the vibrations met with loneliness once again.

Faythe slumped back down in a heap, and the tears started to fall. Everyone she loved was dead because of her. It had started with her mother and ended with Marlowe and Jakon. The pain was so overwhelming she screamed and let her anguish ricochet off the stone and iron cage. When they came for her, she would make it count. No matter what she had to do, she would make them suffer as she now suffered. And the crown prince would be her target.

She didn't know when she fell asleep again. Days could have passed, and she'd be none the wiser as she confined herself to that dark, restful pit. She couldn't bear to stay inside her own mind for long; didn't want to conjure the images of her friends for fear she would find some way to end her own suffering. She would meet her end, but not until she achieved something in her last moments. Not until she had the chance to unleash her retribution on the King of High Farrow.

"Be wary of colorless eyes."

Had Aurialis known this day would come? Was that some sort of warning about the trap she'd naïvely fallen into? First with Captain Varis, and now with the *king* Both had the same haunting black orbs.

Faythe cast away the thought of the Spirit of Life, even cursed her, as she had failed her friends. She forced herself to sit up, her bones aching from the solid ground as they had not provided her with hay or any form of padding. She sat limp, with her hands on her stretched-out legs. The dripping sound actually kept her sane— it was like a metronome for her thoughts. She should have been smarter; should have forced Jakon to stay home so at least one of them would have a life. She had been on a fool's mission from the beginning.

The block door cried open again, and Faythe tipped her head back against the wall with a groan. She was far too low on emotional energy for another round of insults and taunting from Captain Varis.

But it was not the black-eyed monster who greeted her this time. Instead, the demon bore eyes of striking green and a mask of cunning deceit.

Two other guards were behind the prince. His stare never left her as he said to them, "Leave us." They hesitated but reluctantly shuffled out, foolishly leaving her alone with her intended target of revenge.

She straightened her head to look at him. "A visit from the Crown Prince of High Farrow himself. I should be honored," she drawled.

"Faythe, I—"

"You don't get to call me that," she snapped. "You don't get to call me anything. I am nothing to you, as you are nothing to me."

She could have sworn his eyes twinkled with sadness. Another game. One she wouldn't fall for this time. She heard the keys jingle in his hand a moment before he twisted them into the lock and the door swung open. Foolish prince. He stepped inside but remained at a distance. If he came a little closer, she would throw everything into breaking his *damned* wall, and she would tear him from the inside out.

"I had to tell him, or he would have killed you right there," he said quietly.

She laughed without humor. "Don't act like you give a damn."

Her eyes met his—still too far away in the dark. "I have to give you some credit though: you played the role perfectly. Or perhaps I'm simply more of a fool than I thought."

He took another step toward her. "I was never pretending, Faythe. Never with you."

She ignored him. "I hope I at least satisfied your *human curiosities*. Tell me, are we as *fragile* as you thought?"

A pained look shot across his face.

She shrugged nonchalantly. "It's just a pity you never got to sample the full-course menu..." She clicked her tongue. "Might have hindered your findings a little."

He took a small step closer, and it was enough. As soon as she felt his mind, she slammed into the black wall with everything she had and saw him physically wince. It was starting to crack, and she pushed harder. He didn't retreat, when he could have in a matter of seconds. Instead, he walked toward her, and when he was right in front, he crouched to where she sat.

"I'm going to let you in. To show you it was all real," he said, heartbreakingly soft.

At his closeness and tender voice, tears welled in her eyes from better memories. But they were lies and disillusioned feelings. She didn't break focus.

The strain lifted as he granted her access, and she stumbled into his mind. Flashes of thoughts and feelings came her way, but she pushed them aside and dove deeper and deeper until she found the part of his mind she was searching for.

Nik audibly gasped. "Faythe—"

She told his lungs to stop breathing air, and a choked sound came from him. She forced his knees to meet the hard stone, and she too shifted herself to kneel in front of him.

His eyes were wide as he gasped for breath. She took his face in her hands. Tears trailed down her cheeks, but she made no sound as she watched the prince before her flounder for breath, unable to inhale. He would suffocate soon, and for what felt real on her part

—the days they had spent and kisses they shared—she would hold him until the light in his eyes went out. Even though he had betrayed her, even though her body trembled in pain to do so, she could kill him. For Marlowe, for Jakon, for his role in their deaths, and to punish the king. She could do it.

He gripped her arms as she felt him start to fade, but one message shot through the walls she'd put around herself in his mind.

"They're alive."

Faythe inhaled sharply, and the mental shield she'd erected around herself wavered. He showed her an image of her friends in a cell, huddled together, cold and scared but...alive.

"How do I know that wasn't days ago?"

She wouldn't let him breathe again, not yet—not when he could force her back out of his mind the moment she released control.

"You have to trust me."

"Not good enough."

Then all his feelings were thrown at her at once, and she was living through familiar memories from a different perspective. Everything they'd seen together; every moment they'd shared together—it was real. His emotions wracked through her like a storm, and she sobbed. Not in relief or happiness. She sobbed in sadness and frustration. This changed everything and nothing at the same time.

His grip on her arms loosened, and his hands fell as his mind began to fade to blackness...

Faythe let his body fall.

CHAPTER 51

F AYTHE SAT BACK against the cell wall, bringing her knees up to her chest as she watched Nik's still figure lying in front of her. Unconscious, but breathing. After a short moment, he came around and groggily rose to a sitting position.

He groaned. "I suppose I deserved that." His voice croaked.

She remained emotionless. "I'm not finished with you yet."

His face fell, and then he stood, brushing himself off. She took in his appearance as he did, and it was so obvious she wanted to slap herself. Prince Nikalias Silvergriff of High Farrow. Though he wore casual clothes when they met, his poise, his grace, his secretiveness... It was right there in front of her the whole time. She had been too blinded by her own problems to really *look* at him. Maybe if she had, she would have figured it out sooner.

"I'm sorry, Faythe—truly. I never meant to deceive you by not telling you who I really was. Nothing would have been the same if you knew. You would never have trusted me to help you."

She wanted to laugh at the irony. "And I'm supposed to trust you now? Trust built on the foundation of a lie is always doomed to fall."

"When you assumed I was a guard from the solstice...it was the perfect cover. I never lied, only concealed my true name and standing."

"Semantics."

She had seen it in his mind—the truth he couldn't hide from her; his feelings for her. While it comforted her to know she was not alone in those, nothing would ever be the same for them.

"Who I am—it changes nothing."

"It changes everything."

"Not the way I feel about you."

Her heart splintered, and she had to turn her gaze from his. "It can never be between us. It never really *was* anything. The fae guard I fell for...he was never real."

Nik opened his mouth to respond, but the main door interrupted his words as the same two guards entered through it. Taking in the open cell door and the risk to their prince, both guards darted for the hilt of their swords.

Faythe rolled her eyes.

One cleared his throat. "Your Majesty requires your presence in the throne room, Your Highness. We're to escort the prisoner."

She would never get used to him being addressed with such a foreign title.

Nik sighed as he looked down at Faythe. The unspoken words he had for her would remain so, possibly forever, if she was to head to her death. She was ready. If Nik hadn't lied, Marlowe and Jakon were still alive. There was still hope, and she would do everything in her power to see them walk out of here, free.

Nik left her with one last longing look before he stalked out of the cell and then out of her view completely.

The guards warily stepped inside. Faythe smiled slyly at them, and they flinched a little, both of them taking extra caution to avert their eyes. She could at least have fun with their obvious unease about what she could do.

They mercifully removed her chains, and she rubbed her tender wrists, which had formed thick red abrasions. Each guard held her tightly by the arm so she couldn't make any quick maneuvers. She didn't plan to fight or struggle anyway. Words would have to be her weapon if she stood a chance of getting her friends set free.

They took her down familiar hallways. She'd tried to note as much detail as she could in her previous short tours. A lot of them looked the same, and she knew she wouldn't stand much chance of navigating her way out easily—if at all. She glanced at her guards, but they didn't dare look back, and she smirked to herself. They passed a few others, and she picked up on the sound of a couple more joining her escort.

Faythe had to admit, she was kind of flattered the king considered her such a threat to warrant so many. They approached the familiar double doors of the great hall, and the two fae posted outside swiftly opened them before they arrived. Her guards didn't falter a step as they guided her in.

Inside, she beheld the king atop the dais on his throne, his ward on the smaller throne to his right, and Nik on his left. She allowed herself one quick glance at the prince, and his eyes met hers with cool impassiveness. It made her realize he must have kept the knowledge of just how *well* he knew her from his father.

Faythe then cast her gaze to the ward and was struck as she only now took in the full appearance of her hostage. Her skin was a glowing golden brown, and her long, dark brunette hair fell like a waterfall of silk, elegantly half-braided back to show off her delicately pointed ears, which were decorated beautifully with gold accents. She sat perfectly poised in a deep green flowing gown, appearing like a monarch in her own right. But what stunned Faythe the most was the bright, eager smile she cast back to her. Not exactly the reaction she expected when she'd held the ward at knifepoint and threatened to end her life.

Finally, her eyes fell on the king who stalked her carefully, calculating. Perhaps deciding how best to make a show of her death as the human girl who brought a fae to his knees and took hostile action against another.

The guards halted a few paces before the throne and bowed. Faythe remained upright, and the king's eyes narrowed in irritation at the disrespect. She felt hands on her back about to force her down, but the king raised a hand, and they released her, stepping to the side but remaining close.

"It seems you are something that has not existed before, *Faythe*," the king began. "And I fear what you may be capable of if left… unchecked." This was it: her death sentence. She squared her shoulders, about to plead for the life of her friends with her last breath, but he continued. "That is why, at my son's wise counsel, I have decided you may be of use to me here in the castle."

Faythe couldn't have heard right. Her eyes flashed to Nik's in accusation, but he showed no emotion.

"Just listen."

She heard it at the edge of his mind. She wanted to scowl at him, but instead, she reluctantly turned back to the king.

"You can't be serious," she said.

His jaw flexed at her informal tone. "Oh, I assure you, I am very serious. In return for my sparing your life and dismissing your treason, the rest of your days will be bound to my service as my spymaster. However, you will live here under an alias as emissary to the humans in the presence of any…guests."

It took her a moment to register his words and be sure she heard them correctly. Faythe laughed breathily. She looked around the hall, but no one shared her incredulous humor at the completely absurd idea. Her laughter faltered as she took in every-one's straight faces and realized this was no joke. Then it dawned on her exactly what he was asking. No—not asking; *ordering*, or it would indeed be her life. But to be his *spymaster*…

"I won't."

His eyes flashed at her defiance. "I throw you a lifeline—a *very* generous offer—and you have the audacity to decline me?" His voice dropped low.

She tried not to let the dark tone rattle her. "I will not do your dirty work. If you can't trust those in your company, Your Majesty, I suggest you seek new counsel."

His nostrils flared, and he shot to his feet. The sudden movement made her flinch, but she did not retreat back as he stepped down to her level, still casting a shadow as he stood a foot taller.

"You would rather die? Miserable, pathetic human," he spat. "Perhaps I didn't make myself clear enough." He motioned his hand to a guard, and a second later, she heard a clamor to her right.

Her head snapped to the side at the commotion, and her entire body fell with relief upon seeing her friends alive. Shaken, but *alive*.

"It was not a request." He gave a small nod in their direction.

Steel flashed and sang through the hall as the guards who held them drew their weapons, poised to strike the instant the command was made.

"Wait!" she screamed. "I—I'll do it. *Please*. If you let them go, I'll do everything you ask. I won't resist it." Her eyes met those of her friends, and her heart shattered at the sight. Even Jakon looked weak and exhausted, but the fire in his stare remained at least. How would she ever get them to forgive her?

The king scoffed. "So weak, you humans." He stalked back up to the dais. "I'm glad we could come to an agreement. Your friends will be free to leave tonight. You, however, will remain."

She sagged in overwhelming relief. They would live and get to go back to their homes; to be with each other. That was all that mattered. She had tethered herself to the Netherworld to do it, but she supposed that was always her end destination anyway.

"All I ask is a moment to say goodbye. *Please,*" she begged.

The king contemplated. As if deciding it wasn't worth the argument or her outcry if he denied her, he simply waved a bored hand, permitting her to go to them.

She briskly made the short walk to the side of the hall, and the guards stepped away from her friends as she fell into them with an arm hooked around both. They all held each other in silence for a moment, relieved none of them would be meeting an inevitable end. Then she pulled back, unsure of how many precious minutes the king would have mercy for before they were snatched away from her again.

"I'm so sorry. I know you can never forgive me, but—"

"There is nothing to forgive," Marlowe said softly. "Thank you for coming for me. I will never forget it."

"What have you promised them, Faythe? I'm not leaving without you," Jakon growled.

"I'll be okay. They're keeping me alive at least. They seem to think I might actually be useful to them." She huffed a laugh to disguise her revulsion at what they had planned for her. "You need to go and promise me you'll look after each other. This is not goodbye—not even close. I'll find a way to see you again soon." Her throat burned with a painful lump as she tried to keep her voice steady and not break down completely.

Jakon pulled her to him, his arms tightening as if he planned to screw the odds and run off with her. "One word. You get one word to me, and I'll tear the damned wall down to get you out," he mumbled into her hair.

Gods, she knew he would—or would at least die trying.

"I'll be okay," she repeated.

When Jakon released her, Marlowe immediately pulled her into her own bone-crushing embrace. The quiet whisper of her voice in her ear sent a shiver through her.

"This is the right path, Faythe."

She could have collapsed as a million thoughts hit her at once at those words. Did Marlowe know the captain would come for her? Had she simply played her role, knowing this would always be the outcome?

Faythe didn't get to ask any of it out loud as Marlowe went on to answer her unspoken questions quietly but cryptically. "Nothing is certain. Fate can change. Good may not always triumph. But you are on the right path toward the beginning of the end."

It was all riddles to Faythe, but she understood Marlowe's gift as an oracle meant she couldn't press for information—at the risk of altering far more than her own life, it seemed. The Spirits worked through her; knowledge was both a blessing and a curse for the blacksmith. She had the power to guide the light but the burden of knowing impending darkness and being helpless to change the order of events. There could be no victory without suffering; no compassion without pain.

Faythe's grip tightened on Marlowe. "It doesn't feel like the right path," she admitted, perhaps selfishly as she thought of her wicked role for the king.

They released each other, and Faythe cursed the tear that rolled down her cheek. Marlowe wiped it away with a sad smile.

"That's enough! Take them away and escort them to the wall," the king's voice boomed from across the hall.

Faythe quickly reached under her suit and tugged hard at the pendant hanging there. The thin rope snapped, and she pressed it into the blacksmith's hand, looking her dead in the eye.

"Its effects are true."

Marlowe's eyes widened as she heard Faythe's thought in her mind. She glanced at the slab of magestone and then gave Faythe a subtle nod of understanding. She let out a sob as Marlowe was roughly pulled from her grasp by nearby guards.

"Look after each other," Faythe called again when they were dragged further out of reach.

She tunneled into hollow despair with each stride they made away from her, until they were both gone through the wooden side door. She would have collapsed right then if she wasn't all too aware of the audience behind her. Quickly wiping her face, she straightened, holding back her sadness for when she could finally be alone again.

CHAPTER 52

AFTER HER FRIENDS' departure, a guard approached Faythe, and she snapped her eyes to him. He quickly averted his gaze. These guards were quick studies.

She heard movement from behind and twisted to see the king and his ward stalking toward her. Faythe straightened nervously at the dark approaching force.

His voice dropped deadly low. "Make no mistake, girl. If you try a single mind trick or try to attack or escape, I will personally see to your agonizing execution."

She swallowed hard at the lingering threat.

Then his voice perked, and the mood turned chillingly jovial. "Lady Tauria will find suitable living quarters for you. I trust there are some apologies to be made for your earlier antics." He gestured a lazy hand to his ward, who kept a sweet smile as she looked at Faythe.

Honestly, she would admit Tauria made her more anxious than the king in that moment. Did she plan to settle the score between them the second she got Faythe alone?

Tauria walked gracefully past her and mumbled for her to

follow. She did so without a glance back at where Nik stood atop the dais.

Six guards flanked them, and Faythe refrained from huffing at the excessive protection detail. It wasn't as if she could hold the minds of more than one person—or, at least, she had never tried and supposed they were just as unknowing about the full extent of her powers as she.

They weaved through a maze of hallways that all looked the same, and neither female spoke. The pristine splendor of the palace was more daunting than welcoming, making Faythe feel hideously out of place at the stark contrast to her humble hut. This was to be her new *home?* It shocked her to hear she was even getting living quarters as she had highly anticipated she would spend her life in the cells given the king's obvious distaste for her. But she was to be integrated as a member of his counsel; spymaster to those in the know, and human emissary to any outsiders. She knew such a title had never existed in High Farrow's history—or likely any kingdom's past. The fae couldn't care less about the affairs and lives of the humans in the towns below them.

Jakon and Marlowe—they were the reason she would submit to it. As much as the thought twisted a knot in her stomach, it would ensure their safety, for she had no doubt his offer of execution would extend to them also if she refused or stepped out of line.

They walked down another wide, bright hallway that looked just like the last—except a few paintings were different, she noted.

"It might look like an endless loop of halls at first, but you'll learn the differences quite quickly," Tauria said, observing Faythe as she scanned her surroundings.

Faythe met her deep brown stare. "I'm sorry...about before. I just needed the king to hear me," she said sheepishly.

Tauria shrugged in dismissal. "I wanted him to hear you too." A sly smile appeared at the corners of her mouth, and Faythe's brow rose. The ward stopped in front of a large wood door. "This should do nicely." She opened the door and glided inside.

Faythe hesitated for a second before following her in with four guards. Two others remained outside.

She stood and gaped when she entered. She was sure the bedroom was big enough to fit the whole feeble structure of the hut inside, with an excessively large bed a prominent focal feature along the wall. She walked a few steps further in, eyes grazing the finery in admiration. She spotted a separate wardrobe ready to be filled with clothes, and a private bathroom complete with its own bath. Another door to her right led off into a small dining area.

Gods, she had never seen such a luxurious living space, and this was to be where she stayed?

"A little ostentatious, I know, but I'm sure you'll find yourself quite comfortable." Tauria's eyes twinkled in amusement at Faythe's dumbfounded gawking. Then the ward headed to the far end of the room that was lined with full-length glass double doors leading onto a stone-walled balcony. She pushed them open and stepped outside.

Faythe read her silent invitation to follow, where they might talk semi-privately out of earshot of the four guards.

It was night, and the cloudless sky opened up to a view of the bright blanket of stars and a glorious full moon that illuminated where they stood. Tauria braced her palms on the balcony's stone rail, and Faythe stepped up to join her. The view that unfolded from the vantage point took the breath from her. The entire inner city sparkled as if the sky had rained its stars below.

"Beautiful, isn't it?" Tauria commented.

Faythe didn't reply. Instead, she asked, "Why are you being kind to me?" It wasn't an accusation or a lack of appreciation, but Faythe didn't expect the warm reception from any fae female, never mind one whose life she had threatened.

Tauria looked at her, eyes turning a bright hazel in the moonlight. "Why shouldn't I be?" When Faythe didn't reply again, not seeing the need to state the obvious, Tauria sighed sadly. "We're not all the heartless, human-hating monsters your people have come to see us as, Faythe. I hope in time you will see that."

Faythe winced. "It's hard to believe your kind has any regard for us when you live like this while so many suffer in those towns outside the wall." She nodded to the city below.

Tauria was quiet in contemplation of her words. "There are a lot of us who would like to see that changed."

Faythe turned to the ward, glancing briefly at the delicate points of her ears that set the two females apart. For a moment, she imagined what it would be like for their two species to get along in friendship and equality rather than live in a divided coexistence. It struck her then that in Tauria's voice, she heard the words and wisdom of Nik. It warmed and broke her heart at the same time.

"Do you think it's possible?" Faythe said quietly.

The ward gave a wholesome smile. "When Prince Nikalias takes the throne, I think it will be the dawning of a new age for the citizens of High Farrow—for both races." Tauria spoke in loving admiration of Nik, and it had her wondering what kind of history lay between them.

They stood in silent thought, and Faythe tried to imagine her kind living side by side with the fae in the star-kissed city below. The image put a smile of hope on her face.

Tauria released a long breath. "I'll leave you to get acquainted with your rooms." She turned for the glass doors. "I'll have one of the servants stock the wardrobe with clothing for you, and you'll have a uniform for any meetings and formal business the king requires your presence for." Tauria glanced over her, and Faythe shifted. "You can bathe and freshen up in the washroom. I'll have fresh clothing sent up and a hot meal." Tauria twisted and strolled back into the room.

"Thank you," Faythe called.

The ward paused to look back over her shoulder. She answered with nod and a small smile.

Faythe welcomed the solitude when the guards filed out behind her and the door clicked shut. She remained on the balcony, letting the cool, crisp air engulf her, while she pondered her new twist of fate. She looked past the sea of lights, over the waves of uneven rooftops, and reminded herself of one thing: Though she was now physically chained within the castle, her spirit would remain free and unbroken.

True to Tauria's word, a short while later, there was a quiet knock on her door. When Faythe answered, two young women stood holding fresh clothing and a meal tray. Her stomach grumbled and ached at the sight, and she wondered when she last ate.

She let them inside and went immediately for the food they left on the dining table before even considering a bath.

"Is there anything else we can get you?" one spoke timidly.

Faythe looked up at her and smiled gratefully. They were both human, and it was a comfort she desperately needed. "No. This is perfect, thank you."

The women looked a little taken back at her warm response, and it pained Faythe to think of what kind of reception the human servants in the castle were used to from the fae. They bent over in a short bow and went to leave.

"Wait," Faythe said quickly. "What are your names?"

They blinked at each other and didn't immediately respond. "I'm Elise, and this is Ingrid. We'll be your personal servants, Lady."

Faythe nearly choked on her bread. "Please—my name is Faythe. *Just* Faythe."

Elise gave her a small answering nod.

Faythe had not expected to have anyone tend to her, and she would have refused their service, but she had to admit, having frequent human company might just keep her sane in this place.

"Would you like us to help you bathe and dress for bed?" Ingrid asked.

Faythe shook her head. "No. Thanks again, Elise and Ingrid."

They both took their leave, and Faythe greedily devoured everything they had brought for her: stew and bread with a side of cheese, grapes, and wine. The food was glorious, and she couldn't help but feel guilty for fine dining while all the people she loved still lived in poverty in comparison. At least she knew Jakon would have all her coin from The Cave. It would keep him and Marlowe comfortable for a while.

She stretched from the dining table and wandered into the bedroom. Elise and Ingrid had laid out a short silk nightgown and a soft robe for tonight as well as a rather lavish gown for tomorrow. She was to be blended into the court as one of its *ladies*, so the fae wouldn't undermine her presence when it came to the important tasks. They could dress her in all their best finery, but it would never disguise her human heritage, and she was sure she would never truly feel at home among the fae—at least, not under the current social divide and friction.

Tauria's earlier words echoed through her mind, offering hope for the future.

There was a sharp knock on her door and then a pause before it opened. A familiar head of sleek black hair cautiously stepped inside, deliberately closing the door slowly to give her the chance to cast him out.

Nik lingered just in front of the closed doorway, and they stared at each other for a moment.

He cleared his throat. "I just wanted to see how you were settling in," he said awkwardly.

It pained her to see Nik standing before her now as a different male to the one she'd opened her heart to. She pushed back the ache and huffed lightly.

"It'll take time to adjust, for sure."

He nodded in understanding. "The views are—"

"Why are you really here, Nik?" she cut in, not in the mood for idle chatter.

His face fell, and he came a few steps closer. "I need to know you don't hate me for who I am."

"I hate that you lied to me," she admitted.

"Can you forgive me?"

"I don't know."

It was the truth, and she refused to meet his eye. Instead, she distracted herself with the folds in the dress splayed out on the bed.

He stepped closer again, and out of the corner of her eye, she caught his hand going to her face.

Faythe retreated a step. "Don't," she warned.

Pain flashed across his face. Then it was gone, and he straightened.

"We can't pretend anymore—not here." Her heart cracked. She couldn't hide her sadness as she looked him in the eye. "You're a crown prince and will one day be the King of High Farrow. Maybe not in my lifetime. We were doomed from the start, Nik." She blinked back the burning in her eyes. It wasn't just *who* he was; there had always been the fact of *what* he was that Faythe had tried so hard to forget. But no one could outrun time. She would grow old and pass away, while his immortality would keep him young and thriving.

She wanted so badly to take away the despair in his eyes at the cruel reality they had both avoided confronting until now.

"When you said the fae guard you felt for was never real…did you mean it?" he asked in no more than a whisper.

"Yes."

He winced a fraction.

"And no." She held his intense stare. "What we had between us was real. But I have no idea who you really are, *Nikalias.*"

He bowed his head in understanding. "Will you give me a chance—to find out? The real me, no more secrets?"

She smiled then—a warm, genuine smile. "I'd like to."

His shoulders loosened in relief. "I will always care for you,

Faythe."

It was all the closure she needed. Though it was torture to have him close and not be able to find comfort in his touch, she would be able to move on knowing she had a true friend in him for as long as she lived. There was no denying the bond between them.

"I will always care for you too, Nik."

They went out onto the balcony and sat chatting together on the cushioned chairs. She listened, awestruck, while he talked passionately about his life as the Prince of High Farrow. It was liberating to finally learn more about the fae male she had spent months in the company of—the one who had saved her from herself, and then from his father. Despite everything, she would always owe him a great debt for what he had risked—more so now, as she discovered how difficult it must have been for the prince to roam incognito through the town.

"Tauria seems like an interesting female," Faythe commented when Nik mentioned the ward.

He huffed a laugh. "You two could wreak havoc in this castle."

Faythe grinned wide, and for the first time in what felt like a lifetime, it was genuine happiness she felt. Her friends were safe, she was alive, and her ability had become her salvation instead of her doom in the face of the king. Her secrets were out and could no longer destroy her. She despised the reason why she'd ended up in the castle, but she was exactly where she needed to be—to find the temple ruin and free her soul, which was still anchored to the eternal woods. Whatever else she learned about herself from the Spirit Aurialis, she would be ready for it.

I knew your path would lead you to the royal household. That is all.

A small smile tugged at her lips in awe and disbelief. Whether Marlowe had known before exactly *how* she'd come to be here, Faythe couldn't be sure. She supposed it didn't matter.

She turned her head to look over the glittering city. If she had to now call this home, she could at least make the most of it.

With a mischievous smile, she said, "I can't wait."

EPILOGUE

- Reuben -

THE FAINT INTERMITTENT scraping of scuttling rodents had been the only sound for some time now. Still, Reuben remained silently cramped in his small wooden cell, not even daring to breathe too loud. Every time a rat screeched or clawed at the ground, the disruption of the deafening stillness sent his heart into a frenzy.

He knew they had docked from the loud commotion of exiting crew members a while ago and the fact he no longer swayed nause-atingly with the motion of wild, thrashing waves. He was relieved he had managed to hold back the vomit that rose in his stomach too many times on their journey across the sea. He couldn't be sure how many days had passed since leaving High Farrow or how many hours since they'd finally reached their destination of Lakelaria.

His whole body had ached during the first stretch of the grueling journey, and he'd tried to shuffle his position routinely as best he could within the painful confines of the crate. Now, he was completely numb all over and worried about the functionality of his limbs.

Deciding no one was coming back for the cargo anytime soon, Reuben braced his splayed palms against the lid above his head. His pulse drummed in his ears in anticipation of being free from his confines and setting foot on completely new land; unknown territory. He strained against the enclosure and would have tasted the fresh air sooner were it not for his dead muscles that were agony to stretch, protesting against the strength it took.

Finally, the lid popped off, and he slid it to the side with steady caution.

He tuned his hearing again. Silence. Though he couldn't be sure if there were any fae stationed outside the ship, they were likely to detect him from inside if he was brazen in his movements.

Reuben was slow to rise from his crouched position as pain started shooting up every muscle and bone that had sat dormant for days. He knew it was dark in the cargo hold from the small cracks in the barrel, but he could barely make out the distorted shapes of the other containers around him when he fully emerged. He felt around and braced against the solid form beside him. Then, as stealthily as he could, he hauled himself free at last.

When his feet met solid ground to stand straight, he almost buckled under his own weight. He took a moment to stretch and then reached back into the barrel for his very few belongings. Turning, he spotted a rectangular slither of light: *a door!* The only one he could see. He crept toward it, wincing with every creak of the cursed floorboards.

When he crossed to it, he paused for a moment to press his ear to the exit. Nothing alerted him to any man or fae within hearing distance. With his heart a wild rattle in his chest, he grasped the handle and slowly pulled it open. He dared a wary peek out the door first, finding no bodies in the dimly lit cabin—to his great relief.

Reuben didn't have a plan, but once he made it off the ship, he supposed he would be able to find another human and beg for refuge…if the fae didn't catch him as a stowaway first. He was never blessed with the skill of stealth—not like his childhood friend, Faythe. The thought of her, the thought of every friend, and his *mother!* He'd been forced to leave them behind, and it sent him into a dark pit of despair. He couldn't think of them right now. Not until he at least got to safety, or he would be crippled with grief.

Reuben felt the wisp of wind before he found a sure exit off the ship. He followed that wind, and it took him up a set of narrow, winding stairs, down another damp and dingy hallway, until…

The outside at last!

Moonlight signaled the way out where it pooled in from a door-less gap at the end of the passage. His steps quickened, so eager to feel the force of fresh air on his face that he momentarily forgot his life depended on him being slow and quiet. He approached the exit with caution, stopping to crane his neck around and scan the main deck. Surprisingly, there was not a soul—man or fae—left on the ship or the sandy shore.

Reuben straightened and strolled out of the cabin.

Out in the open, he filled his lungs with the salty fresh air and welcomed the blissful freedom. He didn't feel the need to hide or remain inconspicuous as it was clear the docks were abandoned and unpatrolled during the night. A relief, since it was unlike High Farrow where fae soldiers crawled at all hours.

He disembarked the ship with a slight skip in his step. Perhaps this kingdom wouldn't be so bad after all if they were lax on security and control.

The thought made him smile, and he crossed the sandy shore to head into the woodland. It reminded him a lot of Westland Forest, though he supposed little could be different about a woods. It was too dark to pick out anything that might set the scene apart from his homeland. It was quiet, however—almost *too* quiet—but he put that down to the late hour and the fact there maybe weren't as many small woodland creatures in Lakelaria.

There wasn't much he could remember about the mighty land from old teachings in school, but he knew from maps that Lakelaria was famously named for its channels of water that ran throughout the kingdom. There was one chilling tale that had stuck with him since childhood though. This was once a kingdom ruled and occupied by the sirens, who held the ability of song to lure man into their waters. Of course, it was all myth and scary stories, but Reuben would be keeping far away from the lake paths…just in case.

Walking through the crooked rows of trees, he was eager to get out of the woods that were starting to make his skin crawl. But he stopped dead in his tracks, certain he caught one of the skinnier tree trunks…moving.

His calm heart picked up a rapid, uneven rhythm, caught between remaining paralyzed in fear or taking off in flight. He decided on something in the middle, pressing forward slowly while clutching the straps of his backpack painfully tight should he need to make a run for it.

Capturing another flinch of movement out of the corner of his eye, he whipped his head around.

It could just be the leaves.

He reeled in his panic. There were infinite things that moved in woodland areas; his mind was simply jumping to irrational conclusions in fear, triggering mild paranoia that he was being tracked. Still, he quickened his pace.

Just as he took his next step and a branch cracked underfoot, all went black.

Reuben cried out when something was thrown over his head, followed impossibly quickly by someone restraining his arms and binding them behind his back. He didn't even catch a breath before he was fully captured by his stealthy assailant.

"*Please!* I—I mean no harm! Please, let me go!" Reuben cried frantically in his panic.

No one spoke back to him. Still, he knew the first attacker wasn't alone when he felt an arm hook around each of his elbows and begin to drag him away. He didn't have it in him to fight as his crippling fear froze his movement, triggering an incoherent slur of pleas and protests instead.

His captors paid him no attention and didn't loosen their grip or slow their fast pace that had Reuben tripping over his own feet. He soon gave up trying to walk and let them drag him.

It was the most agonizingly long few minutes of his short life, and it shook him into a frenzy to imagine they would be his last if he was being led to his death. He heard the screech of door hinges, then he felt the change in the ground. His toes didn't turn up dirt or catch over sharp branches. Now, they glided over a far smoother and much more even surface.

Then they halted, and he was suddenly released.

Reuben went from dangling limply in his captor's arms to falling against the cold ground, his shoulder taking the brunt of the force thanks to his bound hands. He shuffled himself to his knees, and then the bag over his head was roughly snatched away. His neck snapped back painfully with it, and he blinked rapidly to the beat of his heart as he adjusted to his new surroundings.

He was now indoors, in a shoddy hut that was barely illuminated by some nearby torches. He glanced to his side and shrieked, flinching back at the sight of two huge fae males, cloaked and hooded in a black uniform. He knew that uniform, and when realization hit, Reuben thought he would pass out from the wave of flashbacks to his last encounter with such a force.

Valgard.

He stared at them wide-eyed and wide-mouthed, unable to speak, move, or switch emotion from cold-blooded terror. The fae remained stationary and didn't return his stare as they stood straight and poised, eyes fixed behind him.

The floorboards creaked, signaling a new presence in the room.

Reuben snapped out of his shock to whip his head around. Only, when he did, he wasn't met with the death-promising, brute-force male he expected.

Instead, his horror soothed into gawking awe at the tall female fae who emerged from the dark hole in the wall. He was struck by her beauty—it was matched by no fae or human he had seen before. Her hair blazed such a dark amber it was almost red, and it moved like real flames. Her face was delicate, pale, *perfect.* But when he looked into her *eyes...*

He'd seen those eyes before—their color.

No. It's only a coincidence.

She came to a stop in front of him. The female crouched down to where he knelt paralyzed by bewilderment more than fear. She wore a feline smile that made every hair on his body stand on end. She was beautiful—but *dangerous.* He didn't know what it was, but something told him not to be fooled by her graceful exterior. With the beauty of the leopard came the capacity to kill.

Finally, the temptress spoke. "Yes," she said in an elegant melody. "I think you'll be of great use to me." Even her voice sounded not of this world; hypnotizing.

And he felt it too, as he couldn't tear his gaze from her. Perhaps he was still in a deep stupor at the thought of who else surfaced in his mind at seeing her eyes—eyes of glittering *gold.* There was only one other he knew whose irises shared such a color, except the female's in front burned slightly brighter, almost glowing, in comparison. The ethereal beauty's rouge painted lips twitched in a cruel smile that had him trembling violently. Reuben stared and stared into those blazing orbs, straining his mind to not let the face morph...into Faythe's.

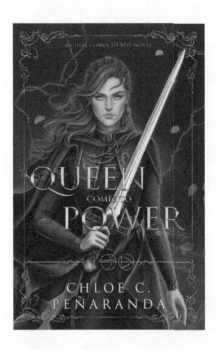

When courts collide, blood may be spilled. But when destinies collide, blood may hold power.

A DUTY...

Bound in service to the king within the city, Faythe grapples with morality to keep herself and her friends safe. Nik's loyalty is tested as he struggles against his father's cruel ways. When blood and duty divide the heart, *can* love conquer all?

AN ALLIANCE...

While the kingdoms prepare to unite, Faythe is forced to remain hidden in plain sight. But suspicions quickly arise with the mysterious fae general from an ally court. Getting close to Reylan could unravel truths she longed for, but trust is hard to gain and even harder to hold. When lurking evil threatens the alliance that keeps them all safe, Faythe may find herself on the side where danger meets desire in a force that could break past the guard on her heart.

A CHOICE...

For the threat of battle isn't the only conflict to fear. Faythe can't forget the deal she struck in the woods to save her friend's life–and it's time to fulfil. Finding the temple ruin leads them to harrowing discoveries within the castle...and something far more sinister than the war that lingers. It seems everyone will receive more than they bargained for. A history that haunts, truths that destroy, and a tangled destiny they didn't expect.

Out Now!

PRONOUNCIATION GUIDE

NAMES

Faythe: faith
Nik: nick
Jakon: jack-on
Marlowe: mar-low
Tauria: tor-ee-a
Orlon: or-lon
Reuben: ru-ben
Ferris: fer-iss
Varis: var-iss
Aurialis: orr-ee-a-liss
Marvellas: mar-vell-as

PLACES

Ungardia: un-gar-dee-a
Farrowhold: farrow-hold
Galmire: gal-my-er
High Farrow: high-farrow
Lakelaria: lake-la-ree-a
Rhyenelle: rye-en-elle
Olmstone: Olm-stone
Fenstead: fen-stead
Dalrune: dal-rune

OTHER

Riscillius: risk-ill-ee-us
Lumarias: lou-ma-ree-as
Yucolites: you-co-lights

ACKNOWLEDGMENTS

It's been a journey. A wonderful, fantastic journey of introducing my world of Ungardia to you, and I have many people to thank as part of my creative and support team who without each and every one this book would not have come together.

To my mum Yvonne, who never once thought my dreams were too big and encouraged me to reach for the stars. The one who listened to my stresses, crushed my self-doubts, and gave me belief in myself. Thank you for being you.

To my sister Eva, the first reader of the raw and unedited version of AHCTR. Thank you for your enthusiasm and encouragement for this series. Reuben is a character forever dedicated to you.

To my niece Chiara, also a first reader of the unedited book. Thank you for your honesty and encouragement, which helped me make changes that strengthened the plot of this book.

To my dad, who has always been a number one supporter. Thank you. And to the rest of the family unit, I owe credit to you all in your own special way who have given me confidence and drive to pursue this book. Thank you for your love and support.

To my extraordinary editor, Bryony Leah, I thank my lucky stars for you. Your edits and suggestions are invaluable, your encouragement and praise inspiring, and your dedication and attention admirable. Thank you for being so professional, accommodating, and going above and beyond for this book.

To Alice Maria Power, for the absolutely stunning cover illustra-tion. Your work is honestly as close to real-life magic as it gets.

Thank you for being so wonderful and attentive to every detail. I cannot wait to illustrate this series with you.

Finally, and perhaps most importantly, I wouldn't get to do what I love without you—the readers! Thank you from the bottom of my heart for choosing to pick up my book and begin the journey through Ungardia. This is only the beginning, and I hope to see you all along for the trials and tribulations of Faythe's story, and those of many other characters to come! Here's to you.

ABOUT THE AUTHOR

CHLOE C. PEÑARANDA is the Scottish author of the compelling epic fantasy series *An Heir Comes to Rise*.

A lifelong avid reader and writer, Chloe discovered her passion for storytelling in her early teens. An Heir Comes to Rise has been built upon from years' worth of building on fictional characters and exploring Tolkien-like quests in made up worlds. During her time at the University of the West of Scotland, Chloe immersed herself in writing for short film, producing animations, and spending class time dreaming of far off lands.

In her spare time from writing in her home in scenic Scotland, Chloe enjoys digital art, graphic design, and down time with her three furry companions. When the real world calls...she rarely listens.

www.ccpenaranda.com

Made in the USA
Coppell, TX
28 March 2024

30659321R00236